Praise for

W. D. Gagliani

"Gagliani has brought bite back to the werewolf novel!"
—CNN Headline News Book Lizard

"The best werewolf novel since *The Howling*!"
—J.A. Konrath, author of *Whiskey Sour*, on *Wolf's Trap*

"Riveting. Werewolf fans should be more than pleased."
  —*Flesh & Blood Magazine* on *Wolf's Trap*

"*Wolf's Bluff* will keep you biting your nails right up to its blood-drenched finale. Gagliani sets a relentless pace from the first page and never lets up."
—John Everson, Bram Stoker Award-winning author of *The 13th*

"Gagliani is a natural storyteller."
—P.D. Cacek, World Fantasy Award winner, author of *Night Prayers*

"Riveting, disturbing, gut-wrenching—and entertaining as all get-out—and I loved every page!
—Jay Bonansinga, author of *The Black Mariah*, on *Wolf's Trap*

Look for these titles by
W. D. Gagliani

Coming Soon:

Wolf's Trap

Wolf's Edge

W. D. Gagliani

Samhain Publishing, Ltd.
11821 Mason Montgomery Road, 4B
Cincinnati, OH 45249
www.samhainpublishing.com

First Samhain Publishing, Ltd. electronic publication: October 2011
First Samhain Publishing, Ltd. print publication: January 2012

Acknowledgments

As always, I'd like to dedicate this book to my Mom and Janis, and in memory of my dad. Also my good friend, the writer Joel S. Ross, who was taken from us suddenly and much too soon.

I'd also like to acknowledge the stories my grandmother and parents told me of their childhood in Italy 1943-44, under German occupation and Allied bombing. Some of those stories and experiences have made their way into this novel.

Thanks for various reasons due to: Regina Allen, Jim Argendeli, Gary A. Braunbeck, Judy Bridges, John Everson, Gary Jonas, A.G. Kent, Don Kinney, Edward Lee, Jonathan Maberry, Lisa Mannetti, Len Maynard, David Morrell and Hank Wagner, Keith Petersen, Brian Pinkerton, Tim Powers, Michael Slade, the Starbucks at 8880 South Howell Avenue, Tamara Thorne, Christopher and S-A Welch, and Mark and Jennie Zirbel, among many others.

Special thanks to Don D'Auria and to David Benton for going above and beyond the call of duty...

I will always miss the lyrics Eric Woolfson would have written... I'm glad I had the chance to tell him how much his work meant to me.

Author's Note

The real Minocqua is located in Oneida County, and the real Eagle River is in Vilas County of northern Wisconsin. The real Milwaukee is located in the far southeast corner of the state on the shores of the great Lake Michigan. Once again I have altered these places as needed (geographically, socially, and with regard to local city and police department organization) in order to suit my purposes. All characters in these alternate versions of Minocqua, Eagle River, and Milwaukee are either fictional or used fictitiously and in no way resemble their real-world counterparts. However, some things are unalterably true. If you drive up Highway 45 or 51 from Milwaukee, and find yourself entering the North Woods, after dusk you might notice the shadows keeping pace with you just outside of your view in the thick undergrowth that crowds the shoulder. The shadows seem to move effortlessly between the tightly packed pines. If you look up you might see the moon's silvery sheen filtering through the swaying treetops. Don't roll down your windows—you might hear the howling.

Never, ever stop the car when you hear the howling...

"He who fights with monsters should beware lest he thereby become a monster. And if thou gaze long into an abyss, the abyss will also gaze into thee."
—Friedrich Nietzsche, *Beyond Good and Evil*

Prologue

Somewhere between Minocqua and Eagle River, WI

The keys clicked lightly under his fingers, and he watched the short paragraph take shape on the laptop's screen before him. The light it emitted was enough to cast a blue-white glow across the room and over his shape. He hunched over slightly, refocusing his eyes and positioning the bifocals to give him a clear look at the text he was leaving behind. He moused over a phrase, adjusted it, cut another word here and added several words there.

He was very quiet. His family slept, and he didn't want to complicate things by awakening them. Karina snored softly in the adjacent room, her form stretched under the sheet in the sideways position she preferred. Down the hall, the nearest room was where Katerina slumbered the innocent sleep of the six-year-old, a favorite bear watching over her from one side of the pillow and an animal—a jolly looking dog from the latest Pixar movie—was crushed in her sleepy embrace. The boys slept in the far room, across the hall from the main upstairs bath.

He smiled sadly as he thought of his family, asleep and unencumbered by what ate at him like acid. His smile turned into a frown and then a grimace as he tasted the acid column that rose in his throat. Real or not, he felt the vomit push its way into the back of his throat, and he fought to swallow it down.

Hands shaking, he typed a few more words, reread the six lines or so he had written into the blank file, then he moused over to the Print command and heard the sheet work its way through the elderly Epson below his desk. Then he highlighted and copied the text, clicked into the open browser, scrolled to where the text box sat waiting, empty, its cursor blinking like a clown's evil wink. He pasted the text and Submitted it, then closed the page and clicked into the Preview function. There it was, his text posted on his website's main page where the counter would soon begin to click upward as his regulars checked his blog and news.

He closed the browser but left the computer on. It really didn't matter.

Behind him, where the bottom of the built-in bookcase met the lower cabinets, their shelves hidden behind cherry-wood doors, he flicked the disguised switch and waited for the upper bookcase to disengage from its lock. It hissed open a few inches, and he reached between its edge and the frame and opened wide the secret compartment. Behind the movable bookcase were several shelves of items and a built-in safe. He ignored everything but one item. He took it from its resting place inside the red velvet-lined case, then pushed the compartment door shut again.

He took the object and held it up where moonlight entering the wide picture window could illuminate it. The huge, silver disk above shed light over the lake and its surroundings, leaking into the living room and over his hands. The heavy object shone in the light. It was a dagger perhaps nine inches in length, sheathed in lightweight wood criss-crossed with carved symbols. The dagger's grip was set with several irregular shaped jewels in a line above the straight cross-guard. The moonlight blackened the jewels so they looked like pools of darkness in the hilt.

His eyes suddenly filled, and he tilted his head as if tears could be coaxed to clear his pupils on their own. His motion achieved nothing, and the tears swelled up until they were heavy enough to seek their own ways across his cheeks. He repressed a sob.

He had decades to sob over.

He tucked the sheathed dagger into his belt, leaving his hands free.

Almost without realizing how he had gotten there, he stood in front of a door down the hall. Now holding the dagger in one hand, he used the other to edge the door open just enough to slip inside, where his daughter slept among stuffed animals and at least one doll. Her golden hair was made into a silver halo by the moonlight filtered through the blinds. She was tucked in all the way to her chin, her tiny hands wrapped around the plush dog.

He let his tears fall onto her pillow for a moment, looking at her one last time. Then he swiftly slid the blade from its scabbard, placed one hand over the top of her face and pressed down hard, effectively preventing her scream and keeping her from seeing what he was about to do.

Forgive me, he prayed as he quickly drew the blade once across her throat. He wasn't sure who would grant the forgiveness, however.

Dodging the hot spray, he held her head down on the pillow until it and the bed were sodden, and her tiny struggles were finished.

Not long. It didn't take long at all.

Sobbing quietly, snot bubbling from his nostrils, he left his daughter's room and entered the next, where the boys slept.

Thankfully they had given up the bunk beds, preferring two

individual singles set perpendicular to each other. He approached the closest, his younger son, and said his quiet good-bye.

Then he repeated the procedure with the heavy hand, pressure downward holding his son's neck in position and keeping him quiet and blind. The blade sang through the young skin with nary a hitch, but this time the blood gush half-caught him as he swayed to evade it. His older son grumbled in his sleep, muttered, and snored after shifting sideways on his pillow. In a moment the large hand, the father's hand, was holding the small head down, and the other hand was doing the deed almost as if they were independent of each other and of his control. He barely moved this time, letting more of his son's blood bathe him as he suppressed the struggling boy beneath. This son had been his favorite.

He waited again for the bleed-out, snot now coating his chin. He was unmindful of the snot and tears and saliva that ran freely from his open mouth.

Then he headed for the master bedroom, where his wife waited.

Her eyes were open and questioning when he approached, apparently having heard either his walking or the children's struggling. She probably hadn't processed what she'd heard, because her instinctive alarm had not forced the issue and fully awakened her fear.

"What—" she began, but his hand covered her lips and eyes, and his one motion took the blooded silver blade through her neck. Even as the curtain of blood jetted out from her, he could feel the scream under his hand, the accusation, the terror.

"*Why?*"

It didn't matter whether she asked the question, it was what he heard. His body covered hers, lovingly, feeling her struggles diminish until finally it went still beneath his. He was drenched with his family's blood now, a symbolic sacrifice of everything he had ever loved.

Carefully, he replaced the blooded dagger in its hiding place. The box contained two dagger-shaped cradles, and his filled one of them. The other cradle was dusty—it hadn't held its dagger in decades.

Then he took a pistol from its hooks above where the case holding the blade lay among other items. He closed the secret compartment's door.

He dragged himself through the hallway and to the living room, with its view of the woods and the lake. He surveyed the moonlit scene one last time.

He felt nothing, really. Did he?

His family's fresh blood soaked his clothes and clogged his nostrils with its sweet, metallic stench.

No time for regrets. It was too late. Better decisions would have led

13

to better outcomes.

The pistol in his hand was an antique, but he had kept it oiled and in good condition. And the magazine was filled with his best home loads. He pulled the toggle and cocked the German war-issue 1908 Parabellum model, which most people knew as the *Luger*. He felt the weight of the pistol, its superb balance, and he allowed himself one small, sad smile.

He stood with his back to the wide, white wall. Twisted the gun around in his grip. Rested the oily barrel on his forehead.

When he squeezed the trigger, the last thing he saw was the frozen face of his wife, asking *Why?* Her staring, accusing eyes registered for a fraction of a second, and then it was over.

His body spasmed once against the wall now ruined by the shower of blood and bits of skull, spasmed then slumped to the hardwood floor. A lake grew quickly below him like a crimson outline.

One hour later, the sound of breaking glass washed over the frozen tableau inside the house. Heavy boot falls marked the intruder's trek through the rooms, one by one, ending at the wall where a man's body lay slumped, his head collapsed like a deflated child's balloon.

The blood was black in the reflected moonlight.

The intruder shook his head, then set about the search, which had just become more complicated.

Another hour passed, and the intruder found what he knew was there to be found. Not much effort had been made to keep the secret storage area truly hidden. With a laser measuring device, the intruder quickly located the several discrepancies that signaled secret compartments behind false walls.

Still almost two hours before dawn, the intruder found the main gas valve in the rear of the basement, the portion behind a door located in the cedar-paneled bar area dominated by a regulation pool table and various rich man's toys. Behind the door, the house's systems were ensconced in a room with walls of reinforced poured concrete. The intruder flicked on the lights, located the gas line and took a few moments to follow it with his eyes, then he took a wrench from his waist pack and loosened a couple connectors. He waited for a minute until he could smell the gas quickly escaping the pipe, then retreated through the open door.

Back upstairs, he set an innocuous-looking cell phone housing on a hallway table near the back door and basement entrance. Inside was a tiny, remote-operated device that would ignite upon receipt of a certain signal text. When it did, it would at the same time provide the needed spark and destroy itself. It would be indistinguishable from the kind of slag left by any sort of cell phone upon melting.

Confusion was the intended result. The crime scene would be a mess. Suicide? Murder? Murder-suicide? Unlawful entry, or fakery? The man whose body lay slumped against the wall would be blamed, and they'd stop looking for the rest of the story. Small-town cops would never go beyond the obvious in this one. There was plenty of the obvious on which to concentrate.

The intruder left the premises undetected. Two hours later—and a fair number of miles away—the time he knew was needed to fill the enclosed space with gas, he sent the text message.

Imagining the fireball, he smiled slightly.

In his trunk lay the wooden case he had removed from the scene.

Chapter One
Endgame: First Day

Lupo

The bitter breeze blowing off the lake cut through his leather jacket and, instinctively, he dug his large hands into the pockets. He made fists, but he wasn't aware he had.

The usual clanking of small boat rigging was down to a dozen or so stragglers still in the water of the North Point Marina. Lupo stood with his back to the old roundhouse, which was boarded up for the season. Wistfully, he recalled warm days on the lake, playing dominoes and drinking overpriced canned beer from the roundhouse deli, getting greasy with chips and sandwiches wrapped in waxed paper. Across the weathered picnic table in his memory was Caroline Stewart, laughing as they struggled to play the old man's game they had somehow both enjoyed picking up.

Lupo's fists started to hurt from the pressure, and then they started to itch.

It was strange, after all these years, having such clear memories of Caroline. She'd been his professor, confessor and confidante, and then lover.

And then he had killed her.

"Jesus, Nick, could you just let it go?" The voice from behind him startled him, but he pretended otherwise.

"You've beaten yourself up for too many years. You have good reason to move on now, and accept the past and what you are and what you will always be."

Lupo wanted to stifle the raspy voice, but he already knew the old man would have his say.

He had killed Caroline Stewart, and that act of violence, while not completely his fault, had damned him forever, as far as he could tell. It had confirmed his suspicions—he really was a monster.

"Get over yourself," said the old-man voice.

He resisted for a few moments, then whirled around.

There was no one there. Ghost Sam liked these surgical strikes, making his point in as bloody a manner as possible, then disappearing...wherever he disappeared to. Most likely Lupo's head, which was definitely not a healthy place to be.

He *was* a monster, Ghost Sam's platitudes notwithstanding.

How could a werewolf not be a monster?

"You've faced real monsters. I know monsters. You're not much of a monster."

"Christ, Sam, you still have a sick sense of humor even after death, you know that?"

"Laugh away, cop boy. But will you ever listen to me? No, you won't. Apparently you inherited that stubbornness you always accuse your dad of having."

Actually Lupo listened to Ghost Sam fairly often, both when he saw him and when he didn't. But there had to be an end to it, a line he could draw.

His mind wandered back to Caroline, and what the Creature had done to her. The guilt was still tangible. She had backed his decision to become a cop, and he'd been on his way to being a good one when the most traumatic incident of his life took place. The Creature had done it, he knew it intellectually, but he couldn't stop thinking that the Creature was still part of him, or that he could have controlled its rage. Miraculously, he had managed to evade suspicion, though he'd lived in fear for years, and then he'd climbed the ranks of the Milwaukee Police Department, all the way to Homicide Detective.

Until his past—and his secret—had come back to torment him and endanger the woman he now loved. He had managed to protect her so far, when she wasn't protecting *him*, but he had a lousy record when it came to women who became attached to him.

He stifled what he had to admit was a sob.

Jessie.

Things weren't so smooth now, and it was all his fault.

Again.

He'd tried to get her some help, but she was either at her meeting right now or at the casino. He couldn't quite grasp why a woman as successful, intelligent, beautiful, and perfect in every way had succumbed to a strangely warped version of the same gambling addiction he saw manifested in old folks who flushed their life savings away while standing blank-eyed at slot machines.

What the hell was he supposed to do, lock her up? Keep her out of the casino?

He snorted in spurious laughter. He remembered when *he* was the one who needed to be locked up, when he feared the full moon would take him and force him to commit murder after grisly murder. In fact, the moon had indeed caused him to do some bad things, but he'd learned to beat the moon's influence.

Usually.

He had a lot on his mind today. It wasn't just Caroline's memory, or Jessie's gambling. It was the look in Tom Arnow's eyes as he'd died, after Lupo had flicked that damned dagger squarely into his chest. And it was what he'd done even later.

That damned cursed dagger.

He turned away from the gray water, his fists itching like a delicate torture. He wished he could flay the skin off his hands.

His iPhone buzzed in his pocket. Damn it, somebody always interrupting his life. He dug it out with an itchy hand.

"Yeah?" he barked.

He listened for a minute, verified the address, and clicked off. Third Ward, crime scene. He was practically there already. Just a hop down Lake Drive and then a few blocks south of downtown. DiSanto was meeting him there.

He turned and half expected to see Sam Waters standing nearby, his gray hair gathered in its usual ponytail and his small but somehow still imposing frame tucked into a too-large leather parka. But he was alone.

He crossed the deserted parking lot between the boarded-up roundhouse and the yacht club and climbed into the slightly battered Maxima he clung to stubbornly. Rich DiSanto, his partner of two years, hounded him ceaselessly about the car. As a homicide detective, Lupo had the choice to drive his own vehicle while on duty, and he preferred comfort to style.

"At least get a Mustang or a Camaro, one of those new ones," DiSanto had a habit of nagging almost weekly.

"If I did," Lupo usually reminded him, "you wouldn't be very comfortable." It was true—the Maxima had the horsepower he wanted, thanks to some custom work, and the leather seats were comfortably worn. DiSanto's long legs needed the ample space below the seat.

No way would he confess to the childish DiSanto that he'd been, in fact, tempted by the recent Mustangs.

Lupo sat for a minute. A strange tingle centered on the back of his neck made him turn and scan the rest of the lot. A couple cars in slots near the yacht club and a minivan toward the beach side were his only company. They were deserted, probably people who worked maintenance at the club. He shrugged.

Paranoia strikes deep.

He'd given Wolfpaw Security Services—or whatever they were

calling themselves these days—enough to chew on for a long while, and right now the congressional hearings were gearing up in D.C. He had to be the last thing on their minds at the moment.

He shrugged, then started up and zipped onto Lake Drive, heading south along the coastline. The trees that dotted the parkland around the pond beside the curvy road were already half bare. He chafed at the thought of another case, on top of the half dozen he and DiSanto still had pending. It was just that kind of fall season, he mused, with people losing their cool after having lost their money or their house, or their family. Tended to make people a little crazy, as did the weather, which had been gray and drizzly or downright cold for three weeks already.

Lupo knew, because the Creature within also wanted out. The depression that had set in to harass his human side had begun to affect the Creature, too. Bleed-through had started to increase a year ago, and Lupo wondered if it was an age thing.

The shitty fact of it was that he didn't know, and he couldn't ask, because all the other shapeshifters he had met so far he'd had to kill. There was no asking for fatherly advice in his world. He hadn't even realized there were others like him until they showed up and started killing people he cared about and trying their damndest to kill him, too.

He checked again the address they'd texted him as he passed under the U.S. Bank building, Wisconsin's tallest skyscraper at a conservative 601 feet, and headed for Water Street, which would take him into the heart of the Third Ward a few blocks south.

He had ambivalent memories of the Third Ward, since his friend Corinne had been involved with a porn outfit that had set up shop in a loft in one of the renovated warehouses there. She'd been murdered by Martin Stewart and a long nightmare had begun to unfold, the only positive aspect of which was his new and sudden relationship with Jessie Hawkins, whom he'd known for years but hadn't realized he had fallen in love with until they were both targeted by the serial killer.

First she'd been his landlord Up North, where he went a few days a month to distance himself from people he might hurt when the moon turned full. They had certainly been friends for years, since she'd first taken over her family's properties near Eagle River. In that time she had begun her practice inside the reservation, tied to it and its people because they were her own people, too. Jessie Hawkins came from a mixed marriage, her father having been a prominent physician and surgeon and part-time coroner, and she'd followed his footsteps in all the best ways. But neither Jessie nor Lupo had realized their attraction until the killer Martin Stewart began targeting everyone Lupo knew, including Jessie.

Now Lupo was hip to the fact that she was beautiful, a sort of earthier version of a famous model, as he had been told. Her flaming, highlighted chestnut hair either left to bounce off her shoulders in a controlled blaze or harnessed in a ponytail still made him want to comb it with his fingers. Her dark eyes were limpid, light-reflecting pools set above a long, straight but slightly upturned nose and a generous, smile-ready but sensuous mouth.

She had moved in with him recently, after he had brought them more trouble by kicking the sleeping wolf that was Wolfpaw Security Services.

Just thinking of them and what they had done—and almost managed to do—to everyone he cared about brought a rage so severe he worried about his own self-control. He shook his head.

"You're right to worry," Ghost Sam said, speaking from the passenger seat. He was translucent.

Lupo was used to the sudden appearances. "Damn right. But I almost took care of it, didn't I?"

"If running away is *taking care of it*, then yes, you almost did." Ghost Sam had a way of speaking sarcastically that made Don Rickles look like a comedian for children.

Damn it, Sam, I miss you.

"I know. I miss those Bloody Marys we used to have Up North," the apparition said wistfully. "I miss the better Bond movies...Daniel Craig's good, but they've sacrificed character for non-stop action."

"It's a reboot," he pointed out.

No answer.

The passenger seat was empty again.

Shit, talking to myself again.

Except he always felt slightly better afterwards.

He was almost there.

He zigzagged, taking Buffalo east, then Jefferson south, a stone's throw from the Italian Community Center. Three squads were parked in front of a not-quite renovated warehouse with a couple furniture stores on the first level, more or less blocking the street with their light-bars' strobes reflecting onto the tall windows. A Coroner's wagon stood open near the main door, and on the other side of the street he could make out DiSanto's late-model Charger pulled up at an angle facing the door. A uniform stood outside, and Lupo nodded at him as he climbed out of his car and headed inside.

"Up on three, detective," the cop said.

Lupo thanked him and took the decrepit stairs up.

It was an eclectic building with several suites listed on the cracked board in the lobby and several floors in various stages of being gutted.

Suites might have been a bit pretentious. At the door of suite 301, with a fading hand-painted sign proclaiming it was Midnight Studios, Lupo found another uniform.

"Hey," Lupo said. "In here?"

"Yeah, but it's not pretty." The cop shook his head. "Thought I'd seen it all."

"We all do," Lupo said, "until we see more."

"Fuckin' degenerates..."

Lupo patted the guy on the arm. "You'll get used to it."

"Thought I was. But not this shit."

Lupo nodded and stepped through the paint-flecked doorway. It was clearly a low-rent movie studio with a wooden floor reception area leading to a series of office rooms at the far end, and an arch leading the other way to the floor's main space, a gutted loft with random mountains of crappy furniture piled up throughout. He stood for a second wondering which way to head, and then DiSanto came out of one of the office doors to the left, and Lupo saw that the other cops were in there, too.

"It's a nice one, Nick. The meatwagon guys are just waiting for you before scooping up the vic."

"Gee, thanks, it's so thoughtful of them."

"Aim to please," said DiSanto.

"What's the deal?" Lupo said quickly. His partner would head into total cliché-mode if not stopped.

"Looks like a low-budget movie outfit. The guy's apparently an accountant and camera operator. We're checking on the name. He might have interrupted a robbery, or at least an intruder. But it looks like he was punished way beyond what would have been necessary."

"Witnesses?"

"Uniforms are hittin' the other tenants, but except for the stores on the first level, these other places are fly by night. Nobody home most of the time. Doesn't look like anybody saw a thing."

"Who called it in?" Lupo was at the door by now.

DiSanto rolled his eyes. "Anonymous phone tip."

"I hate those," Lupo growled.

"Yeah."

Anonymous tips always meant an agenda.

Lupo waved him off and stood looking at the doorjamb and the open door itself. It was one of those industrial loft doors, covered in riveted sheet metal panels and painted with sloppy, white brush strokes. There was no sign of tampering that he could see. The lock's bolt was simply open, retracted into the door. Inside, a dead bolt stood

21

open. Lupo backed onto the landing and down the top few stairs, searching carefully for any recognizable signs left by the deadly visitor. Gravel, dirt, grass, twigs. But there was nothing.

Surreptitiously, Lupo sniffed the air. He was learning more and more about scents, honing an ability to catch, separate, and memorize them. This skill had helped with the Martin Stewart case, but not at all with identifying other shapeshifters. Perhaps it was an innate defense mechanism—if they could sense each other too easily, they'd tear each other apart on meeting.

The stairs held a mélange of scents he could identify. Paint and thinner and wood varnish were foremost. Then there was a layer of rotting food, maybe salads and rancid Chinese takeout. He figured the people who worked on the films, whatever they were, probably ate nothing but boxed food. He figured there'd be a barrel of trash inside the gutted space.

Of course he smelled people smells, but they were normal and nondescript. Normal in that he caught notes of sweat and hair spray, cologne and aftershave, rancid breath, urine, and probably flatulence. And even semen, like maybe some trysts had taken place inside the film studio offices. *A casting couch? More porn?*

Whatever. It was meaningless. Probably dozens of people had trooped up these stairs. Film folks, actors, extras, friends of friends, and at least one murderer.

Lupo grinned mirthlessly. Maybe if he forced a Change the Creature inside could detect something he'd missed. Maybe he'd come back later, after hours, and try it. His mentor and lover Caroline had nurtured his experimental fugues. But he needed quiet and no interruptions.

His control was still limited and the Creature cranky. It was just too risky to jump into recklessly.

He heard more footsteps on the stairs below and snagged a certain scent—Lieutenant Bakke—surging toward him.

Shit.

"Who caught the squeal?" he barked upward.

The lieutenant was nothing if not a people person. He was all business, everyone knew that, but what was he doing at a crime scene?

"DiSanto and I got it," Lupo said, making way for the short, wide-bodied cop. "What's up?"

"I hear this is pretty disgusting. Came to see for myself."

"Feel free," Lupo said. Knock yourself out, he wanted to say.

The older cop bulled his way inside. Lupo glanced at his watch.

"Jesus!" Bakke said, edging out the door.

Two minutes twenty. He'd lasted longer than Lupo thought he would.

Bakke's hand shook as he fumbled out a cigarette and struggled with a lighter. Then he saw Lupo's look and realized he wasn't supposed to smoke at a crime scene and put the cigarette away, crushing it in the process. His hand shook as he finally got the lighter back in his pocket.

He sighed. "Now, that's why I got off the streets."

"Yes, sir. It's a bad one." *You don't know the half of it.*

"I hadda check it out. Somehow this has filtered up the ranks, and I got some probing questions from—" He straightened suddenly. "Well, no matter. I checked it out. You guys have it in hand?"

"Scene's secure. The lab guys have been through. Coroner's van is on its way. Clean-up's gonna be a bitch. We're sifting through stuff, figuring ID, possible motives, you know the drill."

"Yeah, Lupo, I remember," Bakke said. "I ain't been flying a desk that long."

"No sir."

"Carry on, then. But keep me in the loop." He stared at Lupo, his eyes narrowing. "And I mean that. No whitewash. Except with the press. Keep sordid details out of any statements. In fact, don't make any. I'll take care of it."

"Sure." Lupo shrugged.

"All right." Bakke nodded as if to convince himself, then made his way unsteadily down the steps.

"What was that all about?" DiSanto said from behind him, standing in the doorway.

"I'm not exactly sure," he said. "But I bet it'll end up bad news for us."

Chapter Two

Mordred

He was watching when Lupo squealed out of the parking lot.

He was named Mordred, but he didn't know who had given him the name.

One of his earliest memories was of being stung by a stick he would one day learn to call a *cattle prod.*

He hadn't cared who had given him the strange name, nor what the stick was called, but he had cared about avoiding its tip when one of the men came to roust him from his sleep or his play.

Now he shook the memory with a physical shrug.

Always in the middle of the night.

No wonder he rarely slept. That twilight time between wakefulness and sleep always attacked his thoughts and ate at him like a disease devouring him from the inside out, leaving him wrung and sodden and unrested.

His body's need for very little sleep coincided with the majority of his assignments. The only reaction he felt was a spell of violent, cold shivers for a time in the morning, but compared to the cattle prod days, the sensation was merely an inconvenience.

He swung in a few cars behind Lupo's junker but without much hurry. He knew where the cop was headed. The minivan was well-equipped for surveillance, and he himself had not been visible even though he could have read the label on Lupo's briefs. But now he didn't have to keep him in sight, because his scrambled anonymous call had summoned the cocky homicide cop right to where he had prepared things.

He flicked a button on his all-purpose remote, and the screen on the dash switched from GPS display to a rather sharp camera image of the hallway of a building in the Third Ward. A uniformed cop stood outside. Mordred enjoyed imagining how pale he must be after the vomiting. Broad, dark-clothed bodies obscured the picture for a few seconds. More cops arriving as the word spread. One more made his way back onto the landing and stumbled downward out of view. Another walked out slowly and sank out of sight, probably sitting on the steps below the hidden camera's field of view.

Mordred chuckled.

Probably sitting and hyperventilating, trying to keep his throat muscles from contracting and erupting his stomach's contents up and into his mouth.

Lupo would not be so affected. He experienced worse crime scenes fairly regularly, and he himself had caused similar damage to a human body, so there was no chance he would be impressed, except perhaps with the brutality of the murder, which was not typical in this particular metro area. Here a 9mm fusillade in the inner city was king of the crime scene sweepstakes.

Mordred let Lupo's Maxima lose him and tooled along the cold lake coastline, occasionally eying the display. There, that was Richard DiSanto, Lupo's younger partner. Mordred licked his lips unconsciously. He had no specific instructions regarding Detective DiSanto, but as far as he was concerned that meant he could do as he wished. When the switch was flicked, he would take some pleasure in dropping this cop, too.

He half-whistled something he had learned in the lab years ago, though he had no idea what the song or composition might have been. The melody was horribly mangled by his whistle, but it sounded perfect to his ears.

Jessie

Frustrated, she started chewing her nails again.

The meeting was over and she was grateful for that, but the itch was starting already. She sat in her car, the same old Pathfinder she'd driven for almost fifteen years, and turned the heat way up for a few seconds. It wasn't cold yet, not really, but she still felt the same shiver that usually engulfed her after a meeting, when she seemed more vulnerable, more likely to break her discipline and head for the Valley, where the huge Milwaukee Indian casino rose out of the industrial neighborhood like a pyramid on the plain of Giza.

Almost robotically, she chewed the corners of one thumbnail, then the other. She heard them crack under her teeth and it made her hesitate.

Her move here would have been more effective if there hadn't been such a good establishment so near, such a temptation that made it hard for her to ignore the itch. The big casino seemed to be calling to her. She willed herself to visualize Nick and his disapproving face, but it wasn't enough to beat the itch.

Jessie Hawkins couldn't quite place her finger on when the gambling became a problem. As far as she was concerned, it had just happened. She'd never been much of a gambler, but then the tribe had voted to build a casino near Eagle River. After some rather incredible opposition—which eventually included multiple murders and the revelation that Nick Lupo wasn't the only human-wolf hybrid in the woods—the casino was erected in record time, just across from her new hospital.

Her visits had started as mere boredom relief. She pulled her fair share of late shifts in the small ER and the free clinic, and occasionally she was just bored and trying to stay awake at two or three in the morning. The cafeteria was shut down, the vending machines disgusted her, and those blazing lights she saw from her office window promised food in four themed restaurants, including a diner and sports bar, as well as the gambling itself. She'd taken to crossing the street and the parking lots just to grab a bite to eat during the doldrums of her shift.

At least, that was how it started. Then at some point the continuous C Major chord played interminably by the hundreds of slot machines in the barn-like building had drawn her attention. During the day they were crowded with retirees and poor reservation folks looking for a payoff, and of course whites from all over the county who hoped to make their fortune with a few dollars' investment. But at night, traffic was lighter, and she could have her pick of dozens of bright and noisy attention-getting slots emblazoned with a variety of thematic images.

Jessie was a doctor and being analytical was second nature. She knew the gambling was bad, especially financially. The casinos had learned to reduce people's hard-earned money to a simple number, *credits*, to nudge them toward forgetting those *credits* could also pay the rent and buy groceries. She knew her situation was like the long-time smoker who knows smoking is harming him, but does it anyway without too much thought as to why.

She sat in the Pathfinder a while longer, letting the warm air from the vents cascade over her and chase away the worst of the shivers. She chewed and ripped her thumbnails until she tasted blood.

Then she put the truck in gear and headed for the casino.

She just wasn't ready to stop.

A passing thought suggested that maybe she was looking for Nick to rescue her, pull her out of the casino and back into his heart.

She dismissed the passing thought.

"Keep passing," she said, feeling wetness in her eyes.

In a few minutes, she entered the industrial valley southwest of the downtown area and made for the casino, a gargantuan building with seemingly a new wing or addition always under construction. It was like an octopus, reaching out its tentacles to snag unwary passersby.

She fixed her eyes and spruced up a little so as to not appear like one of the lifeless slot machine zombies she had once ridiculed.

There but for the grace of God, wasn't that what they said? She chose not to finish the familiar phrase.

The parking structure was almost full already. She parked on the skywalk level, and a few minutes' walk had her inside, where something seemed to inject itself directly into her bloodstream.

No, she wasn't ready to stop.

Not by herself.

Lupo

After they'd closed down the crime scene and watched the body rolled into the meatwagon, Lupo and DiSanto waited for the uniforms to finish the canvass. But there wasn't all that much to do—there were few tenants around, for the most part.

Lupo had given orders for the canvass to be completed by splitting the remainder so half would be done that night by the late shift cops, and the other the next day by the early shift.

"We'll need lists of everybody your people talked to," Lupo told a veteran sergeant named Golinski. "Get as many as you can on them."

Golinski nodded. He was a good one to work crime scenes. If he had been younger, he might look good for a gold detective's badge, Lupo thought. He watched Golinski talk to each of his men in turn.

DiSanto mimed washing his hands. "Done here, Nick?"

Lupo didn't answer right away. He still felt the tingle of someone watching, but it seemed ridiculous—a trite and trivial cliché at best. He scanned the cavernous room and ticked off everything they had done. It was all covered. Vic's hands had been bagged in special paper, hundreds of digital photographs shot from every angle, every possible surface dusted. The dusting had yielded hundreds of prints—*good luck with that!*—and every aspect of the gruesome crime had been recorded.

"Nick?"

"Uh, yeah, sorry." Lupo sighed. "I think we got it covered."

"What makes people do this shit?" DiSanto asked, probably not expecting an answer.

They had wondered the same thing earlier, as soon as they'd seen the victim's head, removed—*torn off*—and propped up on a corner shelf where its dull staring eyes could survey the room. Below it was a spreading triangle of gore too terrible to contemplate, oozing down the wood shelf to the wall and making like molasses as it reached for the floor like a ghostly talon.

"And why?" DiSanto said.

Lupo wasn't in a philosophical mood. He grunted a noncommittal answer followed by a half shrug. Bakke's expression as he'd stepped out the door had said it all.

"I mean, fuckin' decapitation. It's like a Tarantino movie in here."

The blood had spread from the pyramid and pooled like a shag carpet throughout the room, a half-inch thick lake of darkening crimson. The first cop on the scene had slipped and gone sliding into it face-first. *He* would never forget this one.

"Shit, I don't know," Lupo said.

But he did know.

This reminded him of what those Wolfpaw assholes had done to Tom Arnow's family. Lupo thought if he Changed right now, let the Creature out and let him get a deep sniff, he was convinced he would catch the scent of yet another fucking shapeshifter.

Goddamn it.

"Have to face it, Nick," said Ghost Sam from right beside a clueless DiSanto, "the genie is out of the bottle. And the only way is for you to kill the genie and smash the bottle."

Lupo turned away so fast he figured DiSanto had to think it was an intentional slight. Then he turned back, slowly, regaining his composure while DiSanto eyed him curiously.

Ghost Sam had gone again. Left the air around them slightly skewed.

Awry, he thought. *Different.*

Lupo shrugged. Let that be DiSanto's answer.

"Meet you back in the shop in an hour," Lupo said. "Keep Bakke busy."

Jessie

She slid the gaming card into a charging machine and only caught herself after she'd fed three twenties into its hungry slit mouth.

The doctor part of her wanted to step back and study the reason she had become so weak. She realized, maybe for the first time, that she weakened as soon as she entered the casino. Was it the flashing lights? The continuous C-Major chord that seemed capable of hypnotizing its victims? The lure of easy money?

But she'd never lusted for money before. Never craved it, or obsessed about it. And, in fact, money was reduced to benign numbers when using a card—you forgot the "credits" were quarters, or dollars, or fives, or tens, or hundreds. Which was intelligent psychology practiced by the casinos, like the "free" drinks and the lack of windows.

So why this irresistible urge to flush her money down the toilet?

She realized that she'd moved from the cash machine to a nearby slot machine without being aware of the walk. This sudden realization shocked her, though it didn't keep her from pressing the big red Play button after she'd inserted her card and watching the numbers on the panel display decrease as the dials spun.

Then the dials stopped on the same stylized icon, a king's head, and her numbers ticked upward rapidly, light flashing as the machine played a rousing little tune of victory. A minor win.

About seventy-five dollars, she thought as she did the math in her head. Good enough to cash out ahead. Good enough to take Nick out to dinner, someplace fancier than they usually managed.

She pressed the red button and watched the numbers start their downward trek again.

Simonson

He watched.

Watching had become his mission. That was how he perceived it.

The thing with the house up north was an exception he was forced to make, in order to cover up certain aspects he couldn't have local cops bumbling over.

That had been a surprise. He had himself stumbled over it in the course of a recon, but it had to fit in somewhere.

So besides that wipe action, watching had become his mission, and sometimes that mission included watching other watchers.

That's what he was doing now, watching a watcher.

It could make your head spin.

There was a chess game in progress. Everywhere he looked was a chess game. Occasionally a few pawns and a bishop or rook were eliminated, but for the most part there were many moves the result of which you couldn't see for a while. And his place on the chessboard—that he couldn't see either. He considered himself invisible but he wasn't, not really. He made himself visible now and then, pulling up into radar range and doing something to affect the outcome of the game without being blamed. Or noticed.

Playing God.

Why choose to handle things this way? Maybe because he'd been damned good at it in the military, where he'd gotten his training, and then in the so-called private sector, where his eyes had been opened. And it had all gone bad.

Not really playing God, he mused. But casting about for ways to affect the chess game without becoming too much a piece himself that he could be scooped off the board. Occasionally he lent a hand, but those days were few and very far between.

So Simonson watched.

He had been watching when the scientist decided to play God for his family. That location—it had to have been connected to the cop in some way. He'd only found it by watching and paying attention. But now that he'd stuck his hand in, maybe they'd come after him.

Maybe not. He could never predict what *They* would do. ,

No matter how he tried, he could never out-think them, and that was why he had given himself over to watching.

Watching and waiting.

For the moment.

He put his eyes to the eyepieces and watched as his subject disappeared into the building. He expected a meet, maybe a walk and talk, but as he adjusted the eyepiece he held tightly on the right window, he saw a flash of quick movement followed by a sudden spurt of blood...

It couldn't be anything else.

Blood spattered one of the loft-size windows.

He watched as his subject committed the very same depravity Simonson had pledged to stop.

But as was so often the case he was too far away, in a precarious position, and if he interfered he would most certainly be too late to save the victim while at the same time making himself too visible on the chessboard. Becoming a target ruined a piece's chances of survival.

He bit his tongue, clenched his teeth, felt his muscles tighten and relax over and over as if they were being jolted by a torturer's electric prod, and in the end all he could do was watch.

He purposely kept his eyes open, absorbing the details of what he saw.

His breathing had slowed to a pace more akin to death, and he realized he had simply forgotten to breathe.

Time passed almost quicker than his watch could catch. He watched, but his subject had disappeared after the deed was done. He hadn't expected it, but he should have predicted it, and it bothered him that once again he had been unable to out-think one of *Them.*

The damned headaches were affecting his thought patterns, his logic, his critical thinking.

He swallowed a half dozen aspirin.

So then he watched as the cops came and did their thing, amazed at how quickly they came. He watched as they ran the crime scene about as well as they could, knowing some of what they'd find would make them shake their heads and doubt their collection abilities or their instruments. He watched as the one specific cop he wanted to see stayed back. He used his equipment to assure himself of what was happening with that cop.

Simonson already knew about *him*. But he didn't only watch the cop, he also watched the Watcher.

The Watcher had killed the innocent victim. *Slaughtered* him, more like. Then he had settled back to watch from afar.

Simonson watched *him*, too.

And the cop.

This was very interesting. Interesting how they were both watching.

He kept watching.

Chapter Three

Lupo

He checked for stragglers. The lieutenant had bugged out quick, the crime scene techs had left, the useless EMTs had sidled out, the coroner's staff had booked it with the vic's body, and the last uniform now stood in front of the sealed door.

"Pull this duty, Officer?" Lupo asked him. The guy was young, barely a rookie. It was almost like hazing—make the new kid haunt the sealed door.

The kid sighed. He knew it. "Yes, sir. Orders."

At least he was smart about it.

Lupo nodded. "What's your name?"

"Baranski, sir."

"Okay, then, Baranski. I'm heading up to check out the rest of this stairwell. Don't mind any noise I make, all right?"

The kid looked at him with a funny expression crossing his baby-fat features. "I think that's already been done, sir."

"Sure, but I like to check some details myself," Lupo said casually. "My case, my details, my responsibility. I'm the one who caught this, so you got to humor me, Officer Baranski. Keep me happy, I put in a good word for you down the line."

The kid blushed. "Thank you, sir, Detective Lupo."

"Cool. Actually, can you head down to the first floor and see if those other neighbors can give a statement now?" He spoke lower. "Maybe you won't have to be back tomorrow to finish the canvass, you get those statements now."

The young cop nodded slowly. This was an assignment he could wrap his mind around, while standing indefinitely in front of a dead guy's door seemed like a dead end.

As soon as the kid started down the stairs, Lupo went up. The staircase was dingy and grimy, with here and there the exposed bare brick of the outside wall and crumbling cinderblock on the inside. A building on the wrong side of the development line. Here, the Cream City brick so valued elsewhere was just too deteriorated for restoration.

He took the stairs by twos, finding nothing but locked doors on every landing. Gray light intruded through greasy, glass block windows that faced the back of the building. The dust on the stairs seemed to have been disturbed by one passing set of footprints. Three flights up, the dust had been kicked up in a confusion of smudges.

But there was something worse.

The footprints leading up to the next landing were typical of shoes. The prints that emerged from the kicked-up area were made by a wolf.

It could have been a dog, and to the average eye it would have been easy to dismiss the marks as having been made by somebody's guard dog. Except Lupo knew wolf's prints when he saw them.

A shiver worked its way down Lupo's back like a trickle of ice water. A growl worked its way up his throat. The Creature was trying to get out. *Needed to get out.*

Now.

Lupo suppressed the growl, but in a minute he'd stripped off his clothes and tucked them onto the window ledge. He'd planned a recon already, but the wolf prints meant he had to be in wolf form—both for the Creature's nose and in case he stumbled onto this new adversary.

Another like him.

Another *monster.*

Lupo concentrated, visualizing his transformation from muscled, naked human to wolf.

He was getting faster. He'd barely begun to visualize himself running on four giant paws when he felt the transition begin and complete and just like that—*it's a fact, Jack!*—he was over and leaping up the same steps, his paws obscuring the other wolf's marks.

This territory's now mine! the Creature seemed to say.

The usual multitude of sharp scents was like a lancet driven through his nostrils and straight into his brain.

Chemicals made his nose twitch—*paint and thinner and glue.* But there were other scents, too. Rotting food, urine, various intermixed perfumes and colognes, sweat, scorched hair, feces, semen, cheap air freshener...

And another shapeshifter.

Just as he had thought.

Now that he was over, the Creature wanted full control, and Lupo felt his influence slipping as the other shapeshifter's scent grew stronger in his nostrils. Another growl built up from down in his throat, and the Creature's jaws opened in anticipation of a confrontation.

It craved conflict. It was a territorial monster, after all, and this other shapeshifter whose scent was in his nostrils was on *his* turf now.

Lupo considered how much easier his life had been when he was the only shapeshifter around, even though it had seemed incredibly complex to him. But only being faced with enemies like him, who knew more than him, and who outnumbered him—only now could he see how naïve he had been.

He let the wolf have its head. Maybe the Creature would lead him to the enemy, though it was unlikely the perp would still be here. Lupo was still trying to figure out the best way to exploit his shapeshifting abilities, but he'd learned quickly they often caused as many complications as they resolved.

The wolf nosed its way into the open loft on this floor, a wide-open space that had been gutted in preparation for a future tenant.

The Creature's almost involuntary growl was a signal it had caught the scent.

The scent of the werewolf who had been here earlier, waiting for the right time to slaughter the guy downstairs...

But why?

Lupo couldn't help wondering the *why* of the crime.

The Creature stalked the space, checking the tall windows, sniffing the unpolished floor, catching the smells of other activity, but also the enemy wolf's scent and letting it infiltrate its memory. If the Creature came across the same scent, it would remember.

And that was useful. But how did it help Lupo now? There was no apparent clue as to the motive. The perp had wandered this space, then made his way down the stairs either as human or wolf, and then he'd ripped the poor, dumb, helpless bastard down there to shreds. *But why?*

And Lupo had to wonder, then, whether he was the reason. Was *he* himself the motive? Was the enemy wolf simply raising a challenge flag, marking his territory in blood rather than in the traditional method?

Was Lupo inadvertently responsible for the poor guy's death?

His *murder?*

Jesus.

Mordred

The band around his head threatened to squeeze his brain out his ears like bloody toothpaste.

He put his trembling hands up and tried to massage his temples. His bones felt sharp and brittle under the thin layer of skin.

He closed his eyes and he was back in the lab.

In the lab.

The long, bare strips of neon lighting stabbed his pupils and made him shiver with their implied cold.

No, it *was* cold.

He heard voices behind the glass partition, the one that reflected his own distorted image. He knew they huddled back there, watching him like a freak.

Watching...

They watched as he reacted to the drugs and to whatever else they put in the syringes. They watched, sometimes, as he writhed on the bare concrete floor like a fish flopping on the grass after having been plucked out of a pond. They watched as he bruised his body and broke his limbs and sometimes as he bled all over their floor, always judging, measuring what their evil would do to him.

They watched because he *was* a freak.

The harsh pressure he applied to his temples started to do the trick, and he came back, thankfully leaving the lab behind. *Again.* But it was always there, the lab, ready to encroach on him when he was least prepared.

But now the call of the mission took over his focus, and he knew he was back on track.

He had left several tiny cams in place throughout the loft itself and also in the staircase, and now he paned the software across the large screen to monitor all the angles simultaneously.

And then he was watching the cop go through his Change and then sniff the loft.

Ah, the game's afoot.

He chuckled.

He noted Lupo's wolf form with interest. He was an oversized black wolf, definitely an aberration. His surveillance logs and videos would formulate a thorough report.

Doctor Schlosser would be pleased.

Lupo

Back at Central, Lupo ripped off his crooked tie. He'd retied it too quickly. He hated those things. Choked him, and he hated to have his neck constricted.

Maybe it was a wolf thing.

He stuffed the silver silk tie Jessie had picked out for him into his pocket and hoped she wouldn't find it. He'd catch hell for that.

Now that he shared his city space with her, he was acutely aware of how often their different styles somehow managed to clash. His living style was to let things lie where they landed when he tossed them in disgust, anger, or frustration. Her living style was to obsessively pick up after him, criticize his lack of organization when she couldn't figure out where his stuff belonged, and then nag him about changing.

Nag?

Did I really think that about her? About Jessie?

She'd never been a nag before, but their close proximity lately seemed to bring it out of her. And he had been alone for so long that he hadn't quite yet managed to relearn how to diplomatically navigate around someone sharing his space for more than a few hours. Which was probably why she'd taken to being away from his place whenever she thought he might be on his way home.

It was like being married, he figured, without any of the good parts.

How did we get from there to here?

She wasn't really a nag. He chided himself for thinking these thoughts. No, not a nag, but Jessie Hawkins knew she had rights, and she used them.

"Hey!"

Lupo turned and shot a blank look at DiSanto, who gave him his version of the Seinfeldian raised eyebrow, pop-eyed headshake that meant *What's wrong with you?*

"What?" He tucked the last of the guilty tie into the evidence-suppressing pocket.

"I was asking you if you found anything else worth sharing on your whatever you call it, personal canvass?" DiSanto waited for Lupo to swing into his desk chair before finishing in a whisper. "Cause the Loo wants to know what we've got. The Third Ward's too ritzy for disgusting crimes like this, you know that."

Lieutenant Walter C. Bakke was the new guy in the homicide squad leader's office. The last two guys had retired young. Very young. Bakke was trying to buck the trend.

DiSanto looked around to make sure Bakke wasn't skulking about. "I hear he's already gotten a call from the mayor."

"The fuck, already?" Lupo made a sour face. "There's gotta be a mole on the squad. How could he know to get worked up over this already?" But this explained the hurried crime scene visit, the personal interest.

"You know the Loo. If this were the Inner City, he'd just wave us off to do our thing. But the Third Ward, that's money. Got to keep the richies happy."

Lupo sighed. DiSanto's humor was dangerous sometimes. He called Bakke "Loo" ostensibly because he was the *loo-tenant*, but no one other than Lupo had caught on yet that he was also riffing subtly on the boss's initials.

God help us the day he figures it out.

"What about Killian, the bastard? Is he our little underground rat-mammal? He call the mayor?"

Lupo's dislike for Griff Killian was well known if not acknowledged, but no one other than the two of them knew the mutual circumstances. Lupo could sense Killian wanted to trap him, but the Arnow killing and its hazy culpability effectively muzzled him.

For the moment.

"I don't know who the rat is," said DiSanto, "but it doesn't matter right now. What matters is that we're taking heat for this thing already, and we don't have any real leads."

Lupo said, "I didn't find much of anything above or below that loft. Maybe the CSI boys have something. No report yet?"

"Nah, they're down a couple with the flu. Maybe tomorrow."

"They're not terribly quick even on a good day."

Lupo glanced at Killian's office window and tried to see through the blinds. His thoughts wandered. There was too much to keep quiet, too much he couldn't explain. How was he supposed to keep all these secrets when they were about to blow up in his face?

"Maybe it's time you trusted DiSanto with your secret," Ghost Sam said. He was sitting on Lupo's guest chair. "Maybe it's time you stopped carrying all the burdens of the world."

Lupo tried to ignore the ghostly interruption, but he stayed where he was.

"You can't fight them alone," said Ghost Sam obstinately.

Go away! You're dead, Sam. Leave me alone!

"We have anything new on the victim?"

DiSanto nodded, checking a notebook teetering on top of a stack of folders. "Yeah, we were right about him being an accountant and camera operator, kind of. Lenny A. Wolf. He's also listing himself as an independent producer. Midnight Films is his baby. And..."

"And?"

"And based on the recordings we found, most of their product is low-grade porn, with a smattering of really cheap horror flicks sold direct to DVD for a pittance."

Delayed effect. Lupo felt his ears pop as if the pressure in the squad room had changed.

"What was that name again?"

Chapter Four

Killian

The day had turned into another haze.

It was routine by now. He could awaken clear-eyed and filled with purpose, but by noon or one o'clock the haze took over and his brain turned to mush. As if overloaded, the organ would simply refuse to keep two thoughts simultaneously in mind. No matter how many lists, journal entries, freewriting exercises, sessions with the shrink, and whispers in the confessional of the bar he attempted, the haze took over, and he became a diminished version of himself.

The headache began as soon as he opened his eyes, banged on his temples all day long, and faded only after he drifted off into unsettled sleep. His nights were filled with images of large animals stalking him, galloping on all fours as he ran in place, their hot breath on his neck. He awoke unrefreshed every day, his eyes aching and his head beginning its normal throb. Eventually, his brain packed it in, and he set his forehead down on the desk as long as he could stand it.

Griff Killian felt hunger as well as the haze lapping at his edges, so he selected a burrito blindly from his cold stash and groaned as he bent to give it a nuking in his tiny microwave stacked on top of his child-size refrigerator. The calories and fat were beginning to take their toll. He wasn't quite as dashing and imposing a figure as when he had been brought here to the ailing Milwaukee PD to ramp up Internal Affairs and seek out any departmental "bad apples."

And he'd been successful, too.

Maybe too successful. He'd been dubbed the Grim Reaper, and it was said when he walked the halls of the precinct he was recruiting for hell.

He sniffed the air, enjoying the food's plastic but somehow appealing aroma as it bubbled in the microwave. He'd had the habit for years, but now no matter how he enjoyed the smell of the heating processed food, when the haze caught him full square, he was barely able to acknowledge that in which he would normally bask.

Yeah, he'd been very successful, taking the Milwaukee PD into the 21st Century in terms of rooting out its less motivated—or downright criminal—elements. He had become a legend, mostly respected but always with that edge of hatred because Killian's IA went after even the most mundane corruption, the free concert ticket or occasional coffee handed over unpaid. But for the real bad apples, he *was* the Grim Reaper.

Now he had made Detective Dominic Lupo—he sneered, thinking how they called him "Nick"—his pet project. Of course, the curve ball the bastard had thrown him with the Tom Arnow incident had taken him out of the game. But not for long.

Not for long, you asshole. Not for long.

Nobody beats Killian.

They'd said it in grade school, in high school he'd beaten it into them, and in college he'd proven the saying right in so many ways.

He watched from the narrow slits in his office blinds as Lupo came waltzing in and limped to his desk.

But that was it, wasn't it? The bastard didn't limp to his desk. He didn't limp at all.

Arrogant sonofabitch. If he could only prove the mangy cop was faking the injury...

Old Julia Barrett had been right after all.

Killian seethed.

But the cop seemed to have friends in high places. Despite the revolving door in the homicide lieutenant's office as of late, Lupo just kept skating by. Who protected him? He'd have to check with David Marcowicz and see if he had any theories. He had his own session with Marcowicz, trying to deal with the shooting with which he had been saddled.

He kept an eye on Lupo. *Now* the bastard seemed to remember, and he started limping.

Start-stop, start-stop. Sure as hell not consistent.

Killian took a bite of his congealed burrito, and his chest seized up for a moment. This "Hot Flaming" stamp they put on there wasn't kidding. He felt the reflux starting to happen, but swallowed down the acid bile that rose up and mixed with the beany, cheesy flavor. His belly rumbled.

He watched as Lupo and the dipshit DiSanto hobnobbed. They didn't seem so concerned about the gruesome homicide on their blotter, did they? The homicide lieutenant, a new guy named Bakke, was squealing like a pig about pressure, but Killian couldn't see any of it. The pace in the squad room hadn't picked up.

He snagged the phone off his desk and dialed.

"Marcowicz? It's Killian," he said when the whiny voice answered. "I need to see you."

He eyed Lupo, who was on the phone now. He hated dirty cops, and Lupo just had to be dirty. Besides what the bastard had done to Killian.

Why couldn't he remember exactly what Lupo had done to him? Why did he watch the scene replay itself over and over in the middle of the night, but it remained mostly a haze of indistinct images? There was a chase, a takedown, and a fight, but he simply could not put it in focus. Then suddenly the fucker Lupo shot the other cop, the sheriff, and then from that moment on Killian remembered all too well that Lupo owned him.

Lupo fucking owned him.

Killian had survived politically because the inquest had ruled "his" shot had been accidental. What the fuck did *they* know? Killian knew enough about what had happened to know Lupo had engineered some kind of wild con on everyone. Including him, because he knew he'd seen *something* he had since blocked. Multiple visits to Marcowicz's office had not unlocked the truth of what he had seen, but he knew Lupo had him—that what he had seen would get him deep-sixed, dumped, psycho-labeled. Retired, if he was lucky. Otherwise, institutionalized.

He had to find a way...

But how to trap him without succumbing to the bastard's blackmail? Whatever had really happened out there, Lupo seemed sure it would hurt Killian if he squawked.

Cocksure, actually.

He had to find a way to trip up the cop that didn't directly involve him.

Killian chewed the cold burrito paste thoughtfully. He felt the air build up in his chest and ignored it.

He dialed again and hunched over the phone.

Lupo

"The privilege of rank," said DiSanto as they slid into a dark booth at the Ale House, still in the Third Ward.

"You can't delegate the whole investigation," Lupo said.

They'd started some uniforms on various tasks, started some automated searches, and called it quits for some sleep. But DiSanto complained he needed food. Lupo wasn't very comfortable making the stop when he thought he should go home and check on Jessie. On the other hand, a quick sandwich and something non-alcoholic would help settle his stomach.

DiSanto ordered a designer cheeseburger and a Bloody Mary when the waitress stopped by. She eyed them suspiciously. DiSanto wore a suit, but not so stylish as to suggest attorney or accountant. *Cop!* She was the type who seemed to be normally bubbly but tonight she'd forgotten how to be. She looked at them strangely.

Lupo asked for a steak sandwich, rare, skip the fries, and a tall iced tea.

"Man, not even a beer?" DiSanto shook his head sadly.

Sitting across from him in the booth, Ghost Sam disagreed. "You need to stay sharp, Nick. Something's in the wind. I can feel it."

Crap, did he have to have his own clairvoyant shaman?

Some people had angels, some devils. Some might have been hounded by their consciences. In Ghost Sam, Nick thought he had all three.

"Don't forget comedian," the Indian said. "Thank you, I'll be here all week."

Jesus.

Being haunted could be very inconvenient.

The food came and he chewed the meat unhappily. As usual, they hadn't believed he wanted the steak *actually* rare, so they'd given it a thorough grilling anyway. It pleased the Creature not at all.

"What do you drink when you're not enjoying a brew? You're kind of a connoisseur, right?" DiSanto asked.

DiSanto was in need of a life, a girlfriend, or something to do.

"I like beer, the less mass-produced the better. Harder stuff, I usually order rum and tonic or a Manhattan. At home, I make my own version I call the Midtown Manhattan."

"Oh yeah, you invented it? What's in it?" DiSanto clearly wanted to avoid discussing the butchery they'd just seen.

"Manhattans are usually made with whiskey, but since this is Wisconsin, I use brandy. Equal parts, brandy and sweet vermouth, plus a half shot of Triple Sec or Cointreau. Tall glass, lots of rocks. A tiny splash of bitters, olive or cherry optional."

"Sounds sweet."

"Well, you could use the whiskey, less vermouth, and stick to olives or onions."

"I meant *sweet* as in *just fine*," said DiSanto, who liked clichés.

"Ah."

They chewed in silence. Sometimes DiSanto was just a bit too enthusiastic for Lupo. He missed his old partner, Ben Sabatini, for his cynical silences.

"If you'd confide in him, he'd be able to help you more." Ghost Sam was back, eyeing the food he couldn't eat.

Lupo shook his head.

No, Ghost Sam was a manifestation of his needs, not the dead person, no matter how much he'd come to like that dead person. He closed his eyes and when he reopened them Ghost Sam was gone.

"—been kinda quiet about this one, Nick. What's up? You're not worried about this so-called pressure from the mayor, are you?"

"I'm worried about where it came from. Got to be Killian. He has it in for me, and this is a good way to get under my skin."

"Sure, I get you guys don't like each other, but why would he try to torpedo your case? Doesn't make sense, does it? We're all on the same team."

"Are we?"

"Well, I thought so. Fucking politics."

Lupo wasn't about to go into details, but it was more than just politics—it was a feud that was going to get worse before it got better.

That's what happens when the basis of anything is murder.

They paid the waitress, who was still avoiding their eyes.

Only when they walked out into the lighted lobby did DiSanto notice the dried bloodstains on the back of Lupo's leather jacket.

"Good thing I wear my badge on my belt," joked DiSanto. "Otherwise she'd have called the cops on us."

Lupo nodded.

He hadn't taken the jacket off except when he'd wolfed and checked out the staircase and the other loft. So how'd he get blood on it?

Mordred

He had them in the crosshairs when they were standing in the lobby. Looked like they'd spotted the blood he had left as a gift.

Lupo would get it. The other guy was not even on the board.

If he'd gotten the word right then, he could have taken them both out in about ten seconds. The temptation was great. But Sigfried had him on a tight leash. Mordred did not know what the plan was, or what he would be required to do for the endgame, but he knew he was only to trace, record, and interpret. What Sigfried planned to do with the information was not for him to question, although the beast within him wanted a piece of this Lupo character. Whatever Lupo had done to Sigfried, it was enough to split his time between the big hearings and whatever Mordred told him.

He'd been recording video, too, directly from the van with a long-range rig. But he was especially proud of his walk into the crowded bar and slouching past the booth the two cops occupied. He had planted a tiny cam below the ledge that ran around the large saloon-style room at waist level. And now what he heard about this Killian guy sounded intriguing.

Mordred itched to terminate something.

The cop.

The mission.

He wasn't used to being outside the loop. Sigfried had given him more responsibility than this. Why was he playing his cards close to the chest?

Jesus!

His finger tightened on the trigger and he mimed squeezing it, ever so slowly.

Boom.

Boom.

Lupo

He found her more or less where he thought he would.

He'd split from DiSanto at the Ale House. DiSanto was heading back to the shop to check on leads and searches. They'd both had to eat, so it wasn't like they were taking time off the job.

But Lupo had pulled rank on him, too. He had to check on Jessie.

He hated to admit it to himself, but he was worried about her fragile state. Ever since the casino shoot-out, she'd been slipping into a dark zone—with the uncontrollable gambling, for instance.

And he also hated to admit that his dalliance—did they use that word anymore?—with Heather Wilson had shaken her faith in him more than he had imagined. They hadn't committed to each other in any official capacity, that was true, but there was an implied commitment.

Dammit, he was uncomfortable with commitment.

Not because he had anything against it, but because everyone he'd ever committed to wound up hurt, or worse. His track record with commitment was lousy, and now that he had someone worth cherishing, he was afraid it would end badly. And it would be his fault.

Then again, maybe it's just my guilt trying to disguise itself.

He had plenty of guilt.

The darkness had almost claimed him for good. He hadn't confessed to Jessie that he had stepped off the ledge and fallen deeply into a spiral that led to a self-destructive moment.

He was still vague on how it had happened, but even worse, on how it had ended. And he was still around.

He had used the dagger...

The damned dagger that had saved him, and others, but then it had killed Tom Arnow.

Fuck that.

I *killed Tom Arnow.*

And Lupo had decided he shouldn't live, either. He'd unsheathed the dagger from its—*magical*—protective scabbard, which exposed the deadly silver blade. With the heat already starting to scorch his skin, he had sought the final release.

And somebody had stopped him.

Lupo had been close to death, unconscious, the blade doing its work inside his body, liquefying his insides and killing both him and the Creature inside him...

But when he awoke, Lupo wasn't in some afterlife or in some netherworld. He was at home, and the dagger had been withdrawn from the wound. The damage it had done was healing, repairing itself, and the dagger—safely sheathed—had been left on his dresser.

Through the pain of the knitting wounds, which had been nearly fatal, he had rethought his position on living.

Sometimes all you need is a friend.

Even if you don't know who it is.

So now he hoped to return the favor, even if he didn't know whom to thank. Perhaps it was Jessie. He'd considered asking her, but if he was wrong then he would have been confessing that he'd sought a way out. And if it had been her, he knew her well enough to know she couldn't treat it like a secret...

He owed Jessie, far more than just for having been willing to put up with *him* and his condition. He owed her for tangible, gun-in-hand help and back-up like he'd gotten from almost no one else.

So now, as he walked the length of the barn-like Indian casino, he knew he'd find her at one of her favorite rows of slots.

The human brain was a mystery.

Shit, add the heart to that list...

Some people took adversity and used it to become religious. Some did good works and volunteered. Some became aid workers. Some didn't make lemonade, after all—they withdrew and sought a way out, like he had.

Jessie had taken her adversity and turned it into an addiction the likes of which he could never have predicted.

So he was here, surveying the long rows of stools, searching for her lustrous hair among the shorter, elderly people who made up the majority of the clientele.

There she was...

He stopped and stepped aside, out of the flow, watching her from afar.

Even here, at her worst, pushing the bet button with robotic movements so unlike her...even here she was magnificent.

A thoroughbred among elderly plow horses.

Was that a bad way to describe her?

Fuck it, no one has to know.

He smiled, a little sadly, and watched her for a few minutes from afar.

Her profile was superb. Her breasts strained the front of her blouse, which was rather conservative. Her leather coat gave her a sort of Indiana Jones look, but no one who looked into those smoldering dark eyes or saw the curl of those perfect smiling lips would have mistaken her for Harrison Ford.

He admired her for a while, letting the day's events slide off. Let DiSanto worry about it until tomorrow.

He approached her from behind and put a hand lightly on her back. Sadly, he felt her stiffen under his touch.

Chapter Five

Jessie

When Nick found her at the slot machines, she felt fury.

Fury at having been caught indulging her weakness. Though she told herself she was furious he had invaded her privacy.

Actually she wasn't pleased to have been so predictable, either.

"Jess, please, we have to talk about this."

His color-shifting eyes were still enticing and romantic, reminiscent of what had attracted her in the first place and had kept them together this long, but now they reflected his hurt.

She turned his hurt into his fault.

He's just a good actor, that's all.

She turned away from his stricken look and pressed the machine's Maximum Bet button with a quick little jab of her finger. The reels spun crazily, the lights and electronic carnival music trivializing the moment between them.

The three pictures that landed across the screen didn't match, and thirty credits disappeared from her card.

Thirty dollars.

When did I switch to the ten-dollar machine?

His hand was on her arm, gentle pressure keeping her from jettisoning more virtual cash.

"Jess!" he said, loud enough that a couple heads turned from nearby slot machines. "Please. Let's at least get some food and talk, okay?"

Her muscles locked up as he steadily prodded her off the vinyl stool.

No!

He was stronger, though, and one by one her defenses broke down, and he had her off the stool, stepping away.

She was crying now, big, fat tears rolling down her face. She reached back and ejected her gaming card, and then Nick was pulling her down the long aisle. Someone slipped into her spot on the stool, and Jessie resented that person, who would reap the benefit of her play. She'd warmed up that machine! Now it would hit a winner.

Nick's hand on her arm steering her through two tight turns, then heading down another aisle, finally broke her connection to the game that wasn't a game.

God, she knew deep down that pressing a button to flush your money down an electronic toilet was no game.

Of course she knew that.

Then why did she continue doing it? Why, even now, did she want to reach out and stop at a blinking slot machine and start again?

They reached the food court, and Nick guided her to a corner table. The place was only lightly busy, for it was too late for dinner. Gamblers ate only when hungry and not by the clock, so there was always some traffic to and from the dozen food kiosks offering a faux version of every kind of cuisine you could name. Much of it would be over-salted, fried, and carb-heavy, just what the doctor ordered to keep people thirsty and on their feet at the games and tables. It was all a cycle.

Nick sat her down, made a *Wait* gesture, then stalked off. He returned a minute later with two cups of free coffee from the self-help station nearby.

"Jess, you need to eat something," he said.

She shrugged. "I had a sandwich."

"When?"

"Sometime today."

"Jess, it's almost midnight." He shucked his coat. "Wait here."

Her muscles seemed to melt into the plastic chair. Suddenly she couldn't have moved if she wanted to.

He returned with a tray bearing two slices of New York-style pizza, a pile of vaguely Chinese chicken tidbits, a cinnamon roll and two forks.

"Best I could do here," he said in apology. "We should have gone to the buffet or the sports bar."

"It's okay, I'm not hungry."

He spread out the food and split the bun.

"Hey, the pizza's not bad," he said, chewing. "Not enough meat for me, but..."

Then she was crying. "What's wrong with me, Nick?" She laid her head in her hands. "What's happened to us?"

He set down the pizza and took her hands in his, forcing her to look at him. She tried to avoid his eyes, but found she couldn't. His gaze had always been entrancing, and now it was especially so.

As if he were gazing into her soul.

Her eyes leaked bitter tears, and she didn't try to stop them. Nick said nothing. He waited her out. The food congealed between them.

In a few minutes, her breath hitched as she tried to inhale through her blocked nostrils. She blew her nose with one of the napkins he had brought, which he held out for her. She half smiled and then picked up her sagging pizza slice.

"You're right, doesn't look bad," she said, taking a bite. He followed suit, obviously giving her space to speak her mind.

Jessie appreciated that he was thoughtful, in his own way. For a few minutes, they picked at the food. She realized she was hungry after all, but her stomach was upset. And her breathing was labored—all that smoke... When would casinos go smokeless, like the rest of the world? Probably never. Why turn off potential customers? And even though the state had banned indoor smoking, the Indian casinos were exempt by virtue of being on sovereign land. Did her clothes reek of smoke when she finally made it home? *Home.* It sounded comforting. Did she deserve comfort?

She finished her slice, forcing down the last bit of crust. Then she looked at him over a forkful of fried rice she didn't really want, either.

"Why are you eating so late?" *And hunting me down.*

He followed her lead and ignored the issues between them for the moment. "I caught another bad one today. Third Ward. It's messy as hell, and it has wolf written all over it."

The food caught in her throat. "What? Oh no," she blurted out. Maybe he wasn't ignoring the issues after all, but doubling down. "Another one? Is it...*them?*"

He sighed. "I don't know. But probably."

"My God..."

"Yeah, I thought we were rid of them. They're in the spotlight daily. I mean, I thought they'd be more careful. But there's no link to us that I can see. The vic was another of those low-level porn guys all the Internet technology's created the last ten years. Did low-budget horror and stuff like that, too. Otherwise, it almost seems random. But it was messy enough—and sloppy—that it just might be a message. To me. The vic's name was Leonard A. Wolf."

Her eyes widened as she sounded it out.

"Jesus, Nick." She rounded up another forkful of cold rice, but put it down. "Not again."

She felt an itch crawling down her arms to her hands, her fingers. As if they yearned to head for the slots, or maybe the roulette wheel. As if they longed for the safe risk. Gambling was safer to face than monstrous hunters bent on tearing you apart and eating your flesh.

"And how awful, murdering someone just because of his name," she added.

Nick tore the cinnamon bun in half and took a bite before setting it aside. "There's no point speculating yet. Right now it looks that way to me, and for some reason we're taking heat on it already. DiSanto's holding down the fort, but I don't have very long. Let's go home, Jess. Please."

"Is it home, Nick?" The words tumbled out before she could stop them. Perhaps it was the knowledge that he had, after all, cheated on her with that disgusting reporter woman.

His eyes registered the blow. "It's home as long as you're there," he said softly.

She nodded. It was the right thing to say.

But how much did it mean, coming from him?

She let herself be led away from the table. He slid their cold food into the trash can slot and stacked the tray with the others. Even though she felt the pull of the games behind her, the siren call of the perpetual C-Major chord created by the clusters of machines waiting to be fed hard-earned cash.

She flashed on Eric Woolfson's *Turn of a Friendly Card* suite, specifically the "Nothing Left to Lose" section, and wondered if it weren't true for her.

Then she followed Nick out to the massive parking structure and tried to ignore the blank-eyed stares of those just wading in. She knew she must look like that, and she didn't like it. Not at all.

Was that *blood* on his jacket? She didn't ask and he didn't mention it. Maybe it had been a bad one for him after all.

The drive home was a blur. Her well-used Pathfinder might as well have followed his car on its own through some mystical autopilot. She didn't remember parking. She didn't remember the stairs. Now she stood in front of the gas fireplace as he flicked on the switch and the heat began to dissipate the long day's cold. Early winter was building up its strength, biding its time.

She looked around. This place, an old, East Side apartment he had adjusted to his needs over the years—bars on the windows, reinforced doors, multiple locks, subtle soundproofing—had become a temporary haven to her since the shoot-out at the casino near Eagle River. But it felt like a prison, too, as did her free time. She was on indefinite leave from the rez hospital, and there was a perfectly fine Indian casino only twenty minutes' drive away. (Nick had taken her to its small theatre to see Alan Parsons and his Live Project recently, and then she had become reacquainted with gaming.) Now the itch to press those buttons had become its own prison, one only she could see.

Nothing left to lose.

Jessie sensed that Nick was acting on borrowed time. DiSanto was a good guy, and an even better partner. Nick teased him mercilessly, but they'd bonded after poor Ben Sabatini's murder. The younger cop

49

was probably on the job, letting Nick get some rest. She noted he'd set his phone where he could grab it quickly.

The fact that he was here, rather than on the job, on a heater case, said a lot. She should feel lucky. But luck was elusive.

"How about a drink?" Nick said.

He slid his iPod into the Bose dock that had recently taken over his stereo needs and hunted up something appropriate. She bet herself it would be one of *their* songs—the Alan Parsons Project, or a Greg Lake ballad. Maybe Genesis from *The Trick of the Tail* days.

She was surprised when the first piano notes cascaded from the speaker. Rick Wakeman's *Sea Airs*. Very romantic.

Gee, I can't get away from gambling even in my mind, she thought as she paid off the lost bet.

"Maybe one drink," she said.

Nick turned and faced her, his look intense in the flickering darkness. He touched her cheek with a rough hand. She felt the scars entrenched through his flesh, where he'd gripped a silver-loaded handgun.

Neither said anything for a long, breathless moment.

Then he swept her into a rough embrace, and she felt her body respond almost independently of her mind, which wanted her to analyze, measure, and step away.

But it was too late. Their mouths found each other, and her need was suddenly overpowering, and it seemed that his was, too. For a long while they tasted each other like teenagers at a drive-in...

Did teenagers even know what a drive-in was, she wondered, her mind once again separating from her body.

Does it matter?

He held her closer and nuzzled her ripe lips, her smooth cheeks, her ears, her neck, all the while stroking her hair with his large hands. Their tongues met, danced, twirled, then retreated, leaving behind a cooling sheen of desire they both felt. Their motions intensified, and in the light of the gas flame in the corner their pupils flickered with the fire of their passion as they stared into each other's eyes. After a few minutes his hands slid from the back of her head, down her back, and to her sides, where his caresses made her breathing quicken. Their lips on each other, their roving hands causing friction heat, they slowly edged toward the maroon leather sofa, sinking into its cool embrace while continuing to explore each other like kids accidentally left alone by overprotective parents.

Oh, Nick. She reacted to his touch, but also felt regret for her behavior. But she couldn't figure out how to force herself to change. The gambling was somehow driving a bigger wedge between them than his fleeting infidelity. Because he had made amends, and continued to do so, while she floundered about in the rising waters of gambling addiction, waters that threatened to drown her if she didn't find a way to get herself free.

His hands were under her blouse now, his hot skin infecting hers with the lovely burning of his lust. She unbuttoned, and he peeled the cotton slowly downward, freeing her covered breasts. Burning fingertips slid under her brassiere, and she felt his touch on her skin and she deftly undid the clasp and then her breasts thrust out at him, her nipples growing from the heat between them. He took them between gentle fingers, one at a time, and followed up with his tongue.

She moaned. This had been magical for them since that first time, up in the cottage he rented from her. There had been heat between them for years, but he had never realized it, and she had been too shy. His confused feelings had been based on how dangerous his *condition* had proven for those he loved. And nothing had changed... In fact, knowing someone had possibly used a murder to send him a message was almost enough to cool her passion.

Almost. What he was doing inexorably drove her into a frenzy, her sensitive nipples tingling under his attention. His tongue slowly traversed the long curve of her belly, around and around the skin of her navel, the warmth-cool of his saliva entering her smooth pucker before it continued down the downy slope toward the top hem of her jeans.

He unsnapped them and slowly stripped them down over her thighs. She laid her hand gently on the back of his head and urged him onward, downward. He unzipped them in front with one hand, the other stroking her buttocks as they were revealed. His tongue trailed down, past where the jeans had been, and reached the top of her panties. His hand, now free, tugged the thin fabric down, and he followed, his lips and tongue softly kissing the skin plunging to her cleft.

On a dare from her friend Donna Banner, a life-loving pediatrician recently hired on at the rez hospital, Jessie had gone from a neatly trimmed mound to a bare one, feeling deliciously wicked as she'd admired the results afterwards. *And Nick...* Nick had certainly reacted to her decision as Donna'd predicted. And why not? She knew how sensual the smoothness could be.

Now Nick tortured her with a slow and deliberate prying open of her smooth folds, kissing her with uninhibited passion as she felt herself melting inside.

He grunted as he ran into the obstacle of her pants and damp panties again and, with endearing impatience, tugged hard until the fabrics reached her ankles, at which point she shucked them completely by stepping out of their tangle and kicking them away. The way clear, Nick homed in on her most sensitive areas, and she spread her feet to allow him access. She used her hands on his head for balance and gave herself to him without reservation.

The white heat of the moment melted any differences they'd had, any issues, and any conflicts. All she could do was concentrate on the pleasure he was intent on giving her, selfless and unbounded by inhibition.

He opened her as if unwrapping the ultimate gift, and his hot tongue electrified her inside and out, exploring and never still, tasting and touching, swirling and lapping. She groaned and pulled him toward her, granting him more and more of herself.

And he took more and more, nuzzling and licking and both zeroing in on and deliciously depriving her most sensitive spot. Harder and harder, then less, hotter and then cooler, wet and dry, he made her the target of all his attention, and she saw red at the edges of her vision whenever she opened her eyes. Then she closed her eyes, and it was just the two of them in the world,

Jessie shrieked softly and melted in waves of ecstasy even as he gave her no reprieve, until she almost had to push him away to let the orgasm peak without causing her to scream in delicious yet incapacitating pleasure.

Panting, she slowly straightened from her awkward position, her legs splayed widely apart with Nick on his knees between them. She looked down at him, and in the gaslight caught the glint in his eye, the small, smug turn of his lips displaying his pride at having brought her to such heights.

In all fairness, she thought as her brain began to work again, they hadn't been all that intimate in a couple weeks. She'd stored it up, she figured, and all he'd had to do was open the door. She had thrown away the key.

She took barely a minute ripping his pants off and pushing him down to thank him with a special approach he had no trouble allowing. She yanked his briefs down to his ankles, waited impatiently as he stepped out of them and kicked them aside, then engulfed him with her loving mouth.

"Jessie," he whispered into the darkness above them. "My dear Jessie…"

She gave and took and gave again, pleasuring him with attention and deprivation and back again, feeling his thrusting at the back of her throat and yet preventing him from finishing, finding that a selfish part of her wanted to save him for herself again.

He groaned in frustration and pleasure, a mix of emotions bubbling under the surface of the words he muttered. Then she left him, her sudden absence leaving him cold for a moment, until she straddled him and guided him inside her cleft, replacing the brief cold with the warmth from her inner core.

He filled her, and she rose and fell on him, their mouths meeting again and staying together as they rocked rhythmically on the leather, united in pleasure—*and love, her mind screamed, and love!*—as they hadn't been for much too long.

The sweet scent of their mingling sweat enveloped them and urged them on.

Mordred

He huddled over his equipment. The infrared camera was paying dividends now. He'd taken a chance on deploying both standard and infrared, and this unexpected interlude was making his extra work worthwhile.

He had wired up the cop's apartment earlier, knowing his scent was effectively masked by Ghost, the hunter's best weapon against sharp olfactory abilities. His professional lockpick equipment had gotten him in the door easily enough, though it hadn't been a picnic.

Not that he knew what a picnic might have been like.

His memory was dominated by strobe and fluorescent-lit laboratory flashes, harsh light glinting off thick steel bars and shiny autopsy tables, their gutters running with thick red blood, bottles filling for later consumption and rewards for work well-done.

No, *hadn't been a picnic* was just a phrase for Mordred. He had little memory of everyday pleasures shared by humans, because he had always been reminded that he wasn't human.

Now he watched the infrared imagery on the monitor and saw that the two of them had switched positions again, their body heat giving away their location and marking the boundaries of their heated bodies. Now *she* was on her knees and *he* was thrusting behind her and Mordred could relate to that one, yes he could, because even in the lab they had given him *subjects* to be with, to play with, to mate with, that he remembered now all too clearly with the hollow pang of loneliness born of an all-consuming mission...

He wiped a sheen of sweat from across his brow and felt the urge to change and find himself a plaything.

No, the mission comes first. He knew his orders, at least as they stood right now.

He watched the two shapes melting together and apart and back together again, separating and rejoining, and then she straddled him again, and they became a red and black blob on the monitor, their rhythm gathering speed until finally they slowed and fell off each other and clearly lay in a sprawling embrace.

Their body heat had peaked, and he was expert enough at reading the colors to know that sweat was cooling on their skin and changing the sensor's readings.

Simonson

The bastard was recording them.

He wondered what Lupo would say if he knew what the pervert was doing. This was more info to pass on to the cop eventually, after he approached him with his proposal. It was likely the guy wouldn't believe him at first, but Simonson had ways of proving what he said, and even now he made a note of what the Wolfpaw operative was up to.

He was almost angry enough to make a move right then, stop the bastard and teach him a lesson.

But that would cause him too much trouble later, because they'd probably dispatch an Alpha Team, and then he and the cop would have too much to deal with. This way, even though he couldn't be sure what their game was, he knew they were in surveillance—*not termination*—mode.

Chances were good the CEO and the rest of the bastards on the board were too occupied with the daily hearings, which had just started and gave every indication of lasting for weeks. They'd be keeping their noses clean for the most part, so he had better not overreact.

He retreated into the darkness and watched without acting.

Once again, he was watching the Watcher.

Sigfried

He ran gnarled hands through his thinning hair, combing it with his spread fingers and wincing as he felt the bumps in his skull. It was short hair and stringy, and it was more gray than it had been even just last year. He sat in a cone of light made by a brass desk lamp. The rest of his office was dark, black to his eyes, and he breathed in the familiar scent of leather from the chairs and the sofa and the dozens of books lined up behind him on shelves. He preferred not seeing the details around him because they tended to distract him.

The first day of hearings had been brutal. Having barely begun, the bloated congressmen had preened and pontificated for the cameras. All his previous influence on Capitol Hill had only bought him one friend appointed to this committee, and this guy could ill afford to make his allegiances known on the first day. So Wolfpaw had been raked over the coals. Sigfried still smarted from the smackdown.

While he appeared to take notes on the congressmen's tirades, Sigfried instead wrote a list of their names for future reference, surreptitiously eyeing their nameplates without listening to half of what they said. His answers were already sculpted anyway, weren't as much answers as brief monologues, and he didn't expect to be there very many days longer. Then he had circled three names on his list and made sure Omega Team received them in order to do research. The three congressmen—one a woman, actually—would find their families' images on crisp photographs taken with a zoom lens in the next day's mail. Their focus would no longer be on these hearings, and the furor would fizzle out. It was a tactic he'd used before, one that worked well by reminding the sanctimonious politicians that *anyone* could be gotten to, no matter what level of protection.

Sigfried chuckled. The press wouldn't know what to make of the sudden disengage maneuver by the politicians, the questions would turn softball, Sigfried's answers would be boring and predictable, and the story would start to fade.

Now, as far as Sigfried could tell, Wolfpaw's greatest enemy was one lone cop whose stubbornness had cost the company plenty. He'd made a mistake with that cop, escalating too fast, not realizing until too late that he was dealing with another shifter. He'd assumed the cop's takedown of Tannhauser, Schwartz and Tef was nothing more than luck. But by the time he realized his mistake, he'd issued orders and dispatched Wagner and her Alpha Team to take care of it. It was one thing to know shapeshifters existed, and another altogether to be a shapeshifter.

No, he'd badly miscalculated. Now the hearings would still occupy his time, and he figured the cop thought he was home free. Well, he was wrong.

He was *very* wrong.

For Sigfried had "loosed the thunder of his terrible swift sword," as he liked to say when golfing with his more aggressive political partners, never mind the misquote.

He withdrew his head from the cone of light, and anyone standing nearby would have seen him almost disappear into the darkness. He knew how to pull that off, too, with accounts in the Caymans ready to fuel a very comfortable retirement indeed, a retirement somewhere out of the reach of extradition. But that was a last resort. For now, Sigfried was staying. He had faith in himself, his plans, his contingencies, and ultimately in his highborn luck.

His wife slept in one of the three master-size bedrooms upstairs. He could join her.

Instead, he picked up the phone and speed-dialed a number. The voice at the other end was sleepy, but awoke when he spoke her name. Idly, he clicked the desktop remote, and a flat monitor flickered into life, one of three mounted across a low credenza not far from his desk. The middle monitor now showed his wife in the dark bedroom, a gray, bulky shape under a thin blanket. He frowned in distaste.

"Be ready in an hour, Margarethe," he said into the phone. "I'm coming over."

There was a sharp intake of breath at the other end. "Now?"

"Now. Have one other there with you. Either blonde or brunette." He rubbed his chin absently. "And have her ready for me."

He could hear she was already getting out of bed. It was inconvenient, but he had an account. Her services didn't run cheap, but when someone like Sigfried requested special service, she knew how to indulge his tastes at any time of day and night. She knew better than to argue, or complain.

When she agreed he was already hanging up.

Jessie

She lay on her side, curled into his body, and remembered to trace the map of his scars in her mind. With the lights on, she'd gotten a look at a whole new set of patterns of which she hadn't been aware.

He had been in trouble he hadn't told her about.

It was both sweet and infuriating.

Nick Lupo was not used to sharing. Anything, from information to personal space.

But she had to admit, he was getting better. And some things he could share just fine. She caressed his stomach and the top of his groin from behind and felt him stir under her touch even though he was asleep.

They'd needed this. She knew she'd been pushing him away. Hell, she was still angry at him for the Heather Wilson slip...

If you could call it that.

But there was all that weird baggage she'd had dumped on her since the massacre, since poor Tom Arnow's accidental death.

She'd seen a therapist twice up at the rez. Nick didn't know about *that*, so maybe they were a little even about those new scars of his. But she had friends and connections—hell, she ran the hospital!

Rosa had pegged it, there was no doubt. Post-traumatic stress disorder. It manifested in different ways for different people. In her case, the bloodbath had led her to seek some kind of release, and apparently spending money gambling with little or no control fit the bill. PTSD affected soldiers most often, but civilians who'd survived catastrophic events came down with it too. As a doctor, she'd suspected it, but it was frustrating that she couldn't make herself stop.

What happened to "Physician, heal thyself?"

Well, she couldn't.

She moved her hand around gently and felt his muscles react, rippling slightly. He never really relaxed. She knew he was worried about Wolfpaw coming after them again. And that he felt guilty because it was his fault. And she suspected he himself suffered a form of PTSD.

Lately they'd just stopped connecting, but she was sure the problems stemmed from the same roots. She didn't even consider Heather Wilson the worst of them.

Though if she ever saw that scheming nymphomaniac ever again, she'd...well, she had a stash of silver ammunition. And Nick had that old silver dagger.

Was that even still a real term, *nymphomaniac?*

What did they say these days? *Sex addict?*

She smiled into his shoulder. She'd just been a good little sex addict herself, not long before. She felt good and fucked. *Fucked good.*

She almost giggled.

Her hand moved in small circles, slowly enlarging them until she reached the part of his groin where...

Yes!

He stirred under her touch, and then Nick himself stirred too. She grinned.

He had a bad case to deal with, and lots of worries, and her own weird problems, and he needed his sleep. But right then, she needed what he had given her earlier even more.

He growled playfully and rolled over, taking her by surprise.

"Haven't you had enough?"

She captured him with her long, slim fingers. "Actually, no."

Her fluttering strokes grew more insistent. Now he lay sideways and faced her, and she felt him below, prodding her mound and sending electricity through her again.

She ran a long fingernail down the length of his resurrected penis until it shuddered on her, flirting with her lips. She smiled into his eyes. "Well, Mr. Lupo, I presume?"

"Uh huh," he whispered.

"Meet your rescuer." Her voice was husky with reawakened desire.

She pushed him gently onto his back and slid off the bed, kneeling in front of him. Her hands first massaged his thighs, then took hold of him.

"Jessie—" he began, but she cut him off.

"Shhh, let's just concentrate on the now."

"I have to be up in a couple hours..."

"Mr. Lupo, you seem to be up right now."

Her lips encircled him, and then she was reminded of what those first times had been like, back when Martin Stewart had been on the hunt for them, and she made him forget about their current problems—and she forgot about her anger, too, she noted—for as long as she could. For as long as *he* could.

Afterwards, with both of them awake and alert, he mixed them a couple of his Midtown Manhattans, which they sipped sitting in his leather chairs set in front of his window, watching the wind whip tree branches around. Winter seemed to be coming early, and leaves had already started leaving the trees. The hardy mix of tastes in his invented drink warmed her belly, and their silence was a comfortable one after all the intimacy.

Lupo's feet touched hers on the leather ottoman they shared.

"What if I ask Marcowicz about trauma and whether your gambling is related?"

She pulled her feet away from his.

"Marcowicz! You can't even stand him." Suddenly she felt cold again.

"Doesn't mean he doesn't know his stuff."

"You do what you think is right," she said, making clear she was done talking.

He sighed audibly.

In the morning she awoke refreshed, but then she remembered his little dig. And she heard him tune into the early local news and their report on the "brutal Third Ward murder," and he said "Shit!" and jumped in the shower.

She rolled over, tears soaking into her pillow.

Sigfried

When he swung open the door to the secret room at the rear of his penthouse in the city, as always Margarethe took his breath away.

She'd entered his lair through the secret underground ramp and used the second private elevator, hidden in the rear of the 20,000 square-foot sky-high abode.

Encased in shiny, black PVC and rows of sharp studs, her full breasts thrust through openings in the plastic and her nipples engorged and lacquered in fire-red, she was the minx of his dreams. Her long, lean legs started from the stiletto heeled knee-high boots and swelled to her muscular thighs, between which the bare mound of her sex glistened with her desire literally dripping down the thin chain that hung from her sparkling labial ring.

Hair a golden honey, a full head of it framed a face highlighted by blood-red lips and blackened eye sockets half hidden behind a leather mask, before cascading down her plastic-corseted back down to exposed buttocks chiseled from flesh-colored marble. Her sleeveless tunic revealed muscular biceps tattooed with SS flashes on the left and an official tilted swastika on the right like an armband.

One spike-gloved hand held a bullwhip coiled like a snake ready to strike.

"Margarethe," he whispered, his voice raspy with desire and lust. He wanted to taste the bite of that snake. He wanted to—

As soon as he entered and the door closed silently behind him, he saw that she did have someone with her even on such short notice. Probably one of her less talented trainees. Manacled to a tilted, grooved table. She was a slight girl, not well fed, but full-breasted, wrapped in a loose uniform tunic in Wehrmacht gray. Her eyes were only half open and glazed.

Stoned, Sigfried realized. *She might be ready…*

Her mouth was gagged with a short, black leather shaft tucked far back into her mouth like a horse's bit.

His eyes roved over the luscious offering, then met Margarethe's piercing blue eyes. With a raised eyebrow, she held out the bullwhip and he took it. It sent a shiver up his arm and down his back.

He unleashed the bullwhip, and its plaited leather length undulated lazily like a narrow snake, tongue flicking wickedly.

Crack!

A line of blood appeared on the girl's abdomen, the skin parted by the leather tip as if with the flick of a scalpel.

Crack!

Another bloody rip appeared between the girl's breasts. This time she reacted, whimpering around the gag as the pain finally registered.

He dropped the bullwhip. Foreplay could only last so long.

Margarethe's gloved hand reached out, encircled Sigfried's erection, and gently tugged him closer to where the bound girl writhed in a sudden effort to free herself. The sharp razor pain of the whip's tip was stripping off the high of whatever drugs the lovely Mistress Margarethe had administered. When Sigfried was close enough, Margarethe's other hand swung a hospital table around and brought it within range.

Sigfried's cock twitched in Margarethe's grip as he perused the silver instruments lined upon the red velour tray. Her fingers traveled lightly and cupped his balls, and he felt himself harden as his hand hovered indecisively over the selection and returned to grasp a long-handled scalpel with triangular blade.

"Ah, the number eleven," Margarethe leaned in and whispered in his ear, her fingers tracing the veins on his cock with gentle pressure. "A very good choice."

Sigfried's breath came in short gasps, the stimuli gaining power over him. Margarethe knew his triggers. She knew his needs and his wants. She made sure his eyes roved over her Nazi tattoos, her dripping red lips, and the bloody slits on the girl's torso, then she applied just enough pressure to his groin and felt his excitement spike.

She knelt slowly beside him and took him into her mouth as he began to cut, the girl's white skin a canvas for his inspiration. Thus thoroughly stimulated, Sigfried indulged in his art.

By the time he came, the girl was unrecognizable, and what was left of her bled out and down the table's grooves, into the drain.

Chapter Six

Seven years ago...

Mordred

Occasionally, he sat in the chair they provided and did not roll around like a freak. Those were the times he could almost hear them scratching their heads, scribbling notes on their computers and pads. To be sure, they also scribbled when he flopped around. But he felt that somehow they were more mystified when his reactions didn't fit their preconceptions.

He raised his head, painfully, and stared into the glass partition. He saw himself and marveled at how much of a stranger's face it was.

His arm throbbed where they had stabbed him yet again with their needle. The throb started with a regular beat, but the tempo increased. He looked down and watched as his blue vein swelled in time to the throb. It pulsed and itched to the point where he needed to scratch the skin stretched like parchment over the blue snake. His hands shuddered in jagged little motions, and he felt his nails lengthen and enlarge into sharp claws.

Suddenly he screamed a full-mouthed scream.

The throb in his veins had become a stabbing-burning-lancing of white-hot fire.

The echo of his scream bouncing from the metal walls hurt his ears, but there was so much pain from inside the veins that snaked through his entire body that he couldn't even feel it.

The liquid burning dug through every limb like a scalpel, scraping bone and muscle like a rusty file.

But his hands were trapped by aluminum bands not even his immense strength could snap, so the claws that craved to scratch the flaming fire infesting his veins could only flutter uselessly. The bands dug into his skin and added to the pain.

His screaming went on and on, until his throat was raw. And then he passed out, his head slumping down onto his chest with a suddenness that seemed final. As if he had expired.

Behind the viewing glass, Dr. Schlosser turned to his team of assistants.

"Note that once the pain has spread throughout his body, it subsides to the level at which he is able to withstand it."

"Could it be he's just so fatigued by the continuous pain that his passing out is a form of escape?" The assistant was fairly new, still wide-eyed at what he had seen and learned in this sublevel laboratory. His expertise in veterinary medicine and physiology had gotten him on the team, but his ruthlessly dangerous and subversive experiments since then kept him there.

"That's what we thought until a couple years ago, Dr. Gavin," Schlosser said, ignoring the slumped figure in the other room. "But we have fairly good evidence that the tolerance therapy works. We took an approach several generations ago that has led us to this day, a day in which a genetically manipulated werewolf has become much more tolerant of the one substance that would otherwise kill it."

Schlosser turned to the bank of video monitors, recently updated along with the archival system so that decades' worth of videotape now resided on hard drives. He keyed up a distorted video that slowly coalesced to show his test subject writhing in pain.

Of course, there were always those damnable daggers. He would come to understand them, in time. Right now, he could celebrate his unqualified success.

Celebrations were held in his playroom.

He was looking forward to it.

He was in the narrow streets of Falluja again, ducking gunfire from hidden AK-47s, knowing they'd targeted him even more because he was a contractor and not one of the "flags," what the Wolfpaw people called American soldiers.

Then he was inside the dingy, barely stocked store, a family of terrified ragheads standing against the back wall. He turned his MP5K's stubby muzzle to cover them while his fellow squad members fanned out behind him, and he heard them smashing the store's wares.

"Where are the insurgents?" he shouted at the cringing locals. "The terrorists? Where are they?"

The family members shrugged, feigning a lack of understanding. The always did that when they didn't like the questions. But he knew they understood his words well enough. Almost everybody in this country spoke some English.

"Where are you hiding them?" he shouted.

But they stared back, unresponsive and full of insolence.

He set down his submachine gun on the dirt floor, stripped off his flak jacket, and unbuttoned his desert cammies. The idiots stared at him as if he'd grown a second head.

Just wait!

Naked in front of them, his penis standing at attention, he repeated his questions. But the family was terrified now, mostly by this foreigner's bizarre behavior. Perhaps they wondered if all foreigners were crazy. *Insane.*

He visualized himself changing, and then he felt the familiar tingle that traversed his veins from head to toe and made him feel as if were bursting. His erection might as well have been made of granite.

When the change took him over, the people's screams excited him all the more.

He waded into them, claws and fangs slashing.

Blood flowed from severed heads, arm and leg stumps, and slit bellies. He was a blur of savagery, no longer caring about what they said, the answers to his questions, or even his mission. The beast ignored their pleas, their screams, their crying. All that mattered was their deaths. He had become an avenging angel, an executioner, driven by an instinctive need to maim, torture and kill.

And then he fed, eating his fill from each of his victims. He sampled from one, then another and another, and finally he left his mark on the territory and left his wolf form behind. He stood, naked, sated, and examined his handiwork.

Mordred retrieved his clothing and dressed, blinking under the harsh lighting. What he had seen earlier as a dingy Falluja mud-brick hovel of a store became something else altogether. The racks of surviving bottles and cans coalesced under his returning vision. Instead of a dirt floor, beneath his feet was a tiled pattern of black and white, now marred by broken glass, spilled liquor, and the bloody remains of everyone who had fallen prey to the beast.

He shook his head to clear it and wondered about the flashback. For the duration of his raging attack, he *had been* back in Iraq. It wasn't the first time. Perhaps he needed to tell Sigfried about these flashbacks. They were occurring too often lately.

He destroyed the tapes from the security system. Then he flicked on the rest of the lights.

On his way out, he flipped the CLOSED sign around to COME IN, WE'RE OPEN.

Chapter Seven

The telephone trilled insistently inside the communications office of the bunker deep below the sidewalks of the *Reichstrasse*. At the switchboard desk, ready to make the connection, sat a buxom blonde Aryan in a smoke-gray uniform. Her manicured fingers manipulated the wires expertly. In less than a year, her job would be done by gray-haired men in rumpled, stained uniforms devoid of rank insignia, the last remaining few of the Führer's last guard detail. But now, for a fleeting moment at least, business as usual seemed to be occurring in the busy underground headquarters of the SS Special Units Division.

Obergruppenführer Helmut vonStumpfahren plucked the receiver from its cradle when the blonde's connection came through and buzzed his office phone. He looked to be in his forties—a hardy, handsome man with leonine salt and pepper hair and a serpentine burn scar on his left cheek.

"Ja," he barked into the receiver. "I was awaiting your call."

Recently promoted to full general, vonStumpfahren was the commanding officer of the top secret Werwolf Division of the SS, a unit known to exist only by a half dozen officers from Heinrich Himmler's staff, and, of course, by the nearly five thousand recruits who had secretly trained in the Bavarian Alps for the glorious last defense of the Fatherland. He had been added to the staff of the Führer's command bunker to coordinate the division's deployment in the face of the predicted enemy advance on the capital. The pincers from Italy and Normandy were closing in, and his job would be to pull the trigger on the various outlying units' assignments in other quadrants of the Fatherland and its annexed territories.

Those quadrants and territories shrank by the day, if one but checked the situation room maps, but no one wished to point out the obvious to the Führer.

Not when he was just as likely to order one's summary execution for the treason of speaking the truth. But the General's belief in his various projects included the conviction that all was not lost. Not if the Werwolf Division was deployed correctly. All would not be lost.

Not for him, anyway.

Currently the pressure of the Führer's expectations and confidence weighed on him greatly. He fingered the "Spezial-SS" flashes on his collar, the lightning bolts woven through a silver wolf's head—only a handful of officers knew its meaning, but everyone knew he was one of few who had the ear of both Himmler and the Führer himself. He also wore the black uniform and *Totenkopf*—death's head—sleeve diamond insignia, the result of which was the abject fear of anyone he approached, for they would gather from the unusual symbols that his rank was special. And therefore to be greatly feared.

Now vonStumpfahren listened as the caller outlined the readiness of some of those units. He tapped his fingers on the desk impatiently, waiting for the long list to end. "What about the Götterdämmerung Projekt? How is the readiness?"

The voice at the other end whined that he was not directly aware of the situation, offering profuse excuses for the lack of detail.

"Damn you," vonStumpfahren whispered, "how dare you waste my time without the information I require?"

There was a moment's silence, then the excuses began again. The general hung up, cutting off the obsequious voice.

He barked into the intercom and waited for the blonde's adroit fingers to make the connection he wanted.

"Ja?"

He spoke his name and heard the responder's breath intake.

He spoke another name.

"*Jawohl!* I shall fetch him, Herr Obergruppenführer. It will only take a moment."

"Very well."

The line was surprisingly clear of static. A minute or less passed, and then a deep voice spoke in his ear.

"I am he."

VonStumpfahren spoke his name again and the other sighed. "I know who you are. This is an interruption, so please let us get to the point of your call."

The general smiled crookedly. He'd ordered executions for less, but this was a special person indeed. The problem was, the bastard knew it.

"Herr Doktor, my apologies for the interruption. May I assume your accommodations are satisfactory? The change from Treblinka has been a positive one?"

"You may not assume, sir." The doctor lowered his voice and hissed into the mouthpiece. "The facilities are hopelessly difficult. There are three camps, and I require a permanent laboratory with access to a wooded area. Treblinka was perfect! Here I am burdened with a backward system, backward facilities, dunce-headed help, and an impossible schedule. You may definitely not assume I am happy."

The general held the telephone away from his ear. "I will attempt to better your situation from my end of things. Perhaps Chelmno, while closer to us here at home, is still too far?"

Chelmno was in occupied Poland, not far from Lodz. Closer than the Treblinka camp, which no longer existed, but still a long distance from Berlin.

"Distance has nothing to do with it. I need better facilities. Your instructions are to complete my experiments in the most expedient way possible. Yet that idiot Mengele has always had more support than I. You wish to expedite my work? Return my laboratory facilities at the university."

"Herr Doktor," the general said with forced patience, "you know that the, er, nature of your work requires a buffer zone. I have much power, but at this point in our struggle I cannot command the funds to build a new facility that fulfills all your requirements. I am only too aware of your needs, but you must be aware of the sacrifices we make daily. If your work should show the results we need sooner rather than later, perhaps we could find a way. But I fear the interruptions have made your chance of success remote."

"Your fear is correct," the scientist said, sighing. "I apologize for my outburst, General. The stress, the long hours—"

"I understand, let us move on. What are your newest results?"

The scientist laid out the pertinent facts. Some of them made vonStumpfahren smile, some made him frown. But all in all, there was much for him to be satisfied with. The time was getting short, and he thanked the harried scientist.

"You are welcome, Herr General. I am certain we are on the verge of a breakthrough. The genetic work is much more ambitious than our friend Mengele's interests, as you know, and the subjects are less, er, desirable. And yet we are having some success."

The general sat back in a rare moment of relaxation, crossing his boots under the massive desk.

At last, the words I want to hear!

"You are taking precautions with the data?"

"Yes, your advice has been most helpful."

Indeed, every month the scientist's junior assistant was taken to the rear of Chelmno manor and forced into the gassing van along with the rest of the human cattle. His body ended up in one of the massive holes in the forest camp four kilometers away. By then a new assistant was being trained by the doctor's associates. This procedure assured a small sphere of knowledge.

66

"And your notes?" the general asked.

"Safe, always safe. In good hands. And the same with the film."

"Very well, I am satisfied."

"I knew you would be, Herr General." There was a ring of pride in the scientist's voice. A burst of static erased his next words.

"Verdammte Bastarde!"

An air raid, likely, somewhere between the bunker and the far eastern frontier.

VonStumpfahren slammed his hand on the desk. The connection had been broken. The wire had been cut, again. He sighed.

Doktor Schlosser was a difficult man to manage. He was proud and arrogant, a prissy type whose personality rankled the general. But his promise to deliver one of the general's greatest wishes had convinced vonStumpfahren that he was worth the resources.

He replaced the receiver slowly, envisioning a new beginning for the Fatherland.

This he should have taken to the Führer in person. Instead, he poured a hefty draught of French Cognac and silently toasted his efforts. There was *some* treasure one had to hoard.

Genova, Italy, 1944

Franco Lupo

The airplane tire was too large and partially melted on one side so it wasn't perfectly round, but still it rolled well enough down the path's slight decline. Franco was helping it along with a length of wood swiped from the ruins of a farmer's house, its frame blown apart by an Allied bomb that had missed the rail crossing nearby.

His friend Pietro had shown him how to do it, using the scorched rod to maneuver the ungainly tire without getting gooey black rubber all over himself. You had to keep the wood rod in motion, alternately touching each edge with its tip, to exert control of its direction, and occasionally using it to brake by jabbing it into the inner circle's edge.

In this way, the two boys walked two huge tires down the path, which was screened from the nearby road by a thicket of pines and interspersed cypresses. The tires were taller than the boys, having come off an American B-17 bomber downed by German anti-aircraft fire the previous week.

The airplane was not much more than a scorched skeleton now, its exposed metal ribs making it resemble a chicken that had been picked over by hungry guests.

Franco's stomach grumbled at the image, which came unbidden into his mind's eye followed rapidly by others: a slab of pork *pancetta*, its edges sizzled just right, and a series of savory side dishes, followed by a beautifully browned and sugar-sprinkled *pandolce* with some of his mother's fresh, hand-whisked cream.

Unfortunately he knew these were just fantasies, and the thought of what really awaited him, a family dinner that consisted of a skimpy vegetable soup made of wilted lettuce and dandelion leaves, parsnips, and a boiled potato or two accompanying a tough old chicken that had been boiled to tolerable tenderness, wasn't enough to ease the hollow feeling inside. His stomach growled again, a double blast.

"So is this plan of yours gonna work?" he asked Pietro, his best friend, who was concentrating so hard at steering his tire that his tongue lolled grotesquely between his clenched teeth.

"Well?" he prodded.

"Huh?" Pietro retrieved his tongue and snuck a quick look at his friend. "What?"

"This plan gonna work?"

"How would I know?" Pietro snapped. "But it's a plan. It's better than waiting until we age like a fine wine or cheese. Can you think of a better way to let the partisans know they can recruit us?"

He went back to concentrating on the tire. The trick was to control its speed, otherwise he would lose it to the slope. He wielded his wooden rod a little like the boys imagined one of those Indian elephant wranglers used to handle their large beasts.

"I hope it works, because I wanna help end this stupid war. If we help the partisans we'll be closer to kicking out the damn Germans!"

"Shhh," Pietro cautioned in a hiss. "You wanna end up in a prison camp? Or worse?"

"We're gonna be risking our lives anyway, no?" Franco pointed out. "What's the difference?"

"We gotta at least get our plan off the ground, is what."

"Okay, okay." Franco seemed to have learned how to handle his tire with ease. He just wished his empty stomach would stop rumbling. But with the wartime rationing and all the "unofficial" shortages—those the government didn't admit to—there was little extra food in the Lupo household pantry for a growing boy. Franco was lucky to get one egg twice a week, and that was if his father went without. Butter and lard were impossible and potatoes often a luxury.

Franco tried hard to put the thought of food far from his mind.

The path curved slightly to their right, and they maneuvered their tires carefully, using rods and hands to keep them captive in the increasing decline.

Suddenly Pietro's tire hit a partially buried rock in the path's center and bounced off the ground just enough for Pietro to lose control as it started to tilt toward him. Though extraordinarily wide, the tire was also quite tall, so its weight immediately caused it to wobble as Pietro tried to shove it back. When it finally toppled sideways it caught Pietro's leg, and he emitted a yelp.

Only Franco's quick thinking saved the other boy's leg from probably snapping under the rubber's weight. Deftly, Franco used his almost unnatural control of the other tire to collapse it sideways, where it landed just below Pietro's tilting tire. Franco's tire wedged itself underneath Pietro's, and both bounced and rolled like huge, spinning coins.

"Help me. My leg!"

With Franco pulling rapidly, Pietro was able to jerk his leg free before the huge, curved length of rubber could roll over him and pinch him against the rocky ground.

The boys fell back painfully and watched the tires wobble against themselves slower and slower until finally they stopped with one laying flat and the other resting on it at a sharp angle. They gasped, barely able to snatch air into their lungs.

But at least Pietro's leg wasn't a mass of ripped skin, torn cartilage and protruding bone.

When they started laughing, the two ridiculous tires became even more amusing. They howled until they hiccupped, all attempts at silent running temporarily forgotten.

"What about the plan?" Pietro said when he finally caught his breath. "The Resistance?"

"Shut up and help me," Franco said, giggling.

Together, they were able to drag the upper tire back on its edge, and then stood it back up, exploiting the angle at which it rested on the other. That tire lay completely flat, and its weight was almost too much, but they put their backs into it, their hands pulling on the inner rim until the tire began to right itself. With two pairs of hands now, and their feet keeping it from sliding, lifting Franco's tire became much easier.

They were a fair distance up in the hills, so apparently no one had heard the commotion. No vehicles had rumbled down the nearby road. Soon they were following another bend in the path. The tangled undergrowth dropped away, and they now stood at the top of a steep hill. The path continued on down to their left, but their destination was the bluff still hidden behind a stand of stubby evergreens with overgrown lower branches.

Somewhat refreshed, Franco and Pietro walked their tires toward the trees and leaned them against thick trunks facing the bluff's edge.

Now Franco felt the fear start to overtake his enthusiasm. The plan had been a good one, if they lived to tell anyone about it. It had all seemed so logical and adventurous. It was an extension of the games and pranks they'd played for years. When the Germans went from being welcome allies to occupiers almost overnight, the boys had felt a stab of nationalism. The rumors and recent underground news of armed resistance had grown rapidly, and now it was an open secret that German supremacy on Italian soil was being challenged every day by common people, many of them ex-soldiers who had taken up arms against the despised invader.

Now, poised with their hands resting on the warm rubber of their unlikely weapons, both boys felt the shiver of last-second fear.

"Ready?" Pietro whispered.

Franco nodded. Sweat trickled down his back. The brilliant, blue sky above and the sun's warmth had heated him up, but the sweat now reminded him of the thin stream of rusty water you could summon with furious pumping of the well handle on his grandmother's farm. It was always ice cold, that water.

He nodded, this time with conviction. "It's our only way of getting recruited," he reminded his friend. "We have to go through with it."

Pietro nodded. He wasn't letting go of his tire just yet, either. "You gonna run?"

Franco felt his hands shaking, his knees week. *Could* he run?

"Yeah," he said. "We better."

He grasped his tire with both hands and manhandled it off its resting place, aiming for the break in the undergrowth they'd made by cutting it down secretly in the previous few days. Beside him, Pietro did the same.

He craned his neck, but couldn't see the target. But he knew where it was. Their reconnaissance had been thorough. Huffing in a loud whisper, Franco gave the tire a hard shove with both arms and a foot, and watched it leap forward off the rise and careen through the thicket and then roll down the hill, gaining speed as it bounced on and off the rocky ground.

Pietro released his tire a few seconds later.

The boys craned their necks, side by side, in order to see.

The two gigantic tires jounced down the steep hillside, gathering speed until they seemed to blur.

Pietro and Franco crept closer to the lip overlooking the bluff. The tires had disappeared out of sight. Crouched to keep their heads below the ragged line of scrub, the boys watched with a mixture of joy and horror as the huge, rolling wheels reached the road below. The road ran parallel to the bottom of the hillside and curved slightly on its way to a freshly painted guardhouse. A sentry stood near the lift gate that blocked the road. His sudden shout brought three more soldiers out of the guardhouse to gawk at the black, bouncing tires that bore down on them.

Before they could do more than shout and point, the tires bounced across the road. One tilted too far to the side and landed flat with a loud cracking sound. Its final bounces were sideways, and then it settled on its side like a gigantic coin.

The soldiers shouted again as the other tire bounced straight and true through the barbed-wire fence and onto the ground beside the road. One soldier pointed up at the boys.

"*Dio mio!*" Franco blurted. They'd been spotted!

The soldier raised his rifle...

But then the remaining tire struck one of the slight indentations in the pocked dirt strip, and a mighty explosion threw up clods of dry soil and stones.

It felt like a slap on their ears.

The soldier was thrown off his feet, rifle flung away from his body, and then there was another explosion as a second pressure mine detonated when the riddled remains of the tire landed on its plunger.

The boys stared at the smoke and fire and then the sound of gunshots reached them, The other soldiers had spotted them and were now on the road, their rifles aimed in the boys' direction. They were bolt-action Mausers and took a moment to chamber a new round between firing, but still the three Germans poured a withering fire above the boys' heads. The oak and cypress trunks behind them were taking the brunt of the volley. Bark and leaf debris flew like shrapnel all around them. Their ears ringing and now frightened for their lives, they dropped to the ground and felt air move just inches away when the big rifle rounds whizzed past and demolished the trees and undergrowth that hid them.

"*Presto! Scappiamo!* We gotta get outta here!" Franco shouted over the gunfire. His ears were still ringing from the mine explosions—he thought he was whispering.

Pietro was stunned frozen. His eyes were wide with fear, his muscles paralyzed. He hadn't expected the sentries would be so eager to bag their hidden attackers.

Nor that they could shoot so well.

Franco risked a peek over the bluff's lip. A command car bristling with guns was speeding toward the guardhouse from behind the fence. It reminded him of a speedy black scorpion. It slowed down and two of the gate sentries piled in, and then it sped up and out of the gate onto the road.

Heading up.

To where the boys were hiding.

Heading up that road *fast.*

"*Andiamo, presto!*" Franco shouted in Pietro's ear. *Let's go, right now!* He grasped the other boy's arm and yanked him back from the top of the hill. Pietro's eyes were wide, staring into somewhere Franco couldn't imagine. The remaining sentry was still concentrating his rifle fire on the spot where the boys had been standing only moments before. Splinters of bark from the trees rained down on them like tiny knives, drawing blood when they hit skin.

Pietro was waking up, starting to run and following Franco through the slashing brush.

"Come on!" Franco shouted.

From below, they heard the grinding of gears as the command car sped up the sloping road toward them.

It was plain to see what had happened. The boys had hoped to detonate a few mines the Germans had laid along both sides of the approach to this particular field command post. But they hadn't counted on the Germans believing they were under attack. Pietro had convinced his friend they'd just shake their fists and swear at them in their comical language like they all did when faced with the ubiquitous boyish thievery that went on all over occupied Italy.

Pietro and Franco had hoped to use their demonstration as a way to deal their way into a local partisan unit commanded by one of his cousins. They knew the rumors about the Resistance as well as anyone, and maybe better. Once the story of their exploit got around, they believed, of two boys disrupting the enemy minefield, all the partisan units would begin to use their tactics—using discarded tires.

But now they were running for their lives, grand plans forgotten.

They heard the command car approach the switchback just below the crest of the hill. The driver crashed through the gears and made the engine scream. Excited German voices were punctuated by stuttering rifle fire from down below.

"*Corri!*" Franco urged his friend. *Run!* They were stumbling through the thickening underbrush. "Avoid the road!" he gasped out. "The path, too!"

They heard the car rounding the curve a ways below, imagining it scuttling along the road like a giant beetle. It threatened to cut them off if they didn't reach—and cross—their section of road first.

Then they could get lost in the thickest part of the woods. The Germans would leave them alone—once on foot in the forest, the uniforms would become likely easy targets for partisan knives in the back and garrotes around the neck.

They ran as fast as their legs could take them, their faces and arms slashed by low-hanging branches that seemed to have become razor-sharp since they had last been there.

Suddenly they broke through the vegetation and found themselves on the paved road.

Unfortunately, the command car had already careened around the curve, and the soldiers on it picked out the boys as live targets. One of the Germans fired a long burst from his submachine gun as the boys dove into the woods, the slugs barely missing them.

"*Il bosco!*" Pietro shouted. "We'll lose them in the woods!"

They slashed through the low-level brush, brambles scraping their skin painfully as they ran.

The loud, ripping burp of a machine gun drove them to hug the ground, and they felt slugs tear up trees and bushes all around them, raining down shrapnel made of bark.

Dio mio, Franco thought. *I'm going to die for this stupid stunt.*

The command car was stuck on the road, so the boys dragged themselves almost upright and slipped further into the wooded grove. Franco hoped the Germans would give up the chase. For what were they but a couple of children? Why were the Bosch so determined to run them to ground and kill them? Their airplane tire had blown a couple mines, so what?

The tree trunks closed in around them. They heard a couple more bursts from the machine gunner, but now barely a tenth of the bullets were penetrating the dense thicket, and as they continued to fight their way through the slashing brambles, the sound of gunfire retreated.

Panting, their muscles trembling with the exertion of their run, the boys slowed and looked at each other. They stood stock still, listening.

Franco thought they might have traversed a full kilometer through the woods, but it was hard to tell. The sound of the car's engine was so muffled by the trees that it was reduced to a faint humming.

It sounds like an angry bee, he thought. He shook his head at the nonsense thought. Then the reality of their plight sank in.

"We could have been killed," he said to Pietro.

For his part, Pietro was shivering like a leaf in a windstorm. All he could do was nod.

"Why did they come after us like that?" Franco scratched his chin, and his fingers came away bloody. Suddenly he could feel that his exposed skin was criss-crossed by thin cuts and slashes. He was going to catch hell at home.

Then he snorted. If he survived.

As they caught their breath and let their tightened leg muscles relax, they listened for sounds of pursuit.

"They can't drive that car into the woods," Franco said, sounding more hopeful than convinced.

"*Cretini!*" Pietro spat out. "I wish we would have killed some."

Franco thought Pietro's tough words came easily, after they'd both run like rabbits. On the other hand, who would have expected such a response?

"Whatever they're guarding in that compound must be pretty important."

"Why?" Pietro said.

"Because they can't be that mad at us for a couple mines. It doesn't make sense." Kids were always playing pranks on soldiers. Most often the soldiers took the abuse good-naturedly.

"We could have killed a few of them," Pietro pointed out. "We *wanted* to kill a few of them."

"Maybe they're just bored."

Franco cocked his head to one side. "I think..."

"What, what's wrong?" Pietro said, anxiety crossing his features.

"I think—" Franco began again. His voice faded as he listened carefully. "Dogs!"

From where they had come, the direction of the road, they could both suddenly hear the snapping of branches and a strange baying.

No, it was...

Not quite barking.

Howling.

The boys looked at each other, their eyes widening.

"That doesn't sound like dogs," Franco said.

Pietro was shaking his head. "I spent last winter visiting my uncle up in the mountains," he whispered. "This sounds like wolves. I heard enough of them."

"Lupi?" Franco shivered.

"Yeah, like your name, idiot!"

Franco Lupo would have smacked Pietro at any other time, but suddenly the fear was upon him. They'd just been shot at by angry soldiers, but this somehow seemed worse. Were the soldiers hunting them with domesticated wolves?

"They have to be guard dogs," he whispered. "German shepherds."

The howling continued.

Coming closer.

From several directions.

Pietro shook his head rapidly.

"*Wolves.* I'm telling you! Not fucking dogs!"

"How—?"

"Doesn't matter," Pietro spat. "We have to keep running!"

Wordlessly, Franco agreed. He started running again, his body crying out in rebellion and his leg muscles tightening again almost immediately. Pietro was right next to him. They ducked under the low-hanging branches and dug deeper into the forest, running blindly to put more distance between themselves and the howling beasts presumably on their trail.

Whatever they were.

Wolves.

Franco instinctively knew his friend was right.

Howling.

Coming closer.

Giovanni Lupo

When the Germans had first come, there had been smiles all around. Italy was allied to Germany, and it was ever so clear that the Italian kingdom, though led by a dictator, could ride German coattails to greatness.

Watching columns of German soldiers and their mechanized horses—tanks, half-tracks, armored personnel carriers, squared-off command cars, and miles of covered two-ton transports—people who lined the streets of the large cities nodded with nervous assent. It was an impressive sight. Perhaps it was time for Italy's rise, aided by their Germanic neighbor.

Mussolini sucks Hitler's dick, some of the more cynical said quietly to their like-minded friends, but most saw the strength of the German forces and imagined their country as a reborn player on the world stage. If it took Mussolini's sycophancy to achieve the old grandeur, then why not? Italians and Germans together, the middle ground people said—who would have thought it possible?

But then the realities of war set in, and early Italian military success was followed sharply by military disasters and losses as campaign after campaign turned bloody and churned up Italian lives like sacrifices to inscrutable gods. Slowly the alliance between Germany and Italy strained, certainly at street level, and German High Command centers began to feel a backlash that was at first political and social, but later began to include acts of domestic terrorism perpetrated by disaffected citizens and soldiers who had deserted and who now flocked to the camps of the partisans in the mountains and hills.

Relatively quickly, it became less and less safe for German soldiers stationed in Italian cities to partake of the nightlife and restaurants, to frequent the whorehouses and the sex parlors, or even just to shop and relax. In far more remote villages and towns, it was even worse. Soon German soldiers began to be found naked, mutilated, throats slit ear to ear, as local frustrations with the war and its impact—and predicted outcome—grew and the populace turned against the minority who still clamored to ride German coattails. For now it seemed such a ride would lead the Italian homeland straight to a hell of its own making.

Giovanni Lupo lived with his family on the outskirts of Genova, the huge port city whose importance to the German war machine had kept it tightly occupied by mechanized German forces. Its factories had turned now to near slave labor to churn out goods for the war effort, but it was Germany's war effort—no longer Italy's. In September 1943, the Italian monarchy and its political backers had signed a secret armistice with the Allies. As soon as it became known that Italy had surrendered, the German forces in Italy overnight turned into an occupation force that would draw Allied bombers who had little choice but to target the ports, the factories, and the bases now reinforced in order to slow the Allied advance from the south with as much resistance as possible. Everyone knew the war was lost except the mad German leadership.

Now, heading home on foot from his meager employment in a local foundry that had miraculously avoided nationalization by the Germans, Giovanni Lupo kept a cautious watch for German patrols. They would sometimes sweep up able-bodied Italian men to fill gaps in factory assembly lines. One could be in the wrong place at the wrong time. Giovanni watched for covered trucks, listening for their loud gearboxes in the distance.

A typical tactic was for such a covered truck to drive to a public square or market, pull up, and disperse its human cargo, a platoon of Wehrmacht infantrymen who would then round up bystanders and passersby and hold them at gunpoint until a cattle van could remove the hapless victims.

Giovanni was convinced his ears were very sensitive. The moment he heard the unforgettable sound of one of those vehicles, he would melt into one of the narrow lanes that lined the street he walked. He had mapped numerous routes home to avoid this very danger. He walked briskly now, avoiding the glances of strangers, hoping he could make it home without trouble. His fellow pedestrians surely thought the same and went their way, avoiding him.

Every day it was a similar prayer, every day the same risk. It drove his wife mad. Young Maria Lupo had suffered through the early days of the war, separated from her own family who lived in the hills near Venice. Only Giovanni's good job and his determination to continue to make a life for his wife and son in the shadow of the big city kept her from fleeing the dead-eyed Italians and the German soldiers—some of whom were courteous and friendly, and some of whom were quite the opposite—and heading for her own family's farm.

Giovanni knew her patience was running thin. Things had steadily worsened since the armistice had become common knowledge and the German army, the legendary Wehrmacht, had clamped down on the populace. Food was expensive, some staples scarce or altogether impossible to find at any price, the streets dangerous, the Allied advance and the partisans' renewed vigor leading to more and more cruelty at the hands of the German occupiers...

Giovanni walked fast, his hands in his pockets, one wrapped around the tubular lead weight he carried in case he needed a little more weight behind his considerable right hook. Wouldn't help against an armed patrol, but a single adversary would pay the price if his jaw got between Giovanni and his escape route. It might be all the advantage he needed to avoid the life of a slave. He walked fast, hoping to beat the rapidly approaching darkness almost as much as the random patrols.

For, as dusk arrived, so would the Allied bombers.

He looked straight ahead, ears attuned to the infrequent roar of a motor vehicle. Bicycles he tuned out, along with handcarts and wheelbarrows.

Maria, I'm coming home. Don't worry too much.

He hoped his son had found his way home from school by now. School was a random affair, sometimes held all day as was required, sometimes dismissed early for completely unpredictable reasons. A month ago, a teacher had disappeared—presumably in a street sweep. The children had been dismissed until a substitute could be coaxed from another school farther away. Hardly anyone wanted to work so close to a German high command, for it was an Allied high-priority target.

The fact of which was on Giovanni's mind more right now than usual.

He had worked a full day for the first time in months, eagerly accepting the opportunity to earn a few extra *lire*. Maybe there would be eggs and some lard in the kitchen tomorrow because of it. He hated watching his son grow up hungry, though Franco was a good boy who didn't complain often.

Again Giovanni thought of his son's walk home from school. It was a long walk, some of it through rural lanes and secondary streets, but he should be safe if he walked straight home without any distractions.

Unfortunately, Franco was the kind of boy for whom *everything* was a distraction. Curious and intelligent beyond his years, the boy made a learning game out of everything. He studied his surroundings with perhaps a bit more enthusiasm than was good in such a setting.

If not for this damnable, senseless war—and its resulting occupation by the goddamned Germans—his son would have been at the top of his class in studies. But the school slowdown had stunted the book learning, and Giovanni was beginning to fear his boy was getting too much of a street education. He spent half his days, sometimes his entire days, running the streets with a few of his fellow students. Some of them were fatherless boys whose moral compass was questionable at best. Some were borderline delinquents.

Giovanni knew enough parents and a couple teachers, and he knew some of what the boys were learning on the streets. But what could he do, tie the boy down every day? Surely his wife would have wanted him to, but most days Giovanni was off to work before the break of dawn, so he couldn't know whether there would be school or not. Sometimes they learned Franco'd been on the streets all day only when he came home to eat the meager supper Maria had spent her day preparing from their thin supplies. This was also why he had jumped at the chance to work for a few more hours. One of the best ways to show his family the depth of his love was to help fill their stomachs.

Some of these additional *lire* he had earned today would also find their way into the pockets of German soldiers willing to part with certain foodstuffs—barter and outright black market dealing were in effect for both sides, an irony of war. German mess halls had plenty of oil and potatoes and salt. What they didn't have was beef and other meats, coffee, tea, and other spices. Urban Italian families lacked eggs, oil, butter, flour. Accommodations could be made. Chocolate, cigarettes and tobacco, lard, and—from nearby farms, freshly-killed chickens, rabbits, ducks and geese, an occasional lamb—became commodities at the center of complex bartering deals that often benefited both sides. German officers, accustomed to the high life preordained by their lofty rank, tended to look the other way when their subordinates engaged in such dealings, for their own messes benefited as well from the illicit trade. Some of the officer corps even ran their own black market schemes. Wartime created many dark avenues of capitalism, not all of them food oriented.

But it was the thought of extra food, especially eggs and meat and oil, all of which he could almost taste—though he suspected that soon the Germans would begin to run out of oil as well, if the rumors of losses in the South were true—that distracted Giovanni from his single-minded route home.

And distracted him from two very important things.

One was the approaching command car, which was crawling along scouting the streets ahead of a "collection" squad.

The other was the exact moment at which dusk would become evening.

Giovanni turned the corner and found himself facing the command car, which swerved toward him with a squeal of tires. Two burly Germans were leaping from the rear in seconds, before the vehicle had even come to a full stop.

Taken by surprise, Giovanni shrank back against the wall behind him, having forgotten it was there. He lost precious time trying to decide whether he should pull his lead-heavy hand from his pocket and fight, or flee the way he'd come. Unfortunately, the momentary indecision tied up both options, for his weighted hand caught in his clothes and at the same time he couldn't reorient his legs and feet in order to allow for a sprint away from the uniformed thugs who were upon him.

Merda!

Shit!

His fist was *trapped*.

His feet tripped over themselves, and he went down sideways even as the two Germans caught him in double steel grips and yanked him off the sidewalk as if he were a child, their guttural orders and commands just a jagged jumble of sounds in his ears.

Oh no, Maria! This wasn't what I wanted!

He struggled in their grasp, his rock-hard muscles straining inside his constricting coat, but the two were larger than average, two bruisers who knew the ropes. They suspected his hand held a weapon and made sure it couldn't clear his damned pocket, and by keeping his feet off the ground they kept him off-balance as well, and he found it impossible to gather enough leverage for a kick.

He had no platform from which to launch an attack.

"Nooooo!" he shouted in frustration. Tears wet the corners of his eyes.

He'd asked for this.

The two uniformed goons manhandled him between them, their faces grim with determination and single-minded purpose. Perhaps their own well-being in the barracks depended on how they performed their thuggish duty.

Whatever their motivation, they were as immovable as boulders, and Giovanni wept with anger and futility as he saw his days of freedom and the love of his family wrenched from him as surely as his heart would be.

But still he struggled in their iron grip even as they dragged him, sweating and screaming, past the waiting command car to where a small, covered truck was just pulling up.

This was why he hadn't heard it. Smaller than the usual vehicle, it had also been driving toward him from around the corner of the adjacent unpaved lane.

A perfect trap.

And he'd stumbled right into it.

His thoughts turned for a split second to the new strategy—if only he'd witnessed it in action before, he might have avoided falling prey to it.

His legs swinging empty kicks at the shins of his attackers, which they mostly avoided, his mouth keeping up a steady stream of curses that would have made his wife blush, he found himself being tossed face-first like a sack of spongy, rotten potatoes over the rear gate and into the back of the truck.

His face stopped its painful slide on the rough planks by smashing into the muddy boots of another German soldier, who thrust the muzzle of his submachine gun brutally into Giovanni's skull.

He almost passed out.

Boots all around him, and at the front of the truck bed scuffed shoes and even bare feet—other conscripted unfortunates.

He couldn't look up, but what was in his range of vision deflated his spirit and took the fight out of him.

A stream of guttural syllables followed him onto the truck bed. One of the two burly thugs telling the other troopers he was probably armed.

His thought was borne out when hands reached out for his arms on both sides and dug his fist out of his pocket as the gun muzzle threatened to burrow straight through his skull and into his brain. Rivulets of blood seeped down his forehead and into his eyes as he felt the gunmetal scraping his cranium like a crowbar. His fist was forcibly removed from his pocket, the fabric tearing loudly, and the lead weight was pried from his fingers with inexorable strength.

My Maria! My son!

Beyond the pain in his head, the only thought he had was of his family and the fact that he would never see them again.

Now pressure on the back of his head was crushing his face into the rough wood of the truck bed, his nose beginning to crumple as other hands roughly patted him down with obscene efficiency. The feeling was as if those hands were not touching his body but someone else's. He wondered if his nose would break before the pressure was relieved. His breathing constricted, he suddenly began to cough and gasp, and blood leaked down his throat and he choked.

He was choking to death right there, on the truck bed.

The other thing that escaped Giovanni happened then.

Giovanni, who was now struggling to breathe through squashed nostrils and swallow blood before it could choke him, couldn't possibly be aware of it. His skull screamed where the gun prodded him still, and his face crushed into the wood was excruciating. And his teeth, his teeth were now grinding into the inside of his lips, which split like ripe grapes and began to leak blood over his chin.

The other thing was the moment dusk became evening.

And almost exactly the next moment, the Allied bombers came.

The air-raid sirens started up all around them, though Giovanni really couldn't hear them through the pain.

Grinding up to a screaming wail, the nearest sirens signaled the arrival of the first wave of the night's bombers. Not every night, not yet, but often enough to keep the Germans—and the innocent populace—guessing, the Allied bombing campaign cranked up when the lights went out. Tonight the raid was slightly too early, with a tendril of daylight left scattered across the darkening sky, but there it was, the bomber squadron was committed. The rumble of airplane engines slowly crawled over the land, and in seconds the *crump-crump-crump* of anti-aircraft fire joined in the cacophony as invisible gunners began to lay down a barrage that would knock a percentage of the Liberators and Fortresses out of the sky before the raid was over.

Waves of American and English long-distance bombers tonight targeted the harbor, the high command, and the factories arrayed in long blocks between them. Typically, the first strings of ordnance fell short and landed in civilian neighborhoods.

Like this one.

Around Giovanni, the results of the early raid were pronounced.

The truck's driver gunned the motor and squealed away from the cobbled curb.

The thugs who had thrown Giovanni onto the back of the truck were left behind, where they no doubt leaped for the command car in their haste to escape the open street. They were in the crosshairs for a direct hit, or burial under rubble if Allied bombs found a nearby building.

The soldiers who'd been frisking Giovanni and driving the gun muzzle into his cranium were thrown clear to the side as the driver swerved.

Giovanni felt the pressure on his body suddenly recede and took his opportunity, ignoring the pain in his head and face and leaping up to dive off the rear of the truck. The soldier with the submachine gun sought to regain his balance and managed to partially block Giovanni's access to the open gate.

Behind them, the cobblestones fled past dizzily as the vehicle gained speed. Another few seconds, and Giovanni's escape attempt would be suicide.

Adding to the confusion, a series of explosions down the street rocked the ground and the truck careened to the right-hand side.

Giovanni's hands wrapped around the barrel of the German's submachine gun as if of their own volition, and he snatched it away. Once the gun was in his grasp, he turned it around.

The short burst cut the soldier in half and threw him against his fellows in a heap.

Giovanni made his split-second decision and dove from the rear of the vehicle.

He hit the cobblestones hard, knocking the air from his lungs even as he rolled over and over toward the gutter.

His hands still grasped the gun.

Down the street, a building collapsed immediately after an Allied bomb struck its roof and ripped out its guts when it exploded. The cloud of dust and debris obscured the street and pelted Giovanni's back as he lay on the cobblestones trying to draw a breath.

Before he could manage to inhale...

A naked arm with a bloody stump crashed to the ground in front of his face and bounced toward him, coming to rest close enough for him to touch it.

Whatever he had eaten that day surged up his throat in a pillar of acid bile, and he coughed up the taste, feeling his throat muscles convulse. Still unable to breathe, he felt like a drowning man. Suppressing the urge to vomit took all his concentration, but he managed to swallow without bringing anything up.

He shook his head to clear it of the cottony fog it had collected in the last few seconds.

He glanced over the obscene debris and saw the careening truck he had leapt from teeter momentarily on two wheels, strike the opposite curb and overturn, spilling its human cargo like sacks of trash.

Maddened by the beating, the explosions, his painful escape, and the bloody evidence of the horror of war, Giovanni struggled to his feet, the submachine gun still in his hands.

Three soldiers spilled from the truck also stood, and one pointed at him, his mouth open in a sort of guttural scream, calling attention to Giovanni's accidental escape as if it were a personal affront.

His hands were bruised, his arms ached. But his right index finger tightened on the trigger as if he'd lost muscular control, and the twitch caused the Schmeisser MP-40 to stutter in his grip. The breech ejected a stream of hot brass casings as the gun spoke in its own guttural dialect.

The soldiers flopped and twitched as the 9mm slugs tore through them in ragged, bloody lines. The muzzle went silent when the magazine was empty, the bolt stuck in the open position.

Giovanni's hands opened after and the smoking gun dropped to the bricks.

He stared at the carnage he had wrought.

Maria!

God, what have I done?

Soldiers were crawling from the truck's sideways cab, and one was reaching for a sidearm. Yet another emerged from the covered rear, struggling to bring a Mauser rifle to bear.

Giovanni closed his eyes.

Addio, Maria. Good-bye, Franco.

He awaited the feel of the slugs tearing out his chest.

Instead, gunfire erupted all around him.

The Germans danced like out of control marionettes, clouds of blood and bone around their bodies, then fell twitching to the gore-slickened road. Masked gunmen sprinted from the cover of dark doorways and narrow lanes, ran to the wounded or dead Germans and shot them repeatedly in the head with pistols. Several with Breda submachine guns motioned other civilian men from the rear of the truck, one of whom had been wounded in the gunfire and had to be carried. When the gunmen had made sure all German soldiers were dead, they stripped the bodies of weapons and ammunition.

A gangly young man in a rakish beret walked up to Giovanni, who stood still stunned by what he had done, grasped his hand and pumped it enthusiastically.

"*Grazie, signore. Lei e' un eroe!*"

You are a hero!

"No!" Giovanni spit at him, breaking into a wracking cough as the dust swirled around them. "No," he repeated softly in disgust.

"*Si, certamente.*" The young man was clearly in command of the rag-tag group of gunmen. He wore a tweed coat crossed by bandoliers shotgun shells, and in his hands he held a fine Beretta hunting shotgun. He had a German Luger pistol holstered on his hip. He smiled broadly under a thin moustache. "I am Corrado Garzanti, field commander of the local brigade."

"*Partigiani?*" Partisans?

"Of course." He gestured at his men, who were finished stripping the dead soldiers and were now standing watch, their guns turned outward in case of attack. "We were about to ambush the collection patrol when you took matters into your own hands, eh? Very nicely done."

"How? How did you know? To be here, right now?"

Corrado waved the question away. "We have sources. People who listen and report. We expected them. We did not expect *you*, however."

Giovanni's head spun a little and he stumbled sideways, almost losing his footing. Ragged bursts of gunfire and screams came from farther down the street, and he whirled, apprehensive.

"It's just my men taking care of the command car. Those dirty German bastards are never going home."

Corrado reached out and steadied Giovanni before he could collapse.

"I think you had better come with us. It won't be safe here very soon. We survived the bombing, but the bastards will be out looking for revenge. Damned bad idea to be out on the street then." He waved at one of his men. "Dario, come here. I want you to escort our hero home to pack."

"No, no, it's not necessary."

"Oh, it is. If they find you, they will hang you from a lamppost with metal wire. It's what they're doing these days. Pack a small bag and come with us. We have a safe haven. It's not a palace, but it's a good home. And they don't know where it is."

"No, you don't understand, I have a wife and a child. I have a family! I can't go away with you. What happens to them?" Giovanni swayed and the partisan leader steadied him again.

"Clearly, you cannot just go home. *Va bene*, we take you home and you take your family with you. We have enough space. Most of us have lost our families, but there are a few."

Giovanni began to argue again. His head throbbed and his body ached in a million places. He wondered if his nose was broken. He felt blood still welling up on his broken lips and dribbling down his chin. He took a breath and felt his bruised ribs poking his lungs...

And the air raid siren ground to life again, its insistent wail gathering strength as the rumbling of invisible aircraft reached them.

"*Arrivano ancora*! Second wave!" Corrado shouted. His men knew what to do. And Corrado's fist jabbed out and caught Giovanni's jaw, snapping his head back and dropping him like a broken doll.

"You and you," he pointed at the strapping Dario and another man. "Take him between you. He's coming to the sanctuary. He has no choice now."

Giovanni moaned as the hands grabbed him.

Maria.

He lost the light at the same moment as the first string of bombs stitched their way toward the harbor, taking down a block of tenements and shops in a cluster of explosions, jetting gas fires, and a spreading cloud of dust and debris.

Giovanni welcomed the darkness as relief from the nightmare his life had become.

Franco

The ragged howling sent chills down his back, and when he glanced at his friend, he saw that Pietro was spooked too. Their eyes locked. The fear was obvious in their open pupils.

They'd been brought up on scary stories featuring wolves—what child wasn't?—but now, upon hearing the sound of pursuit, a strange pursuit completely different from that of the armed sentries, the fear seemed to reach down into the deepest depths of their psyche, strangling any resurgent courage their evasion of the soldiers might have caused.

Suddenly, for a reason he couldn't understand, Franco's heart seemed to grow cold.

Wolves.

Had they come down from the hills?

Wild game was easier pickings at higher elevations. The farmers here protected their flocks and henhouses with their loud guns, mostly trying to keep half-starved German soldiers away unless they had goods with which to barter. Franco had seen his grandmother trading with German officers, whose gratitude shone in their eyes, and whose stiff military bows somehow seemed to contradict the rumored atrocities about which one heard whispers. Even at his young age, Franco understood that there were shades of gray between the extremes. Perhaps not all Germans were monsters.

Since the livestock around these parts was so well protected, wolves tended to keep to the darker woods. Occasionally, a single, starving wolf wandered within range, and the hunters formed a party and tracked it down for execution. A starving wolf was always considered a much more dangerous opponent, for it would attack even

85

greater predators—such as humans—in its desperation.

But this was a pack, judging by the numerous howls and yelps. Multiple animals and large, too, by the sound of them.

Coming closer.

Franco snapped out of his fear-induced spell. He reached out and snagged Pietro's lapels and shook his friend like a doll.

"Listen to me, we have to run!"

"Again?"

"Yes! They're not far away."

"Maybe they don't want us. Everybody knows wolves don't attack people."

"I think we're about to find out for sure if they do." Franco let go of his friend and stepped back.

Pietro's eyes were crazy, wide and unfocused. Spittle flew from his slack lips as he muttered words Franco couldn't understand. His hand whipped out and caught his friend's cheek in a slap. The *smack* brought them both around.

Franco was stunned. It was so much like something his father might have done in a fit of anger.

But it had worked.

Pietro's eyes suddenly shed their watery curtain and focused on his.

"Listen!" he whispered.

They craned their necks, but there was no need. The howling came from three directions, the sound rising in intensity, coming closer. Franco thought he could hear large bodies crashing through the undergrowth, monstrous shapes solidifying in his head. He pictured them hurtling through brambles and bushes, following their prey's scent.

"We *have* to go!" he added, and grabbed Pietro's arm again. "If you don't follow me, I'm going without you. I mean it!"

He pulled his reluctant friend toward where the thicket began its obstruction again. Beyond it were patches of darkness that united to form a false midnight. A dead oak branch lay across their path, and Franco plucked it off the ground then walked back the way they had come, sweeping leaves and pine needles and twigs this way and that, hoping to ruin both their tracks and their scents. He tossed the branch aside and they hurried into the tunnel-like darkness of the old wood that covered this elevation like a mantle. Higher up, there were pines and firs, but here it was a mix, and thin-trunked white pines stood in crooked lines that wove in and out of the denser deciduous groves planted by the Romans centuries before.

The boys only cared that they were putting distance between themselves and their pursuers, whether they were dogs or wolves.

They were wolves. Franco knew it deep inside, though he tried not to think about it as his feet tripped on roots and saplings, throwing off his balance and slowing his headlong rush. Pietro stumbled along next to him, but they sometimes lost sight of each other in pockets of darkness as they wove between tree trunks like needles through thick cloth.

Behind them the wolves ran.

And howled.

And came closer, eating up the ground.

The boys ran. They ran as they had never run before.

Chapter Eight
Endgame: Second Day

Lupo

Satellite radio had been a revelation.

Lupo skimmed through the more interesting channels to find some truly deep tracks for the ride.

Although he still plugged his iPod or phone into the car's upgraded system, and even fed in the occasional CD from his extensive collection of progressive and neoprogressive rock music, or occasionally classical or New Age, he had stumbled onto the satellite phenomenon in DiSanto's new car. Several of the classic rock channels peppered into their playlists bands he had almost never heard on standard radio—the Strawbs, Camel, Procol Harum, Marillion, Dream Theater, Transatlantic, along with the mainstays of prog such as Floyd, Genesis, Yes, Emerson Lake and Palmer, Jethro Tull, Moody Blues, and more.

But today the satellite was killing him. He already felt a deep sadness at the chasm that seemed to be opening between him and Jessie. They'd made love, true, and recaptured some of the magic...but then things had slid back to senseless bickering when he realized she'd go back to the casino no matter how many times she'd agreed not to.

So today every one of his prog-friendly channels stabbed him in the heart with loss. Eric Woolfson's evocative voice on a Parsons Project song, a Floyd classic heavy on Rick Wright's keyboards, a Warren Zevon tune, a Ronnie James Dio song—it seemed he could not avoid being reminded of his icons' mortality. These people had helped him grow up with their music, and now he was watching them die, one by one. It was disconcerting, and he blinked damp eyes rapidly when he climbed from his car. DiSanto wouldn't understand.

Hell, nobody would.

But loss is tough to face. He should know—he'd faced more than his share. *Caused* more than his share.

By the time he reached the homicide squad room, he was back to wearing the pissed-off face that usually got him somewhere with timid suspects in the interrogation rooms. It also kept some cops off his back.

He stalked past the mostly empty cubicles and desks lined up in a maze on the bullpen side of the room and right up to the row of offices along the back wall. Griff Killian was just nosing out of his hole, facing the other way, when Lupo got his hands on him and flipped him around and against the wall.

"What the fuck you doin'—" Killian's New York accent erased any progress he'd made fitting in to the Midwest.

"We need to have a little talk," Lupo snarled, barely controlling the growl that threatened to erupt from deep inside. Rage brought the Creature much closer to the surface than he was usually comfortable with.

"Take your hands off me!"

Lupo increased his grip and yanked the big cop off-balance, twisting him around in a tight circle that took him back into his cubbyhole office.

"What did you do?" he growled. "How did you put the pressure on Bakke?"

"I don't know what you're talking about." Killian tried to shrug his way out of Lupo's grasp, but the cop's hands were like steel bands. "Get the fuck—"

Lupo's grip tightened and fabric tore. His face was inches from Killian's.

"You have connections with the mayor's office. You always did, you bastard. And you pulled strings to get me assigned to this murder, and then you turned around and put the wringer on Bakke."

"No, I—"

"Shut up. Why would you do it when you know what I am, what I can do to you?"

"What you are? Besides a crooked cop and a killer? I saw you kill Arnow—"

"I said shut up."

Lupo's hands had steadily traveled up Killian's clothing, and now his grip cut off the IA cop's breathing. Killian started to choke. Lupo shook him like the proverbial rag doll.

"I wondered why we got pressure so quickly. Usually takes a day or two to get the mayor's office in a tizzy, but they were on us like glue in less than two hours. I wondered about that, Killian, about who'd benefit most if we got our hands tied before we could even start. And it's you—you can't stand me, you want to get rid of me—"

Killian's ruddy face was turning from red to blue as Lupo's grasp cut off his air. Killian's hands batted weakly at Lupo's chest, then down and against the flimsy wall behind him.

"It's what you saw, isn't it?" Lupo sputtered. "You could leave it alone, but you choose not to."

The Creature hovered close to the surface, barely one or two layers below. Conflict tended to grant it greater control.

Which Lupo knew was dangerous.

If he didn't relent, Lupo would change right here and now. He knew it, but he went on, cutting it close.

"Plus you been talking to the shrink, Marcowicz, right?"

Killian's eyes were bulging, his hands still trying to beat a tattoo rhythm on Lupo's chest but faltering fast.

"What did you tell him?"

He shook Killian easily even though the IA cop was bigger. If his hands turned to claws, he'd be ripping Killian's chest cavity open, tearing out organs and steaming entrails. Lupo knew he was on the brink, and yet it was getting him nowhere. Killian's eyes had seemed confused and unfocused even before the choking had begun. This was just his fury being released, focused on Killian because he didn't know where else to focus it. Not yet, anyway.

Lupo loosened his grip and Killian sagged, gasping for air and starting to cough violently. Lupo let him, giving just enough to let the cop realize he still meant business. Then he shook Killian again.

"What. Did. You. Tell. Him?"

Killian wheezed and coughed, his face scarlet. "Nothing!"

"Tell me the truth," Lupo snarled.

Then hands grasped his arms and tore him off Killian so suddenly that he was thrown off-balance and Killian fell back into the wall.

"Nick, what the hell?"

DiSanto's hands on Lupo angered the Creature. The growl that erupted from Lupo's throat was made of raw animal rage and, for a second, Lupo felt control slip away.

Under his clothing, he knew tufts of stiff hair sprouted up his arms and back.

He knew he'd start to ripple in a second.

DiSanto must have seen the kaleidoscopic changes in Lupo's eyes, because he recoiled and released his arms. And stepped back.

"What— what's the problem?" he said, blinking rapidly and retreating further from the animal he saw reflected in his partner. "Killian, you all right?"

Killian was still in the middle of a coughing fit, but he nodded. His face was bleached white, like chalk.

Lupo turned his angry glare from DiSanto, who tried hard to ignore it, to Killian. He thrust a sharpened fingernail at Killian's chest, hard enough to leave a bruise.

"Better hope I don't find out you're lying. I'll finish this if I do. You and the Doc better be on your guard."

"Threatening me?" Killian was recovering color and dignity.

Lupo almost gagged on the smell of cheap burritos that pervaded the office.

"Yeah, matter of fact." He was coming down off the Creature high. Miraculously, because things had almost gotten out of hand.

DiSanto looked from one to the other. "We good here? We done?"

Lupo glared at Killian one last time. "For now."

Outside the office, DiSanto whirled on Lupo. "What the fuck, Nick?"

Lupo sighed, the Creature having retreated back to wherever it rested between changes. He knew the hair had retreated, too. How much to tell DiSanto? His partner had no idea what had happened outside the casino before he'd shown up. No idea what Killian had seen.

"Look, Killian's the reason we've got heat on this case already. The stiff's barely cold, and we're getting the heater routine? Had to be instigated from within. Think about it."

He remembered to limp slightly. Didn't help that he tended to forget he was supposed to be wearing a prosthesis. He did, but it was a fake one designed by his special effects wizard friend. His forgetting to limp probably reminded Killian of the cover-up every day. Something had been building up in the IA cop since the incident, and he'd figured out a way to hassle Lupo—through his cases. There was no way he could know about Lupo's suspicions that Mr. Wolf's murder might have been a message to him after all.

DiSanto was nodding. "Sure, I believe that. I'm not, uh, aware of what exactly went down at that casino, but since then he's been actin' like a dog with a chew-bone, working it around and around. Figure he had to crush it sometime."

"Yeah, whatever." Lupo sighed. His hands and feet tingled. A sort of foiled-wolf adrenaline letdown, maybe. The Creature's disappointment at not being given the chance to rip apart something warm and bloody. "What are you doing here so early?"

"Got the ME's autopsy report on Lenny Wolf. Got more info on Wolf's video business, too." He smirked.

"Start with the autopsy," Lupo said, knowing there was little chance the business angle was relevant. They reached their own corner desk area, a wide, shared cubicle where they could sit back to back, several computer displays spread out next to them showing various law enforcement database log-ons ready for input.

"Funny stuff, Nick."

"Yeah?" *Shit,* he just knew where this was going.

"Yeah. Seems that Wolf's body remains are full of teeth marks. The large enough parts, anyway."

"Teeth?" He knew how to play the game, he'd had enough practice. But it was a pain. "Whaddya mean, *teeth?*"

"Not human teeth. Animal. Dog or dog-like." DiSanto raised an eyebrow. "Remind you of anything?"

Lupo frowned. "Not off-hand."

"Not that long ago, the frat-boy bike gang, remember the one you collared, got his ticket punched later on? Remember, he said *he* was attacked by a giant dog the day of the bust. ME concurred. Found some weird DNA. He called it an error. And..."

"And?"

"Those animal attacks in Wausau? You worked those with that cop, Falken?" He shook his head. "Damn, she was somethin'. Too bad she had to get killed by those casino robbers. Anyway, the *animal attacks*. What's going on, Nick?"

Christ, the facts were closing in on him.

He sighed. "I don't really know, but I've noticed those connections too. Seems like, lately, half the stuff we do is connected."

"What did you and Falken find out about the animal attacks?"

"Unfortunately, nothing. We dropped them when the casino robbery came along. Then Falken got killed, and I hadn't seen any more obvious animal attacks since then. It seemed we were done with those."

"What about wolves?"

Lupo's head snapped sharply around. "What?"

"You know, the reintroduction went too well. Wolves are thriving. The packs are growing in size. Lots of farmers want them off the protected lists, especially if they have to choose between the wolves and their livestock."

"I'm against hunting them," Lupo said, his voice hoarse. "Unless I can get a sick individual in my cross-hairs. That one I'd take out, just to put him out of his misery. Plus it might have been a sick wolf who attacked humans."

"Here in town?" DiSanto said incredulously.

"No, DiSanto," Lupo snorted. "Not here. Here it's a whole other deal."

Lupo's phone buzzed and he snatched it off its cradle. "Yeah, homicide. Lupo."

Crap.

He met DiSanto's eyes and nodded once.

Killian

He resisted the urge to go home and shower.

The bastard had almost killed him, cut off his air.

Strong. He's a lot stronger than he looks. And pissed off. Out of control.

Detective Lupo had to be stopped. Killian rubbed his neck where the other cop's hands had almost crushed his larynx. The bruise would be embarrassing.

Actually, Killian was embarrassed about the fact that he had some sort of hazy memory of having seen something, having been part of something, but he couldn't remember it.

That was one reason he had started to see Marcowicz. The police psychologist had already given him some dirt on one Dominick Lupo, but now Killian also needed the shrink's help. At least, he thought he did. He'd always been solidly pragmatic, his feet on the ground, however you wanted to wrap it, he had taken for granted his own lack of stress-related mental problems.

But now Marcowicz was telling him just that. He theorized Killian had suffered some kind of trauma, and now he'd blocked it—mostly, if not completely—from his memory. Marcowicz had expressed surprise it was Killian's shooting of Tom Arnow he *did* remember. Of course, Killian couldn't cop to the truth there—that he hadn't shot the sheriff...

Isn't there some song about shooting the sheriff?

...because Lupo had done it, using Killian's Glock, and he seemed to believe whatever else Killian knew would get him a section-eight—or whatever cops did to ease out the mental cases.

Well, fuck that, Killian thought. *I'm gonna figure out what I saw and why it's so important to Nick Lupo, and then I'm going to roll the dice.*

In the meantime, Killian would stick with Lupo like a virus, apply heat whenever possible, and try to prepare for his ultimate revenge— serving up the crooked cop to a review board that would strip him of his badge, and hopefully of his freedom.

He closed his office blinds, leaving only a tiny slit through which he could survey Lupo's domain. His phone buzzed and he scooped it off the desk.

"Yeah?"

He listened, grunting. Then he hung up, thought for a second, and dialed quickly. He said very little. Then he pushed the phone away and sat back to wait, closing his eyes and smashing his hands into his eye sockets until he thought his head would burst from the pressure.

Heather

She pulled off I-94 and skirted the downtown exit, choosing to head west through the Marquette interchange and head for the western suburbs where she could find one of the few remaining mom-and-pop motels.

At the wheel of an anonymously sensible black Hyundai Sonata, she regretted having disposed of her beloved silver Lexus SUV—but it was too recognizable, especially by people she was most likely to run into here. She'd never be able to do surveillance in that distinctive vehicle, and she'd decided to make herself match the unflashy sedan. She had dyed her signature honey-blonde mane a convincing shade of black, changing her make-up and clothing to go with the new, more serious look.

A while back she'd considered a nose job to change the planes of her face, but frankly her "condition"—as Nick Lupo would say—made her quite nervous to go under the knife. Who knew what might happen while under general anesthesia? No, she had resorted to the more simplistic methods of disguise, and so far it had worked in various situations—some more interesting than others.

She'd just sat in on the first congressional hearings on Wolfpaw and its crimes in Iraq, and no one in the Washington crowd had recognized her even though she had worked for two New York television stations since ditching her old job and haunts in Wausau, Wisconsin. It was amazing what little alterations could to make one look completely different.

But she was still an imposing figure, an Amazon with patrician features and a figure to drive men—and women—wild, and an enthusiastic interest in indulging herself and experimenting with both whenever the opportunity presented itself.

She smiled tightly as she followed the traffic flowing past the Miller Park baseball stadium. She clearly remembered the threesome she'd had with two hometown baseball players not so long ago, and later she'd slept with the wife of one of them. Well, there'd been very little sleeping, as the wife had clearly meant to exact some payback on her unfaithful husband but had found in Heather such a responsive playmate that all thought of revenge had left her pretty little head— *mostly while receiving head!* Heather recalled.

She remembered another sports urban legend she had personally researched. Someone had once told her (with a smirk) that in the "old days," women who sat in the front row at the famed Lambeau Field, where the beloved Green Bay Packers practiced their craft, would sometimes go commando and spread their legs to give the hunky football players a show. With the intention, of course, of advertising a certain interest in playing another kind of game altogether.

Intrigued, and certainly tingled, Heather had wielded some of her considerable influence to wangle such a seat at the perennially sold-out Lambeau for a late summer game. She'd researched the seating chart and found several areas where the tactic could still be employed, which was difficult because over time the front row had been masked with colorful rubber matting (perhaps as a response to the unofficial entertainment, which increasingly could be caught on network cameras now that technology made it easier).

She had enjoyed the game very much, and flashed her wares at every opportunity—lining up players as well as coaches and assistants and new fans who gawked unabashedly at what she allowed them to see. A new "Brazilian" had given her the weaponry to decimate any competition that might have shown up in one of the few other potential hot seats.

Reaching down to slap-five with passing players and others after the game was won, she had found her hands filled with scraps of white wrapping tape with phone numbers and autographs Sharpied on. What a series of unbridled sexual adventures *that* experiment had led to, she recalled now, feeling the heat creep up on her. She had worked her way through the list and kept the autographs to this day in a bound memory book along with promotional photos of her conquests. A couple of them still emailed her, though they had moved on from Green Bay.

Ah, memories! She turned down the car's heater. She didn't need it, suddenly.

In the suburb of West Allis, she was able to locate a run-down motel of Sixties vintage. Not quite a Bates Motel, but certainly heading in that direction. A U-shaped two-story building with outdoor balcony access wrapped around a dingy pool area covered for the approaching winter. A burned-out sign advertised low rates, perpetual vacancies, and free HBO. A satellite dish, apparently from the early twentieth century, took up a quarter of the tiny concrete lawn. Two semis and a smattering of outdated cars indicated the clientele was sleepy truckers and adulterous liaisons.

Within minutes, Heather had a key card and directions to her new temporary abode, both issued to her new identity. The door to 113 displayed the same poorly done retro-fit of the electronic key system, a window covered from the inside by a thick sheet of plasticized rubber curtain, and a protruding air conditioning unit that probably let in more cold air now than what it kicked into the room intentionally in summer.

Now it was time to reconnect with some of her old friends.

Oh, they'd be real happy to see *her* again, that was for sure.

Well, maybe Nick Lupo would be, if he was free of that do-gooder Jessie Hawkins by now. Heather tingled at the thought of her seduction of the homicide cop. They shared a condition, so they would always be more closely connected than he was with the doctor lady.

Connected, heh.

Heather smiled. She did indeed hope to *connect* with Lupo again.

First to make a couple phone calls, then she would get the lay of the land. She'd only spent a small amount of time in Milwaukee, and while it was no metropolis, at over a million people in the metro area, it wasn't exactly Wausau, either.

She plucked a TracFone out of a bagful she'd picked up from a series of vendors while on the road. She pulled a portable police scanner set from her shoulder bag. An old-fashioned tool of the trade, but still a valuable one, especially when most if not all of her sources here were dried up or shut down. It was a whole new world, a blogger's world, and she felt her beloved journalism career sliding out from under her. In any case, she'd probably be doing an on-line newscast someday soon. She wasn't sentimental—she'd adapt. And lately she'd adapted a lot.

Hell, I gave up almost everything...twice.

This time, I'm getting something out of it and I'm not letting go.

She flicked on the scanner, locked the door, and went to use the dark-streaked shower. Twenty minutes later, dripping with water as hot as she could get it and wrapped in a stiff towel, she stepped back onto the blue carpeting and heard the squawking coming from the scanner.

Lupo

When they walked past the phalanx of uniforms dispatched to keep the neighborhood crowd at bay, it was only after navigating the maze of a dozen police squad cars parked throughout the barricaded street. All the action was in front of a liquor store.

"Jesus, half the department is here. The fuck needs this much shoe leather?"

Lupo shrugged and shook his head. "Must be a bad one. But it's attracting more attention than if they kept it quiet, that's for sure." He flashed his badge at a young uniform he didn't recognize. "Homicide, Lupo."

The cop might have been green, but Lupo realized he was also green in the sense of being *sick*. The kid nodded once and waved them inside with a shivery dip of his head.

"It's bad," he said. His voice was shaky.

"They're all bad, son," Lupo muttered.

"No, I mean *really* bad, sir. I mean fucking Iraq bad. I did two tours there with the Guard, sir, and this is worse than anything I ever seen."

They left him behind, shaking his head.

"Christ, what an intro," DiSanto said.

But then they stepped into the harshly lit interior of the store.

The level of carnage was every bit as bad as the cop at the door promised. Several CSI personnel in white suits stepped in and out of the blood and alcohol lake that stretched across the floor, their faces revealing queasy stomachs. Crimson splashes painted walls and shelves. And body parts lay in heaps throughout the space. A series of severed heads adorned the counter of one of the checkout stations.

"Shit," DiSanto said, his throat bubbling. He turned away and vomited near the door. "Sorry, Nick, this is too fucking much," he said, wiping his mouth.

"Yeah, it is." Lupo waved at a CSI-suit and asked a wordless question. The guy nodded and used gestures to show Lupo where he could step.

He squatted near a stack of severed arms and legs. They'd been gnawed, torn from the bodies with supernatural strength and then chewed like chicken drumsticks.

Fuck.

Another overt message.

"What the hell is this place?" he asked DiSanto, who was mopping his brow with a shaky hand.

"Huh? Liquor store."

"No, what is it called?"

DiSanto made a face to indicate he wasn't all that keen on doing irrelevant research for Lupo. He flipped through his smart phone's screens. "It's called... Wolf Liquor & Wine.

"Goddamn it!"

"What?"

"Just goddamn it, that's all."

"Name mean anything to you?"

"No," he lied. "But there's a coincidence for you..."

DiSanto looked blank, the expression intensified by the lack of color in his face. He shrugged. "I don't get it."

Damn it, if I tell him I have to explain it. If I don't and he gets it—or the task force gets it—then what will they make of it? Can it be spun in some innocuous way?

"Remember our low-rent movie producer vic?"

"Lenny, uh, Wolf." Light dawned on his face. "Ah, Wolf Liquor. You figure the same family?"

"Don't know, but it's worth a shot," Lupo said. They'd bark up the wrong tree, but who would ever make the right connection other than him, anyway?

DiSanto got on the phone and read off the names. "Sandy, be a pal and run some names for us. Check any obvious connections." He spelled out the names and clicked off.

"Maybe a family feud kinda thing? Or an OC deal?"

Lupo shook his head. "I don't see organized crime doing this. This is more Mexican cartel sort of work, and there's no likely connection there. I mean, we'll check, but I doubt it."

"Didn't the Mafia use to cut people up with blowtorches? In the golden age, the Seventies?"

"Yeah, I read those books too. From Valachi to *Mafia, USA* to the Executioner novels. But it was something they did in a few cases. Call it a case-by-case basis. Not a typical policy, or a routine approach. They didn't all go out and buy torches. Anyway, these poor folks don't show any burn marks, and there's no burned flesh stench."

"Plenty of other stench, though," DiSanto said. He pinched his nose. Fecal matter from the disembowelments had been as ubiquitous as blood, staining most of the floor space. They'd had to follow a no-contamination path marked out by the crime scene guys.

"Got that right."

They poked around, staying out of the CSI-folks' way, not touching much. There was little forensic evidence to be found, though Lupo would have bet they'd find some canid hair. Once again, the very slight DNA differences between *canis lupus* and *canis lupus familiaris*—the domesticated dog—would lead the ME's staff into declaring they weren't sure what had shed in there, but since a wolf was unlikely they'd chalk it up to being a dog. Maybe there wasn't a dog in the family, and maybe they'd wonder about the name Wolf and the possible wolf hair, but there wasn't much chance they'd jump to the right conclusion.

Lupo discreetly sniffed several small puddles left near the corners of the sales space. There was no doubt, it was strong-smelling urine. He bet himself that changing now would have given the Creature a good sniff of the rogue wolf who had done all this damage. He had raged, killed sales staff and several customers, and then marked his territory.

Part of the message.

But what was the message?

I know who you are?

Wolfpaw is sniffing around you again?

I'm coming for you, Lupo?

If it was Wolfpaw's work, then why pussyfoot around? Why not just come gunning for him? What was the point of the subtle messages, flags to grab his attention? What was the point of butchering innocent people? Was it to weigh on his conscience? Was it a challenge? A plea for capture?

Jesus, were they toying with him?

And if they were, how much danger was Jessie in?

Chapter Nine

Killian

"Listen, we need to talk again." He snorted. "No, not about me. About our friend and his woman. I've got somebody reporting to me, and it turns out she's spending an inordinate amount of time and cash in the local casino. What's that say to you?"

Marcowicz was silent as he thought about it. "Could be nothing. Maybe she just likes gambling."

"I have it on good authority they argue about it a good deal."

"Hm, then it could be a problem of sorts. Maybe—"

"Look, she was up to her neck in that incident up north, you know, the so-called casino robbery gone wrong."

"Yeah, sure, I'd forgotten about that."

"So she's a doctor, yet she took out a couple of those thugs herself, toting a shotgun no less. Any chance for a reaction there?

"Sure, sure," Marcowicz said thoughtfully. "I guess she could be suffering some latent PTSD. You say she's *gambling*?"

"Like there's no tomorrow. Like somebody's putting a gun to her head."

"Hmm, I'd have to talk with her at length to diagnose, of course—"

"Yeah, yeah, I know. Just diagnose with me, don't worry about her." Killian was getting tired of talking to the psychologist, who tended to get wrapped up in his own little world and forget about the context.

"Yes, I think Post-Traumatic Stress could cause someone to go overboard and indulge in some previously uninteresting activity. The fact that gambling tends to be self-destructive might be a clue. But didn't you tell me she was already gambling before the shoot-out?"

"Seems like it, from what I've been able to find out. The surviving guards all placed her there regularly, dropping good money with a gaming card."

"Maybe, and it's just a guess, she was already trying to process something traumatic by indulging in behavior contradictory to her usual character, and the shootings simply accelerated or exacerbated it and—"

"And made her worse?"

"Sure, possible."

"Maybe she was already pissed—"

"Upset."

"Whatever. Maybe she had a gripe with her boyfriend before that, and now it's just a bigger gripe." Killian wanted it to be clear in his head.

"I'd guess it's possible. Likely, even."

"Maybe if she knew her boyfriend was a murderer, could that do it?"

"*Is* he a murderer?" Marcowicz asked cautiously. It would change everything in their conversation.

Killian gritted his teeth painfully. "Not that I can prove, yet. But it's possible."

He cut off the doc, thanking him. Time to see Bakke? Where did the lieutenant stand?

Lupo

He took a minute to dial up Jessie's phone, but got her voicemail.

"Jess, it's me, call me as soon as you get this. I think there's a chance we're in the crosshairs again, dammit. It's just a feeling, but I'd like to know you're okay." He hesitated. If he sounded too angry, she'd ignore him. "So, wherever you are, give me a call."

He suspected she'd gone to the casino again.

Damn it.

Maybe it was better, being in such a busy place. Maybe it would make a hit or a snatch harder to pull off.

But he figured a pro would handle it just fine, and this new enemy wolf was a pro.

"I love you, Jess," he added just as his recording time cut him off. Did the words get recorded or not?

No way to tell now.

Heather

She stood behind the barricades hastily erected by the uniforms stationed outside the liquor store. Almost two dozen of the cops milled around or held the forming crowd at bay. A CSI van and an SUV from the ME were pulled up at the door, so she couldn't see inside. Lupo's damned Maxima sat farther up the street, outnumbered by enough squad cars to populate a parking lot. Would he ever spring for a ballsier car? He was a Corvette or at least a Mustang kind of guy. But she knew he'd had the Maxima's engine swapped out for something with custom growl.

She frowned at the circus-like quality of the response.

What the fuck happened here?

The scanner chatter she had heard in the motel made it clear this was no typical store robbery. The few veiled references—soon dropped in lieu of a complete lack of details—reached across the police bands, and she heard Lupo's call sign at some point. They used cell phones but also a dispatcher like the old days here, and she'd been able to figure out that Lupo was the lead cop on this one, and that it wasn't the only butchery done recently here in town. Barely in town an hour, and she was already getting dragged into something bizarre. She'd have to work her sources.

She pulled wrinkled clothes from one of her bags almost without looking. Tight jeans, a black, button-down blouse, a thin gray sweater over it, and her leather bomber jacket with the Harley-Davidson logo in conspicuous prominence. Standard undercover look for her, especially here—the center of the Harley universe (after all, the Harley museum was only a couple miles back the way she'd come). She'd finished dressing with impatient little gestures.

The game's afoot!

Then she'd found her way to the crime scene and parked a couple blocks away. Walking in, she did a double take when she saw the store's sign: WOLF LIQUOR & WINE.

Kind of took her breath away, knowing what she did. Coincidence?

Did she believe in those anymore?

Hiding within the crowd gathering behind the barricades, she surveyed as much of the scene as she could. On her turf, she would have used and abused her press credentials, but here she was out of her new haunts, unrecognized, and she thought that remaining under the radar might be best.

Especially since her hasty retreat out of town the last time she'd crossed paths with Nick Lupo. Chances were he wasn't happy with her. She would approach him, of course, but first she wanted to get a sense of what was what.

The hearings had opened up a new area of inquiry for her. Even though Lupo likely held a grudge against her, the fact that she hadn't been the rogue wolf he thought her to be would end up working in her favor. She hadn't expected to get embroiled in a case involving the reviled Wolfpaw, but having been so fortunate, she had now made the bizarre contractor group part of her life.

Not a good batch of enemies to make, now, is it?

What was it about this weird werewolf culture that made her loathe them, made her want to take them down?

Could it be that the only werewolves she'd met were all monstrous killers, especially those she had learned had killed their way through their Iraq assignments?

Or could it be that opposing Wolfpaw put her on the side of Nick Lupo?

A delicious shiver zipped through her favorite body parts and she chuckled. She figured it wouldn't take a lot to steal Nick from that doctor chick. She was cute, no denying, but she was as dull as a ten-year-old knife. Heather figured she and Lupo could share some pretty exciting times. Maybe no more hunting the homeless—*been there, done that!*—and no more sleeping around...

Well, how about being more careful? When she'd taken up with that slut Erica, how could she have known Erica was actually the cop Sheila Falken—the Wolfpaw operative who was framing her for a series of murders in order to expose and kill everyone who knew about werewolves? If she were more careful, she wouldn't get so close to one of the enemy again.

But getting close to Lupo, *that* she was rather looking forward to. She'd had him wrapped around her little you-know-what, until he caught a case of conscience. She could do it again.

"Hey, officer, what's going on?" It was worth a try.

"Official police business," the guy growled without turning around.

"But, sir, I was supposed to meet someone in there!"

The cop turned, and his eyes flicked over the people standing there. Heather raised a hand. "My boyfriend told me to meet him here. We were gonna buy some champagne to celebrate our, um, anniversary."

His glance roved over her face and, of course, down to her breasts. She'd left her jacked unzipped, and her chest was impressive enough to make him miss a beat.

"Ma'am," he stuttered, "are you sure this is the place? His car parked anywhere near here?"

Now that she'd engaged him, he was hooked. She batted her eyes at him, as if she were blinking hard imagining that something had happened to her "boyfriend."

"I don't see his car, but he hasn't shown up, so I don't know." She put just enough near-desperation in her tone to hitch her wagon to his sympathy. "Maybe if I could check inside?"

He grimaced. "Uh, no, ma'am, you wouldn't want to do that."

He looks sick! What the hell happened in there?

"Is there anyone I can talk to?" Why not take the chance? If Lupo came out, she could just melt away before he reached her. The crowd was growing, rubbernecking and jostling her from behind.

"I'll check," he said, but he was shaking his head. He mumbled into his shoulder radio. "Okay," he said. "Somebody's comin'."

Shit! Maybe she'd overplayed her hand. If Lupo came out, he'd recognize her.

She stood on her toes to look from behind a tall guy who hogged the front of the barricade. His crew cut looked fresh, and she could see the tip of an elaborate tattoo on his neck.

Military guy, she thought from force of habit.

Good looking guy, too. Muscles stood out on that neck. His jaw was chiseled to perfection.

She waited a minute, knowing the cop was still checking her out and pretending she didn't notice. She did notice that the hunky military guy seemed to be watching her from the corner of his eye, too. She was ready to duck behind him if Lupo himself took the call.

Nope, she saw the door open, and DiSanto squeezed past the guard and onto the sidewalk, looking for the cop who had called in. They conferred in whispers, then DiSanto looked at her, and his eyes widened slightly.

Did he recognize me? Or was he just admiring?

"Uh, your boyfriend might be in there?"

She nodded, biting a lip. Very worried now.

"Are you the cop—I mean, *officer* in charge?"

"DiSanto, homicide," he said, sidestepping the question.

"Homicide?" she squealed. "Oh, no!"

"Can you describe your boyfriend?"

She hesitated. Made it look good. She'd always been fast on her feet, a good actress even in grade school. She knew how to underplay a role.

"Uh, almost as tall as this guy—" she tilted her head at the guy in front of her, "—but he's got long, dark hair and a goatee, and he wears earrings in both ears. I told him they make him look—"

"No need to worry, ma'am." DiSanto broke into her stream of consciousness with a tight smile. "Nobody in there matches that description. Maybe he's just late."

"Oh, thank God! Thank you, officer."

"No problem." He gave the rest of the crowd a pan, then sidled toward the door again.

She was about to step back, out of the crowd, when she caught the military guy's eye. Or he caught hers.

Undressed her.

She was used to it, but this was a little different. His intense gaze seemed to penetrate her disguise, her motive, her story. She kept going and felt his eyes on her even when she turned away. Even as she walked to her car.

Creep.

Then again, he was just her type.

She forgot about him when she started to plan how she would re-enter Lupo's life. This wasn't the place. He would have shoved her aside so quickly her head would have spun itself back to blonde.

No, maybe this needed a subtler approach.

But what the fuckety-fuck-fuck had gone on in there? DiSanto's look had been grim, and he was a guy who'd eat a chilidog at an autopsy.

She checked back over her shoulder, but big Military Tattoo was nowhere to be seen.

Sigfried

He awoke with a hammering throb in his head, the result of overindulging in his best twelve-year-old single malt after the session with Margarethe.

She had stayed for a drink with him, then attended to the disposal. He had raised her pay grade in Wolfpaw, and her new "section" provided various discreet services to employees both at home and overseas. She'd been very accommodating since her takeover of the dom business, and he saw no problem with using her for other purposes. When the field commanders needed R&R packages for the men, a certain discretion was necessary, and the last people he'd had on had been prone to spilling their guts to the fucking press. It was but one reason he was called up to face those wrinkly old dinosaurs of congress.

Sigfried lay on his back and willed the headache away.

He forced himself to relax, muscle by muscle, first feeling the throb increase as he brought intensity to bear. But then he felt a characteristic melting. He let it wash over him.

Once his muscles relaxed, the rest of his body seemed to follow suit and slowly the pressure abated. He felt more able to face the day's challenges.

His wife of twenty-seven years, Georgina, had long ago given up trying to occupy his time. His "work" came first, he had explained with excruciating detail.

And now part of his work was defending his company in front of the congressional committee. He had explained that his hours would be irregular from now on, and indeed, when he checked the feed from her bedroom he saw that she had dressed and gone hours ago. Today was a recess day for the hearings, and he had indulged himself last night, knowing he could spend today coordinating the Lupo mission.

Wolfpaw Security Services had now been stung twice by the pesky homicide cop, Nick Lupo. Three times, if one counted the original three ex-mercenaries hired by that idiot, the serial killer mayor. The company had often spiritedly discouraged such moonlighting by its employees, but as they had been "former" employees, there had been no easy way to monitor the three shapeshifters' new hobby. Their supervisor had been punished for missing the signs.

Besides opening Wolfpaw to media and public scrutiny, the fact that two of the three, Tannhauser and Schwartz, were descendants of revered *founders* had rankled the council. A shakeup was in order, and a new management team had taken over Wolfpaw. Sigfried had been Wagner's direct supervisor, part of the old Wolfpaw ultra-secret council, some of whom were board members also. Their ancestors' identities determined their rank within the company's hierarchy, which hid the remainder of the werewolf members of the Wehrmacht's Werwolf Division's descendants.

And he sat above it all, CEO and chief scientist. In charge because it was his family's money that had built the company, and his family's work that had staffed it so...innovatingly.

He climbed out of bed and faced his day, at once worried and excited.

These were interesting times, indeed.

Mordred

He uploaded the video clips from his surveillance to the Wolfpaw safe server. The longest video was of the cop and his lady friend screwing for hours. Well, it *seemed* like hours. The other clips showed Lupo from other angles, standing at the lake shore, walking in and out of the house, the café where he often ate, the casino—where he met his gambling-addicted girlfriend—and walking in and out of the central precinct, Milwaukee's main police station.

Mordred figured Sigfried would order him to kill the woman, too, when the time came. It stood to reason that she knew what he knew.

He licked his lips of unconscious drool.

But so far his orders were to hover, targeting anyone around the cop who might know his secret, but make no overt moves. Except he was allowed to send messages, wasn't he? His orders were contradictory, weren't they?

He sensed that Sigfried might request a snatch instead of a hit.

Looked like maybe the lab from which he himself had emerged might get more business. What would Sigfried want to learn from poking and prodding Lupo?

It wasn't his place to question it, or any decisions made by the council. Mordred wondered, though, because his scars still ached from the poking and prodding he had received during those endless years.

Years of glass cages and silver bars, and later the injections, and the torture, and the screaming that had then turned out to be his own, his insides feeling as if they were being melted by hot pokers. Then relief, blessed, sweet relief. And then the melting heat, the torture, the screaming...

All in the name of science...

Mordred's head started to ache, the band tightening as if Sigfried himself were once again visiting the lab and getting a first-hand look at his scientist's creation.

His creation—Mordred.

More than first-hand looks. He remembered Sigfried holding the syringe. He remembered Sigfried holding a glowing blade and slicing, stabbing, cutting. Then stepping back and observing, observing, observing.

All while Mordred screamed in mindless, excruciating pain.

Was it so strange that now he enjoyed causing others pain?

Was it so strange he couldn't wait until Sigfried unclipped the leash and let him have the cop and his lady and everyone else in his sights?

In the meantime, Mordred enjoyed the messages he left for the cop.

He ended the upload and tried to wish the tightening band away with images of Lupo's woman under his claws. And fangs.

If he'd been in the woods, he would have howled.

Killian

Bakke's eyes widened at him, and he looked like an overgrown goldfish.

"Wait, you're running a case on one of my homicide detectives *right now*, while we got this heater case? Are you nuts?"

He was sitting behind his large desk, looking like a moon-faced fish. His complexion was patchy-red, his nose marked by the thin, red vines of a serious drinker.

If only you knew I'm the guy who made it a heater. And that your cop Lupo's the boy... No, not something you should find out.

"Chief—"

"I told you not to call me that."

"Lieutenant, sorry," Killian said. *Good thing you don't know what your men call you, and why.* "Lieutenant, I was given the leeway needed to investigate allegations against anyone, at any time. Your commissioner reiterated this leeway recently. I am not only allowed, I'm encouraged by the City Council. And duty-bound."

"You have allegations against one of my cops? Don't tell me! I don't wanna know yet."

It's way more than allegations, fuckhead.

"I'll work it on the down low until I have something worth bringing you, Lieutenant. You can be sure I'll keep it under wraps until then."

Killian hated to sound obsequious, but sometimes you had to go with what worked best.

They were sitting in Bakke's office, but Killian felt out of place. His little hole downstairs had become home, and the cloying smell of his snacks of choice had become a comforting presence that gave him the sense of separateness on which he had come to rely to do his job. Sure, he was hated by the rank and file, but they feared him and that was best.

All except Lupo. He didn't seem afraid at all.

And that rankled Killian probably most of all the things he could list he had against Lupo.

But Bakke was a strange fish—overgrown guppy or blowfish or whatever he resembled—who was more on top of things going on with his cops than he seemed to be. He was more competent than he appeared, too, and now his trust seemed to lie with Lupo.

Killian figured he'd have to catch Lupo doing something very bad, indeed.

Which also rankled, because he knew he himself could get Lupo for murder, but his prints on his gun would be hard to argue with. Lupo had checkmated him, but Killian still thought there was more. But what was it?

Bakke was talking at him and he tuned back in.

"Everybody's in agreement your IA has done an excellent job cleaning up the typical problems in the department. The MPD is better for it, Killian. But you don't want to go too far, take things to a personal level, know what I mean?"

Killian felt his face heating up.

He opened his mouth, but Bakke went on.

"I have heard rumbles from some corners that you have a personal gripe against one of my best detectives. A *decorated* detective. A fucking *hero*, Killian. I don't care if the two of you can't stand to be in the same room, or if you're constantly comparing your dicks in the john, or if you don't like the way he looks, or whatever the fuck."

Bakke showed some of his rarely seen hardass attitude right then, leaning forward and staring at Killian intensely with those pop-eyes which suddenly didn't seem so comical.

"I don't care what it is that's between you, but I'm warning you. You come at that particular cop with some half-baked shit you can't back up, without a case so solid you could hammer a roof on it and call it a vacation house in a hurricane zone, and *I will have your ass and your badge and your career hung out on the flagpole.*"

He smiled for the first time, and Killian now thought he looked more like a shark.

Fuck.

Killian hated getting his legs cut out from under him like this.

"Do you, ah, understand where I'm comin' from?" Bakke said, clearly demanding a response more definite than a stare.

"Got it, Lieutenant." Killian tried to smile, but he could tell it looked as if he'd swallowed a lemon.

Bakke's smile widened, and Killian swore he could see those multiple rows of shark's teeth set like triangular razors in Bakke's mouth.

Killian hadn't misjudged somebody this badly in quite a while. And he had expected his reputation would have carried more weight.

He left the office stiffly, as if Bakke's shoe were still embedded in his ass. It sure felt like it.

This made Killian twice as determined to stick to Lupo and see what the fucker was doing now. Chances were it was something. He'd already had his little twerpy DiSanto running some names.

He took the stairs and went straight for his office, where he could nuke something, anything from his stash.

His hands shook, and his breathing was rapid.

Marcowicz, here I come.

The Grim Reaper was back.

Chapter Ten

Simonson

Ever since he had removed the second silver dagger from the Minocqua massacre crime scene, Simonson had followed the Watcher.

Sleep-deprived and bone-tired, Geoff Simonson had made Wolfpaw Security his life's work.

Destroying Wolfpaw.

He had served in Iraq as a Ranger, but left the military under shadowy circumstances. He'd found himself recovering from a near-fatal head wound, fighting off massive, unpredictable headaches, and later—when in need of employment—sucked into the war machine that Wolfpaw Security Services had cranked up between its training capacity and actual security services.

Simonson couldn't remember signing the agreement. He'd been in the throes of a miserable, head-rattling, sharp pain jabbing at his temples. But he was well positioned as an asset to a company like Wolfpaw. As soon as he had recovered completely, according to the company doctors, he was already in country and trained to the gills for the very kind of campaign being fought in the streets and alleys of the Iraqi cities.

He advanced through the ranks of Wolfpaw despite his streak of blackouts and forced downtime.

And his anger built.

Anger turned to rage.

Working for Wolfpaw in Iraq, Simonson witnessed not only many of their day-to-day infractions—such as the use of prohibited explosive ammunition, indiscriminate shootings, gun smuggling and even killing for sport, the procuring of prostitutes for employees and other contractors and the occasional diplomat, plus the cover-ups all those required to keep them out of the news—but also the fact that a number of Wolfpaw mercenaries were lycanthropes.

Goddamn werewolves.

Monsters out of cheap horror movies.

Except these were *real*. He had seen them transform, starting out as humans and then suddenly shimmering, seeming to ripple in mid-air, and then becoming larger than average wolves whose fangs went for the throats of their victims, then disemboweled them and consumed the contents of their stomachs. And their limbs.

He had become an expert at recognizing werewolf attacks.

He had witnessed the slaughter caused by werewolf employees of the company, who seemed to hold all the power.

As werewolves, besides killing enemy combatants and identified jihadists, they also made sport of killing innocent people.

Conflicted, Simonson went into a tailspin. Both a moral and physical one that drained him of energy and will.

He'd awakened a month later in a Baghdad flophouse (and *that* was saying something), feverish and unemployed, cut off by his employer and from the normal world. From then on, nothing had been *normal.*

Headaches lanced through his brain with alarming regularity, and he suspected a brain tumor would bring him down like a bull elephant in the crosshairs of a .50-caliber rifle.

Geoff Simonson went "off the grid" and pledged to fight Wolfpaw and its lycanthropes. As part of his surveillance one night, he was surreptitiously observing their Georgia compound when one Dominic Lupo infiltrated it. He'd watched with interest as the rogue cop Lupo took on one of the wolf training teams by enduring pain the level of which Simonson could only imagine, efficiently executing a few of the rawer recruits. Their shapeshifting abilities were no match for Lupo's experience and determination. Even so, Lupo had barely escaped the compound and the state with his human skin intact.

Lupo's actions had given Simonson a direction to follow, but complications with his gear and the sudden onset of one of his lance-like headaches had forced him to the sideline temporarily.

Later, Simonson followed Wolfpaw's reinforced Alpha Team north, which led him directly to Nick Lupo and a strange sequence of events. There, too, he managed to be perfectly positioned and equipped to observe the bloody battle at the new casino. Intrigued by the fact that Lupo was a werewolf but also a sworn enemy of the evil Wolfpaw corporation, he decided to make Lupo the focus of his surveillance. By tailing Lupo and witnessing the events in the casino parking lot, Simonson had spotted the unusual dagger that saved Lupo and his team, but not the poor ex-sheriff, Tom Arnow.

And then Simonson had spotted the Watcher, who also kept surveillance on Lupo and those around him.

Simonson had no doubt the Watcher was one of Wolfpaw's weapons. Why was he holding off like that, observing from afar?

The game's complexity increased.

Simonson bided his time, but looked for the moment he would approach Nick Lupo. When the opportunity came, he could be Lupo's best chance.

And so now he found himself outside Wolf Liquor & Wine, wondering if he could approach Lupo when he came out. Simonson knew the Watcher had butchered the people in that store, but if he approached Lupo now he'd be an obvious suspect. He had to find the right moment. He had to keep an eye on Lupo, but continue tracking the Watcher, too.

And what was up with the dark-haired chick with the make-believe boyfriend? He'd seen through that ploy without much trouble, while the two cops just looked at her rack. He watched her eyes, though, and her lips, and he knew she was spinning a cover story. A spur of the moment cover story, but not one of the worst he'd ever heard. She had experience using her chest to bedazzle men into doing her bidding, and though this hadn't worked, she'd gotten some sort of info. He wasn't sure what, but the partner had gotten a vibe of sorts from her.

Simonson melted through the crowd in the opposite direction from the inquisitive woman. Not sure how he knew, but he figured he'd be seeing her again.

Killian

They met at an Albanian-owned diner a few blocks down, one of those with huge servings and menus that might as well have been photocopied, all offering the same idealized American fare. It was slightly better than that local chain with the twin clocks, but he didn't really like the way they made their hot dogs here—cutting them in half along their length to press them into rolls rather than hot dog buns. As a New Yorker, he hated anything outside of tradition. The diner had a Philly steak, but he'd made the mistake of trying that once and—never again. He ordered a generic hamburger, yanked the over-nuked bacon, left the fried onions and slathered on the mustard. Marcowicz ordered an omelet the size of his plate. Killian snagged the check so the doc would be grateful and talk more.

They went over the same topics as in their phone call.

He started with the usual questions and let the weaselly psychologist talk on, his mouth disgustingly full of eggs flecked with green and red.

Killian wanted material he could use to make his case against Nick Lupo, but it was a delicate balance because of Lupo's stature in the squad—and the department. The wishy-washy Lieutenant Bakke was a jerk, but he seemed willing to allow Lupo rope to hang himself, as all good task force heads are expected to do when things go wrong. The downside of all that rope was that Lupo could easily get himself out of most kinds of trouble with it exactly because it was so loose, and he had plenty of wiggle room.

"What about this whole seeing dead people thing?" he asked the doc, hoping the idiot would stop chewing before answering.

Mordred

He watched the New York cop with the weird name chatting up the bowlegged police psychologist. He wasn't far away, tucked in a booth of his own and slouched behind the figures of an overfed family of four hanging over the edges of their booth in front of him.

The fact that Killian was pumping the little snitch of a doctor meant there was something there for him to learn, about Lupo and about whatever he was forced to waste his time on in therapy.

Mordred flipped on the tiny unit that looked like a bluetooth earpiece, and what appeared to be a cell phone in his hand was an advanced parabolic microphone he positioned just right.

Their words popped into his ear, and he listened intently as he worked on a chunk of gristly, rare meat most humans would have sent back.

What was this about *seeing dead people*?

The psychologist swallowed a huge mouthful of food. "He hasn't talked about seeing Ghost Sam, as he calls the apparition, for quite a while. As a matter of fact, I was encouraged by his progress. The delusion seemed to be slipping away."

"That's good," the cop said sarcastically. "What about that foot?"

"I have seen him limp *less* on occasion, but that could be related to the weather. Understand, I can't just ask him to prove he's injured. I have noticed some new scarring on his right hand, however."

The cop leaned forward eagerly. "Oh? What kind of scarring?"

The weasel swallowed again, getting close to polishing off the monster omelet, then answered.

"I'd say it's most consistent with burns, really, but in weird straight lines, as if the burns were controlled. Very unusual. But they looked quite painful."

"So you think he's what, burning himself? What do those straight lines mean?" The cop was all ears.

So was Mordred. He had some idea where those scars came from.

"I can't determine that by just merely glancing at them, Killian." He pushed his plate away after hoovering up the last crumbs.

"Hm, I guess not." Killian drummed his fingers on the table, and Mordred heard it almost as snare drum rolls through the earpiece.

"What kind of excuse do you need to examine them?"

The doctor shrugged, then leaned in and whispered, "I have made some inquiries along the lines of what we discussed recently. The incidence of animal attacks, the ME's reports with all those errors they've acknowledged. And Lupo's inordinate amount of time off, much of it backed up by his partner. His file's getting thicker by the week, Killian. I'm learning some interesting things about this guy."

"Well?"

The doctor looked at his watch. "Hey, I have to be going. There are intriguing details we can discuss, but it'll have to be our next meeting."

"Christ, Marcowicz, you're fucking stringing me along!"

"I have to move slowly—"

Mordred left them to bicker over the check, paid his own and slipped out of the diner within two minutes. Neither of them saw him or paid any attention.

Marcowicz was worth prodding.

Sigfried

It had been a hell of a day.

Again.

More grandstanding by congressmen and that one woman he would like to have strangled.

More cameras and recorders in his face.

More allegations against Wolfpaw.

Tonight the bastards would get their photographs and start to think twice about what they were asking. Things would get better tomorrow.

But right now he needed release.

And now this. Margarethe was unavailable, for the first time since she had bought the dom business he almost single-handedly supported. (Well, he knew there were other high-powered clients, but they couldn't possibly afford the services he used so often.) Her replacement in charge, Veronika was her name, was certainly well-proportioned and full of assets—among them her multiply pierced labia and nipples, which were even more desirable than Margarethe's, but even so she was no Margarethe. For one thing, she had not been able to provide him with what he needed most, a plaything he could break that she would be willing and able to dispose of, after. He didn't know how Margarethe did it, but she had been able to procure such a plaything every time he'd asked—and lately he was asking more often.

So he'd suffered through a sub-par sloppy blowjob, had paddled her ass half-heartedly until she pretended to come, then had taken her from behind and made her scream by pulling on her labial rings until the mascara ran down her face.

That he'd enjoyed.

He'd have to have a word with Margarethe when she returned...see about a refund. And he hadn't felt generous with a tip, either—unlike the thousand dollars he routinely handed his favorite dom. He dismissed Veronika with a barely disguised frown.

Now he propped open his laptop and connected to the secure server, where he could download the latest Mordred report.

He enjoyed watching the cop and the lady doctor screwing themselves silly. They were supposedly on the outs, but they sure made sparks... In fact, it was more enjoyable than his own session had been, and it gave him another painful erection. He considered summoning Veronika back again, but then gave up and let it frustrate him all the more.

That lady doctor... She was something. Perhaps Mordred should bring him a memento of the mission.

He rewound the clip to the beginning and started touching himself.

Chapter Eleven

1944
Chelmno
Prey

Branches reached down from overhead like skeletal fingers groping for a victim to haul up into the dark maw at the center of the tree.

Jakov's breath plumed around his head as he ran, his bare feet slit by the icy crust on the recent snowfall, his steps stuttering because the snow seemed intent on dragging him down into its frozen depths. At this point, his lungs burning and ready to burst, his skin as hard as marble in the frosty moonlight, he could not have decided which fate was worse. The branches slashed at his face with their Christmas-tree needles suddenly more like those of syringes, while the ice crystals below him cut his soles and ankles with scalpel-like blades.

He stopped running, mind almost too blank from shock and pain to choose whether to risk entering the dark grove or stick to the open. The grove would be somewhat protected from the snow, but the needles covering the ground would prick his feet, and the branches would continue slashing his face and arms. But the snow slowed his progress. And his tracks made his pursuer's work easier.

Barely stopping to consider, he gritted his remaining teeth against the pain and struck out through the trees. Several kilometers to the east, he knew, was a huge hole half filled with fresh corpses. Perhaps he could manage to do what he had been told was impossible.

The loose-fitting clothing, rough on his skin, concealed the pistol he had found just before breaking out of the charnel house the camp sadist called a laboratory.

They called him *der Schnitter.*

The reaper.

Jakov, already nearly frozen to death, shuddered to think of what he had seen.

And when the howling began behind him, he shuffled to a halt. He fumbled the pistol out of his clothes, wondering just then why it had been so easy. It had just been lying there, as if set out for him to find.

He'd been a military man once, long ago. He dropped the magazine into his palm and even in the shadows he could see it was empty. He snarled and almost threw the gun away. But then he pulled back on the toggle and looked and there was one cartridge, seated in the breech.

They wanted him to commit suicide?

He angled the pistol just right and squinted at the bullet, and it gleamed silver in the moonlight that filtered down on his hand.

One bullet.

Jakov understood then that he was a pawn in some fiendish game. What they had done to him wasn't even the end.

He had grown up in a land infested by wolf packs in the winter. He knew their long, mournful howls. While they had frightened him as a child, the howling he now heard from nearby chilled the blood in his veins even more than the snow and ice could.

Gripping the nearly useless gun in one hand, he started running again. Or, rather, shuffling along on his bare feet, made bloodier by the ice. He left red splatters behind on the pointed needles that jabbed his soles until he could no longer keep from screaming with the pain. When he did open his mouth and screech hoarsely, the sound was drowned out by the howling behind him, bare meters away in the woods.

A creature crashed through the shadows of the pine branches just behind him. He heard large paws scrabbling for purchase on the slick forest floor.

The gun.

A silver bullet?

He turned to face the monster that had tracked him from his easy escape in the woods.

The slavering jaws were the first thing he saw, fangs bared and very bright in the moon's intermittent beams. The eyes above those jaws glowed red. A wolf, twice the size of any of the undernourished specimens he had seen near home. The beast's howls turned to mad snarling as he bore down on the helpless human.

Jakov had faced a charge before, and he had not broken.

He waited a second more, until the monstrous creature was almost upon him, then—with a steadier hand than he had any right to have— he fired the one shot he had been granted.

He saw the bullet punch the beast between his glowing, rage-filled eyes and explode a portion of the skull in a cloud of red gore. The beast's snarling was cut off, and it ground to a halt at Jakov's feet.

A perfect shot.

Jakov lowered the gun. The wolf was dead.

He resumed breathing, his lungs wracked by the cold and the exertion.

Suddenly, impossibly, the wolf's eyes opened again and fixed his killer with a red glare.

A wailing scream of pain mixed with rage escaped the snapping jaws even as the beast's entire body leaped up off the ground and landed on Jakov's chest as if he'd not been shot, fangs ripping tender throat flesh before going for the man's unprotected belly.

The last thing Jakov saw before the darkness cut off his own futile scream of frustration was the wound his one bullet had made, mending itself both in front and on top of the wolf's head. In seconds, all signs of the wound disappeared.

Then Jakov was no longer human, just food.

And reward.

Chapter Twelve

Lupo

There was someone standing near his car. No, *leaning* on his car.

"What the fuck?" he whispered to himself, easing the Glock from its holster and quickly, quietly racking the slide as he approached the Maxima, which he'd parked on the street.

He glanced back, but DiSanto had disappeared in the opposite direction.

Holding the gun half hidden at his side, Lupo came up on the guy who leaned on Lupo's car from behind. Seemed like a tall, muscular type. Military or ex-military haircut, wide of body with sleeves filled by huge biceps. Wearing a navy sweatshirt, much too light for the late fall chill.

Lupo was quiet, but the guy turned to face him just as he almost reached him.

Face on, the sweatshirt was a U.S. Navy logo with SEALS stenciled on it. The guy's face was wide and flat, almost Slavic, his jaw strong and heroic, like a comic book hero. Dark, haunted eyes stared at Lupo, noted the drawn Glock, and then smiled widely.

"Detective Lupo, I presume?" He reached out a hand.

Lupo recoiled slightly, turning aside in case this was a set-up. If the guy wanted to attack him, though, why wait for him at his car? Why not try to grab him from behind?

"Yeah, I'm Lupo," he said guardedly. He kept the Glock in hand.

"Sorry, don't be alarmed." The big guy nodded at Lupo's gun. "Careful is good. I could be anybody." He kept his hand out. "Name is Simonson. Geoff Simonson. G-E-O-F-F. I was a Ranger in Iraq."

Still Lupo didn't shake hands. "Your shirt—"

"Says SEALS on it, I know. I had buddies in the Navy. Marines, too." Finally he dropped his hand, now it was obvious Lupo wasn't going to shake.

"Okay, that explains the shirt, but what do you want? I get nervous when guys lean on my car. In my experience, that's somebody about to try and deliver a message. Are you?"

Simonson nodded. "Sure, makes sense. I wasn't sure if I should call and make an appointment. I know you're busy."

"How do you know what keeps me busy?" Lupo narrowed his eyes. This guy was a cool customer.

"Paper today quoted a Lieutenant Bakke as having named you to head a task force. That's always a time-sink." He smiled, as if hoping to increase the potential camaraderie.

"Okay, Simonson," Lupo said, uncocking the Glock and reholstering. This guy had balls, but if he was going to attack, would he do it within sight of the cop shop? "Tell me your story? You want to be a source?"

"Partner, maybe."

Lupo snorted. "I got one of those. I could use information, though. There's some bad shit going down, and if you know something about it..."

"I do know something about it. And I know some of your history with Wolfpaw."

Shit, should have kept the gun cocked and ready.

And: *Shit, I knew all those were connected.*

Simonson held up his hands in surrender when he saw Lupo's flinch back toward his holster.

"Hey, they're my enemies too."

Lupo almost went for the gun anyway. He didn't know anything about this guy, who looked him in the eye with absolute openness.

"All right, Simonson. Two minutes. What you got?"

"Oh, it's not that simple. I've got a lot. A whole lot. But I'd need more than a couple minutes on the sidewalk to get to it all. How to play it? If you don't want to hear what I've got, I'll walk away. I thought we might have some common objectives, man, but if you have trust issues..."

Lupo barked out a laugh. "Trust issues? That's a good one. If you even know anything at all about Wolfpaw, you'd know how funny that is."

"It's because I do know that I said it. You see, I used to work for them. Until I saw way too much, and I got out. Now I'm off the grid."

"You worked for Wolfpaw?"

"Fuckin'-A. Been there, got the T-shirt. Falluja, Basra, I was one of those guys half Western, half native you'd see in those press pieces on the evils of war contractors. I was just doing my job. Left the military and went to work for Wolfpaw making about a thousand dollars a day."

"So why talk to me? What makes you think I have any connection to Wolfpaw?"

Simonson's eyes shifted left and right, checking for listeners. "Maybe it is best we're having this talk here. Too many ears. Wolfpaw has bastards everywhere."

"Again, why talk to me?" Lupo's hands tingled, and he felt ridges of fur sprouting along his spine. The Creature wanted to growl.

Who is this guy?

"You think just because they're sitting in front of some bloated congressmen they've forgotten about you? Man, you're nuts then." The guy wiped a big hand over his head.

Lupo itched to grab his Glock and stick it in this guy's eye. "Tell me why I should listen to you and then tell me what you have to say. No games."

Simonson surrendered again. "No games, Lupo. You hurt Wolfpaw pretty bad. Killed a whole Alpha Team. Well, minus one guy. He'll show up soon, bet on it."

"Goddamnit, lower your voice." Lupo felt sweat colliding with the Creature's manifestations. A growl started way down low. How the hell had this happened?

Simonson smiled as if it caused him pain. "Now you want to go somewhere?"

"Shit, what's your game?"

"No game." He twirled like a model. "See, no guns. Feel free to frisk. Just talk. I'm on your side. I saw what they did there. I did some of those things myself. But most of all, I saw what they did that was...*moon-related*. And I saw you take out half a training team down in Georgia."

This was getting out of hand. Lupo wanted to just find a reason to shoot this guy. He knew way too much, and he seemed casual about it. He knew about the wolves, and he seemed to know about Lupo and his Creature.

Jesus.

The club kept getting larger. Pretty soon everybody and his brother would know.

"You know John Hawk's Pub?" Lupo asked.

"On the river, downtown? I think so."

"It's big, noisy, and has dark corner booths. Meet me there in a half hour."

"Not setting up some sort of ambush, are we?"

Lupo sighed. "If I really wanted to, I'd kill you right here and worry about it afterwards. You know that, don't you?"

"Took my chances, man. We got a common goal. We both hate these Wolfpaw fuckers."

"John Hawk's, a half hour. Three of the corners are dark, and there's even a smaller room with a fireplace that's rarely used. See you there in thirty."

"Sounds fair."

Simonson stepped away from the Maxima and, for one crazy second, Lupo wondered if he'd wired up a bomb. But why hang around, then? He clicked the remote and climbed in, keeping the big military guy in his sight at all times. Simonson waved as Lupo drove off.

No need for back-up yet. Certainly not dragging DiSanto into anything. He was already coming too close to taking care of this problem in a *final* way.

He left Simonson on the sidewalk, an imposing and mysterious figure.

And fucking dangerous.

Mordred

From his vantage point, the meeting between Lupo and the military guy seemed too short and innocuous to mean anything. But Mordred knew he'd seen the big guy around, and he was almost certain there was a Wolfpaw connection.

Was the guy an informant?

He hadn't been prepared right at that moment to capture an image, so using his employer's resources to ID the guy would have to wait.

Big military guy. Looked familiar in a weird way.

He followed Lupo and made up his mind right then and there to terminate the other guy—whatever he had to sell, he couldn't be allowed to sell it to Lupo. He could defer to Sigfried, of course, but Mordred was certain he knew what orders would flow from the office in the command center.

He stuck to Lupo like glue and wondered if he'd spot the big guy again. Maybe they were meeting? Maybe that was what they'd set up?

Mordred hated having to catch up on anything. Sometimes he felt as if his mind was going to burst, his brain leak out of his ears.

The sessions in the lab usually loomed large in his memory during those times. They'd sure messed with him a lot. He rubbed the back of his head.

He hung back as Lupo went through some half-assed counter-intelligence moves, like maybe he'd learned them from a movie or a thriller writer. He watched from afar as Lupo ascertained no one had gotten there before him and found a spot to survey from, but he himself watched Lupo until Lupo came back and parked on the street farther away.

Okay, that was a good move. Unless he needed to get to his car fast. He'd be getting there early, which was a good way to beat a hit—beat the hitman to the meet.

Must be meeting in that big corner building, bank-looking light peach color exterior, about ten stories. Revolving door into big, high-ceilinged marble lobby. Mordred was only watching, so it didn't matter.

He shot some video with the highly advanced, fifteen megapixel camera and zoom hidden in his standard-looking cell phone.

Then he planned his approach to wherever they were meeting inside that building. He'd keep an eye out for the big military guy showing up for his meeting.

He parked a block farther away than Lupo and walked the rest of the way, his eyes roving.

Heather

She was anonymous as hell in the Hyundai and good thing, too, because she had to jam on the brakes and almost had an idiot tailgater smack her in the rear when she saw Lupo approach the guy leaning on his car.

Looked like Lupo had his gun out.

She wanted to flip off the tailgater, but instead when he swung around her she smiled sweetly and licked her lips at him, and he drove away shaking his head. But with a story to tell. At least he hadn't honked at her.

Was Lupo going to have a gunfight on his hands?

No, they weren't doing anything. The gun was still in Lupo's hand, but hidden.

She pulled into the parking structure on her right and slowed down before pulling up to the automated ticket machine. She took one and zoomed up the ramp and around, to where she could park facing the street on which those two were now talking. It'd been about two minutes by the time she got there, and she hoped they hadn't broken up yet.

She parked too damn fast and almost smacked the barrier, then jumped out to look over the ledge.

No, they were still there, but almost done.

There seemed to be tension between them. They seemed to close in and separate, as if they were about to go for each other's throats. The gun was no longer visible though.

They were yakking at each other.

What was up with the guy?

An informant? A stalker? An ally?

An enemy?

They were breaking up down there. By the time she'd driven around to the exit, they were both gone.

Lupo

He dialed DiSanto's phone, expecting to leave a message.

Nobody ever picks up anymore.

But DiSanto did, surprising him.

"Yeah, Nick?"

"Listen, I just had a chat with a total stranger who seems to know way too much about me and this case—and Wolfpaw. I'm meeting him at Hawk's in a half hour, hear what he has to say. Can you do me a favor and run his name, get the whole package?"

"Yeah, but you sure you want to meet him without back-up? I can be somewhere nearby."

"Nah, I can handle him." He spelled out Simonson's name. "Says he was a Ranger, did at least a tour in Iraq."

"Will do. Call me afterwards?"

"Good to hear you care, DiSanto."

"How else am I gonna get to ride in the Lupo-mobile?"

"Now you're gettin' it."

They clicked off and Lupo climbed into his car. He had a few minutes before having to make the meet, enough time to case the block and building that housed the pub. He'd be able to spot anything out of the ordinary, unless they were spooks—which, Lupo realized, wasn't impossible. As far as Simonson went, he could handle the big guy.

Hawk's pub had a nice long corridor running behind it and a garage below. The place had been moved in the nineties from the basement of an old building to this new bank building on the Milwaukee River, so now it featured a long patio overlooking the sluggish water. Lupo reconned Water Street and Wisconsin Avenue, saw nothing unusual, then slid into the building's parking garage. He made a trip through the levels, then slid back out using his badge at the booth.

He zipped back toward Wells and parked on the street almost two blocks away, checking his personal perimeter as he shuffled back toward the building. He kept the spots in front of the door in sight, but saw nothing that implied surveillance—no tinted windows, no vans or minivans with closed-up rears, no obvious heads low in their seats.

His phone buzzed.

"Yeah, DiSanto?"

"Um, this guy you gave me to run."

"I'm listening."

"Well, his name's in the DoD database all right. Comes up with a sealed jacket file, though. This guy exists, but just barely."

"Shit. Try any other DBs?"

"Every one I can think of. VICAP, Interpol, and all the other law enforcement ones, plus armed forces, and even freakin' Google. Nada, zippo, zilch. DoD definitely says he worked for them, but that's as far as it goes."

"You try any of our backdoor ways into Wolfpaw?"

"Fuck, Nick, that's your thing. I don't have any backdoor ways into Wolfpaw. Anyway, since they're private they'd be likely to be even more close-mouthed, wouldn't they?"

"Probably. Shit, the guy looks legit, like he fits the story, but not being able to check on him bugs me. He says he has inside info on their crimes."

Lupo didn't say anything about what the guy had referred to. What was it? *Moon-related.* That was new. Good way to approach him, wink wink, nudge nudge.

Maybe it was time to let DiSanto in on the big secret. Shit, they'd done that with Arnow.

Yeah, look at what happened to him *because of it.*

There was a time he would never have considered letting anyone in on his secret condition, but it had been a long progression from Caroline Stewart to Jessie, and then the arrival of the Wolfpaw mercenaries had necessitated telling Sheriff Arnow, because how do you ask a guy to silver up his slugs without having him ignore you, or worse yet have you committed?

He thought about Simonson's lack of paper. "Could be one other thing," he added. "Could be he's a spook and that's why he's a blank slate."

"Thought of that and tried a couple contacts I have in the DoD, tried to go beyond the obvious, but I got nothing."

"CIA? NSA? If so, we'll never get any sort of conclusive answer."

"You tell me, Nick, does he strike you that way?"

"There's a vibe. He spent time deployed in Iraq. Sealed records could mean a hundred things."

"Anything you want me to do?"

"Keep trying. I'm gonna meet him and hear what he has to say."

"Want back-up?"

"Thanks, but I don't want to spook him. Pun intended."

"Be careful, Nick."

"You got it."

Lupo was early, the best way to avoid an ambush. He had a Harp in front of him, but he hadn't touched it. Mostly as a prop.

The big guy looked sick. That was the first thing Simonson noticed when he came in. He looked like a soldier who'd seen and done too much, like someone suffering from private agony.

"So why are your files sealed, Simonson?"

The big guy chuckled. "You don't lose any time."

"You gave me your name. I ran it. Now answer me."

The guy ordered a Guinness from a roving waiter.

"When I was a Ranger I was involved in enough covert ops that they took me off the radar, stuck me with an official threat, and cut me loose due to battlefield fatigue. But Wolfpaw was more than happy to make use of my talents. Problem was—"

His beer came.

"Thanks," he said and took a long sip. "Problem was that I saw too many unbelievable things."

"Why should I listen to anything you have to say? I don't know you from Adam."

Shit, I sound like DiSanto with the clichés.

"I was in the process of doing my own investigation after I left Wolfpaw. That was when you roared into my line of sight, blasting your way through an Alpha Team at the compound. And then you and your friends took care of another one. You realize what a problem you are to them?" He drank. "You realize how much they want you silenced?"

"I think they're too busy right now to care."

"Trust me, they're never too busy. I know things about this company. And I know about the whole shapeshifting thing."

"So you also know about me."

Simonson nodded, licked brown foam off the rim of his glass.

"What do you want? Blackmail?"

"I want...an ally. I was planning my own raid into Wolfpaw central. Now I figure you and your friends might be interested in doing what I want to do."

"Jesus, Simonson. I can't kill every werewolf in Wolfpaw—there could be dozens."

"Try hundreds."

"Fuck, that's worse."

Simonson looked around, but most of the tables and booths were empty. "They're like a snake, man, so if we cut off the head the body will die."

"I don't even know where the head is."

"The head is in Washington right now, wrangling congress. But soon he's gonna be visiting the main compound a few miles out of D.C. You proved you could get into the training facility down south. I have what you need for further access. We go in, do the deed, get out. It will all collapse."

Lupo stared at him a long time. So the Georgia facility was secondary? None of his research had indicated a Washington compound. This was good insider information. He hoped for more tidbits, but none came. Clearly, the guy's pitch was done.

"I don't know, Simonson. It's tempting, but..."

"But?"

"I have to think about it. I've got things on my plate right now. And I'm gonna need some proof from you. Something to make me trust you."

"Can be done."

"Where do I find you?"

"I move around, so let me find you."

"What's the time line?"

"The head is going to visit the Washington D.C. compound very soon."

"Then we'll talk very soon."

Lupo dropped a ten on the table and walked away, hoping to flush a tail or a possible ambush. But there was no one, and he left Simonson sipping his Guinness.

Mordred

Some of his memories came rushing back as he stalked his new prey.

His vision blurred, and instead of the city shapes around him he was in the woods again, away from the compound, his wolf's blood singing gloriously in his veins...

He heard the rustle twenty feet away. The fur along his back tingled and the hair rose on end. He extended his snout past his paws and crept forward softly, the pine needles silent below him. His nostrils twitched, picking up the scent. His prey was standing still, but his pungent smell pointed him out as easily as a neon sign.

Mordred ordered his wolf's body to sit still, quietly listening for what the prey was doing.

The thin, emaciated Iraqi had been allowed a combat knife. He couldn't kill Mordred, his hunter, with it, and eventually he would be shot anyway, if he managed to give his hunter the slip. The knife, a black Ka-Bar Tanto combat model, was intended to give the prey a sense that he could defend himself and come out the winner of any confrontation. But that, like most everything else he had been told, was either illusion or an outright lie.

The prey was an Iraqi fighter, a member of the insurgency captured sometime in the seven-year history of Wolfpaw's contractor status in the war. He had been held in one of the CIA-sanctioned black prisons run by military contractors and ungoverned by United States civilian or military law. These prisons were either built in the middle of nowhere or relegated to shady allied countries and promptly forgotten by everyone except those who made the dark side of national defense their business.

There were hundreds of such detainees, held without warrant in dungeons with little chance of escape or survival. Some, like the prey now hiding in the undergrowth not far from where Mordred crouched, had been "reverse rendered" by Wolfpaw back to the United States in defiance of law, with the express intent of using them for the Genesis Project training exercises.

Wiry, lean and muscular like mountain goats, they performed beyond expectations in the training exercises. Their bodies were accustomed to the cold desert night, so when they were released into Wolfpaw's wilderness compound, where the overnight temperature might dip to the teens, they were predetermined for survival. For the Genesis Project, they provided information as well as training exercises. For the Genesis trainee, the Iraqis provided practice, training, and...*live food.*

Mordred advanced softly over the carpet of needles, his huge, muscular body hidden by the shadows of the giant pines overhead.

The prey rustled the bushes again, perhaps shivering in the cold. Or maybe he had heard the predator's approach.

Suddenly he broke cover and ran like a rabbit.

Mordred snarled, almost taken by surprise, and hurled his body into the chase, his paws eating up the ground and his eyes focused like lasers on the zig-zagging body. At first he followed the wiry fighter step for step, quickly learning his stride and his thinking. The earthy scent was strong in his nostrils, and beneath the unwashed smell Mordred also caught the scent of the hot blood that would soon be his. The flesh, the delicious organs.

Moments after starting the chase, Mordred had learned the patterns of his prey. He predicted the direction in which the prisoner would turn...

And beat him there.

Mordred's lunge ended on the prey's back, his powerful forepaws breaking the man's collarbones and more than a few ribs with his weight alone. Then he snatched at the man's head with his jaws, but the man shook it from side to side, and Mordred couldn't find purchase there. He snarled in frustration, masking the man's screams as he tore an ear off and swallowed it like a snack, enjoying the bloody squirt that hit his palate.

But this particular prey was tough. He managed to squirm partly out from under Mordred's bulk and twist himself around so he could bring his one weapon, the Ka-Bar knife, to bear.

Mordred felt the blade slip in and out of his torso.

Even knowing the wounds would start closing immediately, the painful pinpricks irritated him, and he bit off the man's hand. The knife fell away under them, and Mordred bit off the other hand just to even things up. Then, his paws holding down the squirming, screaming human, he took his time lapping some of the fresh blood spilling from the stumps.

His eyes locked on the human's, he leaned in and ripped off half the man's face with one powerful bite. Then, bored by now, he tore out the man's throat and drank greedily from the fountain that spurted up and into his waiting gullet.

Once the man squirmed no more, Mordred took his time with the remains, seeking out the choicest bits as reward for the difficulty factor of this one.

In the lab, those monitoring grinned, and money changed hands. This particular specimen had given their super-wolf a better fight than most expected. Those who had predicted it took home a bonus that week.

Now Mordred blinked rapidly and the pleasant memory faded, leaving but an echo. In its place was this new assignment, with its own delights...

He particularly enjoyed the freedom he was given to improvise.

Improvisation is divine, one of his trainers used to say. He'd taken that line to heart.

Here he was now, far away from the sands of Iraq and a fair distance from where he could run down prey for practice. So in this environment, he enjoyed whatever he could get. He made the last adjustments to his camouflage.

Prey

She opened the door just a crack to peer out at the handsome phone company man. The short chain kept the door from opening any more, but she could see his jumpsuit and tool belt just fine. She knew the rules. Old lady (well, older) living alone, she knew better than to throw open her door to strangers.

129

The man (tall and handsome, yes he was, but much too young for her) glanced down at his high-tech clipboard—it was some kind of flat computer, really—apologetically and then looked up at her.

"Mrs. Ellen Kraniewski?"

Amazingly, he barely struggled with her name at all.

"Yes?" She studied his AT&T insignia and ID photo badge hanging on a thin strap around his neck.

"Your phone, ma'am, is it dead?"

"Matter of fact, yes it is. I started to call the phone company, but then I realized I couldn't very well do that with a dead phone, could I?"

"No, ma'am," he said, chuckling, "though a lot of people these days have cell phones, and that would have done the trick for you."

"Yes, well I'm sure, but I don't have one. My daughter says I don't need one."

Why was she standing here talking to this stranger at her door? His eyes were mesmerizing, she noted, swirling and changing colors from blue to green to black. Very black. No, green.

"Your daughter is wrong," the phone man said. "Everyone needs a cell phone. What you don't need is the land line."

"Land line?" *Those eyes!*

Why was he trying to talk her out of the phone she'd had for decades?

"All those unsightly wires," he said. His eyes were soothing her and his smile was captivating. "I could show you some alternatives while I fix your old phone."

"Uh, yes, sure," she said, still captured by his eyes. For a second they reminded her of her grandson's dog, big, brown orbs full of empty compassion, but why would she even think a thing like that? That wasn't like her at all. "Please come in," she said, throwing open the door and stepping aside. She had a vague memory of her daughter telling her never to do that, but then the phone man was stepping past her and when she turned to face him, after closing the door, he was grinning at her.

His teeth!

"Oh my God," she said, gurgling with an excess of something in her throat.

Then she stepped back awkwardly and realized he had just swiped at her with a hand that wasn't a *hand* at all.

It was a claw tipped with long, pointed nails.

And what gurgled in her throat suddenly was a flood of warmth that reminded her of bathwater, except when she swallowed it tasted completely different.

And then the pain began. She held out a hand she'd brought up to her neck, and it was coated in brilliant scarlet.

"Oh," she whispered, but little sound made it through her fleshy lips. The warmth spread over her neck and chest, and she tottered.

She remembered to look at her visitor. Maybe he could help. But he had just stepped out of his belt and jumpsuit and stood before her, naked! He was all planes and angles, tattoos scattered here and there, and his huge...his huge *thing* (she couldn't even *think* the right word!) stood out from between his thighs like a purple-tipped spear.

"Oh," she said again, and she sank to the floor, which was now suddenly wet and very slippery.

Her visitor was lowering his grinning face to hers.

It was blurry, like her old TV had become. And it was *changing*.

And when she stopped looking into his swirling eyes and started to shriek, it was too late.

Chapter Thirteen

Franco

As they ran, dusk slowly overtook the day. The realization came to Franco, who suddenly couldn't see even a meter before his face. They'd been running blind and hadn't known it.

They slowed, breathing raggedly, their clothes disheveled and stained with sweat and blood from all the slashes on their skin.

The wolves were still on their trail.

Why didn't they give up?

It's as if they're smarter than we are! Franco thought.

But how could that be?

Thoughts of his grandmother's stories from the mountain villages near Venice flitted in and out of his memory.

No!

He refused to let himself think of what she had described, the family stories she had told for decades. He refused to let himself dwell on the possibility that she hadn't exaggerated. He refused to let his imagination fill in the images she had left on his impressionable mind.

The wolves seemed very near.

"We have to keep running!"

"I can't! I'm too tired. Too sore." Pietro was bent over, holding his knees. They could barely see each other.

Just like that, it was night.

Franco thought about his parents, how worried they must be. Franco was a growing boy (that was what they always said), and he never missed a meal, no matter what adventure he might have embarked on. He was a good boy that way, made so all the more by the insistent, never-ending hunger that gnawed at the pit of his stomach because the government rationing and the wartime shortages kept so much food from their larder.

His stomach growled after being reminded he was late for dinner.

But hunger was the last thing on his mind.

Those wolves, or whatever they were, had steadily gained on the boys despite their headlong flight through the dark trees.

But now it was night, and both boys knew what *that* meant.

As if a wish were being granted, both boys heard the distant air raid warning horns. The sirens were too far to be from the city, but perhaps they were hearing those from the German base.

Or whatever it was, locked away behind the barbed wire and mine fields.

Franco had a vision of his father, most likely on his way home right this very minute. And he hoped there was a shelter nearby.

Pietro's family lived down the street from Franco's, so he must have had the same frightening thought.

The air raid sirens rarely managed to give ample warning, and the rumble of airplane engines reached them even through the tight canopy of leaves. He visualized the waves of B-17 bombers approaching over the Mediterranean, pulling up like deadly dragonflies to lay their explosive cargo onto the German stronghold.

Franco gasped suddenly. He'd been holding his breath without realizing it.

The leaves rustled not far away.

They were here.

They've been playing with us, like cats with a mouse.

He pulled Pietro to the right and they stumbled into a tiny clearing.

And there was a stone shack squarely in the center of it, its walls irregular with roughly mortared field stones. The roof was thatched and oft-repaired. The door was a black hole, the slit windows like eyes on a skull.

"Come on!"

Franco herded Pietro across the clearing just as, a few miles away and down below the sloping hills, the first bombs began to rain down upon the fat, expectant targets.

Franco prayed they were missing the residential center this time. The harbor was just too easy for the bombers to miss, and the high command and factories huddled too near the city's center. Every raid cost dozens of innocent victims, people who chose not to evacuate into the shelters, or who were just too slow.

They reached the shack and pulled up short in the doorway, panting. The door, a rough wooden affair without a lock, opened like a rickety curtain. Inside was blackness deeper than any he had ever seen before. Suddenly it seemed bright outside the shack.

Across the clearing the branches parted, and Franco spied the first dark silhouette of a monstrously large, four-legged animal.

A wolf.

The largest wolf his imagination could ever have conjured. It was

133

nosing into the edge of the clearing, its head down and nostrils twitching as it tracked their scent. It hadn't seen them yet, but it wouldn't be long before it did. Or it had and it was playing them.

In the distance, the bombs sounded like rolling thunder.

Getting closer.

Pietro hesitated in the doorway. "We'll be trapped!"

"Here we'll die. Inside we can make a stand."

The words sounded ridiculous even to him. *Make a stand with what?* But what else could they do? The wolves would run them down in minutes, if not seconds.

They fell inside the pitch-black interior of the shack, and he smelled mold, rat droppings, and something he couldn't identify.

It had to be the boys' fear, distilled as a sharp, glandular acid that oozed silently from their pores. Franco realized it deep in his gut. His muscles trembled with fatigue and confused fear. The day had begun with an adventure, an act of defiance they'd poorly thought out. But he hadn't expected the result, the chase, the shooting, and now these monsters on their trail.

The darkness began to wash away as their eyes grew accustomed to it. They stood, waiting, but then Franco grabbed his friend's arm.

"Look!" he said.

There was a rickety loft at one end of the one-room shack. Someone had slept up there. It looked like hay piled up just below the roof crossbeams. The ladder didn't look very solid, but the boys were light.

Franco pointed up, then grabbed the rungs. He heaved himself upward as quietly as he could, Pietro crowding him from behind.

It only occurred to him as he climbed onto the loft that now they were truly trapped.

They huddled in the hay pile, their eyes fixed on the door down below hidden by the inky darkness.

And they waited.

Suddenly the snarling, stuttering roar of a misfiring aircraft engine filled the air above and shook the roof over their hiding place.

They ducked instinctively at the sound.

An airplane's diving screech followed the low roaring.

Franco imagined either an Allied bomber hit by German flak coming in like a fireball, or perhaps it was a German fighter scrambled from the outskirts of Genova to harass the Allied formations. He'd heard the sound before over the city skies. *But never this close!*

Before he'd had time to formulate the thought, the screech-snarl-roar simply cut off, and the air was sucked out of the loft, making his ears hurt as if they'd been lanced with an ice pick. He clapped his hands over them and expected to see blood on his fingers. But there was none, and then the silence was gone in an incredible explosion that rattled the roof's timbers and knocked a curtain of dust and sharp wood bits onto the boys' hiding place. The floor shifted, and jagged beams crashed to the floor, lifting a cloud of dust and debris.

The plane had crashed so near he thought the shack would collapse. It shook like a child's toy, and they were nearly knocked out of the loft.

Franco jabbed Pietro in the near darkness.

"Let's go!"

"What? What about the wolf?" Pietro's eyes were wide and very white in the gloom. "And all the other wolves?"

"Don't you think the plane crash scared it? I bet they're all busy. Come on! *Andiamo!*"

He didn't wait, clutching the rough wood of the ladder and swinging out into the void, trusting his feet would find the right rung. He half slid down, slivers jabbing the soft skin of his fingers.

Down below, he grasped Pietro's arm as he came off the ladder and dragged him toward the door. They checked outside and the wolf seemed to be gone.

They stumbled out into the early evening gloom. In the distance, Allied planes still dropped their bomb loads over the harbor and military installations. Behind them, there was a brilliant red glow between and above the trees and a column of thick black smoke billowing into the night sky. The site of the plane's crash into the woods wasn't far away.

The wolves howled again in the near distance.

"I told you," Franco whispered. "We go the other way!"

They ran to the clearing's edge and faded into the woods. Their muscles were stiff now that they'd crouched in the loft for a while, and Franco wondered if he'd made a good decision. Running was out of the question for a while.

He held out a sudden hand. "*Aspetta!*" Wait!

The undergrowth not far from where they hid parted under assault by a running, stumbling figure.

In the dark, they could barely make out who and what he was— but they could see easily that he wasn't a wolf, or a German soldier, whose ammunition belts and pouches tended to rattle when they ran.

They crouched lower behind the shelter of an oak trunk, hoping to fade into the shadows.

The runner was a pilot. Franco saw his leather flying jacket and helmet, his dark woolen trousers and tall boots. A harness belted to his torso dragged thin rope strands behind him as he half-ran, half-stumbled toward the shack the boys had just vacated. In his right hand he gripped a large pistol. As he reached the shack's doorway, he turned to look behind, cocking his head as if trying to listen.

The wolves are after him now!

Franco was a quick study. The fugitive was an Allied pilot or airman from the plane that had crashed nearby. The rope strands and harness were the remains of his parachute.

Franco inhaled harshly, about to call out to the pilot, when Pietro's hand clapped his mouth shut.

"What are you doing?"

"Calling him here. He'll be trapped there."

"Not our affair! We have to get out of here. *We're* trapped between the wolves and the soldiers at the base. We'll never get home if we don't move. *Now!*"

"We can't leave him, he's on our side."

"His side is bombing us and killing people."

"Because of the Germans!"

"I don't care!"

In the meantime, the pilot made his decision and entered the dark shack just as they had only minutes ago.

It seems like ages.

"See, he's already inside," Pietro said, his voice a low hiss. "We have to get going." He shuffled away, looking around to orient himself.

Franco stood to follow, shaking his head. He hoped the pilot would make it, but he had a bad feeling in the pit of his stomach.

The undergrowth across from them crackled again as a large black wolf erupted from the dark woods.

Franco dropped to the ground and motioned his friend to do the same. The boys melted into the ground shadows, but Franco couldn't keep from watching what was about to happen. The wolf approached the shack, its nostrils twitching and its long jaws full of fangs visible despite the darkness.

And then another wolf padded out from between the trees.

And another.

And another.

The three loped quickly behind the first wolf as it approached the shack's doorway.

Franco couldn't move. His joints and limbs felt locked, as if he'd been pinned to a board like a dried butterfly. He stared at the four wolves, who congregated at the shack's doorway as if deciding what to do. Then they split up, surrounded the building and, a minute later, the largest wolf took a running start and lunged at the flimsy door. It splintered under his weight, and he was through the dark hole into the dark shack.

Franco winced when the first shot rang out.

He heard growling and snarling, crazed screaming, and more gunfire.

Another shot, then another.

Bang!

Bang!

Then *bang-bang!*

Then there was nothing but growling and a long, keening scream of fear, which turned into one of pain, abruptly cut off.

His breath caught in his throat.

Pietro was yanking on his arm, pulling him along into the woods.

Franco wanted to shut out the sounds of frenzied feeding from inside the building, but he could not. It sounded as though the wolves growled and fought each other for prime parts, tearing tearing tearing...

Tearing.

Franco thought he would never be able to get the sound of tearing flesh out of his ears and from his memory.

Then one wolf howled, and the others joined in.

A few moments later, the shack's door opened and a man's naked arm poked out first, then his leg, then the rest of him. He was joined by three others, their faces and mouths streaked with dried blood. They stood in a small huddle, naked, their muscular bodies and their penises on display without shame.

Their penises were erect like those of dogs, and very large. He didn't know much about male erections, but he did know they were not usually so...obvious.

Gesu' e Maria, he thought.

It was what his grandmother would have said, crossing herself and perhaps making the sign of the evil eye to protect herself.

Franco remembered to breathe when Pietro's hand snatched shirt fabric and loose skin and pulled insistently.

Pietro was pointing at the four men through the trees as they glided like ghosts into the woods, then pointed at his own nose.

Franco understood and felt sick at the pit of his stomach. *Can they smell us?*

He thought for a moment and shook his head. He was willing to bet they couldn't because their human noses were just that, *human*.

But if they changed into wolves again...

Dio mio! They could change into wolves!

There was nothing human about that.

Franco made the evil eye like his grandmother had taught him, but he doubted it provided any real protection.

The boys tiptoed through the woods as far as they could without letting their fear drive them to running. They had to avoid being heard. When they were far enough away, they started at a jog and soon were sprinting toward the road.

The sounds of explosions from the direction of the city had faded and died. The air raid was over. The sound of sirens had taken over, screaming from many directions as the *pompieri* braved the streets to use their outdated equipment and attempt to vanquish the many infernos the Allied bombs had caused.

The German air raid sirens sounded the all clear about the time the boys reached the road. They kept to the shadows just off the asphalt, ducking behind bushes whenever they heard a car or military vehicle approaching and rumbling past. In the dark, they had little trouble staying out of sight.

Pietro was dazed, walking with an automatic motion and depending on Franco for cues to crouch down or stand up.

As for Franco... In his mind, he fought with himself. He knew what he'd seen and heard.

His grandmother had been right.

There were mysteries in the world, and they could kill you.

Eat you, he amended. Some mysteries could eat you.

Giovanni

He opened his eyes and immediately closed them. His vision was a blur of indistinct shapes and darkness broken only by flickering blobs of light. He thought he was in church. He smelled candles. He tried to move his head and stopped when it seemed his jaw would break.

Somebody had hit him. There had been an air raid. There were guns and a shooting.

Santa Maria, he thought, *I was doing the shooting.*

Bit by bit the memory came nosing back, and he started to put the pieces together. He realized he was shivering. And through the pain in his head, he felt his eyes swell up.

Where was he?

His moan brought one of the blobs suddenly closer. A cool touch on his forehead triggered memories and thoughts, but blinking brought forth only tears and pain.

"*Sono io, Giovanni,*" a calm but shaky voice spoke in his ear. "*Sono io. Stai tranquillo."*

Maria! Thank God!

His fingers moved and then gripped her hand and brought it to his chest. He still couldn't see very well, but the simple gesture slowed his heart from its onrushing pace and brought the tranquility she'd wished upon him. He started to rise up, but she pushed him back down firmly.

"No, you might be hurt. And we have to stay silent."

"What?"

"Shhhhhh." Her hand caressed his face. "Trust me."

He noticed movement behind her, more blurs making jagged little gestures. He smelled sweat and bodies, and frankly his own scent wasn't altogether better. "What— Where are we? Where is—?"

Suddenly he was seized by the thought of what he hadn't heard or felt yet. His son's hand or face nearby, or his voice.

"Where is Franco?" he groaned, his voice rough.

"I don't know," she said, crying. "He was—"

Somebody stepped closer and whispered, in a clipped voice, "Be silent or you'll get us all killed!"

Giovanni felt Maria's hand caress his face and softly cover his lips. He kissed her cool skin, but his mind reeled. His son wasn't there, wherever *there* was. Maria was there, and these others. Men. He thought he heard a female whisper. Maybe some women and children. But not Franco.

His memory slotted into place, and he remembered the firefight in the street. How he had ended up with a machine gun, and turned it on the hated German.

The bombing raid. The partisans.

Corrado.

Corrado had hit him.

Unsteadily, Giovanni tried to stand and slid halfway off the cot. He was hurt!

But no, he felt each of his limbs, and even though his bones ached and where he'd been slugged throbbed and his head pounded, he was really all right. He reached out for Maria, who tried to steady him.

Sounds from above and nearby reached them, and he felt his heart start to race again.

Then Corrado materialized beside him, a blob with his intellectual's glasses pinching his nose.

"Listen to me," he hissed into Giovanni's ear, "they're close to finding one of our secret entrances, and if they do we are all fucked in the ass. You understand? We have to slip out and fight them, kill them all before they can report. Are you up to it?"

"Up to it?"

Up to it?

Killing people?

Who was this idiot, asking him to kill...

Giovanni thought through the last pieces of his memory and found that he had already killed, hadn't he?

Corrado's band of partisans was gathering behind them, facing a wall that until now Giovanni had thought solid. But there was a slit, a sort of narrow, sloping passage, and the men were slipping through one by one.

"We'll need you. Here." Corrado handed Giovanni an old revolver, which he tucked into his belt. Then someone else handed him a Breda submachine gun. It felt strange in his hands, heavy and awkward. He took it, reluctantly, and looked back at Maria—but a tall man behind him was crowding him toward the passage, his arms also cradling a stubby submachine gun.

It appeared he would have to pay his way.

The tall man and another fell in behind him, and all he could do was nod and try to smile at Maria before she disappeared behind them, and then he was stumbling into the passage. It was a ruined staircase, brick and mortar debris underfoot. Boots and shoes scraped in front of him, climbing, so he followed instinctively even though he could barely see. He tripped on an invisible step and was steadied by the man behind him.

They climbed single file up and up, seemingly endlessly, until they reached a collapsed corridor. He started feeling dizzy, the events of the last few hours catching up. But then Giovanni smelled the evening air and then they were outside, emerging from a hidden fissure between leaning stone walls. He filled his lungs gratefully, his head clearing. The short column of men snaked around the corner, and he realized they were attempting to flank the German patrol before the shelter was sniffed out.

He gripped the Breda tightly, his mind a jumble of fears.

They were nearly around the ruined building's front corner when someone's shoe kicked over a pile of debris, which groaned and came tumbling to the ground in a clatter of stone and wood, raising a cloud of dust.

A shout in German, and then another, and then there was a burst of submachine gun fire and Giovanni realized that the partisans, not yet in position, had been forced to open fire without cover.

"*All'attacco, ragazzi!*" Corrado shouted, urging his men on the attack, their surprise flanking shattered by the shouting and the gunfire. "*Per la patria!*"

The enemy was a series of indistinct shapes, like ghosts, and they had cover.

A man went down on Giovanni's left, his chest split raggedly open.

Giovanni screamed and squeezed the Breda's trigger, letting loose a burst. Recoil tugged the barrel upward, and he saw his rounds shatter a surviving window too high up to catch any of the enemy. Another man went down on his right, screaming that he was hit in the head, but then a bullet silenced him altogether. Giovanni was crying now, as he held the barrel down and sprayed lead until his breech locked open, the magazine empty. Someone shoved another magazine at him and he reloaded, somehow catching on instinctively. Tears running, he shot at the ghostly shapes again, this time seeing one of the shapes throw up his arms and collapse, broken, against the bricks.

Gunfire raged around him, and for a moment he thought the partisans were holding the enemy back, their bursts exacting a terrible toll.

Suddenly they heard a series of loud snarls, followed immediately by an unearthly howling. Giovanni stopped short, feeling a shiver shoot down his spine. Despite the gun battle, this sound was viscerally more terrifying.

"*Lupi!*" someone shouted. And then his voice turned to a gurgle as a dark shape lunged from out of the cloudy darkness and ripped out his throat.

Whatever it was, it snarled and shook its long snout and Giovanni heard a slaughterhouse ripping of bone and flesh and the dead man's head came rolling to a stop at his feet.

Dio mio!

Giovanni couldn't help staring for a split-second down into the dead man's terrified eyes, and then he stumbled aside so he couldn't see the head and the jagged piece of spine protruding from its torn neck.

All around him he heard men screaming, and more four-footed shapes materialized. For the first time he saw that they were giant dogs—

No, they were wolves.

Giovanni had spent some time in the mountains working for his father, and he had seen wolf packs on long winter nights. These were wolves, their fur mostly black or gray and mottled, and they were larger than any he had ever seen or heard of.

And they lunged at men who shot at them over and over without any effect, their jaws then snapping and tearing necks and limbs. *Here* was a partisan going down under a slashing, biting jaw full of fangs. *There* was a man with a wolf's snout buried in his belly, tearing out

141

loops of bloody intestines.

Out of the corner of his eye Giovanni saw one man shoot a wolf, and the animal went down, screaming in rage, trying to reach around its back and bite the smoking wound. The tall man who had been behind him on the staircase leaped onto the wolf's back, a silver blade flashing, and stabbed it twice in the neck before slitting the animal's throat.

It was all happening in mere seconds, but Giovanni swore he saw the wolf catch fire and scream in agony as its blood boiled. And then its body blurred, and it became a naked man, a human, whose greasy hair the tall partisan grabbed with a fist and pulled up, using the glowing blade to sever his head. He tossed it aside with a shout of fury and victory, and turned to help another partisan who was being menaced by a wolf.

Giovanni knew he wanted to scream—his mouth was open, but no sound came out. The battle had degenerated into single shots and snarls, and screams of terror and pain, and gurgling sounds of bloody death.

And he heard the tearing of bone and tissue, the howling of victorious wolves.

He turned in time to see a wolf leaping for his throat. With no time to sidestep, he brought up the Breda's barrel and let loose a long burst.

The bullets stitched across the wolf's body and head and should have cut him to pieces, but Giovanni was horrified to see that the deadly lead barely knocked the animal off its stride. Its weight smashed into him and tossed him to the ground, jaws snapping at his neck.

The Breda flew out of his grasp, and he threw his hands up to avert the wolf's continuous attacks. Giovanni risked one hand and scrabbled for the Beretta in his belt, the other hand desperately holding off the biting wolf's snout. Its raging eyes seemed to be red in the near-darkness.

He brought up the pistol by feel and shoved the barrel under the wolf's jaws. Those eyes held his as the wolf gathered for a final push, and Giovanni pulled the trigger once, twice, three times. And then a fourth time. The bullets ripped through the fur and bone and skull.

Giovanni sucked in air and prepared to throw off the dead animal's weight.

But the wounds caused by his bullets began to close up and disappear. The wolf's red eyes found his and it seemed to smile at his shock and terror.

Then he was awash in a gush of gore as an anonymous hand bearing a flashing silver blade slit the wolf's throat just before it could press its advantage and bite off his face.

142

The dead animal was heaved off him, and it was the tall man from the tunnel who'd done it, a grim smile on his face as he nodded and then jumped to the aid of another partisan locked in a struggle for his life.

The tall partisan won, his blade once again slashing open the wolf's throat. The animal's shriek of pain as the blade burned through its flesh and tendons would haunt Giovanni forever, he knew. And so would the sight of the dead wolf blurring into a dead human. He looked at his right and saw that where his own attacking wolf had been now lay sprawled a dead human. The tall partisan severed both heads.

"Must make sure, eh?" he said gruffly.

Giovanni got to his knees unsteadily, his head spinning, his muscles screaming with fatigue and overuse. He realized the battle was over, won—apparently—by Corrado and his men, but at a terrible cost. A half dozen partisans lay dead, their bodies scattered near the side of the building, several grotesquely disemboweled. Four of five naked, decapitated men marked where the wolves had died. Several uniformed German soldiers also lay dead, their bodies riddled with bullets.

Corrado was alive, his coat covered with splattered blood.

"Thank you, Turco," he said, clapping a hand on the tall man's shoulder. "Without you, I don't know—" He stopped, his haunted eyes finding Giovanni's. "You fought well. You're one of us now. We saved the shelter, this time. But now you must not watch. Turco, I don't envy you this job."

The tall man shrugged. Then he went to each of the dead partisans and stabbed them in the heart before sawing off their heads.

Giovanni thought he had been horrified by everything up to now. But this was too much!

He brought up the Beretta pistol, instinctively wishing to defend the dignity of his dead countrymen. But Corrado pushed the barrel down until it pointed at the ground.

"It's necessary, believe me," he said, making a half-hearted sign of the cross. "We must be sure they are dead, and that they were killed with that blade. Otherwise there's a possibility—"

Turco was finished. They rallied the surviving partisans around them, and wounds were inspected. They were minor, and Giovanni noticed that Turco remained nearby, the unsheathed silver blade touching every survivor—including himself.

Corrado noticed Giovanni's questioning look. "We have learned to look after ourselves," he explained, but it was no real explanation as far as Giovanni was concerned.

Exhausted, his body aching and his mind still reeling at all he had seen, all he wanted to do was climb down those stairs and see his wife.

143

And then he would go find his son.
Se Dio vuole, he thought. *God willing.*

Franco

They had watched carefully to avoid vehicles and patrols on the road, but he had not expected the quiet padding of a monster wolf to come up behind them on the path.

Franco led the way, occasionally turning to coax on his friend Pietro, who had been rendered almost catatonic by the horrors he had witnessed. His steps wooden, his eyes glazed and almost unblinking, Pietro followed Franco by rote like a dog whose only guidance is the master's urging.

Now there was a snarl from behind them, and Franco was startled into leaping forward instinctively.

When he turned, knowing in his heart that it was too late, what he saw he knew immediately would be etched into the back of his mind forever, until the day he died.

A huge gray wolf had shadowed them—who knew how long it had been behind them?—and had pounced on Pietro, its claws driving his slight body into the dirt of the path, while its jaws opened and closed on the boy's head, wrenching it up and back until...

Franco screamed as he watched his friend's head suddenly ripped from his body, the jagged remains of his spine indicating where it had been moments before. The gout of blood that erupted from the ruptured arteries in Pietro's neck was like a fountain, and the wolf shook the deflated head like a bone before tossing it aside and tearing into the boy's tender back and ribs with hungry jaws.

Franco stumbled away backward, down the inclined path, until he lost his footing and rolled down the hill, rocks and sharp branches stabbing him painfully.

The sound of the wolf's hungry attack on his friend's corpse would be with him forever. The sight of the headless body being torn asunder like a Sunday roasted chicken sickened him, and the memory brought up a thin stream of vomit.

But having put some distance between himself and the monster, albeit accidentally, Franco now allowed his instinct to take over his legs, and he ran, slid and tumbled down the path toward the city outskirts, where he knew at least one place he might be safe, if the bombers had spared it—and his family.

It was the only place he could think to go.

Giovanni

Corrado had shucked his bloody coat and now wore a thin, once-white dress shirt. He shivered in the night's chill.

"Now you know what we are up against," he told Giovanni. "Since late last year, the Germans have sent those things against us. We lost many good men to their fangs. And again tonight, damn their hearts."

"But...what are they?"

"Do you not remember the stories your parents told you when you were young? They are wolf-men, just like the legends. They are men, but the full moon makes them wolves. We have learned the hard way they can also control their shapeshifting and become wolves whenever they choose."

"It's just too— It's impossible."

"You saw it with your own eyes. One almost tore you apart, but for Turco there. We know what they are, but they are almost impossible to kill. The Germans are retreating, but they have deployed a rear guard made up, partly, of this Werwolf Division. The monsters have done their worst in the hills and used to stay out of the cities, mostly, but now they are being used against us here as well."

"You said you can't kill them? But they did die."

Corrado snorted quietly. "Sure, but at what cost? They can be killed, but it takes special..." He leaned over and whispered even more quietly. "That man there, hunched in the corner?"

Giovanni saw a man whose look was haunted. His eyes seemed feverish, his skin pale. He hadn't been part of the gun battle.

"He's a priest. He has fought with us. He is a Jesuit. You know what that means?"

Giovanni shrugged. He knew who Jesuits were, of course, but...

"He has done exorcisms. He has faced evil before and survived. And he has brought us more than just his own fighting spirit. From Rome, he has brought us a weapon."

"Rome?"

"From the Vatican." Corrado scratched his stubble. "You want to talk with him? Will it make you feel better about what you have seen?"

Giovanni's eyes unfocused as he stared at the priest. Then he nodded once.

"Hey, Babbo, this guy wants to talk to you," Corrado called out across the room.

The priest stood, and he was no longer graceful as he might have been, but moved as if uncertain of his footing. Or as if his feet were submerged. He had been muscular and then run to fat, but now the fat had dissipated and his skin was sallow and bag-like.

He came to a stop near Giovanni and Corrado. His priest's collar was long gone. His eyes were glazed by lack of sleep or war-weariness.

"You're that new one," he said. "You have a pretty wife."

"Yes, and a son. But I don't know what happened to him. I wanted him here with me, but he's missing. And now I'm not sure I want him here. I don't know what I want. I want to know that what I saw out there cannot exist."

Corrado moved away, shaking his head as if there was nothing more disgusting than someone who would deny the evidence he had seen and touched.

The priest sighed and sat stiffly.

He said: "He calls me Babbo, *dad*, because he's not very religious." His expression was more sympathetic now. "I see how much you fear for your son. What happened?"

"I was out working when the Germans picked me up for one of their damned slave-labor details. I didn't intend— I found myself fighting even though it was the last thing I wanted. My son was out with his friend Pietro, playing, as he does every day since school was closed. That was when Corrado's men grabbed my wife too, but my son wasn't home. I'm grateful, they may have saved her, but now I want to find Franco, and they won't let me go."

"My name is Father Tranelli. I will have a word with Corrado. He's a good man, but he feels responsible for his men, and he cannot separate his hate for Germans from his responsibilities. But you saw what the Germans use against us..."

"What are they, Father?" Giovanni's voice betrayed how he felt haunted by the horror. He half-wondered if he had suffered a blow to the head, and all this was hallucination, or a nightmare. Perhaps he would awaken and find that things were no different than two days before, when his world did not include monstrous creatures.

"They are men who have the ability to turn into wolves. You must remember the legend of the *uomo-lupo*, the wolf-man. Mothers still terrify their unruly children with tales of the *uomo-lupo*, or the *lupo mannaro*—the werewolf—and the Middle Ages were full of sightings, convictions, and executions of so-called wolf-men. And women."

Tranelli hung his head lower, as if the burden of holding it up were almost too much.

He continued: "We have always had the legends, especially in the hill villages. But when the Germans became our occupiers after the government finally surrendered to the Allies, they brought in the Werwolf Division as a rear guard. You know the damned Nazis, they like all that occult stuff. Nobody paid any more attention than to anything else they do. They have already a reputation for shooting civilians and imprisoning anyone they deem dangerous. But as Corrado here will tell you, partisan units began coming into contact with groups of these wolves. First they found sentries killed, torn apart and disemboweled. Men on lonely outposts, killed by mysterious animals. Everyone thought so. But then the attacks became brazen, and sometimes several werewolves will attack a patrol or safehouse."

"But what about guns? Why can't you kill them?" Giovanni slapped his hand on the table. "I saw your men shoot them at point blank range, and yet the wolves still reached them, using their claws and their fangs..." He stopped, realizing he had been one of those men.

"Werewolves are magical beings, young man. I have no other explanation. They are of the devil, perhaps. They cannot be killed by normal means."

"Then if there are many of them, we'll all die..."

"These monsters *are* vulnerable to one thing. You saw yourself. They are averse to silver. Any weapon made of silver will have an effect on them, and bullets cast from pure silver can kill them. It acts like liquid fire inside their bodies. We have dispatched quite a few, recently. And tonight. But we are still susceptible to their attacks."

"Why not make silver bullets by the thousands, then?"

"My friend, because there is not so much silver to go around. The people used it for money in the early days of the war, when they needed to buy food for their families. Whatever they hoarded is not nearly enough. We use whatever we can get, but we have to make it count. Whenever new people join us, we ask for their silver."

Giovanni thought his head would explode. If he hadn't seen it for himself, he would not have believed. He was a Thomas when it came to things like this. Maria always said, "You have to stick your hands in the wounds, just like Saint Thomas the Unbeliever."

"How can you still have your faith after seeing...after seeing *that*?"

"Who says I still have faith?" The priest rubbed his tired features with a claw-like hand. "Well, I do, even if it's not like before. I know things have changed in my mind. But I'm a Jesuit, and I can persevere through anything, as Jesus himself was able to do."

Corrado had returned and heard the last part. "Have you told him yet? The worst part?"

"No, but I will now." He sighed a long sigh, and Giovanni thought he heard the rasp of disease coming from him. "We learned that it's much better to be killed by the beasts than merely bitten. A man bitten but not killed will inevitably turn into a monster on the next full moon."

Father Tranelli shook his head. His brown eyes were watery.

"*Dio mio.*" Giovanni crossed himself. Startled, he realized he hadn't done so in years. Not so much faith left for him, was there?

"This is why even the corpses were— stabbed and—"

"God forgive us, yes."

He was reminded of what Corrado had said. "You spoke of the weapon. It was the blade? Something about the Vatican?"

"I was in Rome a year ago," Tranelli said, nodding and rubbing his thinning hair, "but originally I'm from a small village about fifty kilometers from here. It— it *was* a village. Now it's a butcher shop that has been closed a long time. The people there, they were my family and my flock, and this damned Werwolf Division went there and slaughtered all of them because of one shot someone, a boy, took at a German soldier. These hellish things, they were let loose in the town square, and by the time they were finished, there were thirty-eight butchered corpses. It was worse than what they usually do, line people up and shoot them."

His eyes were haunted, and even in the half-light Giovanni saw the welling tears.

"This time they...they hunted them down and tore them to pieces, all for the sake of vengeance. When I heard, it was too late to save anyone from my family. The people I grew up with. Everyone was gone. All I could do was pray over what was left of their corpses, and hire men from the next town to dig a long line of graves. It was all I could do, you see?" His skin seemed feverish.

Giovanni nodded. He shivered, wondering if he was, himself, too late.

The priest clawed through his thinning hair. "But it wasn't all I could do. I made a visit to the Vatican library. The Prefect is a friend of mine, and he has the keys to the secret archives, which almost no one is allowed to see. But I knew he is closely acquainted with the materials stored there, and their nature."

He paused again. "Corrado, do you have wine?"

"No more for you, Babbo," said the wiry partisan leader. "I need you almost sober, which means I need you the way you almost never are, eh?"

Tranelli licked his dry lips, and Giovanni wondered if that was the disease he'd sensed. Or if there was more. It was difficult to tell, because the priest seemed so used up, dried out, and desperate for a drink, that very likely any other physical ailments were covered up.

"*Eh, va bene, figlio mio.*"

Despite his referring to Corrado as *my son*, Giovanni doubted there was any love lost between the younger man and the haunted, religious one.

"You were saying," Giovanni prodded. "About the materials stored in the secret archives."

He wanted to act, to hunt for his son, but something about the priest made Giovanni want to listen to the rest of what he had to say. Despite his ragged quality and obvious need of drink, there was also an intensity in his words, in his look, that demanded Giovanni pay attention or he would never find his son.

Father Tranelli hunched over the rough table. "Yes, there are many secrets in the catacombs below the Vatican."

He whispered, perhaps afraid the Germans would hear. Perhaps afraid something else would hear.

"You see, the archives are located beneath a modern building, but there is an area at the rear of the newer section where walls were breached, and the archives now include a long portion of the maze that makes up the fabled Roman catacombs. This area is under lock and key and watched over by armed guards, for the Vatican has acquired many books and other items in its history about which the world would be amazed and surprised to learn."

Giovanni felt the weight of his worries, but the Jesuit's story captured his interest despite the fear he felt for the life of his son. Instinctively he guessed that if Corrado lent weight to the priest's story it must not have been a drunkard's hallucination or illusion. Corrado was the most serious man his own age he had ever met, an intellectual whose haunted eyes spoke of a difficult past—and even more difficult actions to stomach. He was probably a Communist—their beliefs attracted serious young intellectuals like Corrado. Having seen what the Fascists and the Nazis were capable of, Giovanni was all for letting the Communists have a go. If the damnable war ever ended.

The priest licked his lips before continuing. Clearly, a drink of wine would have been in order. And maybe it was best Corrado had cut him off, for a single drink would not have been enough to dispel the aura of the things he had seen.

"I could bore you with a list of some of those things, many of them dangerous to our immortal souls, but I won't. I'll get right to the point."

Like an omen, air raid sirens started their frightening wail. Tranelli closed his mouth. Dark, haunted eyes met each other across the dim underground room. Giovanni desperately wanted to hold his Maria's hand, but she was at the far end of the space, helping care for two just-wounded men who lay bleeding on rickety cots.

He was certain she appeared to them as an angel.

Moments later the rumble of Allied engines reached them just before the rattle of anti-aircraft batteries and the rolling thunder of bomb drops.

Tranelli shrugged. "And so it continues. Where was I? Ah yes, the

149

silver weapons."

Giovanni leaned forward to listen, but he couldn't help crying out inside. Where was Franco? Was he safe?

Ignoring the explosions of the Allied bombs, Tranelli continued.

"When I spoke to my friend, the Prefect of the Archives, and we discussed these cursed wolves and their aversion to silver, he showed me an old book—medieval, at the least—in which a mystic theorized that silver was a symbol of purity from time immemorial. And, as we all know, thirty silver coins were the payment Judas received for his betrayal of Christ."

Giovanni almost snorted but caught himself. Until he had seen them, he would have reacted the same way if someone had told him werewolves existed.

"But the Prefect went even further than that, my young friend. You see, he told me that another book on his secret shelves contained the description of a pair of weapons fashioned from relics of the crucifixion. Someone was charged with smelting the thirty coins and using the silver to plate two daggers made from a metal spear-point. It was no simple spear, however, but the spear of Longinus, the centurion who stabbed Our Lord Christ while He languished on the cross. The Roman soldier later repented, when he realized his spear was blessed by its contact with the holy flesh. The silver-plated blades were specially intended to kill werewolves, which up to that point had been invulnerable to any weapon. Since then, all silver is abhorrent to wolves. The silver-plated weapons were matched with wood from either the Longinus spear, or from the true cross or from both—the book was imprecise, as old tomes often are—which was then fashioned into scabbards for the daggers."

"What's the value of that?" Giovanni asked, interested despite his meager belief. In the distance, Allied planes pounded the harbor. He hoped this time, at least, they had found their target. Giovanni also hoped the German warships anchored there were taking a beating.

"One thing is that the sanctified wood seems to veil the silver's presence, so a werewolf cannot quickly sense the imminent danger of a formidable opponent, making it easier to take one by surprise. The mystic further theorized that the holy weapon might be used by one man afflicted with the werewolf disease to fight and vanquish another, because he would be able to keep the blade close to his body without himself suffering the excruciating burns the silver would have caused him otherwise. The mystic called the dagger *the werewolf's werewolf killer*."

"Well, all this knowledge is fine and good, and your friend was certainly helpful, but what good has it done here?"

"After showing me the book, the Prefect went to a locked cabinet in this most secret of places, and from it he removed a wooden case which held both daggers. He gave them to me, my friend, and I have brought them to Corrado."

"My God."

"Yes, perhaps it is God giving us an advantage. Perhaps it is something older than God."

"What does your friend think is the origin of these monsters?"

"My friend referenced the legend of Romulus and Remus, the babes who founded Rome—but more importantly, who were abandoned and later suckled by a she-wolf. Every schoolchild has heard this one, but there is an older, lesser-known legend in which the two male babes were not rescued, but were the offspring of the she-wolf, the result of copulation with a human. In this version, the babes Romulus and Remus were the first shapeshifters, and they passed on the gene to their own offspring. Perhaps the full moon's influence on the night of conception has something to do with it. No one knows. But nothing could kill the cursed wolf-men until the Christ's death led to the fashioning of the daggers."

The priest spread his hands. "We may never know the true connection, if there is one, but we know that moonlight has an effect on the wolf-bastards—it seems to call the wolves when they are first made. And we know that since the day of the crucifixion the metal silver is their weakness. That's all we care about."

Outside, the all clear sounded, and the city came crawling out of its holes.

Chapter Fourteen
Endgame: Third Day

Lupo

Nick Lupo liked thinking back to when he only had a few, old secrets. Their influence had been bad enough, keeping him up nights and eventually lending him the label of tragic figure as people—mostly fellow cops—simply assumed he was weighed down by the tragedies in his life.

They were right, but had no idea that some of those tragedies had been caused by his own, occasionally simplistic solutions to problems. Invariably, his solutions had darkened his world in some other way and forged his bond with tragedy anew.

Recently he had been forced to create new secrets, to act in ways that were theoretically against his ethical code. But he had felt boxed in and found himself giving in to the temptation of the easy fix once again. He'd found that when you chose the easy fix, the complications didn't arrive until later, bringing with them their own widening cracks of consequences.

He wondered what had happened to break—or certainly bend—the bond he and Jessie had forged under fire.

But when he thought clearly, he saw that she simply had responded to the trauma he had brought into her life by changing and giving in to her secret weaknesses.

It wasn't all that different from what his response had been, though they had taken divergent paths.

The question was, could they force those paths to merge once again?

Jessie

She had taken to crying a lot when Lupo wasn't around.

She would cry, and then a coldness would envelop her heart, and she would feel a draw, an attraction to the very thing she had once laughed Nick would never have to worry about.

After all, they'd discussed visiting Vegas once, but had given up the thought since neither was very enthused about it.

Though Nick had remembered a fantasy trilogy by Tim Powers, a favorite author, whose novel *Last Call* dealt directly with the unseen magic of destiny and chance swirling around the city of Las Vegas.

When he described it like that, she'd joked, maybe it would be fascinating to go. But then they'd had their shares of trouble, and gaming casinos on Indian lands had begun an incredible rise.

When her tribe had hustled through a vote to build a casino and hotel complex, it had seemed a mistake. But slowly and surely, the call of the lights—like *the sign in the desert that lies to the West*, she thought, channeling Eric Woolfson's lyric—had eaten into her.

And now she had a problem.

And it was aimed directly at the heart of their relationship.

Damn it, Nick Lupo, why do things have to change?

Lupo

The call came in while he was driving, so it wasn't a problem swinging by to pick up DiSanto.

"What about your meet with this guy you had me check out, the spook?"

Nick tapped his fingers on the wheel, keeping beat to a song only he could hear. It was a song by Fish, the big Scotsman who'd once fronted Marillion. "Credo" had a Peter Gabriel vibe, and he liked its percussiveness. He wanted to dial it up on the iPod, but he didn't.

"Nick, you listening?"

Lupo grunted and lost the beat.

"Hey, is that how it's gonna be? You and secrets again? Like the animal attacks in Wausau? Like the weird terrorists and mercenaries that always show up in Eagle River when you're there? And let's not forget serial fucking killers! Uh, Nick?"

Lupo glanced at him and caught a glimpse of Ghost Sam in the back seat, comfortable despite its limited dimensions. His friend's ghost seemed amused by Lupo's discomfort. He glared at the ghost in the mirror.

"DiSanto," Lupo started patiently, "it's just a bunch of weird coincidences. Remember, this is 'Weird Wisconsin.' We've had Dahmer and Gein, and Al Capone and Dillinger, and American Motors and—"

"Don't condescend," DiSanto warned, a finger extended.

"I'm not, I'm just saying we have our share of the bizarre here, so it's not unusual some of it follows me around. Half the people in Eagle River swear they've seen UFOs. Doesn't mean they're nutcases or hiding something."

He glanced in the mirror again. Ghost Sam was gone.

Talk about the bizarre following him around.

Lupo double checked and figured the lit-up squad car in the street was indication enough they were in the right place.

"Homicide, Lupo and DiSanto," he told a uniform he didn't recognize. There were a lot of them lately. They flashed their badges and the cop pointed at the house, a modest duplex, well kept. His face was drained of blood.

Shit, here we go again.

Lupo led the way inside the front door, where the smell assailed his human nostrils and tickled his Creature's.

Christ, it's another one. Same thing.

It was a slaughter scene, body parts spread all over, blood splatters like pop art on the cream-colored walls, and the wolves.

The wolves.

The lady's name meant nothing to him when another cop read it out of his notebook, but Lupo already knew what the message was and for whom it was meant.

The elderly woman had collected wolves—anything wolf-related. There were wolf figurines, wolf prints, wolf photographs, wolf tapestries, wolf rugs, wolf decorative plates, wolf collector cups and mugs, and even a small but impressive library of nonfiction wolf books.

First a vic named Lenny A. Wolf.

Wolf Liquor.

Then a woman whose hobby was wolves.

What the fuck does he want, and why kill innocent people?

The bastard was insane. Could he be insane? What if a shapeshifter had lost his mind, literally?

Maybe he was conflicted and wanted sympathy.

"Jesus, Nick, not again," DiSanto was saying, as he surveyed the damage and the butchery.

They did their thing, checking the scene for any obvious points of entry. No windows were broken. No sign of forced entry anywhere. The door was intact, so she either knew the caller or trusted him. Lupo didn't say it, but it was clear to him there were bite marks on the remains. He found a puddle and sniffed it. Sure enough, another marking. He wasn't sure what the techs, who were swarming over everything, would think about it, but it didn't matter because he knew what it meant.

Lupo also noticed DiSanto looking at him strangely after examining gnawed remains. *He's spotted the teeth marks, too.*

Lupo wanted to punch a wall. There was no telling what this guy wanted to communicate to him, and no one could guess how many dead innocent people it would take him to either back off or make a move against Lupo.

As if he hadn't felt guilty enough, here was another wacko targeting him.

How long before Jessie became a target?

Mordred

Far away from where Lupo was now receiving his newest message, Mordred was waiting in his van, the side door slightly ajar. He had covered his sensitive surveillance equipment with tarps and had handcuffs, a gag, and a syringe ready.

When David Marcowicz stepped out the side door of the downtown precinct house and walked his bow-legged walk down the street to whatever bar or diner he frequented, he was on a path that would take him past the door.

At the right moment, Mordred slid the door open with a crash and leaned his large-framed body out of the van, snatching up the smaller man as if he were a mannequin. One of his hands was a wolf's paw, its claws long and sharp as knives. The glasses slipped sideways, the eyes widening in disbelief—*and terror.* Before the studious doctor could even begin to utter a scream, the long needle had pierced his neck, and whatever the syringe held was making its way to his brain with nary a roadblock.

His body sagging, Marcowicz slipped to the floor of the van as Mordred slammed the side door shut. He slipped the gag into the guy's mouth, checked his eyes under the twitching lids, rolled him half around so he wouldn't choke, and kicked another tarp over him. Then he slid into the driver's seat, turned the key and slipped out of the parking space. In the mirror he saw only normal traffic, which was light on the side street. And no nosy cops.

Whistling one of those unrecognizable tunes from the lab, Mordred headed for the warehouse he was squatting. His head throbbed, but he forced himself to ignore it. The cattle prods had taught him how to ignore the pain.

He had work to do, and he needed to focus.

DiSanto

"Nick, talk to me."

DiSanto waited for the CSI guys to continue doing their thing. Lupo was stalking around the crime scene, now ignoring the vic altogether. He seemed fascinated by the damned wolf figurines and wolf-related everythings that lay scattered about.

Many of the wolves were speckled with the vic's blood, giving them a certain realism that almost tickled DiSanto's sense of humor. But Lupo seemed on a mission and ready to erupt, so he kept it to himself.

Sure as shit, he'd seen those teeth marks, and he wanted to point them out to Nick, but it looked like he'd already seen them and now he was acting out some sort of anger. DiSanto remembered how often the term "animal attack" had been used in the great forested state of Wisconsin lately, and—if he thought about it at length, which he might do later—he knew that many of those instances ended up involving Nick Lupo. Whether it was Eagle River, Wausau, or just right here in metro Milwaukee, the guy to call for those fucking "animal attacks" was Nick Lupo.

Coincidence?

DiSanto didn't think so.

But what did it mean?

He followed Lupo around and saw him crouch to sniff a stain on the carpeting.

What the hell...?

The big cop stood, making a face, as if what he'd smelled had been very bad indeed. But he made no effort to share with DiSanto whether this new thing was a clue of some sort or not.

DiSanto eyed his partner as he made like a ghost and disappeared into his own observations.

"Hey, watch it!" one of the techs blurted out as he stepped into one of the bloodstains.

"Sorry," he muttered, one eye still on Lupo.

It was clear Lupo was working the scene his own way, in his head.

DiSanto swallowed his rising anger and settled back to watch Lupo until they agreed they were finished. Lupo made calls, got calls, and played the role of task force head even though DiSanto could see his heart wasn't in it.

Heather

The local press had gotten a whiff of this new murder—*brutal* murder, they would say on the newscasts, though by definition *all* murders are brutal—and connected it to the other senseless ones. And then probably Bakke had given them Lupo in a fit of generosity, so when Lupo and DiSanto finally sidled out from the duplex they found themselves facing a ragged row of microphones and recorders held over the barricades by the most dogged of the local television reporters.

Uniforms looked to Lupo for the order to disperse the vultures, but Lupo shook his head imperceptibly. He made an off the cuff statement so generic the reporters could have written it for him. *Leads were being followed, the investigation was ongoing, progress was being made.*

Heather was concealed once again by the small crowd of onlookers that had gathered, tearful neighbors and total strangers. Lupo didn't see her, but she was sure the big military guy from the other crime scene did—though he ignored her.

Was he *the guy?* Getting his jollies by ogling at the scene like a textbook firebug?

Her instinct had always been good, but this time her instinct was confused. As much as he appeared to be connected, it also could be that his only connection was similar to hers. After all, she herself had been to both crime scenes, and *she* hadn't committed the murders.

She wanted to snap a picture of the military guy and wrestled with her cell phone, but he seemed to know what she was up to and managed to keep several spectators between them. She gave up.

Heather would have bet he was involved in her investigation, but how? She put her cell away, and when she looked up, he had disappeared.

Definitely involved.

Lupo had finished up, taken a couple questions with non-answers, then he and DiSanto had retreated away from the menacing microphones.

It was time to make her approach.

Jessie

She felt a presence standing over her shoulder and somehow just knew it wasn't merely a spectator or someone waiting for her to clear off. She pressed MAX BET and watched the reels turn, trying to catch the person's reflection. All she got was a hint of dark hair.

Jessie whirled—as much as one can whirl while seated on a stool—and faced her visitor, muscles tense.

A stranger, at first.

Tall woman, luscious figure, face fit for centerfold or cover, or...television?

No, it can't be...

Glance up—the hair was too dark, almost blue-black.

The make-up dark and almost menacing. Certainly too serious.

But there was no mistaking those large, penetrating eyes, and the long, straight nose. And that porn star mouth.

"Heather," Jessie said. Inside, she wanted to pummel the woman.

"Hello, Jessie," Heather Wilson said, extending her hand.

Jessie ignored it and, after a few awkward moments, Heather

157

pulled it back.

Not gonna happen, Jessie thought. If she touched that woman, it would be to kill her.

"So, you're back," she said. "Unfinished business? Plan to see Nick?"

"Not that it's any of your concern, but I did see Nick already. He just didn't see me."

Jessie felt a wave or rage wash over her. Who was this woman kidding? What did she want from her?

"Look, I know you don't like me."

"That's an understatement." Jessie couldn't help herself.

"But you didn't like me from the start, even before Nick...and I—"

"Just get to the point." Jessie could feel her face scrunching up like a prune.

"Okay, okay. So I'm not here to sweep your boyfriend away. Far as I'm concerned, you two deserve each other. I'm here because I've been following the Wolfpaw hearings, and I have some information Nick will probably want to hear. I'd like you to smooth the way for me—"

"No way, sister. You want to talk to him, you do it yourself. What's it all about, anyway?

"If you won't help me, why should I tell you?"

Jessie had second thoughts. Given Nick's fears, maybe it was foolish to turn this woman away, if she was a source of information he didn't have.

"All right." She nodded. "All right, I'll talk to him. What about those hearings?"

Heather looked entirely different, but still ravishing and enticing. Jessie could see how people fell over themselves to help her.

But she was now a werewolf, too, and that made her dangerous, as ally as well as enemy.

"The hearings aren't the biggest news. I have information on what Wolfpaw is up to, and believe me, it's more than just about some petty crimes in Iraq."

"I wouldn't say *petty*..." Jessie said.

"They're petty in the bigger context. They're symptoms of the disease at the heart of the company. It's not a company, in philosophy. It sees itself as a movement."

"So let's talk."

"How about a coffee or something? There's too many people around here. Maybe the corner of the cafeteria?"

"Lead on." Jessie followed, barely believing she had given in so easily.

Sigfried

When his cell burped and vibrated across the vast desk in his inner office, Sigfried was occupied. His hands were cupped around the woman's ears, and he was forcing her up and down on his aching erection.

He'd just been grinning widely, enjoying one of those moments of privilege.

Lowly "everymen" suspected captains of industry indulged themselves in such base ways, and joked about it, but probably didn't realize how much head was given from below the ornate desks located in the middle of basketball court-sized offices. Offices tastefully appointed with multi-million-dollar trinkets plundered from the world's art galleries and collections.

Her golden hair, a requirement today, was silken beneath his strong fingers. Her eyes were closed. Her mouth, very talented indeed. Sensual and accommodating, opened wide and receiving his deep thrusts with practiced ease. A long line of drool connected her chin to his groin, and more saliva dribbled down his cock. Her sucking sounds blended with her rapid nose-breathing and perfectly matched the rhythm of his thrusting.

Her knees were probably screaming by now, because Sigfried was known to require a very long session. But Margarethe's stand-in, Veronika, had sent the best she could find, and his instructions had been followed to the letter. The kneeling woman wore a typical Bavarian beer hall maiden's outfit, although he had pulled down her dirndl and bared her impressive breasts before pushing her down to worship in front of him. Her hair was tied up in two braids on the sides and piled up high, giving his hands plenty of purchase for his grunted maneuvering of her face in relation to his shining erection.

But now the damned cell phone had interrupted his concentration, and he felt himself soften a bit between her fleshy lips. She noticed, for her eyes opened, and she blinked up at him inquiringly. Mascara ran down her cheeks in black-marker lines. He'd been at this a while, and her eyes had started to water. Now he sensed that she wondered silently whether she should go on, or did he want to take that?

"Just keep sucking," he growled. "Voice mail."

So she bore down on him, and he ignored the vibrating phone until it stopped, satisfied, and he finally felt the enormous climax rising from down low and finally he screamed in German as it resolved in a gush that filled her mouth and choked her. He held her head so she couldn't go anywhere—*the privilege of rank, baby*—and made her lick him clean.

He was still hard, as usual, so he continued to thrust long after she had finished.

Take that, Everyman. Bet you wish you were me.

Goddamn it, those hearings had emasculated him for hours, the preening, primping, bloated camera-whore congressmen scoring their points against him with their self-important rhetoric and barely veiled insults that ultimately simply hid their envy for his money, his lifestyle, his *power.* They'd publicly emasculated him, but right now he felt a million times the man any one of them was, and he finally pulled the woman off the floor and allowed her to half-collapse on his lap.

He'd taken notes. Several unfortunate "accidents" would shake the Washington establishment in the next year. Maybe they'd even tilt the balance of power. Either way, he'd have the last laugh even if he was forced to wear orange.

And he knew he wouldn't.

He manhandled her lithe body around sideways, and she went slack, following his very specific instructions, and then he flipped up her frilly skirt. No underwear impeded him. First he paddled her ass cheeks until they glowed a healthy red—wonderful globes, beautifully shaped—and then he worked his fingers into her and manipulated her shaved folds until she squealed. He continued, alternating the paddling and the fingering, until she screamed and went slack on his lap. Unsurprisingly, he was hard again. When he moved her off himself, she looked at him, a question in her glazed eyes.

"Nah," he said, waving her off. "Tell Veronika she's a treasure. I'll tell her boss to give her a raise." He plucked a stack of cash from a drawer and handed it over, dismissing her with a tiny wave. She collected herself and exited hastily. He waited for his second erection to fade before standing to re-button.

Maybe later.

After the next round of fucking hearings.

He snatched the phone off the shining mahogany and fumbled with it until the voice mail played.

They were informing him that the council was assembled, waiting for him. He grinned without any humor. Well, they'd damn well wait until he changed his pants. This pair was speckled with bodily fluids— his, hers, both, it didn't matter.

When he entered the conference room located far down his private corridor, he stopped to survey his hand-picked inner council. Several would be known to television cameras. Several would most definitely not be known, ever. And several would not last the month.

He believed in turnover, Sigfried did.

He liked keeping them waiting.

"Come to order," be barked, and a couple of them jumped.

Good.

He liked them afraid.

"Damage control?"

One at the far end spoke up. "Editorials in five major papers and sixteen websites, all negative but three websites. Reporting on major networks, negative except for one."

His money spoke loudly, but it would have to speak louder.

"Response?"

Another, to the right this time, piped in. "Press releases forwarded to all usual outlets. PR section has created a half dozen YouTube videos that show the congressmen in negative lights based on their stupid and/or incomprehensible comments and questions. Another half dozen YouTube clips show your answers to be balanced and well-structured."

Sigfried nodded. "More?"

A third voice, shakier, responded. "We still have teams scouring the Internet for illicit video of, uh, questionable activities. Where appropriate, servers will be sabotaged and posters will be, uh, discouraged from further posting. Problem is many of these things go viral and get mailed back and forth. We have a tough time controlling such traffic."

"Do a better job of it," Sigfried said, making a mental note. It was time to promote someone from outside to the inner circle. It was time to clean house.

"Yes sir," said the doomed man, wiping his brow.

Sigfried detested weakness of any kind.

"Any other reports?"

"Financial, sir. Profits are still up. Stock price has stabilized after a dip last week. Your appearance, while somewhat damaging, assured stockholders we are on top of the problems. The 'bad apples' defense is working. Public opinion is easily swayed when the stockholders are happy."

"Good. Contracts?"

The appropriate voice arose from a corner. "Several new from the African continent. One cancellation, but Legal is investigating a lawsuit to halt it. U.S. Army has requested pricing on several new contracts, despite being warned by congress to withdraw support. Oh, and Bell has accepted our request for new fleet attack helicopters based on our own design. We are haggling, but the bid will be lowered even more by next week."

Sigfried nodded. The company his father had built on the foundation laid down so long ago was thriving despite some setbacks.

The government's misguided witch-hunt notwithstanding, Wolfpaw's health looked good.

"Send in our guest."

Near the door, one of the members stood and hurried out. He returned a few moments later with a large, muscular man in a black Wolfpaw Land Forces uniform. He moved stiffly and limped slightly. A network of scars across his face extended below the collar of his starched tunic. His beret was tucked neatly through an epaulet. He stood at attention as well as he could, given his recent injuries.

"Major Wilcox?"

"Sir."

"You have a report for the council?" Sigfried lounged in the huge leather armchair and rocked imperceptibly.

"Yes."

"Well, go ahead, man." Sigfried waved impatiently.

"Thank you, sir." Wilcox clicked a remote in his hand, and an LCD screen slid down from the ceiling where they could all see it.

"I'm grateful for the second chance, sir," Wilcox blurted out.

Sigfried frowned. Poor decorum. But the soldier had his uses, though he had been bested. "Carry on."

Wilcox flicked on the screen and video began.

"Regarding the problem up north," he said, "our agent Mordred sent this report."

First there was some dark footage of a couple fucking.

Can you still use the word "footage" when there's no film?

Regular light and infrared gave all the necessary details, and a tinny soundtrack provided the grunting.

"This is our infiltrator, you're sure?"

"Yes, sir. Dominic Lupo, a homicide cop. A good one. He is one of us, and he has proven to be stubborn and ridiculously lucky."

"And his ladyfriend?"

"A woman doctor who works on the reservation. Jessie Hawkins. Self-reliant and tougher than she looks." He cleared his throat. "Sir, Mordred could switch from surveillance mode to elimination with ease."

"No, Wilcox. I know all that. I am intrigued by this shifter's origins, and I want him watched for now. I may want him tortured a bit, later on, but I don't want him eliminated yet. He's caused us some great damage, but we're busy right now with our own problems. You may have noticed me in front of that rogues' gallery of so-called lawmakers, allowing them to aim their barbs. But we'll see about that last laugh, won't we?"

"Yes, sir."

The video ended. Another began. This one was of a different nature.

"Mordred's questioning session of the local police psychologist, David Marcowicz. He was reluctant at first to provide any information, though we knew he'd been speaking to other players. Then he became interested in cooperating."

The screaming startled a few council members. Others licked dry lips. One wiped a brow. No one looked away.

On the screen, an indistinct set of backyard clippers was snipping off the fingertips of the screaming subject, who was manacled to a chair.

Snip, snip, snip.

Over the screaming, a voice intoned: "Those are the first knuckles. No need to worry about trimming nails, eh?"

The screams degenerated into snot-distorted bawling. Making out the words was difficult due to all the whimpering and crying and snorting.

"Now let's make the other hand match, shall we?"

"Noooooooooooooo! Wait, wait, I'll tell you what you want! Please!"

"Yes you will," the quiet voice said, "but I want to make sure you'll tell me the truth. And I want you to be able to avoid the need for manicures. We'll talk in a minute, you and I."

Snip-snip-snip-snip.

The victim's screaming degenerated into incoherent syllables strung together with the sound of saliva and snot hitting the concrete floor.

Snip.

"There, Doctor Marcowicz. Now we can continue our chat." He patted the bleeding fingers dry with a red-blotted towel, waited, and patted again. Meanwhile, Marcowicz had fainted.

For the next half hour, Mordred poked and prodded with a variety of implements. He cut, sliced, yanked, sawed, and stabbed, and finally the ragged, high-pitched and increasingly incoherent voice of Marcowicz turned into a pathetic gurgle and then he died, whatever was left of him hunched over in the slick chair.

Sigfried nodded at Wilcox. "A good lesson, I'd say. Thank you for sharing it with us. Find out more about this *Griff Killian* and forward it to me. You will travel there and provide Mordred with some back-up, as well as another assignment we'll discuss. Mordred has my orders, and now so will you. Wait for me outside."

"Sir." Wilcox saluted stiffly and exited the conference room.

Sigfried surveyed his council members. He noted those who

163

seemed the most nervous, made mental notes for confirmation of his conclusions, then arose.

"I'm off to the next set of hearings. Needless to say, I will not be in a mood to be kind on my return. Wolfpaw will survive and thrive. And today you have seen the culmination of several lines of valuable research. Thank you all very much."

He strode from the room.

The microphones would pick up everything he needed to know. The council would look decidedly different in a week.

Chapter Fifteen

Jessie

"What in the hell are you telling me?" Lupo's voice soared a bit. Fortunately the diner was nearly empty, and the waitresses were reluctant to wade amongst the empty tables and booths unless summoned.

"Nick, I know it doesn't make sense, but Heather says she has information you need. She connected it to the case you have now."

"You mean cases, plural. The guy's escalating. And he's definitely trying to tell me something, but the message is garbled."

"What do you mean?" She reached out and took his callused, scarred hand in hers.

His hand was *very* badly scarred.

"He's either warning me or threatening me, but I can't figure out which. But he's killing innocent people to do it, so he's got to be stopped no matter what. Now tell me about Heather."

She shared a quick version of how Heather had approached her, how she looked different, and what she had said—but also that there was more she would only share with Lupo himself.

"Well, shit, Jess, I don't have anything much to say to her. She helped Arnow—" He stopped suddenly in mid-sentence.

"Helped Arnow what?"

Suddenly he seemed evasive. "She helped him get over his grief, kind of, but then she dumped him and took off. Again. She has a history of running, doesn't she? And now that she's one of—like *me*, she's even harder to trust because I can't ever figure out her motives."

"Hm, kind of like this guy who's leaving you the messages. Could it be *her*, Nick? Could she be the one?"

He rubbed his neck absently. "Good theory, but I let the Creature check one of the crime scenes, and it's definitely a male. I'd know if it's a female." He stopped for a second. "Though not if she was in on it, I guess."

"Nick..."

"I'm gonna have to talk to her, aren't I? Even if I don't trust her. Maybe she's legit."

"That would be a first."

"Yeah, it would."

His anger had settled a bit, and then their food came and they stopped talking long enough to fuel up. When she looked in his eyes, though, she saw only mystery and uncertainty.

Sigfried

"Wilcox, step into my office." Sigfried held his door, enjoying the flash of fear he'd caused in the big man.

"Yes, sir." He sat where Sigfried motioned him. "At ease."

"Major Wilcox, as a former Alpha Team commander, you no doubt know that when my predecessor dispatched your group to this Wisconsin backwater, there was a purpose beside taking out those who know about the werewolf gene."

Wilcox nodded, relaxing slightly now that he didn't think he would be summarily executed.

Sigfried continued. He was in a talkative mood. "There was a reason we were interested in that area, and why we built a laboratory facility nearby and staffed it with several of our brilliant scientists. That reason was the cop, Dominic Lupo. The cop was of interest because his strain had been created with the input of a minor player who turned out to be somewhat more—he's of no interest to you, because he's long gone."

Sigfried stroked his goatee, which made him look Satanic, a look he wasn't altogether unhappy with.

"Wilcox, you're to provide Mordred with back-up if he needs it, as I said, but I also want you to scout our laboratory facility near Minocqua. Quaint place, that. You'll be using my personal plane."

"Yes, sir," Wilcox said, listening to the rest of his orders.

Heather

They were sitting in a booth, waiting for her. The diner was half empty, and she ordered coffee and a bagel before sliding in across from them.

Nice psychology, she thought. Sitting across from her, they were consciously together and also united against her, in case she was wondering. This wasn't going to be a friendly meeting, but then she hadn't expected it to be.

She'd been surprised by the quick call, and that they were willing to meet her right then.

She looked from Jessie to Lupo and smiled slightly. Jessie was stifling her irritation. Lupo's nostrils were flaring, and Heather wasn't sure whether it was anger or awakened lust, but she found them sexy all the same. She knew one of her feet was touching one of his under the table—her long legs always caused her trouble in booths. In this case, she liked it.

Lupo moved his foot just enough to break the connection.

She smiled more widely.

"Well, it's nice to see you two still together. What you went through, most couples would have broken up over. I'm happy for you."

They said nothing, but Jessie rolled her eyes.

Given the gambling thing, Heather figured not all waters were smooth in *that* harbor.

Her coffee came and she wrapped her long fingers around the mug.

"Nick, how's your case? I hear you're the task force guy."

She took a long sip and left a dark smudge on the rim of her mug. She saw Lupo staring at it before he looked up and into her eyes.

Inside, she smiled. He was still hers, if only physically.

The long silence was deafening. But she was adept at riding out pauses and letting her interviewees nervously spill guts.

"You look different," Lupo said finally, assessing.

Jessie obviously felt the vibe between them, and Heather sensed her muscles tightening from across the table.

"But not that different," he continued. "I saw you, caught a glance of you at the scene. I should have looked more closely."

"You like it?" She fanned her very dark hair.

"It suits you."

"Can we get back to why you're here?" Jessie erupted, clearly annoyed by the preliminaries.

The chunky waitress came with her bagel and more coffee for all three. Jessie and Lupo didn't touch their mugs, but Heather spread cream cheese over half her bagel and took a bite.

A seductive bite, perhaps. Her eyes never left Lupo's, not until he broke away.

Then she put down the bagel, licked the corner of her lip, and smiled crookedly. "I guess a rare steak would have been a better choice."

Lupo glared at her. "Heather," he started.

She held up a hand.

"Okay, I have information you need. I'm not asking anything in exchange for it, because I think it affects us all. But I've been investigating our friends over at Wolfpaw and, believe me, we only saw the tip of the iceberg up to now."

They leaned in unconsciously and she smiled to herself.

At least they were listening.

"I found out more than even I expected. The stuff is out there, if you know where to look. Our old friends the mercenaries were just three of the many wolves they have in the ranks. Two of them were direct descendants of Nazi bastards from the Werwolf Division. Ring a bell, Nick?"

"Shit, yeah, Tom started by doing a little research, and then we both did. We found out they'd been all over northern Italy at the end of the war. My father had some history there that my grandmother and he wouldn't talk much about."

Heather nodded. "So anyway, apparently the Werwolf Division guys weren't all werewolves, but enough of them were. But what's more is that when they were commissioned, the head honcho—a sadistic asshole named vonStumpfahren..."

"Sounds like a Volkswagen ad," Jessie said, shaking her head.

"Yeah, well, he was something else. But he wasn't the worst. He employed another one of those sadistic bastard concentration camp doctors, like Mengele, and funded his research."

"On humans?" Jessie made a face.

"Yes and no. On humans, and on...werewolves."

"You're going to connect this to Wolfpaw?" Lupo was hooked. This *was* interesting stuff. *If only they weren't after your ass.*

"Yeah, so like I said Wolfpaw seems to have been born as a front for remaining descendants of the Werwolf group. They incorporated to do what they'd always done well—wage war. Somewhere along the line, these two things intertwined—whoever in the Werwolf Division survived the war, and a modern right-wing paramilitary group with grandiose ideas of selling their services to high bidder nations."

"Okay, so what?" Lupo said, leaning back. "I already know about some of that. I mean, we heard about Werwolf from Tom Arnow, and we have that strange silver dagger."

"You still have that?"

"Yes, of course. It's a useful weapon against one of *us*."

The way he said it, Heather understood she was included on the short list of those who might be at the receiving end of that sharp implement.

"Well, I know a few more things about that dagger."

"How did you find out this kind of information?" Jessie said.

Heather fixed her with an intentionally condescending stare. "I *am* an investigative journalist."

"What else did you find out?" Lupo looked askance at Jessie for one quick second.

"I know there was a matched set, and one of them ended up with the tribe. That's the one you have."

"What about the other one?"

"Missing, right now, but I gather it's not supposed to be."

Lupo took a pull of his coffee. He made a face. "Any idea what the story is behind them? And where the missing one might be?"

"I think the missing dagger wasn't far from its partner, so it would have been up north. But I don't think the tribe had it. Somebody on the inside gave one to them, but kept the other one. As for as their story, I'm afraid I only have some speculative tidbits."

"Why are you keeping us in suspense?" Jessie asked. "We're not your mindless television audience, waiting for the exciting part."

Heather had to laugh. Jessie's feelings about her were quite clear.

"Look, you know the whole werewolf thing isn't exactly normal. We've got to come from somewhere—but we're not on the evolutionary chart, know what I mean? There's some supernatural aspect we just don't know about. That's the bottom line. Whoever made those daggers, and whoever has them, must know. I don't know—yet. The reason I'm talking to you is more directly related to Wolfpaw."

"So what is it?" Lupo asked.

Heather chuckled. "Always to the point, eh? As I told Jessie here, I've sat in on the first set of hearings. They look like they're gonna throw the book at the company. But I have sources who tell me Wolfpaw has begun a campaign of secret threats against the congressmen, and the one woman, that's guaranteed to make them all back off. They're not going to have to pay for all those crimes their werewolves committed in Iraq and a dozen other places. They make other contractors look like fucking angels by comparison, mostly because the others are human."

She drank some coffee and looked at Lupo over the mug, smiling wickedly.

"The werewolves have greater *needs*," she said. "You know that as well as I do."

"I keep my needs under control," he said.

"Not always, Nick, not always." She didn't look at Jessie, but she sure felt the doctor's eyes on her. Like gun sights.

"Come on," he growled. "There's got to be more. Not surprising to think they're planning to weasel and squirm their way out of paying for the crimes. What else?"

Heather paused for effect.

"I have it on good authority that Wolfpaw has been infiltrating the U.S. armed services, both leadership and ranks, with the intention of launching a silent coup on the government. With the intent to create a

169

sort of American Fourth Reich, a secretly Nazi regime."

"*What?*"

"Don't get your panties in an uproar," Heather whispered, glancing around. Fortunately the diner was still mostly empty. "It's a long-term plan. You know we age more slowly than average humans. They expect it to take a while. But they're well on their way. Some obstacles they kill, some they buy. Some they *convert*. Being brought up on these federal charges was a speed bump. *You* are a speed bump. But they have time."

"Shit, I didn't expect this sort of grandiose super-villain stuff."

"You poke the hornets' nest, though, and you get stung. Plus you never know what the hornets are doing in there."

Jessie said, "And what about us? Why are you here? We can't really figure in their plans for world domination."

"Not world, just United States."

"Whatever." Jessie waved her off.

"I'm here because Nick is a big speed bump. So am I, but I haven't hurt them like he has. He knows what they are, how to fight them. He has that dagger. He can fight werewolves with silver, which they can't do. And I'm here because there's something going on here, too, and I don't exactly know what it is. I'd expect them to move against you, Nick, especially after what you did to them, and what you know, but there's no Alpha Team on its way. They're being more subtle. But there's a buzz about someone, an assassin, being sent to..."

"Sent to *what?*" Lupo asked, his nostrils really flaring now.

"That's just it, I couldn't find out what they're planning. The CEO, you've seen him on TV, is this mysterious person whose name is supposedly Sigfried... That's probably an alias—they like their Arthurian and Wagner references, just like their ancestors, the Nazis. Anyway, I know he's sent one of his most secret operatives here, but not what he's supposed to do."

"Know who?"

"No. But there's this big military guy who was at one of the crime scenes. He looks good for it."

"I know about him."

"Nick?" Jessie said, surprised. She reached for his hand but more angrily than with concern.

"Relax, Jess. His name is Geoff Simonson. He's on our side. He approached me, told me he was ex-military, a Ranger, then with Wolfpaw in Iraq. Witnessed the crimes our, uh, friends committed."

"You had him checked out, of course?"

"Yeah, but so far he's under the radar. Says he's gotten off the grid on purpose, to fight them. DiSanto's tried every database on the planet, but no luck."

"Well, do you need a roadmap? He's got to be one of them."

"Then why approach me? Why not put a bullet through me? Or stab me with a silver spear?"

Heather shrugged. "He was at both crime scenes."

"Sure, and I've met with him."

"Nick!" Jessie's eyes showed her sense of betrayal.

"I just talked to him a little while ago."

"And you didn't tell me?"

"Jess, I didn't tell you *yet.*"

"You meet with a potential assassin and I have to hear it from *her?*"

Heather couldn't help but grin. This was classic.

"Well, I just wanted to share my information. You guys can sort it out." She told them where she was staying.

"What are you going to do?" Lupo asked.

"Follow the story." She had some ideas.

She stood and left and wished she could listen in to the argument that would surely erupt.

Lupo

He was driving, but aimlessly.

Sometimes he felt the weight of history and destiny colliding and settling on his shoulders.

And sometimes he felt that he was buffeted by events and people he couldn't control.

Like Heather Wilson.

He wasn't sure how he felt about her.

He felt lust. He knew that.

Who wouldn't? The woman exuded sexuality. She transcended gender and the normal, avoiding convention even as she maneuvered those around her into doing her bidding.

Heather and he had a history.

Jessie wasn't any too happy about that, which should have made things easier for him.

But it didn't.

He combed his hair roughly with his hand, a mannerism picked up recently. A nervous, obsessive tic.

Jesus Christ, Heather.

Was there some destiny there? And how did he relate to it?

171

No matter how much he tried to deny it, Heather shared a bond with him now, a bond Jessie did not.

Heather was a werewolf.

Werewolves had increased libido.

He realized he was sweating. He rolled down his window and let in the cold fall air until his teeth chattered.

Chapter Sixteen

1944
Chelmno, on the Polish border
Schlosser

He waited for the wolf to return. The conditioning had taken quite well with this one. They could barely control their own impulses, so it was almost an impossibility to expect that he would have been able to train them as if they were dogs.

But this one had shown a good response to both the training and the experiments. Even though it spent most of its time as a wolf in excruciating pain, it was almost ready to display to that insufferable bore vonStumpfahren.

Schlosser imagined the exhibition. Like his own field trials, he would use prisoners let loose into the frozen forest as prey. In one swoop, he could proudly display both how well his conditioning of the Werwolf beasts took root, and also how well his silver injection therapy and its offshoots had prepared them to survive wounds inflicted by the mysteriously lethal element.

No one who knew of the werewolf gene understood why silver caused the reaction it did when it was shot, stabbed, or injected into the subject's bloodstream. The burning suffered by the unfortunate guinea pig spanned the gamut from minor, when the amount was minuscule, to devastating. At the upper end of the range, the subject died a terrible death as his inner organs, veins, and muscles burned like fuses melting flesh, tissue, and bone.

Schlosser had gone through several dozen subjects this way, carefully studying how each wound-infliction affected the subhumans whose bodies became wolves.

And he had gone farther, noting how a non-lethal bite spread the evil malady—perhaps through infected saliva—to the bite's recipient. During the next full moon cycle, those bitten would inevitably become wolves themselves, completely disoriented and confused by their new condition. The scientist observed these subjects as they went into the Change, using specially constructed cement cells outfitted with double-thick panes of aircraft glass.

Let Mengele match that!

His rival for the Führer's favor had manipulated himself into a perfect position of power. But Schlosser's work would ensure the survival of the Reich and its Fatherland where Mengele's could not.

Since they were research subjects, Schlosser considered each of those bitten victims expendable—and he used them to further his silver aversion therapy research, most often by torturing them until they died, their screams filling the soundproof cellblock of first Treblinka camp and later Chelmno, where he had been forced to move reluctantly when the former extermination camp was ordered closed and razed.

Thinking of this made the taste in Schlosser's mouth bitter and hard to swallow.

Here in Chelmno—on the border between occupied Poland and the portion of old Poland known as West Prussia—he had been forced to make do with the insanely spread-out camp functions. At the Treblinka facility, a perfectly suitable, thickly wooded forest spread from the camp's perimeter and allowed for his field experiments done under cover of darkness and moonlight, away from prying eyes thanks to the special death's head SS guards sworn to secrecy. But now the local wooded area was four kilometers away from the Chelmno manor house that housed the administration, the extermination facilities, and his larger cellblock and laboratory.

At the perimeter of the forest camp facility, where mass graves were dug, Schlosser had directed the construction of a satellite research facility housed in a series of transportable huts. From here, he would release specially selected prisoners to provide sport and prey for his "hybrids" and, he hoped with increasing excitement, to further his research into extending the man-wolves' tolerance to the pain caused by the dreaded silver.

The old legends were correct, he had written. *The* why *may be a point of debate, but modern science will find a solution to reverse this effect, which will result in hardier shapeshifting subjects for the Werwolf Division and, in future, for the entire German armed forces.*

His proposal to the Führer had emphasized the practical applications of werewolves who could be trained like dogs, which Germans had been doing for ages, and who would be impervious to the one substance dangerous to them.

A race of super-werewolves was in sight, and it would be Klaus Schlosser who created it.

He would be celebrated as the greatest German scientist in history, father of a whole race. And therefore savior of the Aryan race.

When he squinted, he saw statues of himself in all major German capitals of the world. But for now he went about his usual end-of-the-day procedure, selecting a half dozen inmates healthy enough to withstand his experimental procedures, then set about preparing to have his current favorite werewolf bite them in order to provide the next cycle of experiments.

One of the inmates he selected became violent after being brought into the facility, and Schlosser smiled grimly at the subhuman's struggles. He called back the guards, who owed only him allegiance.

"Hold this one down," he ordered, and the two hulking SS men did so with their muscular arms. The prisoner continued to rave in a foreign tongue. Schlosser curled his lip. It sounded like a stream of an inferior language, perhaps something Slavic.

"Silence!" he roared.

But the prisoner paid him no mind, half-babbling and half-muttering when he wasn't screaming.

Schlosser scooped a used syringe from a tray, drew in a column of air, and plunged the needle into the inmate's neck. Even though the struggling form nearly broke the syringe, Schlosser was able to press the plunger home.

The shouter's eyes rolled up into his head, and in a few moments the convulsions began. Schlosser watched with some casual interest. There was always something to learn, even from common animals such as this specimen. The guards held the beast until he expired, finally, his mouth rimed with white specks.

Schlosser motioned for them to clear his laboratory of the corpse. Expressionless, they complied with economic movements, dragging out the slug for disposal in the usual manner. Then the scientist gathered his journals and notes for the day and locked them in his safe. He thought of his wife Gerte and his teenage son, Hans, two hundred kilometers away, and smiled slightly. He would see them soon. In the meantime, he would seek a meal in the manor house officers' mess hall, then return to his small but relatively luxurious flat in town until tomorrow, when he could continue the experiments so valuable to the Fatherland.

Perhaps in the next year he would bring his son to work with him as an assistant. The boy already showed signs of an interest in the sciences, and Schlosser could think of no more noble a cause than that which he had been given by that boorish Prussian, vonStumpfahren. In his hands, and his family's, perhaps lay the means to win this war which—if rumors were true—had begun to go badly.

His meal was forgettable—a glue-like stew of turnips, potatoes, and gristly lumps of meat he could not identify.

But at his flat, Anneliese awaited him, and what she wore brought a smile to his tired face. The ivory phallus protruding from between her muscular thighs was ready, slick with Vaseline. The paddle she wielded on his bare buttocks brought the sort of joy he found in his laboratory.

Later, he screamed joyfully into his favorite leather gag as she sweated and grunted behind him.

And the night was young.

When the air raid sirens started their wail, leaving was the last thing on his mind. *Coming* was the first.

Bombs like thunder sounded in the distance.

Chapter Seventeen

Sigfried

He was preparing his last day testimony—well, closing statements, really—for when those congressmen cowed by the covert photographs would let him publicly off the hook. He would be humble and accept their implied apology to show how big-hearted even the CEO of Wolfpaw Security Services could be. He would be very convincing, staring into the cameras arrayed in a half circle in front of his table, and tell the people of America that they could trust Wolfpaw and its leadership to fight their wars for them.

And then he would continue to seed the military services with his own people, to prepare for the day when true command of the country's military would be handed over to Wolfpaw officers—field-marshals, he wanted to call them—and the bloodless coup would have begun. It would take a decade or two, but the takeover would gradually account for all of government, not only the military.

He assumed it would be the last day. The photographs of helpless, innocent families would have done their best work overnight, while the bastards tried to sleep, the implied threat gathering force as the night darkened and the hours dragged toward a much more dangerous dawn.

His software gave him a blip. New report filed on the secure server, but not Mordred. Had to be Wilcox. The big team leader had been trying hard to get back into Sigfried's good graces since he'd been outplayed at the Eagle River casino. Once, Sigfried had considered him for conversion, making Wilcox a possible Mordred. But his lapse had cost him status, rank, trust—you name it.

Sigfried typed the appropriate logins and prompts and soon had the software confirming it was Wilcox's voice, safely unscrambled, relating a brief report.

"Report starts." Wilcox's voice was reduced to a tinny babble by the small laptop speakers. "New player needs background check. Seems to be helping the cop, Nick Lupo, against operative known as Mordred. Name is Simonson, Geoff." He spelled it slowly. "Will follow up after further surveillance. Report ends. Wilcox out."

Simonson? he thought. *What the hell?*

Why was that familiar?

Sigfried keyboarded himself to a different login, slipped in his password, and clicked into the Wolfpaw database. He waited for the search engine to return a page, read it and smiled.

This is a good twist.

Smiling placidly, he went back to work on his statement for the cameras and the treasonous congressmen. And woman.

Let's not forget her.

He had something special planned for her family. He hoped he'd get to put it in motion.

Chapter Eighteen

1944

Giovanni

He blinked as they led him out of the air raid shelter they called Sanctuary.

It was dark already, but even so it was brighter than in the candle-lit cavern below the bombed-out tenement whose ruined brick walls had caved in and hid the several entrance tunnels the partisan brigade had dug.

After the all clear, Corrado had assigned two men to accompany him to his apartment, where he hoped to find Franco unhurt. Alone and frightened, perhaps, but unhurt.

He prayed as he had, indeed, never prayed before.

He also prayed they would not face any werewolves.

Giovanni followed the tall, strangely nicknamed, bespectacled werewolf killer Turco (who didn't appear in the least Turkish) and the taciturn hulking giant of a man named Manfredo. They had given him a newer German P-38 pistol he had again tucked into his belt and a commando-style knife, and in his hands he carried another Breda submachine gun.

Just like that, it seemed, Giovanni had become a partisan.

Porca fortuna!

He was content to know Maria was as safe as she could be in the shelter, which was extensive and well stocked, but his son's safety was on his mind. And, if he were honest with himself, his own—now if he were stopped by the Germans, he would be summarily executed. Orders had come down from the local High Command that stipulated all units consider any armed Italian a partisan and as such a threat to the defense of the city and outlying territories.

Corrado had shown him a bloody, tattered telegraph flimsy captured from a German—now dead, surely—which made the orders official.

And so here he was, creeping through the ruined buildings on this street, hoping that when he reached his own there would be buildings left standing. No one expected bombs to be accurate all the time, but the amount of civilian devastation ringing the port was incredible. Parts of buildings spilled out debris and belongings, some still smoldering from this last Allied bombing run, which had partly missed the harbor after all.

Here and there he saw a bloody arm or leg protruding from piles of brick and cement rubble. Some places, confused survivors stumbled over the broken remainders of their lives, searching for loved ones or memories to salvage, or just trying to recover from the trauma of the war suddenly intruding on their lives.

Giovanni followed Turco and Manfredo as they led him in redundant zigzags down the street.

Turco held up a hand and they stopped, crouching low behind the remains of a brick wall. The thin, bearded academic didn't look like a seasoned partisan, but Corrado had called him one of the best.

Giovanni couldn't see what had caused Turco to stop them so suddenly.

But then a match flared only a couple meters away on the other side of the broken wall, and Giovanni made out a reflection on a German coal-shuttle helmet and the glint of a long bayonet fitted to the muzzle of a Mauser rifle. A sentry, posted to catch partisans as they crawled from their holes, most likely.

Posted to catch us, Giovanni thought, his throat seizing up and his heart racing.

Turco pressed his index finger on his lips, then waved Manfredo up closer. His hand told Giovanni to wait there, under cover.

The two partisans crawled silently along their side of the wall until they reached a demolished corner. Shattered bricks lay all about. Giovanni could barely see, but these men had lived as outlaws for so long he assumed they'd developed night vision. They were now positioned immediately behind the unsuspecting sentry, as far as he could tell.

Suddenly there was a rattle of equipment and clothes and debris, as Turco went in high and dragged the German backward, his hand clasped tightly over the unfortunate's face to keep him from shouting.

Manfredo lunged in from the side with the silver-bladed knife, plunging its length into the German's side a half dozen times. While Turco pulled the dying soldier back over the wall, Manfredo finished the job by slitting his throat with one savage motion.

They laid the bleeding, dying soldier on a bed of shattered bricks and raided his pockets and belt pouches for ammunition and food, all of which Manfredo silently fed into a bag he carried slung over one shoulder.

Turco nodded at Giovanni and they were on their way.

The whole encounter had taken less than a half minute.

And the local commander would likely round up innocent civilians and have them shot in retaliation when the murdered sentry was found.

Giovanni gritted his teeth.

He had to find Franco. There was no other way to assure the child wouldn't be rounded up and killed. Giovanni never entertained the thought his son might be dead. No, his intuition said the boy was fine, maybe at home, maybe hiding out with his friend. But as time passed, he knew the chances of something befalling his son increased exponentially.

All he had to do was remember how his day had begun, and how it had ended. His world was tilted, and he teetered on the edge, ready to fall. His mind was cracking, and along with that his will to live—if his son was dead, would he not be a failure?

They continued, carefully avoiding the flickering light of fires that marked where gas lines had erupted, crossing from shadow to shadow, occasionally hearing screams of pain and fear from people trapped in the ruins of their buildings. Giovanni's heart cried, but Turco motioned them on, indicating that they had to ignore the victims or they would themselves be sacrificed.

"We stop, we die," he whispered.

Soon they left the devastated section behind, with only a glow from the fires to mark what they had seen. As they approached Giovanni's neighborhood, he was grateful to see that his building still stood—a seven-story, stucco-sided tenement with solid marble floors and a heavy clay tile roof. It looked intact, unharmed, and his heart swelled at the thought of finding Franco at home.

"Watch out!" Turco cried, and lunged past.

Giovanni saw the glint of silver.

And heard snarling behind him.

He turned.

By the time he managed to whirl around, the wolf was on him.

But Turco had also lunged at the attacking beast and intercepted the muscular body in mid-air. They both crashed into Giovanni, and the three went down in a tangle of arms and claws and fangs.

Giovanni dropped the Breda and tried to wrestle the wolf with his bare hands, while Turco attempted to bring his magical blade to bear and still avoid the slashing teeth and claws. The wolf was damnably quick, though, outmaneuvering both men and keeping the three a rolling, tumbling blur that the giant Manfredo could do nothing about.

Giovanni could only keep the jaws away from his throat by pushing the red-eyed head away. Turco struggled with the sheathed dagger. If the priest had been right, then the wood scabbard was actively shielding the wolf from the feared silver on the blade. Giovanni

181

tried to shift the balance of the three squirming bodies to give Turco an advantage, a chance to draw the blade.

But the wolf seemed to predict each attempt, and Giovanni could either avoid the snapping jaws or help Turco, but not both. And the wolf knew it. He could read the monster's intelligence in its demon eyes, which were neither animal nor entirely human.

Turco first grunted when the wolf managed to claw his face, but his grunt turned to a tortured scream of pain as his brain realized that his cheek had been torn open and his jaw dislocated. Right then, lying below the struggling forms, still barely managing to deflect the dangerous fangs, Giovanni realized with horror that the monster's swipe had ripped Turco's left eye from its socket, and it hung from its optic nerve, leaving behind a black hole in which he swore he could see hell itself.

"Shoot him!" he shouted at Manfredo, who was frozen in place with his pistol extended, trying to draw a bead on the monster without striking either human. "Damn you, shoot him!"

But it was too late.

Turco opened his mouth and screamed incoherently as the wolf suddenly gained the advantage and its snapping jaws tore the partisan's clothing to shreds and dug savagely into his belly like a shark shaking a smaller fish.

Giovanni felt the gush of hot blood and intestines wash over his chest and pried himself out from under the dying partisan and the savaging monster. He rolled out from under the two and saw as he did so that Turco was already dead.

"Bastard, shoot him now!"

Manfredo snapped out of his trance and leaned in close enough to put the pistol mere centimeters from the back of the wolf's head. The beast had succumbed to his frenzy and paid no attention.

The crash of the pistol deafened Giovanni. Manfredo fired again and again, hot brass splattering from the breech. The slugs tore through the wolf's skull and exploded through Turco's head.

Unaffected, the wolf snarled and turned its blood-spattered muzzle toward Manfredo.

Before the big man could retreat, the wolf lunged and clamped its jaws on his gun-hand. Manfredo screamed as the wolf shook his head and tossed the severed hand and the pistol into the darkness.

Manfredo desperately tried to stem the bleeding from his jagged stump, but by then the wolf had leaped off the dead Turco, and now its jaws closed on the giant's groin and shook him violently like a child's doll, blood gushing into its mouth and scattering like raindrops over the ground beneath them.

Without time for any thought and operating solely on instinct and self-preservation, Giovanni scooped up the dagger from the ground near Turco's savaged body and slid it out of its wooden sheath.

In the darkness, the blade seemed to glow as if with a moonlit sheen.

Growling incoherently, he attacked the frenzied wolf.

He drew the wolf's attention from Manfredo, but before pulling away, the beast ripped into the wounded giant's groin once more. Giovanni knew enough anatomy to figure he'd nicked a major artery, judging from the jetting blood.

Manfredo would bleed out if he didn't kill the wolf.

Quickly.

But as soon as the werewolf's attention was focused on him, Giovanni questioned his own sanity.

The monstrous wolf's eyes glowed with supernatural intelligence and, very likely, much experience in savage combat.

What did Giovanni have?

A touch of madness, desperation, and a damned dagger from the Vatican—or so the old drunken priest said.

And he had a son to find...

No time to consider a course of attack, because the wolf took all choice away by advancing straight for him. His bloody muzzle seemed to smile as Giovanni took small steps backwards, leading the wolf to the nearest brick wall.

The wolf advanced, snarling, its jaws bracing for a lunge. Giovanni felt the wall with his back and used it to regain his balance. Before he could refine his spontaneous plan, the monster was in the air.

Giovanni feinted left, the wolf went for him, then Giovanni sidestepped to the right. The wolf was on him now, the stench of blood and offal in Giovanni's nostrils. And at the last second he brought the glowing blade up and jabbed it into the wolf's side before sawing with heart-clenching fury.

The wolf shrieked in unholy pain and surprise and crashed into the wall.

Giovanni was also taken by surprise by the ease with which the blade furrowed the beast's fur and skin, parting its flesh as if he were made of dough.

The stench of burning flesh and fur and blood rose up along with a plume of disgusting smoke.

The wolf fell in a heap and flipped, attempting to simultaneously lick his blackening wound closed and snap at Giovanni, who'd stepped away in surprise.

The wolf's side was split, its organs and intestines were spilling out in a bloody jumble, and the smoking continued as if its insides had caught on fire.

Holy fire?

Could it be true?

Giovanni managed to avoid the snapping jaws and stabbed the beast in the side, the blade sinking in to the hilt, and the wolf screamed out, obviously mortally wounded. Pressing his advantage, Giovanni then slid the blade from the smoking, putrefying flesh and plunged it through the beast's right eye and into its brain.

It died as soon as the blade slid out again, collapsing in a smoking heap at the bottom of the wall.

Its body quivering like a hooked fish, the wolf seemed to blur, and Giovanni watched in wonder as it flipped from animal to human and back again until it finally took the form of a naked human. A dead one, with horrific wounds where Giovanni's blade had struck.

Gulping air he hadn't realized he needed, gasping and wheezing, Giovanni stumbled away from the horror.

He cried dry tears for the two partisans who had given their lives to help him find his son.

Franco!

What might have happened to him?

Giovanni found the scabbard he had dropped to the ground and bent to retrieve it.

Suddenly his right upper chest felt as if it had been split open, and he gasped in horror and pain and straightened so quickly he almost fainted. He patted his destroyed clothing—it was covered in a grotesque, mad artist's palette made of blood and worse—and realized that some of the blood on the slit fabric was his own. He riffled through the ruined shirt and hissed in pain as he found the source, a series of deep gashes and a ragged, round wound.

Gesu' e Maria, he whispered, *I'm wounded.*

Fangs or claws?

Did it matter?

His skin was black and rippled around the ragged wounds, the flesh beneath bruising into a series of plum-colored circles. The bleeding appeared to have stopped. A blackened crust of blood and pus was already hardening around each laceration.

Hastily he rearranged the torn clothing to cover the hideous wound, hissing at the excruciating pain he felt as the scratchy fabric dragged across his flayed skin.

Gently he bent again, wincing, and retrieved the scabbard. Then he sheathed the dagger.

Did it hum in his grip?

He gathered his wits, found his bearings, and realized he was only a couple of buildings away from his own. He retrieved the Breda and slung it painfully over his shoulder. One of his friends' pistols went into a pocket. The dagger remained in his hand.

Hunched over in pain and fearful of being spotted by another German patrol, either human or monstrous or composed of both, he hugged the shadows and found his way home.

The building seemed unfamiliar, a stranger, and he had to check the address plate twice to make sure he had indeed reached his own home. His family's airy apartment was one of four located on the fifth floor. The lights were out, but there was moonlight filtering through the skylight way above him.

He shuffled up the stairs, the preternatural quiet frightening, each scrape threatening to send him running for cover. The marble stairs and corridor allowed him to muffle his steps, and soon he was on his own floor. In the near-darkness, he saw that his apartment door was ajar.

Inside, the foyer was dark, and he tripped on a chair Maria had insisted should be there for guests to take off their shoes if they wished. The chair legs scraped on the floor. His heart beat rapidly, a prisoner in his chest but not resting quietly. His wound throbbed, and he resisted the urge to touch it.

"Franco?" he whispered hoarsely. "Franco, are you here, it's your father."

After checking the small bedroom off the foyer, he advanced down the long corridor along which there were two more rooms. Franco's room was empty, though at first he thought his boy was lying in bed. But it was jumbled bedclothes. The next room was the bedroom Giovanni shared with his wife, and Maria's penchant for oversized furniture gave him pause, as each piece looked like a German in hiding or a wolf-man about to pounce.

But there was nothing there, either. And no one.

The last two rooms were a long, narrow bath, which was empty, and the kitchen, a huge, old-fashioned room beside the bath. Standing in the kitchen, he swore he could hear a small heart beating nearby.

"Franco?" he called out in a whisper that threatened to become weeping. His heartbeat throbbed in time with his wound.

A tiny whisper came from a cabinet he had built below the large ceramic sink in the corner.

"Papá?"

"Franco! *Dio mio*, is it you?" He ignored the pain in his chest and

185

sank to his knees, crawling toward the sink, sobbing the whole way.

The boy's face that peeked from behind Maria's frilly curtain was Franco's, all right, but his eyes had aged since Giovanni had last looked into them so many hours-days-years ago. It was only early on the same day, but a lifetime had happened in the meantime. Apparently for Franco, too.

"Are you all right, my son?" He didn't let him answer, but instead gathered the boy in his arms and they rocked together, tears flowing, for a few minutes.

"I'm okay," Franco said. "Mamma?" His voice trembled.

"She's fine, she's fine! We're in a shelter."

"I thought you were dead! Killed by those...*things.*" Franco sighed, laying his head on his father's shoulder. "Hey, there's a lot of blood! Papá, are you—"

"I'm fine. It's the blood of some brave men who helped me, God rest their souls." He slowly shifted Franco's face so he could see him better. "What about your friend Pietro?"

The boy suddenly started to weep. "We were great, we took them on, we saw them turn to wolves, we saw them kill that pilot, and then we ran and ran, but—oh, it was terrible! He caught us by surprise, and it took Pietro, then he did terrible things to him. I ran away, Papá. When I could have helped him, I ran away, I ran all the way home and I hid like a baby."

Giovanni couldn't imagine what his boy had gone through that day, but from the little he'd said it sounded as if it had been more than enough for a child.

"No, Franco," he soothed, "you couldn't have helped him. If you saw the wolves, you know you couldn't have fought them."

"But you did, didn't you?" The boy had always been sensitive.

"I had help," he said. "I had lots of help." He touched the dagger in his pocket.

"Let's go," he said, and they stood up. "We can be with your mother in a short while, if we're careful."

He retrieved his submachine gun from the floor, checked to make sure it was cocked, and then took Franco's hand. "We have a lot to talk about," he said.

As they walked out of the building and into the dangerous night, Giovanni wondered why his wound hadn't bothered him in a while.

Chapter Nineteen
Endgame: Fourth Day

Killian

He padded to the door with vague thoughts of the paper, a breakfast burrito, and then yet another day of trying to find something he could pin on Nick Lupo.

He'd heard the telltale *thump* of the paper hitting his condo door, but it was later than usual. Killian was always one of the first cops on the job, but today he'd lain in bed longer, both thinking about Lupo and dreading going to work.

The Grim Reaper having a crisis?

Nothing a few minutes under the shower wouldn't help, then a pasty burrito with today's headlines, and finally a thoughtful drive in to work.

He opened the door.

And jumped back, startled, when a bloody head that had been propped against the door flopped inside and landed on his bare feet, leaving them bloody.

"Jesus Christ!" he burst out.

It was David Marcowicz, but barely recognizable.

Killian crouched and reached down to touch the corpse. Marcowicz's head had been partially scalped, and several abrasions were still leaking blood. He was missing his fingertips and the tips of his toes, and Killian could see various cuts, jabs, slashes, slices, spread out here and there on the white-skinned doctor's pear-shaped body.

"Lupo!" he whispered, fury making his veins cold.

The fucking bastard had killed Marcowicz and dumped him on Killian's door, literally on his doorstep.

My God, what won't the bastard do to get me?

First there had been the Tom Arnow blackmail, and taking the blame for an accidental shooting that wasn't accidental. Now Lupo was upping the ante. The rogue cop would do anything to get him, Killian realized.

There was still no one in the hallway.

He stumbled back inside and snatched his cell from the foyer table. He started dialing Bakke's direct number to report the crime, but his finger halted after five numbers.

"*Goddamn it!*"

He dropped the cell back inside and instead grabbed poor Marcowicz under the armpits, dragging him inside his place. The stumps of the sheared-off fingers and toes leaked a small amount of blood—he'd been killed hours ago, fortunately—and Killian made sure no one had seen him with the body, then closed the door, gathered up some cleaning supplies and scrubbed the hallway carpeting as best he could with a light bleach mix.

The smell of death and bleach cloyingly in his nose, Killian locked his door and looked down at the psychologist, who'd never break confidentiality on anyone else.

Clearly, Lupo had learned of the doctor's indiscretions and paid them both back in the only way a thug knew—with murder and a murder charge.

"Fuck him," Killian muttered.

Lupo

He had a fucking appointment with that idiot, Marcowicz, and although he'd intended to blow it off—blame the task force work, of course—part of him had to admit that talking about some of his problems had been helpful. Even talking to that idiot, who did say all the right words.

Marcowicz hadn't laughed in his face when Lupo had confessed that he sometimes saw and talked to that ghost version of his friend Sam Waters. Well, he'd low-balled the number of occasions, of course. He'd said he *sometimes* saw Ghost Sam, when in fact it was fairly often.

Lupo was a little worried that Marcowicz was feeding Killian information. He'd suspected it, but couldn't prove it. Part of him wanted to catch the good doctor at it. Part of him just wanted to talk. He'd been able to talk to Jessie before, but lately they were bickering too much. The sex was still great, but it was starting to become a rarer and rarer occurrence—too often they weren't together, and when they were they didn't talk for fear of each other's problems.

He stood at the doctor's office door and knocked. He'd sent off the dozen officers Bakke had assigned him on various tasks, one of them to haunt the ME's office until paper came out of it. Others followed up minor leads for which Lupo had little hope, and otherwise he was free until DiSanto tracked him down.

No Marcowicz. No note, no email, no voicemail, no hand-written "be back shortly" note on the door.

Shit, he's blowing me off.

That was too funny.

Okay, he decided he'd leave the doc a *what-the-fuck* voicemail and get on with his day's work. Bakke had popped in to ask about progress. Lupo stonewalled. Bakke said he'd hold off the pressure a while longer, but soon it would hit the fan. He hoped no other little old ladies got themselves butchered in the meantime.

Lupo knew he had a day or two at most, then they'd feed him to the wolves.

All he could do was pray the enemy wolf wouldn't be one of them.

Killian

Fuck!

He couldn't take the chance of calling Bakke. He'd be nuts to accuse pretty-boy Lupo of this fucking murder without any proof, and in the meantime *he* looked pretty good for the murder himself.

After all, he couldn't explain it other than being Lupo's handiwork. And Bakke had already made clear that he'd take his homicide cops' word over that of the IA guy.

Goddamn that bastard Lupo.

All Killian's work, achieving his status, doing his bit to clean up a spotty department, all turned to shit.

Maybe his Grim Reaper days were over here in Milwaukee.

As soon as he figured out how to get the body out of his place, he was going to return Lupo's favor.

Somehow.

Lupo

Simonson and Lupo were standing on the corner near the downtown precinct. Simonson had called Lupo just after Bakke had implied how little time they had before the story blew up. Lupo wouldn't have given Simonson the time right then, but since he was convinced his interest in Wolfpaw and the current murder cases were connected, he decided to listen to what the guy had to say.

"I got some inside intel on the big guy's visit to the Washington compound," Simonson said, his voice rising to beat the cold wind that had arisen suddenly. "We might have a window of opportunity without part of his protection detail. He's got an Alpha Team permanently assigned to him, but he gave them an assignment out of state."

He huddled in his coat, the tip of his neck tattoo peeking from his collar. The time he'd spent in the desert had spoiled him, he admitted, and the blustery cold of the winter's early arrival was hard to take. His breath bloomed in a cloud around his ruddy face.

"How do you know?" Lupo rubbed his face in unconscious skepticism.

"Man, I was highly placed, for a while. I still have contacts."

"That you can trust?"

"Rock solid. Not everyone in the company likes to see the wolves terrorizing innocent people before butchering them. There's others like me, getting ready to do some damage. I latched on to you 'cause you're already responsible for doing some. Man, they hate you."

Lupo smiled thinly. "I tried, but not hard enough. I miscalculated. Thought there were a few wolves in the ranks, not that the whole outfit was based around them."

"Yeah, well, there's a shitload you don't know, and it'd take us a month to get you on the page. But all that matters is taking down the head. The snake dies, man."

Lupo nodded. "I see it, but I'm kinda busy right here with these murders. You gotta give me some time."

"Time's running out. The window I mentioned will close. Sigfried's gonna walk from the hearings clean as the snow on Mt. Everest. And when he does, he'll be free to deal with you, with me, and with every other wart on his ass."

"Okay, okay. Let me clear my desk. We'll talk—"

"Well, well, Lupo, aren't you going to introduce me to your friend?"

Shit.

"Heather. I was just pointedly not thinking about you."

"I'm sure. Well, what about that intro?"

She'd approached on his blind side, all legs and breasts and newly dark hair. Her leather Harley jacket heightened the shape of her body. Simonson smiled appreciatively.

"Geoff Simonson, this here's Heather Wilson, investigative journalist and sometime news anchor."

And werewolf, and fulltime royal pain in the ass.

They shook hands as both said "Pleased to meet you" at the same time and laughed.

"Investigative journalist, huh?" added Simonson. "I saw you behind the barricade at a crime scene, didn't I? No inside access?"

"Yeah, well, some people are always putting rods through your spokes, you know?" Heather smiled widely and tilted her head at Lupo. "He's tough to get through to."

"So that was the boyfriend ploy?"

"Um," she started, and faltered.

190

"What boyfriend ploy?" Lupo said. He looked from one to the other until the two of them broke into laughter.

"Had to be there," Simonson said.

"Yeah," Heather agreed. They eyed each other.

Is this lust? Seriously?

Lupo frowned, disgusted. "Look, I got things to do. You want to carry on, go ahead without me. Simonson, I'll get back to you." He nodded and stalked away, feeling their eyes on his back.

Wilcox

He'd lost her in the casino, its barn-like structure and rows and rows of slot machines stretching in every direction the eye could see perfect for losing a tail.

Not that she could know.

She might have recognized Wilcox, once. But the scars had changed his looks enough that he was just another accident survivor looking to parlay a settlement into a fortune. He fit right in.

Unfortunately, he just couldn't pick up her trail. He might have tried sniffing her scent—she had a nice one, very tender—but there were too many conflicting smells inside the giant building.

Shit.

His instructions were to stick with Jessie, the woman doctor, and to snatch her if the word came down that Mordred wanted a lever to use against Lupo.

He wasn't sure he understood his role in the plan, but it was not his to wonder why, as the man had said. His was but to do and die. Except the dying part.

If he could find a way to get some payback against that bastard Lupo, though, it would be sweet.

Eating his lovely fucking girlfriend would sure be perfect payback, Wilcox figured.

Killian

He scarfed down another convenience store burrito, felt the bloating in his gut and belched aromatically in the car.

Fuck, at least it helped cover up the smell coming from Marcowicz.

The psychologist was stashed in the trunk.

What the fuck else could he have done, Killian thought, mentally berating himself for allowing himself to play Lupo's obscene game.

He'd watched enough bad movies to have an idea what he could do. He'd known enough about cleaning up crime scenes to know that if he avoided getting his own DNA on the body, it might still have Lupo's, and he could plant the body outside Lupo's place and call in the cavalry. He'd used an old carpet he'd seen in the basement of his building. It had been there for months, and who knew what weird cocktail of DNA it would have—but not his. He was very careful.

Sure, it was unorthodox.

Hell, it was madness!

But Lupo had changed the rules when he'd shot that cop and implicated Killian. His life had swirled down the toilet after that point, his reputation on the line, his sanity taking a hit, and his memory playing tricks on him. The nightmares, the sweats, the trembling hands. The already poor digestion going to hell whether or not he indulged his obsession for the mushy packaged burritos.

Carrying poor old Marcowicz down the stairs and tossing him into the car had almost been too much. The only good thing about the little guy was that he hadn't been as heavy as he looked.

Turning the tables on Lupo had become so much a part of his daily life that he'd been neglecting other IA business. Now finally was his chance to fuck Lupo over. The bastard had hoped to fluster him with his handiwork, but it was Killian who'd get the last laugh.

The pressure and burning built up in his chest.

As he drove toward Lupo's, Killian wondered whether perhaps he hadn't lost his mind.

DiSanto

He hung up the landline and stared off into space for a long minute. Now, what was the deal? He was technically off the clock, because this had come out of nowhere and wasn't related to the task force.

Or was it?

At the very least, it was of interest to Lupo due to the name Wolfpaw entering into it. What to do? Tell Lupo and risk him wasting his time on this? Not telling him would probably piss him off.

DiSanto'd reached out over the state PDs for any weird crimes that had anything to do with wolves. Given Lupo's facial expressions, he'd connected the Lenny Wolf murder to the Wolf Liquor massacre to the "wolf lady" slaughter through the word "wolf." Shit, DiSanto wasn't the best cop ever, he knew that, but he didn't have to be told the connection was there, however weird.

So he'd put out the word, and now he was getting something back.

Minocqua PD had just gotten off the phone with news of a recent fire that had burned down a fancy house on the lake. Now, Minocqua wasn't so far from Eagle River, so the location set DiSanto's alarm bells ringing right there. Eagle River was where half the weird stuff Lupo'd been involved in had gone down.

So, strike one.

The fire had been set to cover up evidence in a bunch of killings. Maybe murders, maybe murders and a suicide. Maybe the fire was related to the murderer or maybe not. The cops had gotten lucky, though, because the house had been built out of cinderblock, as many all-season homes in that North Woods area had been in the past, and the fire had missed some secret improvements built into the house's tough core. Several secret compartments had yielded intriguing finds— weapons and relics melted into slag but still identifiable. And a small laboratory beneath the house, with a fair amount of notes seemingly pointing to the study of wolves.

Strike two.

The family who'd lived in the house, husband and wife and three kids, had all been dead. Looked like the husband had done the rest of the family, then posted a sort of suicide note on a blog they'd found coincidentally.

Shit, took some fucking balls to slit your kids' throats.

Anyway, Minocqua cops had done some digging and found the husband was a scientist—a fancy-ass biologist or whatever—and he worked at a mysterious laboratory facility near Eagle River. A facility owned by a shell corporation and then apparently traced to Wolfpaw Security Services.

Strike three.

DiSanto tapped a pen against his teeth. Checked his watch. Tapped some more.

What to do?

Tell Lupo and he'd go off half-cocked.

Not tell him and there'd be hell to pay, especially if this *did* wrap around to link with their murder spree. The connections to Wolfpaw had to mean something. DiSanto had left his name with the Minocqua cop, assuring him they'd be in touch.

No percentage in keeping it quiet. He called Lupo. He got voicemail, left a cryptic message. Lupo'd tried to see Marcowicz and then had taken off. Maybe Lupo would want to drive up there. The house and laboratory were both still crime scenes, and the cop had whispered something about them being "weird as fuck-all," a phrase DiSanto fully committed to swiping.

He itched to get hold of Lupo and decide whether they'd drive up or commandeer the MPD's chopper. He'd always wanted to do that.

He left Lupo a Post-it in case he showed up, then headed down for a fresh Starbucks and a cookie.

Mordred

Good surveillance software was part of the package, and Mordred had the best. Way back when that bitch Falken had hacked into Lupo's email, they'd been able to stay ahead of the unpredictable cop. But Mordred had gone a step farther. Wolfpaw's connections as a government contractor included feelers into the nation's cell phone providers, and that included one of the easiest to intimidate, AT&T. Mordred had been able to call in and listen to recordings of Lupo's ingoing and outgoing calls and voicemail.

This partner of Lupo's had made a jump Mordred couldn't have predicted. The Minocqua mess was hanging out there. They hadn't even been able to send out a wipe team—not once the cops were involved. The jackass white-coat who'd cracked—what was his name?—had left a fucking blog entry behind, and maybe had started the fire, but he'd fucked it up, and now there were clues out there that hadn't been expected.

DiSanto's message to Lupo had been detailed but only to a point. He'd left the best for a face-to-face.

Mordred was in the van, idling, when he spotted the young buck leaving the precinct.

Mordred had been bred for instinct. He remembered his lessons well. All too well.

He drove the van to within ten feet of the oblivious cop, pacing him from behind. Clearly, it would have been better if he could Change and lunge from the van, tearing the fucker apart. But this was a fairly busy downtown area, and not the woods. Better to strike out in a more urban way. The cop turned the corner and seemed to be heading for the coffee shop a ways down, past the alley.

Mordred made the turn, then gunned the engine and jumped the sidewalk, trying to pin the bastard against the wall.

At the last second, DiSanto must have come out of his daydream, heard the engine. He turned and saw the van coming. And leaped out of the way, the bumper hooking his jacket and nearly flipping him.

Fuck!

The van's nose was now edging into the alley, and the cop was still within his crosshairs. The window was down, and the silenced HK 9mm was in his hand.

He started to bring up the bulky muzzle to end it right there. His finger was bringing pressure on the very light trigger.

But he stopped and lowered the pistol.

A small crowd had just exited the coffee shop, and one of them pointed at the van-and-pedestrian tableau.

Mordred was already risking the operation, trying to take out the cop on the street. Taking out a group of witnesses would only complicate things.

Swearing, he dropped the pistol, hauled on the wheel and swerved back onto the street, jamming the accelerator and making the van smoke as it burned rubber.

Behind him, a stunned DiSanto stood on the street, checking his torn coat and shaking his head.

Bad move, thought Mordred. Sigfried wouldn't be pleased at his ineffectiveness this time.

His head started to throb.

Heather

After meeting, they'd exchanged cell numbers. Heather called him, and he'd said he was busy right then, but free later.

So later they'd gone for drinks at one of the Water Street watering holes—which one? Heather had forgotten, they were all similar—and she'd bought him a beer because he seemed a beer type.

He'd bought her a gimlet, and she'd laughed at him and gotten herself an extra dry martini.

Simonson seemed haunted by what he had seen. His eyes were like deep-water pools, like *cenote*, the sacrificial wells of Central America. Deeper than they looked, possibly full of treasure—and skeletons.

He told her some of what he had seen, both in and out of Wolfpaw uniform. He'd seen things done by his own friends and colleagues, and he'd seen things done by the military—most of it done to innocents, and he swore it had changed him.

He suggested he was suffering from a form of PTSD. She couldn't contradict, for she wasn't at all sure. But he seemed to get more and more tense the longer he talked about it, and his eyes suddenly seemed to have glazed over. His voice faltered.

"Simonson," she said again.

He was somewhere else. One of his hands trembled. His muscles stiffened under his clothing. His breathing turned rapidly ragged until she thought he would hyperventilate.

"Simonson, are you all right?"

He looked at her as if they'd not met.

Shit, how do you use a source who's going wobbly on you? Was this guy in need of a hospital?

"Simonson!" She grabbed his trembling hand and felt the muscles and nerves under his skin rippling like writhing snakes.

Jesus.

She looked around for inspiration. The place was half empty, a barn-like room kept under capacity by the late hour and a shaky economy. Not much help to count on. She gave him her water glass.

"Here Simonson, drink."

He took the glass as if it were an explosive device.

Maybe in his mind, it was.

Veins stood out under his neck tattoo, in his arms, and the backs of his hands. He put the glass down.

There went any help she could get from this guy. If he was so unreliable, how much could Lupo count on him? Of course, Nick Lupo was annoyingly naïve, so he probably didn't see a problem. But as far as she could tell, Simonson was a basket case ready to spill its goods.

Suddenly his breathing slowed and his large body seemed to relax, his muscles slackening. He seemed to be coming back, wherever he'd been. Maybe there was something to the post-traumatic stress thing.

"You all right?"

He blinked and glanced around as if he'd been asleep and unaware of where he was waking up. "Yeah," he said. "Where were we?"

They spent a few minutes going over what he had seen in Iraq and elsewhere, and he assured her he was committed to bringing them down. "They did something to me, and I want them to pay for it."

She couldn't help admiring his ripped physique. His muscles rippled when he moved. When he smiled, which was rare, the dark and scary eyes lit up for a moment. His hair would have been a lustrous color, if not cut military length. His jaw was strong, his neck below corded with muscle. He could have passed for a linebacker. She'd had a few.

"Have to make a visit," she said, smiling into his eyes and patting his hand. "Be right back."

He nodded absently, as if he were about to take that other road again.

The bathroom was large and surprisingly clean. She stared at herself in the mirror and liked the new look. It was too bad she'd have to shed it soon. She fixed her dark make-up and wondered about Simonson. Almost made her wet, right there, thinking of that strong body all over hers.

He was playing some sort of game with Lupo. She sensed it. Was he using Lupo? Maybe Lupo thought he was using *him.* Either way, the distrust she'd seen on Lupo had faded a bit, and he seemed ready to partner with this guy.

And she had to admit, he *was* fascinating.

The door opened behind her, and she started to turn away to leave the space to the newcomer, when she heard the *click* of the lock.

"No, don't move."

It was Simonson.

He was behind her, his outline visible in the mirror. His hands were on her back.

"What are you—" she started, hoarsely.

"Shh, let me feel you," he whispered, and his voice was gentle, belying the rough exterior.

She felt his hands on her back, spreading, kneading downwards. His fingers were strong, like ten steel rods applying gentle pressure that she sensed could become rough at any second. It made her tingle in all the right places.

She looked for his face in the mirror, moved her head, and saw him sniffing her hair.

Shit.

Had she known it would end up like this all along?

His hands roved on her back, but then they slowly wrapped around her torso and cupped her breasts. His groin ground her pelvis into the sink, and she had no trouble feeling his excitement growing behind her. She let her head loll back, and now his rough face scraped her cheek and she inhaled his scent that reminded her of wood smoke, gunpowder, and some kind of manly soap, like Lava. Did they still make that? It reminded her of her father's workshop.

His fingers found her nipples, squeezed, alternating.

It drove her crazy, and she felt herself melting, melting. *Damn him.*

His tongue then started twirling around her ear, circling a few times before leaving a cooling trail on and around her lobe.

She *hadn't* known it would end like this, but she'd been hoping, hadn't she?

The alternating attention to her ear and her nipples was maddening.

Since he was silent anyway, she pulled her head away from him and angled it so she could trap his tongue with her lips, and he let her. She sucked on its squirming tip and then nipped at it with her teeth, then he resumed the assault, and she took more of it into her mouth as if she could swallow it whole. Their lips met as they tasted each other's tongues, and his fingers squeezed her nipples harder and harder, making her groan with desire into his mouth.

He stopped suddenly and pulled away, and she thought she'd go crazy, but then he was ripping at the buttons of her pants and peeling the fabric down her thighs. His nose buried in her neck now, his hands went for her panties, which were wet by now, and he twisted them down her thighs as well, exposing her buttocks to his hands.

Kneading her flesh there, he nosed her head around again and fitted his lips over hers and they stood like that, their heads almost touching the mirror, his body cupping hers from behind.

If he doesn't unleash himself soon, she thought, *I'm going to rip his pants apart.*

She needn't have worried. He groaned now and, without breaking the wet connection of their lips, took his hands off her tingling butt cheeks. She felt his pants sliding roughly down his thighs, and then he was freed and prodding at her crack.

Jesus, he's enormous.

Heather opened her eyes and looked into his as they kissed. His erection parted her folds below and entered her slowly, maddeningly. His eyes were swirling like kaleidoscopes with specks of gold dust floating in and out.

She groaned as his full length entered her and found herself grasping the sink as if she intended to crack the porcelain into pieces. Her head was angled painfully so she could continue their rough kiss, but she didn't care about a sore neck tomorrow. All she cared about was taking as much of him as she could into her body. They ground together as he thrust slowly in and out, reaching her depths and then depriving her over and over. His fingers pinched her nipples oh, so painfully through her blouse.

She could see the two of them in the mirror from the corner of her eye, and they seemed to be a two-faced creature joined at the lips and at the genitals, rocking in their spooning position and moaning with pleasure.

He withdrew once again and she pushed into him, wanting him back, but he backed up and lowered his hands from her nipples and spread her legs farther apart so he could have better access.

Heather knew where he was headed, and she changed the angle of her body so that he could maneuver more easily. She felt the thick head of his erection tickling her puckered hole and forcing its way in. She spread her legs even farther and hissed at the intensity of his inexorable thrust. Her lips mashed on his, tongues wrestling, their eyes locked on each other's. He slowly invaded her with his fullness and took her breath away. He was breaking her in half, and she rammed herself backward onto him, crazed with the sensations.

She closed her eyes and let him ride her and taste her and gobble her up.

She felt the wolf inside howling to break free and pushed her down, trying to keep her from erupting out of control. Then she opened her eyes and—

Jesus, he'd started to change, and the eyes that stared into hers were the cold, gray-green eyes of a monstrous wolf.

The hands on her nipples were paws, and she knew that he had gone over.

Simonson was a werewolf?

His thrusting and panting intensified, and she felt herself coming and...

Jesus Christ, I'm going over!

She knew the gray fur was shooting up along her torso and back, and she was not really quite human anymore as his massive orgasm rocked her altering body and triggered her own orgasm and she turned her fangs and nipped his face and he yelped and bit her shoulder and then they were riding out the waves and there was pounding at the door and a voice asking if she was all right.

And then he was Simonson again, still thrusting into her but becoming flaccid now and the sweat was pouring off him and onto her clammy skin—and she was no longer certain he'd gone over at all. No, she'd come close, but she had imagined it. She hadn't gone over, but she'd *felt* as if she were about to. And he hadn't, but part of her fantasy had included his Change—except he wasn't a wolf.

He *was* panting with exertion, however.

The pounding at the door finally broke her reverie, and they pulled apart and covered up, replacing peeled clothing as well as possible. Heather opened the door while he hid behind it and assured the woman, a waitress, that she was fine, just overcome with a quick illness.

He grinned at her as she pushed the door shut in the woman's face.

"You're, uh, quite something," he said. "I could have dreamed wild dreams of you in the middle of every fucking Iraqi night I ever had to live through."

"That was good, Simonson. Now let's get out of here before they call the EMTs and a Jaws of Life to break me free." She did a quick repair job on her smeared face.

Then they sidled out one at a time, and he pretended to emerge from the men's. They met at their table, disheveled and hungry.

"Did you feel anything...*strange*...going on during that?" she asked him after they'd ordered new drinks and started cooling off.

"Like what?" His eyes, now gone back to military-cold, gave nothing away.

"Nothing. I just had a really intense experience, that's all."

199

"Me too, Wilson, me too."

"So are you helping Nick Lupo with his takedown of Wolfpaw?" She was all business now. Pleasure was over. Great, but done. Now it was back to what she'd wanted to talk about.

"I plan to. I know where the company's inner council is meeting, and I can get us in there."

"And then what?"

He grimaced. "Depends on how dirty your friend Lupo is willing to get. If he's on the level, then we can end it."

Suddenly his eyes widened as if lightning had just struck him.

He rubbed his head so hard the veins in his forearms threatened to pop.

"What's wrong?" she said, concerned despite herself.

"Nothing, just a headache." He groaned.

She reached out a hand to touch him, but he pulled away. Not before she felt the intense heat of his skin.

"I'm all right," he insisted, but his eyes evaded hers. He gathered up his jacket and stood, a bit unsteadily, and tossed money on the table. "I'll be in touch."

"Sure," she said, but he was already walking away. She wondered what had just happened. She'd call Lupo and warn him about Simonson's flakiness. Then again, Lupo was a big boy.

Heather stood, feeling the violence of their union from her pelvis all the way down to her toes. She was still tingling.

The wolf inside was restless, aroused and feeling thwarted by her reversal.

Chapter Twenty

DiSanto

He showed off his torn coat and related the story of the van's near miss.

"He almost pancaked me against the wall, Nick. But then it's like he regained control and steered off the curb and zoomed off. Like the movies."

"No tag number?" Lupo said, shaking his head.

"Oh, I fucking well looked, but it was obscured. Mud, maybe."

"It could be our guy, but why would he be gunning for you? And then why not finish the job?" He grinned. "Not that I'm saying he should've…"

"He had a window half down. I saw a flash, could have been a muzzle. Maybe he was gonna do me. But he spooked. There were people on the sidewalk, coming out of the coffee shop."

"Hm. Go back to the first question. Why?"

DiSanto smiled a secretive little smile. He sure liked having something to share that Lupo didn't have.

"I did get some info from up north that might link to your old friends, and maybe if you're right about this guy with the wolf obsession being connected too, then it's a linear connection, right?"

He explained about the Minocqua killings and the fire, plus the strange findings in the burned-out house. He said, "Maybe we need to make a quick trip up there, check this Wolfpaw lab for ourselves. Whattya think, will Bakke spring for the chopper?"

"Unlikely, plus we'd better not imply we're checking into something too far afield. We know the possible connections, but Bakke's a hard sell."

"Okay, it's a long drive. When?"

Lupo considered. "Tomorrow. Get all our ducks in a row."

DiSanto looked around the squad room. All detectives under them had been assigned to canvass the three crime scenes. The others were handling the squad's regular caseload. The place was deserted. Even Killian's office was dark, and DiSanto didn't think even he was creepy enough to hang out secretly. He frowned.

"Nick, I think it's time you told me what the fuck's going on with you and this Wolfpaw outfit. I ain't stupid. Mrs. DiSanto didn't raise no hayseed. I get all the wolf shit connecting these things, and I get the whole evil contractor thing. But then there's all those fucked up animal attacks. Eagle River, Wausau, here..."

Lupo said nothing.

"Also, tell me why Killian has it in for you—or I'm asking for a new partner."

Lupo still said nothing.

DiSanto snapped his fingers in front of Lupo's face.

"Earth to Mr. Lupo." He pointed at his own chest. "Me, partner. Me, not stranger."

Lupo grimaced. "I'm not keeping you out for any reason other than to protect you—"

"That's not working," DiSanto pointed out. "Look at what happened to my coat."

"I'll get back to you."

DiSanto grinned. He knew when Lupo was backing down.

Lupo

They argued about it half the night, but in the end Jessie had to agree that Nick's back was against the wall on this one.

"He laid it on the line with me, Jess. He said: 'Tell me why Killian has it in for you—or I'm asking for a new partner.'"

She looked pained. The younger cop was a good guy, and she clearly hated to hear he was feeling trapped by secrets.

But he was, of course. They all were.

"You know what happened after we told Tom," she reminded him.

"But knowing about me and the condition isn't what got him killed," he retorted.

At least, not as far as you know.

No, she didn't know that Tom had asked Heather to make him a werewolf so he could seek revenge for the slaughter of his family. She didn't know that it was Ghost Sam who had whispered in Lupo's ear all about it, giving Lupo no choice but to murder his friend—how many revenge-seeking werewolves could he allow to exist? He had just recently learned that lycanthropy wasn't isolated to just him, or even just a few individuals, but that there were many more like him. Allowing Tom Arnow to be one of them would have made life more difficult, though now his conscience wouldn't be bothering him so much.

And he'd second-guessed himself ever since.

Why kill Tom Arnow but allow Heather Wilson to live?

Only Ghost Sam suggested he'd done the right thing, and who thought it was a good idea, listening to ghosts?

"It may not have gotten him killed directly," Jessie agreed, "but it sure led to it in the end."

"Jess, I can't keep lying to DiSanto. He's my partner."

"You could lie to him if it's for his own good. We lie to each other all the time. For good reasons, I mean."

Wow, touché—I didn't see that one coming.

He let it go. "Issues are separate. How can he really have my back—and me his—if he's unaware of everything that complicates my life? Maybe this would all be useful in the long run. Maybe keeping less secrets is the key."

"And maybe he'll consider you a monster and put a bullet in your back the first chance he gets."

"You still have a stash of silver ammo, Jess," he said, very quietly.

She flared up. "I thought we'd agreed it was important to have some handy—not so I could put you down, but because of those others. You're trying to blend the two, but they're separate issues too."

"Okay, stalemate," he said. He was tired of fighting.

"But?"

"But it doesn't help me deal with DiSanto, who's hot to know why Killian wants to get me. If I show him the truth, I can also be more truthful about the complications that caused me—us—to do some things we're not always proud of."

"Yeah, and maybe he'd still see you as a monster and bide his time."

He raised his voice. "Welcome to it, then. Some days I wouldn't mind being put down. What's the point of trying to do good things if you keep getting shoved against the wall?"

Jessie looked at him as if she could read his mind. He had to be careful. He'd done things he wasn't proud of, sure, but did he want to come clean on any of it?

"Nick," she said softly, "I don't want us to fight anymore. If you think your partner needs to know, then I'll back you up." She tried to smile, but her lips quivered. "I don't want us to lose what we have, not over silly arguments."

But it wasn't silly, was it? Bringing DiSanto into the fold meant Lupo's cover would be blown and, on a daily basis, Lupo would be exposed to his partner's whims, biases, and fears. Nothing would ever be the same.

He told her that.

She nodded gravely. "Nothing will ever be the same."

DiSanto

The drive to Kettle Moraine State Park, a ways west, wasn't particularly long, but he couldn't help wondering what all the secrecy was about.

If this had been an episode of *The Sopranos* he'd have to worry they were gonna whack him when they finally reached the woods. They were following Dr. Hawkins's banged-up Pathfinder in Lupo's Maxima. They'd set the whole thing up and sprung it on him over coffee. He liked coffee enough to go along, but they'd talked to him about how serious this thing they were going to share with him was, and he wondered jokingly if they wanted him to help them with a threesome.

Ha!

He knew it wasn't that. Those two were so pissed at each other half the time they had to be crazy about each other, too, because that was how it worked, wasn't it? It was when you really cared that you took the time and energy to fight. His wife and he had lost that spark a long time ago. She only nagged at him when he was pulled away from a family function she thought he should attend. But otherwise she didn't much care what he did about anything. So if these two fought like cats and dogs, then it meant they were still in the heat of the moment. Or something like that.

Which brought him back to the whole secret trip.

They had a serial killer at large, a strange connection up north to something Nick had already finished with, and then he had that asshole Killian on his ass, but here they were, heading for the woods. Maybe a campfire and a weenie roast would solve all their ills.

"Anything you want to tell me now that we're almost there?"

Lupo drove with exaggerated concentration. Traffic was light—duck and goose season was over for both hunters and huggers, and it was now officially too cold to hang out in the woods without a reason.

"DiSanto, I told you before, this is something you have to see to appreciate. It's not easy for me to share this with you, but I want you to know it's for our own good—all of us—because if we don't go ahead there's a good possibility the lack of knowledge will get you killed. Wolfpaw doesn't fuck around."

"Oh, I know that. There's some pretty bad dudes. You see any clips of the hearings?" He pulled down the shade mirror and finger-combed his hair. He wore it long in the rear, so his natural curls made a little duck tail behind his skull.

"Not much. Believe me, I know more than I need to know about them."

"Yeah, that CEO is a real motherfucker, you can just see it. They're starting to back off on him. Almost like suddenly they're afraid of him, you know?"

Lupo snapped his head around and stared at him a long second before focusing on the dull road again.

"What did you say?"

"Uh, let's— Like some of the congressmen are afraid of 'im now. They're kinda backing off, you know, after reading him the riot act over and over.

"Shit, he's getting to them."

"You think so? I mean, they're congressmen. And a woman."

"Believe me, this guy is the face of the board of directors of that company—and their inner council. They're more connected to the government than an octopus. I think they may have pulled some kind of strings to cow the panel."

Up ahead, Jessie was signaling for a turn off the main road. Looked like a DNR access road and maybe a hidden parking area for rangers and other park workers.

Lupo followed her in and pulled up nearby, not right next to her.

This was a strange place for a meeting. Thoughts of movie rub-outs ran through DiSanto's mind. Would they Luca Brasi him, or would Silvio step out from behind a tree with a rod in his hand? Was Lupo his Michael, regretfully but with steely nerves betraying his partner?

DiSanto was surprised to feel his hands shaking.

"So, we're here, eh?" He felt sticky in the seat. He'd sweated a lot more than he had expected.

Lupo held the wheel a minute longer and bowed his head, sighing.

DiSanto was startled when he saw Jessie Hawkins step out of her SUV with a shotgun in hand.

"What the fuck, Nick?"

This was going too far.

Lupo turned in his seat and looked at him, weary.

DiSanto hadn't noticed before how tired and worn-out Lupo looked suddenly. He powered down the windows a couple inches on each side.

"Listen, nothing's happening to you. The shotgun's for *me*. In case something goes wrong. You don't even have to get out of the car until Jessie calls you. Then you're driving back to town with her. Leave my car here, okay?"

"Shit, man! What the hell are you babbling about?"

"I've done this once before, with Tom Arnow. He knew, and he dealt with it. Now I'm asking you to keep an open mind. I'm not faking anything, and I don't plan to cause you any harm, but what you're

205

about to see will probably change a lot of things you think you know."

Before DiSanto could reply, Lupo climbed out of the car and stepped closer to Jessie's Pathfinder. Jessie kept the shotgun at the ready, not quite aimed. She nodded at DiSanto through the windshield, and he thought he recognized fear and some anger, maybe disagreement with how things were going.

He turned back to where Lupo had disappeared behind the SUV just in time to see him step back out.

Except now he was naked.

"The fuck—"

Then DiSanto shut his mouth with an audible *clack* as his teeth came together hard.

"Jesus H. Christ on a stick," he whispered and almost made a sign of the cross from habit, but his hand lost its way over his chest.

Through the windshield he saw his partner, Nick Lupo, standing naked in the cold country air. He might have checked out Lupo's equipment, nervously, or wonder about the chill, but he was just too flustered. It was cold, but Lupo didn't shiver, no, he suddenly seemed to *shimmer,* and then he blurred as if he were in a photograph and the background stayed in focus but the figure in the foreground didn't... And then Nick Lupo was no longer standing there, but an oversize black wolf turned his head and stared at DiSanto through the auto glass—

And it was Nick Lupo's eyes staring at him!

He swore it was Lupo's eyes, but they were changing color, in fact spinning through a weird range of colors, and his fangs were visible when the beast opened its snout and let out a howl that chilled DiSanto's spine like nothing had in decades, since he'd been a kid.

But something tickled him, too, because this was, after all, something so incredible, so bizarre, that it made him tremble with discovery and wonder.

And he believed.

No smoke, no mirrors.

No, Nick Lupo had become a goddamned wolf, like on TV and in the movies.

Lupo howled again, glanced back at DiSanto and at Jessie, who stood back with the shotgun lowered—but ready—and lunged away from the vehicles, making for the woods in an incredibly fast, four-legged gallop.

DiSanto remembered to breathe when Jessie knocked on his window. She had collected Lupo's clothes, badge and gun, and opened the door and handed them to him.

"Can you put these on his seat, please?"

DiSanto wanted to sound eloquent, but he blubbered.

"I know. Weird, huh? That's our Nick. It's not an easy thing for him, believe me." She glanced around then gestured with a nod. "He's gone for a run. Safe for you to switch cars. We have to be careful." She held up the shotgun slightly. "Silver slugs, just like in the comics."

"Uh uh," he said, nodding. *Sure, why not?*

His hands shook and his fingertips tingled.

"Come on, I'll fill you in a little. And he'll follow us later. Sounds like you guys have a road trip planned."

"Uh uh." He nodded.

Cat got your tongue?

No, the wolf did.

DiSanto

They hadn't been out of the hilly Kettle Moraine area for long when he suddenly grabbed the dashboard and held on as if falling off a cliff.

"Gotta stop the car!" he said, his jaw clenched.

Jessie glanced sideways and saw that the color had drained from DiSanto's face.

The Pathfinder wobbled a little as she scanned the road ahead. Fortunately, there was one of those cloverleafs coming up that would offer limited choices in Gas, Food, and Lodging—looked like the Food was a choice between the ubiquitous McDonald's, a Burger King, a convenience mart and a truck stop with a built-in diner. She swerved off the road and zoomed down the snaky ramp, turned right and zipped into the lot between a half dozen parked rigs and a short row of family sedans near the doors.

The second she pulled to a stop, he popped his belt and door and loped for the restaurant door, leaving her wondering in the car.

DiSanto shoved his way into the place, brushed past an elderly bow-legged trucker with toothpicks in his mouth, found the bathrooms and lunged into the men's.

Thankfully, it was empty. Tinny, stringy Muzak did the opposite of soothe him. He locked himself in, leaned against the sink, and stared at himself. He was pale and drawn, his eyes hooded as if he hadn't slept in days. He held up his hands and watched their reflections shaking. He put his hands down and gripped the sink, but then he felt the vibration in his forearms and when he looked up again, his own face was a stranger's.

Jesus, Nick Lupo was a freaking...

What, what was he—*a werewolf?*

DiSanto allowed his breathing to slow and forced himself to take long, deep draughts of fresh air.

Well, it wasn't quite *fresh*, but it was better than being in the car. Jessie Hawkins was great, and hot, and he'd just seen her tote a shotgun filled with silver slugs in case her boyfriend, *the werewolf*, went crazy and...

Great Scott, Larry Talbot!

He breathed as regularly as possible and replayed the scene in his mind. There was little doubt. He'd already pinched himself. No smoke, no mirrors. He had seen what he had seen.

His heart slowed. Maybe he wouldn't upchuck after all.

Come to think of it, he realized that now some things about his partner made more sense. Some things that he'd almost rather not think about.

When he climbed back in the car, she asked, "You okay?"

"Yeah," he said. "Didn't even hurl."

"Well, that's a start."

"Look, Doc, I like Nick. He's been a great partner. Sometimes he's a little gruff, you know, a little impatient..."

"He's Italian." She smiled.

He liked seeing her smile. And if *she* could smile, maybe things weren't so bad.

"So am I. But I'm a little less tightly wound. But maybe now I know why he's the way he is."

"He's not happy about it. Or much of anything, really."

She started up and nosed the car back onto the road to the freeway.

"I'm sorry about that, back there."

"Don't be." Her eyes seemed suddenly a little watery. "You could have wanted to shoot him. He's normal, you know, except for—"

"The wolf thing."

"Yeah." She chuckled. "The wolf thing."

"Kinda cool, really."

"You'd think. Gets messy though."

They drove in silence for a while.

"Is he worried I won't accept him now?" DiSanto asked nervously.

"We both were."

"No worries. It's kinda like being friends with Bruce Wayne, you know. He's got a secret identity."

She laughed, and he relaxed.

Facing him would be weird, though.

And now that he was on board, where would it all lead?

Chapter Twenty-One

Lupo

He ran on his four massive paws and reveled in the feeling of freedom, the cool fall air riffling though his fur. His nostrils were filled with the myriad scents that made the wolf form so pleasurable to be in.

It was almost like sex, and Lupo had learned over the years that the Change increased libido levels in humans. Though he hadn't advertised the fact with the people with whom he had shared his secret, now he could enjoy the release that made his every cell, sinew, and nerve sing with a strangely alien chorus.

His jaws open to playfully catch the air, his eyes roving the woods as they went past in a blur, the shed leaves crunching under his paws, he loped in a great circle through the strongly scented wilderness area.

Lupo kept himself forcefully in control of the Creature, which would have taken over and hunted fresh meat had he loosened his hold. He'd fought hard to be able to stay in charge of the great animal's body, and even though occasionally the Creature rebelled, Lupo had learned to maintain his human perspective. Even when it was filtered through the animal's eyes, it was still human. When the Creature's instincts were needed, Lupo could allow it more leeway, but if he gave too much it could be difficult to bring himself back.

His nose twitched as he caught the scent of a nearby snack, a rabbit who'd realized too late he was in the open. The rodent made a desperate attempt to zigzag its way out of trouble, but Lupo's Creature was with him every step, his paws reaching out to bat the small, furry speedster to the forest floor now and then.

After a few minutes' fun and games, the Creature accepted Lupo's control and allowed the rabbit to roll himself into a ball and out of the way and hop back into the cover of the woods, mostly not the worse for wear.

Lupo gave the Creature another gallop back to where they'd met and he had left his car.

The Creature couldn't help itself. A loud, ragged howl warned others in his territory that it was there and still hungry.

Just as he reached his car, the Creature's nose caught the scent.

The scent.

The wolf who had murdered the innocent people had been sniffing around his car. And he'd urinated on it, a challenge the Creature chafed to accept. His fur standing up, his snout scrunched and his fangs flashing, Lupo chased around and around the car, growling and finally howling in frustration.

The enemy wolf had circled his car and disappeared in his own vehicle.

Lupo calmed the Creature's rage—but not easily—and changed back. He took his clothes from where Jessie had left them and dressed in quick, jerky motions.

Why was his watcher making himself so obvious? And what was his game?

Safely on the road home, he checked his voice mail and heard Jessie's brief message, which sounded pretty good. He voice-dialed DiSanto's phone, not at all sure what DiSanto would say to him.

"Hey," he said when DiSanto picked up.

"Hey, it's Wolfman Jack."

Lupo wasn't sure whether to grin or frown. Sometimes you just couldn't tell with DiSanto.

"*Teen Wolf. I Was a Teenage Werewolf. The Howling. The Wolf Man. An American Werewolf in London.*"

"What's your fucking point," Lupo growled.

"Just that I've seen those all a dozen times each and never expected I'd be, uh, talking to one of them. Of you. You know."

"*Teen Wolf?*"

"Hey, it's better than Nicholson in *Wolf.*"

"Ironically, in that one they got it kind of right."

"Really?"

"Strange but true."

"Like you."

"Plus they did have Michelle Pfeiffer."

"You've got Jessie—she's, uh, *something*, too." His eyes widened. "Hey, is she also—?"

"No. Remember, she was holding the silver-loaded shotgun."

"Oh, yeah."

"Look, are we still partners? Or are you thinking of sharpening the family silver?"

DiSanto paused to think. "Let's give it a try, Lupo."

"Only if I don't have to watch my back, DiSanto."

"Okay. Can we get a pizza now? I'm starving."

"Me too."

He clicked off and let himself smile a little. Things were going to hell again, but maybe he'd done the right thing, opening DiSanto's

211

eyes. Maybe now his partner would run interference for him with Killian.

While Lupo tried to figure out what the game was.

He was tired of being on one board only to find out the game was different.

Later he dropped DiSanto at his own car and turned back into traffic. They were meeting at the precinct to shuffle reports from the various canvasses and check on the autopsies, which were not likely to be done yet. They'd take some shit from Bakke, who'd taken it from the captain, who'd taken it from the commissioner, who most likely had heard from the mayor.

His phone buzzed and he popped it out of his pocket. It was Heather.

Thought about letting it go, but dammit, she'd brought them some useful information. Did he have to freeze out Heather just because Jessie disapproved?

Granted, he'd been bad. But that was then. He was much more solidly centered now. There was little chance he'd slip up again. Jessie was too good to lose.

"Yeah, Heather," he said after making the quick decision.

"Hey, Lupo. I have some more information to pass on, where are you?"

"On the road back to the squad room."

"I can swing by and talk to you there."

He imagined DiSanto getting a load of Heather and realizing she was a wolf, too. Might not be the best idea.

"Heather, I'd rather come to you."

"Promise?" Said with an obvious chuckle in her voice.

He sighed. "Where are you, I'll drive over and you can fill me in."

She gave him the name and address of her motel.

"No expense account?" he joked.

"Just get here."

Killian

He parked his car right in front of Lupo's old building and belched. The burning in his chest barely subsided.

He had a good set of burglar tools. In New York, he'd had connections in various communities, and he'd been known to bend the rules when necessary in his pre-IA days. He'd planted evidence, he'd conducted illegal searches, he'd tapped a phone or two—all strictly informational, of course. Anyway, he'd been taught by one of the best lockmen he'd ever arrested. He was in Lupo's lobby in seconds, and at his door with his ear to the metal-reinforced door. He listened at the door, but there was nothing. The hall was empty. He popped the several locks easily—paranoid bastard, wasn't he?—and pushed the door open to total silence.

Why hadn't he done this before? All part of a misguided attempt to play by the rules. But when the bad cops didn't play by the rules, why did he have to?

He went downstairs to fetch Marcowicz in his carpet roll. Killian was strong, so he got the whole bundle over one shoulder relatively easily. It was a work day, and the cold weather kept wanderers home. No one saw him. He was up the stairs and dropping the doctor's bundle inside Lupo's door in a minute flat. The halls were empty.

When he turned, a big guy was standing there, right in his face.

He was naked.

Killian looked down, despite himself. *What the fuck?*

The guy's massive dick stood at attention mere inches from Killian. He recoiled back two stuttering steps. Then he looked up again, and the guy's eyes seemed to swirl and change color and, before Killian could process it, the guy's shape blurred. Killian blinked, his throat so tight he couldn't have made a sound.

And then a black wolf stood there, where the guy had been.

Killian didn't have time to make a sound, even if he could have.

Claws flashed, and fangs, and Killian's raggedly severed head went bouncing back into Lupo's place. His blood-spewing body sagged in place and fell in a heap on the doorsill.

The wolf licked its chops, dragged Killian like a sack into the room, then took his time slitting open the belly and nosing inside the squishy guts.

Mmmmmm, burritos.

Wilcox ate his fill.

Heather

When Lupo knocked, she called out, "It's open."

He came in and she was reclining on the stripped bed, her naked breasts thrusting at him like accusations.

"Jesus, Heather, cover up."

She grinned. "Are you afraid, Lupo? Come on, don't be a stranger."

She had always been highly sexual, but the werewolf DNA passed on by the bite of that cruel Adonis, Tef, had somehow entwined with her already enhanced libido and made her even more outrageously hungry for pleasure.

Lupo stood near the bed but far enough away. He was clearly distressed. She cupped her own breasts and pointed the full nipples at him. "You could have these right now."

He sighed. "Heather, I've got things to do. What do you want? Besides *that*?"

She grinned widely and rolled off the bed like a panther. She knew she'd have made a *great* panther. She wondered if there were any werepanthers in the world.

"Oh, okay, spoilsport. Go back to your girl next door. I bet she doesn't do what I can do."

"She does just fine," Lupo growled.

"Oooh, maybe she does. I like that anger, Lupo."

"Get to the fucking point!"

"Mostly I wanted to see you—"

He burst out, "What?"

She continued, "But I also wanted to tell you something about your friend Simonson."

"Simonson? What do you—" His eyes widened. "Oh, no, not him too."

Her eyes flashed. She smiled and came forward quickly, her violet-tipped hand cupping his genitals through his pants.

"Don't tell me you don't like this," she said, panting. "I can tell you do."

Lupo clearly wanted to back up, but he was trapped in her spell. She knew she did this to men. She'd done it to the best of them. She gave his bulge a long, slow caress, then released him. But then she reached his face with her lips and licked him like a she-wolf might her mate.

A low growl erupted from deep in her throat, and she nipped at his lips with her teeth.

He groaned, and she saw him starting to blur. His Creature, as he called the wolf within, wanted a piece of this. She chuckled and let herself start to go over. After Simonson, she'd had a taste for this, a new sensation.

But then he resolidified as Nick Lupo, and his strong right hand snatched her arm and squeezed painfully.

"Cut it out, Heather! I mean it. Don't waste my time with your games."

"You're hurting me," she said. He wasn't, but she liked playing games.

"Simonson. What?"

214

She stared into his eyes and saw that he was no longer hers. She yanked her arm back, pouting playfully.

"Okay, Simonson and I got acquainted. I—can't be sure, but I think he might be one of us."

"A werewolf? Makes no sense. He kept talking about how disgusting he found them."

"Well, maybe he means the bad ones. He knows you wolf, right?"

"He saw my recon into the Georgia compound."

"Where you almost got killed," she said.

"Either way, he's against the bad guys. He knows I killed a bunch of them, and he was glad. Did you see him turn?"

"No, I sensed that he—we—did. Well, we almost did. Maybe it was...just me." She thought about it. Maybe she'd been wrong. "Whatever else he may be, I think he's flaky. If you're going into a situation with him, watch your back."

"Is that it?" Lupo said coldly.

"I wanted to feel you inside me..." she said, hopefully.

"Good-bye, Heather," he said, and slammed the door as he left.

Lupo

He couldn't reach Jessie. She probably had her phone off, so should he try her at home or at the damned casino?

Damn it.

Heather made him angry, but her tidbit about Simonson was useful. The guy seemed wracked with PTSD. Could he trust him?

He still hadn't seen any sign of Marcowicz. There hadn't been any calls of illness or emergencies. Lupo had to wonder—had something happened to the doc because of him? And DiSanto's close call? If so, wasn't Jessie in danger?

He smacked the wheel.

Swing home or hit the casino?

Home was closer, so he zipped through the Marquette and swung north, aiming for the East Side. A throbbing rhythm in the back of his head started up, and he couldn't get the traffic to move any faster. He wished he had a squad car.

Finally he pulled into his street, lined with newly bared trees like the naked arms of famine victims.

He recognized Killian's car right away. He pulled into a space down the block and jogged back to his building.

What the fuck was Killian doing here?

Lupo nodded at a first-floor neighbor. On his floor, his door was ajar.

215

Lupo drew his Glock, racked the slide, and cautiously approached the gap. He nudged the door inward with the pistol's muzzle. He had no idea what to expect, but his mind offered up images of a slaughtered female body. His heart pumped blood loudly through his body, pounding in his ears and all the way down to his fingertips. The Creature stirred down below, but he kept him down.

The door stopped suddenly, and Lupo did indeed glimpse a body lying in a bloody pool, its chest and belly sliced open. But he could see its hands, and they were male hands.

Killian.

He heaved a sigh.

He stepped in, covering the interior of his apartment with the steady pistol. There was another damned body, rolled up in a carpet. After he cleared the rest of the place, finding no trace of Jessie, he closed and locked the door and checked his two guests.

Killian. And Marcowicz.

The enemy wolf had done Killian, obviously.

Marcowicz had been tortured.

Either they knew something, or they were just meant to complicate his life.

He knew the building's super pretty well, and he knew there were several utility carts stashed in the basement. He brought up one of them and loaded in Marcowicz. Then he sacrificed a brand new blanket Jessie'd bought when she moved in and did the best he could with Killian. There were bloody splashes all over, but they were inside the apartment.

He should have called in. These murders were cold-blooded and infuriating, and he was in over his head.

But fuck, how else to play it?

It was well known in the department that he and Killian hated each other, and Marcowicz had probably blabbed about his problems all over. Who'd believe someone had killed them and left them in Lupo's place just to be difficult? He'd be in handcuffs in an hour.

He wiped his brow and stood panting, trying to clarify thoughts in his mind.

He shuttled the bodies down into Killian's car, then called DiSanto and asked him to meet in a couple hours.

Lupo locked up, then drove to where he thought he could keep Killian and Marcowicz on ice. Not too long, but he could make a few calls. Favors were owed him, by some not so nice contractors. There were a half dozen freeway ramps under construction out on the west side. Put the two together?

The worst part would be trying to explain the disappearances. And pretending to look for the missing cops. Lupo wouldn't shed a whole lot of tears for either of them, but this business was now officially out of hand.

He wiped his brow, kept to the speed limit, and drove to the temporary gravesite.

Jessie still didn't answer her phone.

Then he took a call from the nursing home.

He reached the hospital an hour after the initial call.

DiSanto had met him, asked no questions—though he wanted to—and dropped him at his car. His partner had also covered for him at headquarters, where they expected some reports he didn't really want to see from the ME. Bakke was making some noises about his task force head never being around, but following leads was a fairly good excuse.

The hospital smell he loathed immediately lanced into his brain. An artificial flower potpourri valiantly tried to cover it, but couldn't. The stench of decay, deterioration and death lurked beneath the cloying syrupy-sweet. He saw a blank-eyed family in obvious vigil sitting uncomfortably in the lobby. *Add desperation to the stench.*

"We had to send her, Mr. Lupo," the home's administrator had told him on the phone. "I think it's time. She's been in and out with her mind the whole last week, and she insists the pain is unbearable. She refuses to eat and her organs are shutting down. We can only do so much here at the Courtyards, as you know."

He was barely aware of the nurse's gaze as she sized him up. She pointed down the hall and smiled sympathetically when he asked for his mother's room. His mind was cold and blank, or he might have appreciated her interest. It seemed as though the moment was here, much as he had dreaded it the past two years.

His mother had been residing at the assisted living facility of the Courtyards since Frank Lupo had died down in Florida, when she had begun sliding steadily and inexorably into dementia. The cancer had come quickly, recently, and completed the job of destroying this once fiercely independent woman. A woman who had been able to withstand Frank Lupo's tough love.

She lay dwarfed by the bed and the monitors, tubes and cords enveloping her slight form like a science project gone awry. She was a ghost of herself, her body already morphing from life to death. Her eyes were closed but there was motion below the lids.

He knew the administrator was right. It wouldn't be long.

"Ah, Ma," he whispered, "I'm here."

She stirred but didn't awaken. Quietly he slid a chair closer to the bed and found her hand on the white linen covers, grasping the gnarled fingers gently in his. She had fed him and clothed him with this hand, changed his diapers and occasionally even slapped him when he was deemed bad (but those times were few, and she never slapped hard...he always suspected she was protecting him from harsher punishment by his father), and now her skin was turning to lifeless rubber. Closing his eyes, he caressed her hand and forearm up to where the IV fed her nutrients, and feeling her sluggish veins under his touch made dampness squeeze from between his lids.

He sat with her almost an hour before she stirred. He'd turned off his phone—*let'em leave voice-mail, dammit*—and he had pulled the room door shut for some privacy from the scurryings outside. The nurses seemed to understand his need for quiet time. In the near dark, her eyes opened suddenly, and she recognized him immediately.

"*Ciao, tesoro,*" she said. She'd always called him a "treasure" when he was little, and she'd never broken the habit.

"*Ciao, Mamma.*" He couldn't break habits either.

"I knew you'd come," she whispered.

"I always come," he said, sounding defensive despite himself. Tough to spend time with her when his phone buzzed at all hours.

"I know, I mean *this* time. I don't have much...time, you know." She coughed, and it was as if her lung walls vibrated inside her. Pain wrote new lines across her features.

"Don't say that, Ma," he whispered.

She squeezed his fingers with hers. "It's okay. It was a good life. But I want to tell you a story before it's time for me to join your father."

"Ma," he began, settling into his child's role again, and she shushed him with a small smile on the features pinched by pain and disease. Was this her dementia kicking in? So far, she sounded more lucid than she had been in a week or two.

"Let me finish. I have to get this out—it's been in my head a long time." She sighed. "And I never know what's going on in here. I can tell I'm not...not *right*. Like your uncle, remember?"

He did. Did dementia run in the family?

"There are things, Nicolino, things about your grandmother...and your father, that you do not know. I think it's time you knew some of them, before I go away."

The pressure of her hand increased on his, and it was so sudden he thought the moment had come, that death would steal her away before she could finish, anyway. Before he could say goodbye.

But she sighed and said, "It's a little pain, but it's starting to leave me."

"We don't have to talk now," he said. But he knew it had to be, and he *was* intrigued.

She shook her head slightly, almost imperceptibly. "We do have to, Nicolino."

It was what his grandmother had called him. *Nicky* was a diminutive of Nicola, which wasn't really his name, either. He'd always wondered who had chosen *Dominic.* Everybody always preferred Nicholas.

"Your grandmother," she said. "It's about her name."

"What about her name?"

She made a gesture with her other hand, indistinct in the dark room. "More than just that. She wasn't my mother."

The shock made him doubt his ears.

"*Cosa?*" he said. *What?*

The dementia, he thought. *It's back...*

But she looked so *aware.*

"I know it sounds crazy, but I swear I am all here. Whatever is wrong with me is not clouding my mind right now. It might not last long, but..."

She emitted a long, labored breath. Decades of smoking had taken their toll even before the cancer. "I need to tell you. Your Grandmother Saltini was your father's mother. She was a Lupo."

Lupo started to take his hand out of her grasp. "Shhh," he whispered. This was too much.

Her fingers moved more rapidly than they had any right to, snatching his hand before he could pull it away. Her eyes shone brightly in the darkness. "*Listen to me!* She pressured your father when you were very young. My own mother, well, she died while you were still a baby. So Maria made him—both of us—swear never to tell you. And your grandpa, my father, she made him swear too. He was a gentle man, but weak, and he went along even though he didn't like it."

"But—but *why?*" Lupo couldn't believe it. This sounded like something out of *General Hospital*, not his real life. But then, various aspects of his life weren't terribly likely either, were they?

"There were...reasons. They made sense at the time. Many things happened to us when we were children in the war. You know, your father told you some stories."

Frank Lupo had, mostly stories of trouble he and his friends had gotten into. He had talked about the Allied bombings, about the various occupation forces and some soldiers who had befriended him.

Possibly, Frank Lupo had had very little idea how many stories his mother had told young Nick. Or how she had suddenly stopped talking about the war when he had reached a certain age.

"But what were the reasons? Why would she make you deceive me like this?"

Her labored breathing reminded him that she didn't have long. The call had implied she wouldn't last the night, yet now she seemed strangely energized, as if baring her soul had carved out more earthly time. Lupo wasn't sure whether to be thankful for knowing these strange truths, or to be annoyed. But to be fair, could he be annoyed for something that had happened three or four decades earlier?

"You remember your grandmother. She was a...forceful woman. She had very strong ideas. She had lived through some very tough things, along with your father, things she would not speak of very often. There were dark things between your father and his mother— secrets they shared—that they would never divulge to me, or to anyone. I don't think they ever talked about them even between them. They were simply buried, but we all knew they were there."

Her voice faded and she lay, breathing with difficulty, rallying her strength.

"Ma, you should rest now," Lupo said, once again caressing her arm. Then he touched her face and felt the wrinkles there, and—for a second—they all disappeared, and she was the lovely woman his father had married. He wondered what his father would have said if he were here now. Or what he wouldn't have said.

She smiled her motherly smile. She'd always done that when he disappointed her in some way, or when she disagreed with him.

"I'll rest soon," she said. "Don't worry. I wanted you to know about this...this deception because I never liked it. And I wanted to tell you that your grandmother left a letter...for you." She sighed, paused to breathe again.

She continued. "I think maybe she wanted to explain what happened and why, but I don't know. I kept my word. I never opened the letter."

Lupo kissed her forehead. "Thanks, Ma. I'll— Where can I find the letter?"

"I put it with my important documents. It's unmarked, sealed. Yellow edges by now, it's so old. I'm not really sure it was meant for you, but I can't imagine who else she would have wanted to confess to. We didn't discuss it, and then she was gone so suddenly, still young."

His grandmother had died while he was in college, when she was barely seventy.

"I think your father wasn't happy with the deception, Nicky. I think they felt they had to do it, for some reason they wouldn't tell me. It was all about things that happened back in the war, when your father was almost killed right at the end. Nicky, I'm glad you're here."

"It's no problem, Ma," he said. "You know I like spending time with you."

He leaned over to kiss her forehead again.

"Ma?"

And he knew.

Unburdened, and in his company, she had been released.

He touched her face and kissed her skin, which seemed colder already, and let the tears come.

It seemed death was his only friend today.

Later he remembered she had called him Nicky, and the memories tumbled together and laid out events he hadn't thought about in many years.

Chapter Twenty-Two

1968
Nick Lupo

Nicky sat with his grandmother. His hands were splayed across a *Spider-Man* comic book, a really great one in which Spidey was manacled to the center of a huge tank rapidly being filled by huge faucets. *The Kingpin sure looks like he's gonna win this one!* But Nicky knew the big villain didn't. He knew because it was probably the tenth time he'd read this episode.

It was Saturday and Nicky knew he was gonna have to start working on his grandma if he was gonna get to watch *Creature Features* that night. Grampa would gladly watch it with him, but there was no way Grampa would go against anything Grandma said.

Grandma gave all the orders, earned most of the money, and kept both husband and grandson in line with the proverbial velvet-gloved iron fist. Nicky often spent several days at a time with his grandparents because his mother worked long hours and his father was away months at a time, but he enjoyed his stays.

His grandparents—especially Grampa, a gentle man with a soft voice and an artisan's hands—indulged his every whim. Except letting him watch scary movies. Nicky couldn't understand why Grandma was so against the movies he liked best, but he often managed to enlist Grampa in schemes to participate in illegal television watching while she worked, napped, or shopped.

Grampa enjoyed the old Universal horror movies as much as Nicky did. For him it was a treat to sit with his grandson, sipping from a never-ending glass of sweet red wine and thrilling to the antics of heroes and monsters.

Westerns were good, too, but they had Grandma's stamp of approval and therefore proved pedestrian for the young boy who much preferred the forbidden over the mundane. Grampa helped Nicky disguise his television habits so as to avoid Maria Saltini's anger. Nicky often thought of his grandfather more as an older brother, one who needed protection despite his own better instincts.

"There's a monster movie on tonight," Nicky whispered, speaking their Italian-English hybrid. Grampa made a slow, deliberate shrug and tipped his head once, briefly, toward the door through which his wife could be seen, seated in the old armchair with sewing needle and thread engaged in the art of prolonging the life of yet another pair of men's socks.

"Do you wanna watch it?" Nicky persisted.

"*Va bene.*" *All right,* the elder Saltini whispered. "But we'll have to look innocent. She worked today, so she'll be tired tonight. If we don't say anything, it will be okay."

Nicky knew that, for Grampa, staying up late to watch a movie meant a few more illicit sips from the bottle. There was nothing wrong with a little complicity—that way they both got something they wanted. Nicky nodded and they shook hands. The boy's tiny hand was buried in the old man's calloused but gentle grip. His janitor's job had worked the delicateness out of his hands, cleaning toilets somehow eroding the artistry a benevolent God had seen fit to bestow on him in his youth.

Nicky had not noticed this change in his beloved co-conspirator, play partner and friend, but he knew that Arturo Saltini was no longer happy. He didn't know why, really, but there had been much whispering coming from his grandparents' bedroom in the last few weeks, and they didn't realize that the old vents brought the sound right to his headboard. But if watching a monster movie with his grandson and a glass of wine could make him happy, then Nicky was happy, too.

"What are you children whispering about in there, eh?" His grandmother's formidable presence hovered in the doorway.

"We are praying," Grampa said with a sideways wink at Nicky.

"Amen."

The bond was strong, and the conspiracy held. In the silence that followed, Nicky turned another page of the *Spider-Man* comic and waited for Grandma to object. She knew full well they weren't praying—neither the Saltinis nor the Lupos were particularly religious, though all had been raised Catholic.

"I can just imagine what kind of trouble the two of you would get into if I wasn't here to watch over you!" Grandma held her arms akimbo, and she wasn't smiling. "What are you reading?"

"*Spider-Man,*" Nicky stammered. This was an unexpected development. "It's my favorite."

"Let the boy alone, Maria," Grampa began, but Grandma cut him off.

"What about your homework?"

"It's Saturday!" Nicky retorted, his voice rising despite his attempt to control it. "I can do my homework tomorrow." His voice became timid again.

"Half today and half tomorrow," she relented. "No *Spider-Man* until after dinner." She held out her hand and waited until Nicky placed the comic into her palm.

Nicky saw the displeasure cross his Grampa's face, but then he was out of the room and collecting his satchel—which he knew had cost them a lot of money. He felt guilty, listening to the urgent whispering as the argument raged. Grandma won, as he knew she would, and then he was buried in vocabulary and spelling exercises.

After a huge dinner of screw-shaped pasta and chicken simmered in tomato sauce, Nicky eyed Grandma warily when she lowered her arthritis-wracked body into her favorite green cloth armchair. She released a contented sigh and settled back to watch *Mannix* even though the dialogue was too quick for her to catch fully. The images helped her relax and soon she was asleep, lightly snoring while Nicky and his grandfather enjoyed the end of the show.

Mannix was cool, Nicky thought, always getting his man and all, but he wasn't as cool as James West and Artemus Gordon. And he couldn't even compete with the best of *Creature Features*. That theme music, the fog, and those human-beast paws stalking the night!

Now Nicky fidgeted, wondering whether Grandma would go to bed or sleep in the chair—which she said soothed her aching back—because her decision would affect his plans greatly. If she slept in the chair, when she awoke and saw what he was watching she would make him turn it off. If she went to bed, however, he and his Grampa had unimpeded television control. To his relief, Grandma was startled awake during the lame newscast and groaned as she raised her tired body out of the armchair and headed for bed. Nicky smiled at his Grampa, who winked and poured himself another glass of wine. WGN's *Creature Features* it was!

By the time the familiar theme came on and "The Wolf Man" started, Nicky and Grampa were all set with crackers, soda, wine and Oreo cookies. From Talbot's first horrifying transformation, Nicky grabbed hold of his grandfather's hand and watched intently, occasionally sneaking a peek at his hand to see if a pentagram were visible. Or was someone else supposed to see it? He'd have to ask Grampa later.

The movie was so scary that Nicky forgot to eat, and when Grandma suddenly threw open the door and stood surveying their criminal behavior, he screamed and jumped out of his seat.

"What are you watching?" Grandma screeched.

But her eyes bulged as she saw for herself. The wolf man was prowling the foggy English countryside while a pack of hounds bayed in the distance. A close-up of the wolf man's tortured, horrifying visage made her mutter under her breath, and her hand dashed off the sign of the cross in quick, desperate motions.

"Maria," Grampa said, rising.

"Turn it off!" Grandma's scream was so abrupt, so unimaginably loud, that both Grampa and Nicky froze. Grampa stood near the table, and Nicky sat half in and half out of his chair.

She fixed both of them in turn with a foreign stare, her eyes almost glazed with—

With what? What's wrong with Grandma?

And then he saw it. Out of the corner of his eye he saw on the screen the mob close in on the wolf man, whom they would no doubt kill. His grandmother's eyes were riveted on the movie, too, but instead of anger they displayed utter terror.

His grandmother was terrified by the movie, and that made Nicky scared, too.

He looked at his grandmother and her fear, then saw that Grampa clutched his chest for a long second before stepping around the table to go to his wife. He led her out of the room, whispering soothingly and putting his arm around her shoulders, which now seemed slumped and no longer as strong as they had earlier.

Nicky turned again to the movie, but his eyes didn't want to focus on it and so he ran to the set and clicked it off as if the monster inside might get out and attack him.

Even in his youth, Nicky realized that his fears were twofold now. His grandmother's fear had scared him, and badly, but Grampa's sudden movement replayed over and over in his mind. The table seemed strangely prophetic, with the half-empty wine glass on Grampa's placemat. Nicky heard his grandparents' urgent voices from the bedroom, and he wondered if he hadn't just seen the future.

He didn't know where that thought had come from, but he couldn't shake the image until he fell into a dreamless sleep, long after the lights were out.

Chapter Twenty-Three

1970

Nick Lupo

Nicky was only ten, but now he read both Italian and English, due to his mother and grandmother's efforts. Nicky's father, too, had fueled the boy's curiosity since he'd been little, stimulating his desire to learn but in a different way, by answering the many questions the boy posed in his childishly serious way. Frank Lupo was hardly ever faced with a question he couldn't field.

Though the elder Lupo's influence in the boy's life was great, as it often is in an Italian household, his father's long absences working overseas with one European firm after another had given Nicky reason to grow closer to his grandparents and, later, to his mother and grandmother. Grampa would have read with him, too, but Grampa was gone now—taken by a heart attack in the night the previous February.

There had been no monster movies since the night of the *Creature Features* argument, and then a real monster had come for his Grampa and left his Grandma bitter and much older. It had slowly sunk in to Nicky that Grampa would never return.

Then came the shock of the newspaper article that his grandmother would not let him read.

The article was in an Italian-American newspaper from New York that his grandmother read religiously in three- and four-day tightly rolled packets the mailman left on the porch.

Nicky had been lying on the floor, drawing one of his elaborate military dioramas. Sheet after sheet he carefully filled with two-dimensional renderings of a waiting, dug in army, followed by separate drawings showing an advancing, challenging army. The final series always showed the battle in snapshot-like flashes, with explosions and flying bodies just like in the movies. It was a childish blend of art and propaganda-bred militarism.

On days like this, in the middle of a fantasy war as real as the Vietnam images he saw daily on television, Nicky wanted to add realism to his drawings. He reached out and snatched one of Grandma's papers from where it lay, beside her armchair. She was busy reading a different one, wearing a hand-crocheted shawl over her rounded shoulders and her cheap, large-framed man's Woolworth's reading glasses.

Maria Saltini herself was still a large-framed woman but her aches and pains had finally forced her to retire—her arthritis and rheumatism made walking and the handling of objects difficult. She used a cane and could barely lift her silverware off the table. But there was no sharper card player and no social drinker quite like her in the family. As a young girl, she had traipsed the hills of her native village in northern Italy and sung lusty songs of sweet love and bitter parting with her friends, sharing many a flask of hearty wine in the process. The love she had for life was almost as profound as that she had for her family, and her grandson especially.

But when she saw his hand remove the newspaper from the pile near her chair, she reached out much more quickly than her years and her physical condition should have allowed, grasping the crinkly pages and removing them from Nicky's grip in one smooth motion.

"*Non oggi, Nicolino.*" *Not today.*

"Why not? I want to read about the battles."

She began handing the paper back, but then she looked down and read something near the bottom of the front page and made up her mind. "I'm sorry, no. You can read another one." Her voice was stern.

Nicky was a smart boy. He had seen where she'd looked.

He noted also the strange gesture she had made with her left hand and quickly hidden.

"Okay, Grandma," he said, sinking back down to the floor and his battle drawings. He kept the corner of his eye on the coveted newspaper. When she shuffled the pile of newspapers and slid that particular issue into the middle, Nicky could still tell its wrinkled corner apart from the others. He *would* see that article she wanted to keep from him. If not now, then later. He was persistent and cunning. And he knew it.

Nick thoughtfully drew an explosion that tossed coolie-hat-wearing bodies all around. *Howitzer*, he thought, sketching it in inside the good guys' fortress with a series of practiced pen strokes. *They just forgot they had it.*

Later, the house was quiet and Nicky had finished his battle and started on another. It was afternoon naptime, and he was supposed to rest just like the adults. The afternoon nap was sacrosanct, a holdover from the Italian custom of taking a long lunch and a nap and then being productive later into the evening. Nicky knew that in parts of Europe you couldn't even find an open store from noon to three. He liked that custom, and he enjoyed being alone for a while as his elders rested.

He knew his grandmother had forgotten about the newspaper

she'd intended to keep from him because she had left the stack of newsprint near the armchair. Nicky pretended to nap until he heard gentle snores and deep breathing coming from the bedroom and the den.

He held his head up for three full minutes, ready to lower it immediately and feign sleep. Then he rolled to the chair and waited for any sound that might signal he was about to be caught by Grandma, awakened from her nap by the urgent need to keep him from...from what?

His curious fingers located the newspaper in question, and he pinched and gently tugged it out from between the others.

Mission accomplished—just like Mr. Phelps and the IM team.

He rolled back to his original spot and shuffled some of his diorama scenes onto the majority of the unrolled newspaper, whose edges kept curling until he finally tamed it with his own body weight.

Now, what was he not supposed to see?

Nicky could read the Italian words well enough to get the gist of most stories. Common, everyday news stories and reports from Vietnam were simple for him, and his parents or grandmother were always ready to help with unfamiliar words.

The front page headlines this day were political, so he skipped them. There was a brief report of some engagement in Vietnam, but there weren't enough details for him, so he scanned it and moved on.

The bottom of the page. A small, boxed item.

Nicky's heart raced as he read it.

"Uomo-Lupo Siciliano."

Sicilian Wolf-Man.

His breath caught in his throat as the headline sank in. His eyes wide, Nicky read the story from Palermo. His heart quickened and his pulse throbbed in his throat. This had to be what Grandma didn't want him to see.

But why?

Various witnesses swore they had been attacked by a creature that was not a man and yet was too large to have been a wolf. Others reported seeing a naked man in the vicinity of the attacks, fueling speculation that the creature was indeed a man in wolf form during the full moon. Livestock had been butchered and partially eaten. Children had disappeared. Hunting parties armed with the *lupara*, or wolf-gun, had criss-crossed the nearby hills to no avail. Perhaps the wolf-man had swum to the mainland, one hunter said.

Nicky felt the shiver in his back. This was too good!

He'd loved "The Wolf-Man" and the other Universal movies when he managed to see them, but here was a *real* newspaper talking about a *real* wolf-man. He wondered how long of a swim it was from Palermo to the mainland. And from mainland Italy—could such a creature take a plane to North America?

Why, there could be *hundreds* of wolf-men on this side of the Atlantic already!

Now Nicky understood why Grandma didn't want him to see the story. Maria Saltini made no bones about her beliefs. She had seen *things* in her life. He had heard her hushed whispers over the years.

He remembered the story of a suspected witch who was forced by townspeople to attend holy mass in the village church only to break down into hysterical fits when given Communion, and then spitting out a sacred host while shouting obscenities in French, a language she didn't know. He wasn't supposed to have heard that story, of course, but Nicky was accomplished at feigning sleep and enjoyed listening to adults talk when they thought he couldn't hear.

Grandma also told the story of a village witch who sold love potions and revenge spells, and what Italian partisans had done to her when they accused her of betraying their leaders to the German occupiers. Grandma said they had "passed her around" until she was torn and bloody, then they had decapitated her battered corpse and buried it in two graves filled with salt and holy water. Everyone knew that witches could transform themselves into other creatures, and you had to make sure they couldn't come back to their bodies.

While he wasn't quite sure what "passing her around" meant, he was sophisticated enough to let his imagination do the rest. He almost wished he didn't know as much as he did. His bedroom would seem twice as dark tonight, and not nearly safe enough.

Now Nicky reread the news story and let the delicious waves of goose bumps wash over him. Maybe the wolf-man of Sicily was even now stepping off a plane in Chicago. If Grandma had seen such things—and he was certain she had—then his fear of a traveling wolf-man couldn't be so far-fetched. The way his grandmother had tried to keep it from him confirmed his suspicions.

If Grandma's scared, then it has to be true!

Later that night, when the house whispered of darkness and of things too frightening to think about in a bedroom lit only by the crack under the door, Nicky understood why his grandmother didn't want him exposed to the stories of her youth.

He made his usual check of the window, latched and covered by the old-fashioned drawn shade; the sliding closet doors, closed, showing no black gaps; the space under the bed, still vaguely like a dark cavern to Nicky, a cavern out of which some slimy, tentacled thing could crawl.

The Sicilian wolf-man whispered threats to him with a gravelly Italian accent. He had just arrived from the Old Country, menacing all. Nicky was unable to defend himself in any way. The man's gaze, under one long and bushy eyebrow, fixed Nicky with its intensity. The flared nostrils were those of a wild animal.

Nicky knew with absolute conviction that the man could turn into a giant wolf, yet he approached the shadowy form and held out his hand. For a moment the man's face emerged from the shadows and softened, a look something like pity crossing his strong features. He reached out a large hand, slowly, but suddenly it was a claw, and Nicky drew back, frightened.

By the time he looked up again, the man's face had changed—his nose had become a snout, and his clean-shaven cheeks were covered with long, scraggly hair. But it was the eyes which held Nicky entranced... The man's eyes had turned from brown to a shimmering green. In the instant it took for the green eyes to register, Nicky was ensnared by the wolf-man's claws. Fangs had grown in the Sicilian's mouth, now framed by his snarling lips, and he bared the drooling teeth only inches from Nicky's neck.

But when Nicky tried to bring up his *lupara*, the gun was useless, unloaded or jammed. An empty weight.

He dropped the gun and screamed as claws and teeth tore into his skin, shredding layers of fat and flesh, hot wetness flooding from the ragged wounds as he flung himself away from the grasping, red-flecked jaws and into a wet embrace he couldn't identify.

He screamed again as the monster's claws tightened on his arms and he felt the flood at his groin, the sickening hot wetness of his urine released unintentionally into the bedclothes and fouling his underwear and pajamas.

He opened his eyes, his breath coming in hitches.

"No more scary movies for you, Nicolino!" Grandma's voice came from the shadow hunched over his bed, and the claws on his arms were her arthritic hands. Now she pulled away and made the sign of the cross, and that other gesture he had come to know so well.

Her hand made a set of horns. The gesture, his mother had explained, used to ward off evil. He started to cry.

Chapter Twenty-Four

Lupo
>*Christ, I haven't thought about any of that in years.*

At the nursing home, the sympathetic administrator led him to his mother's room, where she left him to meditate. Although he wished to do that, he also wanted to find the letter she'd told him about before dying. He opened drawers, closet doors, and then he turned and Ghost Sam stood before him, his finger pointing at the bedside radio on which his mom had listened to operas before the dementia claimed her interest.

"There?" he asked, and the ghost seemed to nod sadly.

Lupo hefted the old-fashioned radio and flipped it, and there was an envelope duct-taped to the underside.

"Thanks," he muttered, but Ghost Sam was gone.

I'd have found it without his help, he assured himself.

He sat on his mother's bed, smelling her missing presence in the air, and read through the thick sheaf of numbered, yellowed papers covered in his grandmother's spidery hand.

It took him a while, and when he was finished he bowed his head, trying to keep his eyes clear of the tears that clamored to come.

Now he knew so much, and he understood many things no one had ever told him.

He took one last look around at his mother's belongings, all that marked her time on earth other than his memory.

He had to find Jessie. He couldn't lose both women most important to him in one day.

He drove to the casino, his heart heavy.

And his rage building.

Jessie

She turned away from her place at the roulette wheel and there was Nick, staring at her.

It was new to her, the betting on the green felt, and she'd actually doubled her money by judiciously betting on red and black, odd and even, and various spreads on the number columns. She learned by watching, and her chip piles grew. Looked like about five hundred dollars in winnings, give or take a few tens.

The irony was that winning wasn't making her feel better. The opposite—she was miserable.

Could it be that the pathology of her gambling problem centered around her *losing*? Maybe the gambling worked for her only when its effects were negative. Winning, she felt somehow unfulfilled, unhappy. Losing, she felt as if she deserved what she got.

She left a big tip for the croupier, then stepped away while wiping her face in frustration.

How messed up am I, anyway?

Then she saw Nick.

He looked grim, and his eyes radiated sadness.

"What's happened?" she asked, her voice catching.

And he told her about his mother.

Jessie started to cry and lay her head on his shoulder as he led her away from the roulette's rattling ball.

But she smelled Heather on him, her perfume, or her make-up—*or shit, maybe that was her musky scent?*

An image intruded. An image of them romping in the forest as wolves, fucking, like dogs in heat.

And then her bitter tears represented an entire array of emotions. A surprising coldness overtook her, making its way up her arms and into her heart.

Mordred

After receiving the new orders via the secure laptop connection, he felt the shudder working its way through his body.

The prods burned and stung his flesh again and left him powerless again. The people on the other side of the glass or outside the silver-plated bars stared and pointed, took notes, drank foul-smelling coffee, and occasionally laughed as he curled into a ball in the corner and whined like a whipped dog, his body blurring as it partly transformed, human to wolf and back again, his fur smoking where they burned him to see how he would react.

To see how his body would heal.

And they took notes. Schlosser and Gavin and their toadies, assistants with their own sadistic tendencies who sometimes reached in and hurt Mordred for no reason other than to see him suffer. They took notes and entered logs on flashing computer screens that lit the lab at night with their bluish, frightening glow.

Mordred shuddered and sweated, remembering the laboratories, the tables on which he was strapped, the needles with their burning injections—like liquid fire injected into his veins—and then it was the blades and their thin slits and cuts. Razorblades, standard or specially coated with a sheen of silver, with the men in the white coats writing down his actions and looking at the wounds as they healed or didn't heal. Touching, probing, poking, and then stabbing, deeper and deeper and then far enough that he could see the sharp tip protruding from the opposite side of his body, feeling the metal sear flesh and sinew along its length, the wound healing itself but then being renewed when the people in the white coats twisted the blade and cut anew.

Mordred ripped his clothes off and curled up in a sweaty, tight ball in the corner. His body grew its fur, and he blurred into the shape of a wolf.

He whined.

Lupo

After tucking Jessie into a hotel room at the downtown Hilton, he called DiSanto. Jessie'd been acting strange since he told her about his mother, but the women had bucked the odds and had gotten along, so maybe this had hit Jessie as hard as it had hit him.

Then, his heart steeled, he met DiSanto and drove to the meet he had called with Geoff Simonson.

It was time to end this.

First, their road trip—a quick run up to Minocqua to check the Wolfpaw lab the local cops had no reason to do much with. Bakke had laughed at DiSanto's request for a chopper and kicked him out of his office. Lupo's name hadn't come up, and Lupo's swift but brief appearance in the squad room had at least quieted the lieutenant's unpredictable anger.

"Told you so," Lupo said to DiSanto. "I got somebody I want you to meet."

"Lead on."

"You okay?"

The younger cop nodded, not quite convincingly.

He'd prepared DiSanto for Geoff Simonson, explaining that he was an ally in the Wolfpaw situation—whether or not it was separate from the three "wolf" murders—and, since he couldn't tell his partner all the details of his own Georgia compound recon, he used Simonson as the witness.

DiSanto recognized him.

"You're the guy outside the liquor store." He didn't seem ready to trust the ex-soldier.

"Yeah, I was trying to hook up with Lupo here," Simonson said, shaking hands. "I knew we could work together, since we both knew *things*. Nick tells me you now know more *things* than before."

DiSanto nodded uncertainly, clearly still uncomfortable with the whole shapeshifter concept.

Simonson detailed his military career and his many gripes with Wolfpaw while DiSanto mostly listened.

Later, Lupo and DiSanto drove in the Maxima, and Simonson followed in his rented, nondescript Toyota.

Lupo hoped like hell there'd be no wolf-related murders in Milwaukee while he was gone.

Later he dialed up some Leonard Cohen, a recent addition to his tastes, and listened to the melancholy voice, letting his mind wander over memories of his mother. Even though he dreaded making the arrangements, he had already started making phone calls. There would be no funeral—his mom had insisted on cremation and a tiny service for her son and girlfriend and partner and a friend or two. The Lupo family would be no more, unless Nick Lupo changed his mind on procreation. But there were too many issues he had to address, too many complications.

The drive was long, and he chased the Cohen with some atmospheric, theremin-laced Reverend Wolf, and then his standard "up north music" from the Alan Parsons Project, music he and Jessie had shared as special from the start of their relationship.

It brought a lump to his throat. Many of his major life moments related directly to music, which was both a blessing and curse as far as he was concerned.

They made good time, and soon they were following DiSanto's Googled map and directions to the Minocqua PD, where the lead investigator—a jovial fisherman-type named Carver—gave them crime scene photos from the fire and murders and a copy of the posted suicide note, then detailed the stalled investigation, including the fire-damaged World War II weapons found in the secret compartment.

"Looks like German guns," DiSanto said.

"Yeah, that's a P-38," Lupo tapped the paper. "And that toggle action was on a P-08, a Luger."

"Weird stuff all over that house," Carver said. "Looks like there were some old flags and tapestries too. Nazi paraphernalia. Medals."

"Collector stuff?"

He thought. "Maybe, but then why hide it? Just looks like someone who couldn't go public with his interests."

"Definitely suicide?"

"The fire didn't cover up enough, so we're pretty sure Dr. Gavin committed suicide after killing his family. Not sure who set the fire."

Carver drove them to the lab at which Gavin worked. It was a locked-up blockhouse facility carved out of the woods south of Highway J. A tall, square, barbed-wire-topped Cyclone fence surrounded the building, Caution and No Trespassing signs dotted along its length.

"Looks almost like a military set-up," Lupo said. "Can we get in?"

"Technically, no. It's owned by a company called WP Enterprises, listed as a medical research facility. It's private, but I do have the keys. Gavin apparently fired everyone who worked here in the days before his, uh, breakdown. The place is lined with these huge cages, and autopsy slabs, operating rooms." He shuddered. "Everyone who's seen it's been sayin' it looks like a torture chamber for animal experiments. We had PETA callin' last week, they got wind of it."

"You said *technically* no, we can't get in?"

"Not supposed to open up for anyone except company personnel. But this is still a crime scene, and you're law enforcement personnel with an open case interest. I'm making an executive decision."

He reached for the padlock on the gate and had barely touched it with the key when the blockhouse exploded, and a great gout of fire reached far above the collapsing roof.

The four men were flattened by the blast, their eardrums nearly shattered. Hot, flaming debris rained around them.

DiSanto

He picked his head up from the ground, his ears ringing, and saw Carver rolling around, his coat on fire. Simonson looked unconscious. He blinked and watched the flames *whooshing* into the sky. He staggered to his feet and patted down the fire on Carver's back. Lupo had leaped up next to him to help.

Concussed, he couldn't hear what Lupo was saying, only see his lips move. He shook his head and shrugged.

A figure flashed past, highlighted by the raging fire.

Then Lupo was sprinting away, giving chase.

Despite his distressed ears and the headache that was rapidly jabbing his skull, DiSanto stared.

Lupo shed his clothing as he ran, and then he blurred and DiSanto's eyes caught him in mid-leap as a black wolf.

He was chasing a man who had also become a wolf.

"Jesus!" DiSanto screamed. Carver and Simonson seemed okay but still out of it. DiSanto drew his Glock and loped off after Lupo— now the pursuing wolf—and saw that they were headed to where a dark sedan was tucked into a corner of the woods.

Up ahead there was vicious snarling, and then the two wolves clashed.

Lupo

When he recognized Wilcox flashing past in a dead run only seconds after the lab blew up, Lupo gave chase. Wilcox was the only survivor of the casino takedown Alpha Team. Wounded, he had eluded Lupo's search and disappeared.

Lupo's ears hurt from the concussion and his body ached from being battered by the blast. But as soon as visualized himself going over and his DNA realigned, the Creature took over—and his physical wounds began immediately to mend themselves. At full strength, his wolf was on the Wilcox-wolf in seconds.

Wilcox was big, but Lupo was bigger, and his paws ate up ground quicker. He caught Wilcox long before the bastard could reach his getaway car.

Lupo ceded control to the Creature. The wolf was close enough to Wilcox's galloping legs that his open snout caught fur and muscle and bit down hard, sending the fleeing wolf into a crashing heap well short of the car.

Wilcox recovered and turned to face his opponent.

Then the wolves squared off and went for each other's throats.

Lupo feinted to the left. Wilcox went for it with his deadly fangs missing Lupo because he was already not there. Lupo's fangs clamped on the enemy wolf's neck and in one violent tear ripped his throat to shreds in a shower of blood, fur, and flesh.

He tore in again and again, destroying the other wolf's neck and severing his head. Then he shook his muzzle and staggered off to the side, tired. On the ground, the wolf's broken body became that of Wilcox.

When Lupo once again looked out through his human eyes, DiSanto was there, half-sitting on the hard ground, his gun held uselessly in one hand.

Heather

At the wheel of her Hyundai, she watched the Milwaukee skyline retreat in her mirror.

She'd be back.

Count on it, Nick Lupo.

She wasn't done here, not by the proverbial long shot.

But she had plans on which to follow through, and she was

expected, so there was this trip to make. She could have flown, but there was more than an even chance that her name would pop up on a flagged list. It was safer to drive, even if it would take longer.

She needed to be there before Lupo and whoever he wound up taking with him. Maybe he'd take his lady love. She could take care of herself, handle a gun as well as any man, but Heather figured he'd have found a way to protect her. No, it would be down to Geoff Simonson and his unresolved issues, and maybe DiSanto. She wondered if the younger cop was clued in—or was Lupo still sheltering him?

Well, she'd know soon enough, after she dialed his number. But first she had to rack up some miles.

She blended into the thickening traffic on the road east, where the endgame awaited.

Lupo

They'd left Carver with a whole new investigation and a headless body—care of the strangely-timed *animal attack*—and not much else to go on. Lupo knew this was going to take some major smoothing over, but it would have to wait.

Simonson's concussion seemed mild, and he had staggered to his car and followed, but now they were turning into a truck stop and parking off to the side to compare notes and pound down coffee and donuts for fueling purposes.

DiSanto had been driving the Maxima, and he went to buy the supplies.

Simonson dug into the trunk of his rental and came out with a cherrywood box, almost like a finely crafted gun presentation case.

"What the hell?" said Lupo.

"I figure it's time to show you this." Simonson was looking worse than Lupo'd ever seen him. The explosion had awakened his post-traumatic stress, Lupo guessed.

Christ, as if Jessie's problems and his own weren't enough.

Simonson laid the wooden case on the trunk and opened it, stepping aside so Lupo could see.

The sheathed dagger inside the case was almost an exact twin of the one Lupo had strapped to his ankle, down to the strange markings on the old wood. The empty indentation where the other dagger belonged told tales.

"Where did you get this?" Lupo growled.

"I took it from the hidden compartment in the murder house. And I'm the one who set the fire."

"Christ, Simonson, what game are you playing?" Lupo looked for DiSanto, but he was still in the truck stop. He felt his muscles tighten in preparation for self-defense. He studied Simonson's face but saw no threat.

"Look, I wanted to cover the whole Nazi connection. The fire should have done the trick, but I didn't catch on that there was so much cinderblock." He wiped his face with one large hand as if it were a washcloth. "I knew what they were doing, see? The guy was the lead scientist at that fucking lab where they tortured—people like you. People with the wolf gene."

"You had to know they'd find the lab." *Where was DiSanto?*

"Just luck on their part. Everything that made the connection from the guy to the lab was saved along with the Nazi stuff, but it shouldn't have been. I should have hung around to make sure."

"Okay. What do you know about the blade that's missing?"

Lupo wondered about DiSanto. How long to buy donuts and coffee? Did he trust Simonson?

"I can tell you that I pulled it out of your chest not that long ago and left it on your desk."

"*You?*" Lupo's mouth hung open and he closed it with a snap. "That was *you?*"

He'd agonized and then decided to end it all, cliché of clichés, but someone had stopped him. He'd suspected Jessie might have done it, but couldn't ask without admitting he had sought suicide. And it was likely she would have been too emotional to keep the secret.

And he doubted Ghost Sam could have done it.

"Why? Why get involved? And why are you here?" Lupo shook his head. "I don't get it." But maybe he did.

"I needed an ally. Against Wolfpaw. Who else could I hit up but the one guy who's been a thorn in their side?"

DiSanto was approaching, his arms full of greasy bags.

Fuck.

Now Lupo would have preferred DiSanto wasn't in the line of fire. But Simonson seemed relaxed, unthreatening.

"Does he...?" Simonson asked.

"No. Don't spread it around."

"I'm not looking for credit for keeping you alive, no worries."

Lupo nodded as DiSanto reached them.

"What's that?" he said, pointing at the wooden case.

Lupo sighed. It was a long story.

During another rest stop about halfway to Milwaukee, Simonson convinced him their next step had to be the council meeting about to take place at the D.C. compound.

"It's the only way to take them down, man. You can't go to the feds. You can't go to the cops. You got to just do them like the monsters they are." The rage made his voice tremble.

Ghost Sam stood next to Lupo, so when he turned the old Indian leaned in.

"Judge, jury and executioner, eh?" said the ghost.

Lupo ignored him.

"Not sure I would recommend this course of action, Nick."

Go away, go away, go away!

Lupo's scream was entirely in his head. But when he looked for Ghost Sam, the Indian was gone. As always, no one else had seen him. How to silence the haunting? He would have enough trouble with his own conscience after what he'd done with Killian and Marcowicz.

He knew he was sliding in deeper over his head, but what choice did he have? His obsession with the sinister Wolfpaw was going to cost him everything if he wasn't careful, everything including Jessie. Now that his mother was gone, the feeling of being an orphan was starting to set in, and here he was, doing his best to ruin every life he came into contact with, including Jessie's and DiSanto's.

But there was the argument that said he had to finish it now. He had an ally, so why not do what Simonson said and take them out, once and for all?

Simonson said, "The council meeting is tomorrow, Lupo. You got to be in or out. There's no other way. I'm flagged on airline lists so I'm driving, so there isn't any fucking-around time. You go, or you stay."

Lupo said nothing for a long moment. Did he have the balls to follow through?

He'd lost too much to leave it alone.

The cost had been too high.

Once back in the Maxima and heading for Milwaukee, Lupo had a long talk with DiSanto and laid out his plan.

DiSanto didn't like it, but Lupo was convincing.

Next stop, the capital.

Chapter Twenty-Five

1944

Giovanni

The reunion between mother and father and son at the shelter was joyful, though tempered by the loss of two good men who had given their lives to bring it about.

The partisan brigade leader Corrado had flown into a rage when informed that the mission had cost two of his best, most experienced men, but a sober look at the condition of Giovanni's blood-splattered clothes caused him to reconsider. Plus the fact that he had not lost the Vatican dagger redeemed the situation somewhat.

"I have seen the dagger's power with my own eyes," he told Corrado, as he held hands with his son and wife, "and I'd like to be its guardian."

He didn't tell anyone he had been wounded in his life-and-death struggle with the wolf.

He didn't have to, because the wound had disappeared by the time he changed into a borrowed shirt and jacket.

In the coming days, Corrado's men met German patrols made up of humans less frequently, while their encounters with the supernatural members of the Werwolf Division increased. They had been designated rear-guard, and while Hitler's ground forces retreated through Northern Italy and met up with those retreating from Normandy, the last-ditch Werwolf Division took over the duty of harassing the partisans who paved the way for the Allied forces advancing from the south.

And in the coming days, Giovanni Lupo became Corrado's best werewolf fighter. In his hand, the Vatican blade became a scythe that mowed down every wolf who dared attack him.

Father Tranelli noted that Giovanni seemed to have become feverish and reckless in his encounters with the monsters. "He is on a mission," the old priest said. "A holy mission, perhaps. But he may not see the end of this accursed war if he doesn't watch himself. What of his wife and son?"

Franco grieved for his friend Pietro, whom he would never see again. Maria wondered at her husband's newfound obsession with killing werewolves. Although the few wives who remained with their men told her how heroic he was, she wondered what had made him so dedicated to causing death at the constant risk of his own life.

For his part, Giovanni grew silent and, despite his great love for his family, distant to the point of being morose.

Corrado often looked at him with some vague suspicion on the tip of his tongue.

The fighting intensified, and Giovanni found himself celebrated as the unit's best and most skillful wolf-killer.

It was cold at night, so no one questioned why he wore gloves on patrol. Only one person noticed that he wore them in daytime, too.

Franco. Another week later, Giovanni Lupo felt the burden of destiny come crashing down on him.

At dawn, he awoke shivering from a nightmare, bathed in cold sweat. Faint echoes of the dream lingered like the previous night's moonlight, and he shrank at the images of blood and fury. God knew he had known enough of both recently. Where was he? Why was he shivering?

He was curled in a tight ball, trying to keep skin on skin so he could stay warmer. Had Maria opened the window again? She tended to feel hot, whereas he craved warmth in the night.

He shivered more intensely. His head ached, throbbing with a hammer-like cadence that threatened to overwhelm him. Slowly he became aware of the cold wetness covering every part of his skin. The tiny, hard points prickling his side puzzled him, as even the scratchy wool blankets piled on his side of the bed didn't usually feel like pine needles.

Pine needles?

Suddenly his throat screamed for water, as if he had swallowed a bucketful of desert sand.

He remembered then that the shelter they had been forced to inhabit since Corrado had rescued and kidnapped him on the street, was below ground. He wasn't in his own comfortable bedroom, where the creamy stucco walls bore only a crucifix and a portrait of Mary. He almost smiled at the memory, but his head hurt too much. And he remembered that the shelter was windowless.

He opened his eyes finally, sure that he wouldn't like what he saw, and then he leaped up, shivering even more violently, shocked to see that he lay on a gently sloping hillside—in a clearing, trees cluttering his view all around. Over him the drooping branches of an elderly weeping willow seemed to cascade like tears. The long, narrow leaves dotted his arms and chest. His *naked* arms and chest! Where was his nightshirt? Giovanni always wore a thick layer of clothing to bed, but now he was naked, and the leaves tickled his skin above. The pine

241

needles beneath him gouged the skin of his side and leg.

He hugged himself, trembling uncontrollably. Cold, wet dew numbed his toes. His penis had shrunk and sought shelter between his thighs, and small twigs made sticky knots in his pubic hair.

"Ma che cosa—?" What is going on?

He tore his right hand from under his left armpit, where he felt a semblance of warmth, cupping his genitals to preserve some body heat. He brought his left hand close to his face until he could see it clearly in what appeared to be the early morning light. The hand itched, as if ants swarmed under his skin. He shook it, but the feeling raged up and down his arm. He looked at his right hand and its crisscross burn scars, which he had begun hiding with a glove.

It was indeed dawn, the sky dappled with patches of light. A cool wind swept across the overgrown grass of the clearing. Cold and wet, he rolled over and climbed to one knee then stood. The clearing was not familiar. The slope meant he was back in the hills, but where? How had he gotten here? And why had he shed all his clothing? His feet squished in the wet grass as he started in one direction, stopped, then tried another.

It all looked the same. Every side of the clearing faced him with a thick stand of trees. Under the canopy of their leaves it was still dark. He didn't know what had happened to him.

And yet...

He stooped to swipe off some leaves and twigs and recoiled to see that his feet weren't only wet with dew—there were splashes of red. Was it...?

Giovanni's breath caught in his throat.

My blood?

He checked his calves, thighs, and ankles thoroughly, but no, he saw or felt no new wounds.

Then whose blood?

He scraped at the bloodstains. Dry, mostly dry. He looked at his fingers. Dark matter was crusted under his nails.

"Gesu' e Santa Maria," he said softly and crossed himself, forgetting his nakedness for a moment.

He sniffed his fingertips.

It was blood. He had smelled enough of it in the last weeks.

He sidled toward the clearing's edge. The approaching sunrise might well cause him to be seen by people who had awakened for field work or farm chores, or to attend mass or one of the meager markets. He had to find his way home.

Home?

Not home, but the shelter that had become his home.

With a deep breath, he abandoned any modesty that might have crippled him and sprinted through the dew toward the thinnest face of the forest.

Giovanni was still shivering, now with fear as well as cold.

The blood, the naked romp outside, and the lack of memory.

There was no accounting for this, none at all.

Unless...

Giovanni looked at his right forearm, which itched unbearably, as if he had a rash or had dragged it through a patch of poison ivy. Below his right shoulder, the ragged wounds where that monstrous creature had torn and ripped the skin with grotesque fangs or claws was throbbing painfully and itching madly, but incredibly the skin was unbroken and unblemished.

How could this be?

Both arms tingled, and he thought he felt the tingle reach his shoulder and spread across his back. He scratched at the edges of where the inflamed wound had been, but it wasn't enough to slake his need. In fact, the itch seemed to be spreading to the other arm now. He would have given anything for some immediate relief.

He lapped at the tingling arm absentmindedly, his nakedness momentarily forgotten.

Then Giovanni stopped in mid-lap. What the hell was he doing, lapping at his arm like a dog?

Porca Madonna!

He shook his head and scraped the area around his mouth with one hand. Dried bits of red flesh flaked off his skin, leaving bloody smears on his palm. Some of the bits were sharp, bone-like. He sniffed at the debris. Smelled like...like slaughtered meat. He'd seen enough farm slaughters in his youth. This was what remained when meat was sawn and processed by butchers. The smell overtook his senses, and he felt the urge to vomit suddenly. When he forced himself to swallow and breathe deeply, the taste of raw meat and bone and rancid blood came alive inside his mouth.

His throat gurgled and hitched, and a stream of bloody vomit spewed onto the ground, splashing his feet before he could sidestep.

It looks like pieces of my lungs, Giovanni thought as he wiped his mouth. The bloody taste was still on his tongue, but now it didn't seem so foreign, and even though he felt another spasm coming, he was able to avoid coughing up.

What is wrong with me? Giovanni thought, a strangled sob escaping from his lips.

He gagged again, but this time it overwhelmed him, and more pieces of bloody flesh and bone came gurgling into his throat and through his lips in a disgusting stream.

After the spasm passed, he opened his eyes and beheld the grotesque contents of his stomach, now splattered onto the grass. He turned away, dizzy, trying to keep his gorge from rising again.

He first now truly understood madness. The shivers he felt had nothing to do with the chill in the air, and the madness was just beginning.

Because not far from the clearing, Giovanni found his clothes. And the savagely butchered body of...someone. He wasn't sure who the male human was, because his head was missing, his neck a red hole of gore and bone chips.

And Giovanni knew he had been cursed.

Corrado's partisan brigade was pinned down by rifle fire from a crow's nest of granite boulders above the sloping path.

They'd been climbing, their guard lowered because the territory had been recently cleared of Germans. But the first rifle rounds brought down two good men, and Corrado shouted at the rest of his column to seek cover.

While the partisans were kept down by the accurate gunfire, a pair of werewolves pounced on those in the rear.

The snarling of werewolves and the screams of men being slaughtered were punctuated by rifle fire, which kept the rest of the partisans pinned and helpless.

Giovanni started snaking back down the path, retrieving one of the daggers from under his coat. The other dagger was with a second patrol.

"Get down!" Corrado hissed roared. "You can't take them on yourself!"

Giovanni ignored him. The brigade had run out of silver bullets days before, and the wolves would work their way back up the path and butcher each partisan one by one, unless someone counterattacked. And the holy weapon was the only way to win a clash with the shapeshifters.

Corrado knew they had no silver other than the dagger, but he tried to stop Giovanni. He'd become fond of the young, fearless fighter—and he was fond of the man's wife and child, too. His own family had been killed by Germans, shot in reprisal for partisan action. But the reprisal had made a partisan out of Corrado, and his leadership had now cost hundreds of German lives. He lowered his head to avoid the damned German riflemen, helpless.

Giovanni scrambled down the rocky incline, past the huddled partisans, avoiding their eyes. In a minute he had reached the slight turn they had recently traversed. The snarling continued, but the screaming was silenced—the men were surely dead.

The first of two werewolves materialized as if magically on the path just below him, its eyes widening with glee and gluttony at the sight of prey, but Giovanni was ready, the dagger held close to his body until he could smell the beast's breath.

Then, when the wolf's muscular legs propelled it into an uphill lunge for his throat, Giovanni judged the timing perfectly, unsheathing the dagger just as the animal reached him, sidestepping it and throwing it off-balance long enough to drive the dagger's point through its neck.

The wolf's scream of tortured pain effectively hid Giovanni's. His hand smoked where the silver scorched his skin and flesh, turning it black. The pain was excruciating, but he still managed to stab the wolf once in the heart as it collapsed at his feet, its wounds flaming and its blood boiling in its veins.

Giovanni whirled to face the second wolf, but this time he'd misjudged the angle of attack, and the red-eyed demon knocked him painfully to his knees. He tried to bring the dagger around, but it was still buried in the dead wolf, who was flickering like a candle back and forth from monster to human.

By the time he ripped the dagger out of the corpse, the second frenzied wolf snatched his hand with its jaws, and he dropped the dagger with a yelp of pain and frustration.

Holding his wounded hand, Giovanni backed up against the rocky slope, knowing the nearest partisans watched helplessly a few meters away, their guns useless and their heads still pinned down by the sniper fire. The wolf's jaws trailed bloody drool as it approached, staring intensely at this new enemy. Its scrabbling paws avoided the toxic dropped dagger, but its body prevented Giovanni from retrieving it.

Before he knew what he was doing, Giovanni felt the rage take him.

He had learned a little about his new condition in the last few weeks, secretly, but he barely understood how the beast inside his bloodstream could take over.

He tried desperately to reverse the feeling, but he felt the changes in his body and the terrible itch of his fur suddenly sprouting along his arms and back, and then—

—then he was *Over-over-Over*, lost inside the instincts and defensive rage of the Beast he barely understood.

The last his human ears heard was the shouting of his partisan companions, horrified by what they saw: one of their own number taking the form of the wolf, the dreaded enemy.

His clothes dropped, ruined, beneath him as his wolf's body took the enemy wolf by surprise.

Jaws snapping at each other, the two wolves closed and fought, biting and retreating, their claws slashing.

Growling, shrieking, they attacked and feinted, bit and retreated, rolled over and over, the advantage switching.

Bullets struck them both, but did no damage. Their fangs drew blood from wounds that hurt excruciatingly, but which began healing and closing up almost immediately.

Suddenly the beast that had been Giovanni was backed up against the hillside, and his paws lost their purchase on the rocky path, and the other wolf seemed about to go in for the kill.

But instead he regained his human form and, while Giovanni tried to make sense of it, reached down and snatched up the dagger and its scabbard. Naked, he sheathed the dagger and inserted it into his mouth, then—before Giovanni could act—returned to his wolf form and bounded away down the hill and around the curve.

The wolf that had been Giovanni regained its footing and scrambled down the hill, human screams following him until he was gone.

The other wolf had too much of an advantage, and even though Giovanni had the scent in its nostrils, he couldn't see him, and he was forced to run blindly. In his brain, where Giovanni and a terrible monster both jostled for control, all he could think was that he had lost one of the holy daggers.

And that he could never go home, for now he was unmasked as one of the enemy. A monster.

I am banished.

Franco

It had been months since they'd told him his father had died, but he knew they whispered about him and his mother when they thought he was asleep.

Maria wept uncontrollably when Corrado's decimated patrol had finally returned on that fateful day, telling tales that both celebrated and vilified his father.

He was a hero. He was a monster.

He could never return.

Franco understood then that his father was alive, but that he was *dead to them.* Because he had become a monster, and because he had lost one of Father Tranelli's strange daggers.

There was no consolation in anyone's eyes, and Franco felt the hate that suddenly bloomed against his mother and himself. As if they had helped his father fool the partisan brigade! As if Giovanni Lupo had intentionally put one over on them!

"We should have never allowed someone named Lupo to join us!" one shouted in a drunken rage. "Never again!"

Then they turned and stared at his mother. And at him.

Their days with the partisan brigade were numbered.

And early one morning, after the new year had come, he and his mother took their few belongings and stepped into the hidden staircase exit, the staring eyes of Corrado and the Jesuit and the few remaining men and women of the brigade boring into their backs, refusing to stop them or send them off with a wish of luck or farewell.

And they had headed for his uncle's farm in the hills, neither of them knowing whether he still lived. Their trek took two weeks of arduously climbing narrow paths, always on the lookout for desperate German soldiers left behind to die.

At the end of 1944, the partisan resistance had risen up against the weakened German occupiers and formed provisional governments which sought and received foreign recognition as sovereign states, but the Germans and the remainder of the Italian forces still loyal to Mussolini were successful in quelling the rebellion and executing its leaders.

Now, all the disparate partisan units could do was await the Allies, whose painstaking advance had been mired by the vicious rearguard action of suicide patrols who would fight to the last man, and elements of the Werwolf Division.

When the Allies finally arrived, their guns audible in the distance, the withdrawal of the few surviving Wehrmacht and ragged Werwolf units left an almost tangible vacuum.

Franco and his mother had been safe on the desolate farm, but the boy could not forget what had happened to his father, or his friend. The nightmares kept him awake, and his mother worried for his health and sanity. In his sleep, he saw the wolves come for him and his family, but then instead of being a German werewolf who battered in their door it was his father, jaws slavering and red eyes glaring with hate. And hunger.

One morning, when Maria went to wake the boy, he was gone.

Franco had grown rapidly, and in a few weeks he already appeared years older than his actual age. What he had witnessed, suffered, and lived through had toughened him, but those things had also changed him in ways he could only suspect. Frequently he found himself awash in a rage, yet unable to understand or explain why. Until one day, when he realized that he needed to face his father—the partisan hero who had become a monster and shattered their small family.

But where could he find Giovanni? Where would his father have sought refuge?

Instinct and keen insight into his father's mind brought him back to their old neighborhood. Franco sensed that his father would have hidden in their old apartment if he could, perhaps to await their return. Not knowing what he would find, the boy—now just barely a teenager—made his way along the street on which he had grown up. Several buildings had been demolished since the last night he had spent here, and others had been damaged, some walls sheared away to expose their insides like grotesque layer cakes. Mountains of rubble lay at the bases of their surviving structures.

Franco looked at all the places they had played during more innocent times and couldn't help thinking of Pietro. The day of their airplane tire stunt was a hazy memory by now. Everything that had happened since then was a nightmare from which he could not wake up.

He pushed open the door of their old apartment, surprised the building still stood, and was overwhelmed by the stench of rotted meat and dried blood. Franco stood in the doorway, breathing through his mouth to avoid being sick.

"Papá?" His voice was soft and tentative and echoed in the high-ceilinged space. "*Sono io, Franco.*"

He heard a shuffling from the kitchen and stepped into the long corridor that led there. He was reminded of that night, when his father had found *him* hiding here. He pushed the memory aside.

"Papá, I've come to bring you back home with me. Our new home."

He held his nostrils. He remembered this same smell in butcher shops down the street. He entered the kitchen. The lights didn't work, but there was enough light from the balcony door to see the form in the shadows at the far end of the massive room.

It was his father, his clothes ragged and his hair growing wild.

"Papá!" he said, startled by his father's appearance.

"Hello, my son," Giovanni said, and then his voice broke, and he was sobbing. "I knew you would come back. I felt it. And your mother...?"

"She's safe on Uncle's farm, but she sends her love."

"*Dio mio*, what a terrible time it has been."

"Yes, Papá', it has been."

Giovanni stepped farther out of the shadows. Franco gasped when he saw the bloody smears around his mouth, crusted in his father's stubble. Giovanni blinked rapidly, as if this was too much light for him.

"I've been hiding here for weeks, hoping you would return. I—I've changed, Franco, I'm not the way I was. I get these urges, I become hungry as you've never known hunger. I become another person altogether, a creature. I try to control this *hunger*, this cursed hunger, but the moon brings it out in me. Sometimes I think I can control it, but then I cannot, and I do terrible things." He put his head down and wept.

"Papá'," Franco whispered. "It's all right."

"I prayed, you know. I prayed that it would go away and leave me alone. I prayed that I could go back to that day when you were playing with your friend and I was trying to earn some money for food, and if we had both just—just come home. If we hadn't... But it's the past now and we can't change it, can we?"

"No, Papá'." Franco felt the tears squeeze out of his eyes.

Giovanni came closer to his son. He reached out and touched Franco's face.

"Don't cry," he said. "Things will be better now."

"Yes," Franco whispered.

"I hear the Germans are finally on their way out of the city. The Allies are only a few days' march away. The war is almost over for us." He spread his arms. "We can be together again, a family. We'll go and fetch your mother."

Franco stepped into his father's embrace. It felt good for a few moments, like it always had. He laid his head on his father's chest. He felt his father's heartbeat.

Giovanni kissed his son's cheek and caressed his face with rough hands.

"My son—" Suddenly Giovanni's body stiffened, and he began to pull away. "What—? Franco, I feel...Franco?" His voice rose as the fear took him. "My son, what have you done?"

The heat must have become suddenly obvious. Franco held his father close, his strength surprising the older man, while his hand had reached behind his back where he'd tucked the dagger stolen from the priest, the companion dagger to the one Giovanni had lost to the enemy wolf. As soon as the blade was free of the scabbard, Giovanni had sensed the heat of the silver dagger.

Franco brought it around quickly, before his father could free himself of the embrace and flee.

But Giovanni didn't attempt to flee.

Franco buried the dagger in his father's chest, hitting the heart on the first try.

Giovanni screamed, and the wound caught fire, as did his clothing around it, and the boy plunged the blade in and out several times, the reek of scorched flesh and blood enveloping them as they hugged one last time.

The creature within Giovanni began to manifest, the hair lengthening and his face beginning to change, his mouth becoming a snout, and Franco thought his father would take him along to hell. He twisted the knife cruelly within each new wound, each twist and each stab piercing vital organs and liquefying them in a flash of silvery heat.

Franco watched as his father flickered from human to wolf and back again, his eyes bulging and finally exploding in a shower of blood and gore, and his hands—which were now claws and could still have raked Franco's face and head—spreading in helpless surrender.

The boy stepped back, and his father collapsed in a burning, smoking heap onto the marble floor.

"My son," he cried in a ragged whisper through charred lips. "*Grazie...* Thank you."

And then Giovanni Lupo was dead, his body once again resembling that of a human.

Franco's tears came, and wouldn't stop until he had done what he knew must be done.

Later, he would arise from where he had sat in vigil and leave the apartment of his youth, changed forever.

The silver dagger would go with him, but after the war he would seek out a crippled Father Tranelli and return it to him. And then he would try to forget everything.

Until someday in the far future, when neighborhood men in the America where Frank Lupo had made his life with a wife and son would come to him, whispering about a wolf...

Chapter Twenty-Six
Endgame: Fifth Day

Lupo

The card Simonson had snagged from the dead inner perimeter guard got them through the outer doors on the building he pointed out as the compound's hub. The guard had started to question Lupo's visitor tags, but Simonson had acted as if there'd been no choice.

"Goddammit Simonson, don't do that. We could have taken the guy out without killing him."

Minutes before, they had accessed the central guardhouse, knocked out and taped up the guy manning it, then spliced in a loop of what was in the cameras' view. Simonson had it ready, but Lupo wondered how he could have prepared it.

"Sources," Simonson had said, grinning.

The drive into the capital had been long and circuitous, but Simonson had steered them unerringly to this compound in the rolling Maryland hills. It was a miniature Langley, a scale version of the CIA's main facility, but here the Wolfpaw logo was everywhere. And Simonson's access had been good through the compound's outer layer of security, but the inner perimeter guard had argued about Lupo's guest badge—it was the wrong color for the day.

"You're planning to whack the council and killing a guard bothers you?"

"He's not on the council," Lupo growled.

Not for the first time, he wondered if learning that others shared the werewolf gene had dragged his soul to hell.

Now, with blood on their hands, they were committed. It had to end here.

Sigfried

The secret council meeting was scheduled for later, but as excited as Sigfried was about it, he had other plans for now.

His call had revealed that Margarethe was indeed back and available, so he booked her for a special session and prepared the playroom.

What was the point of being incalculably wealthy if he couldn't enjoy himself? The congressional hearing had been cut short today, with several congressmen—and the one woman—suddenly displaying much less dogged determination to accuse Wolfpaw of egregious crimes against people, not to mention numerous human rights violations and felonies here on home soil. The list aired early on was long, but in the shortened session some of the wrinkly old dinosaurs took shots at the list and eventually wiped a fair amount of charges, essentially cutting by over a third the number of wrongdoing incidents by the Wolfpaw rank and file.

To Sigfried, this was worth a celebration. His wife had taken off for a shopping spree in the city and wouldn't miss him until late the next day. Margarethe was back, but she had claimed not to have enough time to procure a plaything for him, so it would just be him and her and whatever favored toys she chose to bring. And of course the playroom was fully stocked.

He whistled a little tune his father and grandparents had taught him. *Deutschland Über Alles.*

Margarethe had already come through the special elevator entrance at the rear of the penthouse and had made herself comfortable on the round bed.

Her leather-clad body was nevertheless displayed for his pleasure. When he walked into the room, he faced her spread legs, and his view of her shaved pubis and its tiny chain was enough to drive him wild. She batted her darkened eyes at him from behind the leather mask and smiled with lust. Her nipples stood at attention, and he knew she had been squeezing them in anticipation.

He saw an array of colorful toys spread out beside her and shed his clothing as quickly as possible so he could stretch out beside her lithe form.

She was perfect in every way. Her hair was a few shades darker, but he didn't mind.

"Hello, Sigfried," she muttered, her voice husky. "I've been keeping these warm for you."

She withdrew a long, slick phallus and offered it for his tongue. He lapped and purred, like a cat.

"My dear, you are worth every dollar..."

"I know," she said.

She took hold of his erection and stroked it with her long hand, making him rock-hard. He slid around and nosed at her groin, reaching her favored spot when she spread her thighs apart. Her hand never left him, massaging downward with increased pressure just as he preferred. He raised himself up on all fours and she knew what he wanted. She twisted sideways and approached his buttocks with her perfect face. The phallus she had allowed him to lick now became her way to fuck him, and he grunted as she buried it to the hilt.

His grunting increased in intensity until he sounded like a pig at the trough.

"Are we a good little Nazi?" she mumbled, working behind him now as he panted. "Are we a good party member? Do we *have* a good party member? Apparently we do!"

He moaned, now speechless in his wild lust. And then he screamed as she worked him over with the phallus in one hand and a studded paddle in the other, sparing neither his buttocks nor his testicles.

By the time she was finished—and so was he—they were both covered in sweat, and Sigfried lay on his flaccid belly gently snoring into the jumbled bedclothes.

Margarethe untangled herself from him and slid off the bed like a panther. Sigfried's satisfied snoring continued, and he snorted once.

She left him in the playroom and made her way to the guest shower, the one with the extra professional drain enclosed within a hidden janitor's closet—perfect for bleeding dead playthings. Margarethe started the shower and backed out of the bathroom, instead stalking on long legs down the corridor to the more public area of his sumptuous penthouse. She used her card key, one of his she had managed to have copied. She entered his office and was at his desk, riffling through papers and folders, in barely a minute.

Then she slid open his inner sanctum, his real office, and checked the rank of wide, flat displays showing his entire penthouse. She figured the "sessions" were recorded to the stack of hard drives blinking in a nearby rack. Sigfried was still asleep. His laptop was open, and she played with the software he had left up and running, working the sleek mouse expertly. She plugged in a series of flash drives and downloaded files, one eye on the door.

When Sigfried startled himself awake, he was handcuffed to the bed and Margarethe was gone, her musky scent lingering over him.

He whined a few minutes about the erection she had left him, but enough toys were nearby that he was able to amuse himself. And the handcuffs were specially made so he could defeat them, and he did.

He prepared for the council meeting, whistling more patriotic tunes that reminded him of his grandparents and the lost grandeur of their fatherland. The car was downstairs, ready for his ride.

He was almost ready to implement his family's plans and schemes, carefully shepherded for decades.

Der Führer would have been pleased.

Lupo

Lupo swiped a key card through the box, and the green light gave him reason to breathe again. His muscles had been poised for flight if alarms had been activated.

He was completely prepared to force a Change and retreat in wolf form, leaving Simonson to his own devices. After all, the guy kept surprising Lupo with his seemingly inexhaustible resources—it had occurred to Lupo once or twice that Simonson might be a CIA or NSA plant, an operative charged with destroying Wolfpaw with no accountability. Publicly they dealt with the company and granted contracts, but privately they either loathed or feared it.

Knowing what he knew, Lupo figured the latter was more likely.

He wondered how many werewolves were on the contractor's payroll.

Once inside, Lupo wanted to access the database, even if he had to torture someone, in order to get an idea how many enemy wolves there might be. And, if possible, to get a list of them.

Jessie wouldn't like it, but Lupo thought they'd both rest easier if he could hunt them down one by one and terminate them.

How's that for a soul dragged to hell? he thought.

The door swung open silently, and they covered each other until both were inside. A long corridor extended in three directions before them.

"You know the layout?" Lupo said into his mike.

Simonson grunted. "Yeah, of the lower-echelon areas. This is the nerve center. A whole other animal."

"Listen, if the roving werewolf patrols get wind of us, they'll tear us apart. I can't hold them all off, and they don't die easily.

"I know, I saw plenty of shit over in the desert."

They moved down the corridor, Simonson in the lead.

"Notice I'm following you," Lupo said. His hackles rose. He felt watched despite the fucked cameras. He gripped his off-the-books .40-caliber Glock, which he had fitted with a suppressor. On his back was an HK MP5 submachine gun, also suppressed.

Tucked securely into his right boot was the Vatican dagger.

If the letter his grandmother had left him was the truth, then it was the dagger his father Frank had used to kill his own father, Giovanni Lupo.

No wonder the thing had always felt strange to him.

Simonson seemed to know his way well enough, and the hallway being empty meant they traversed the building quickly.

Simonson spoke in Lupo's ear, his voice tinny. "The center of the building is where the conference rooms are. The council meets there. The CEO's offices and quarters are there, as well, in a three-story tower smack-dab in the center. There's a courtyard there, too, and several guest apartments with separate entrances."

"How do you know all this?"

"Research."

A door opened just ahead, and two uniformed guards jogged out, drawing up short when they caught sight of the intruders.

"Shit," muttered Simonson, and shot them both with short bursts of his suppressed MP5K.

"How do we know they're not wolves?"

"We don't," Simonson said as he sidled past the dead guards. "If they get up and come after us, we'll know."

"Great."

They dragged the guards behind the door and continued down the hall. The bloodstains were masked somewhat by the dark carpeting.

"How long is the loop?" Lupo asked, glancing at the camera bubbles.

"Continuous. We're okay, that way, but if anyone stumbles on those dead guys..."

"Lead on, Simonson," Lupo said, his silenced Glock racked and ready.

Not for the first time, he wondered if Simonson knew what he was doing. And whether he was taking them into a trap.

They came upon a wide-open area furnished with maroon leather furniture and ebony end tables. War art prints lined the walls, all representations of famous battles. Lupo recognized several at a glance: Rorke's Drift, Bunker Hill, the Ardennes, Tobruk, Dunkirk, Dien Bien Phu, Gettysburg, the Alamo, Stalingrad...

A set of huge wooden doors at one end was where Simonson led them.

"The council should be in there now," he said, checking his watch.

Lupo's neck tingled. "Why no guards?"

"Shit, they're in the middle of their most secure space, why post unsightly guards?"

"You don't find it strange?"

"Hell no." Simonson checked the bolt on his HK. "Ready? This is what we came to do, man. This is gonna topple the company. Get ready to make CNN."

"Fuck it, let's go." Lupo cringed at the thought of the road his association with Wolfpaw had led him down. He steeled himself for the slaughter.

Simonson kicked in the door and it crashed open dramatically.

Behind it, a huge oval conference table. Twenty tall leather chairs. *Unoccupied chairs.*

Sigfried

He swept into the conference room at the far end with no fear.

The dark-haired cop, Nick Lupo, whirled at the sound and extended his hand. His Glock was pointed at Sigfried, and the CEO of Wolfpaw laughed.

Lupo fired two shots, paused a beat, then a third. Any of them would have been a kill shot.

The slugs made cracks in the armored glass wall that crossed the far end of the room, but the wall held as it had been designed to do.

"You can lower your guns. They'll be useless against this reinforced glass wall." He punctuated his words by rapping his knuckles on it.

The look that crossed the cop's face was priceless, and Sigfried thrilled to the feel of the win.

It's such pleasure, being superior.

"Welcome to my little kingdom! As you can see, I was expecting you."

He watched the disgust on Lupo's face with satisfaction.

"You're probably wondering what my game might be. Well, stick around and I'll tell you." He smiled. "After all, it's been both frustrating and fun playing this chess game with you. Just for the hell of it, though, drop your gun."

Then Sigfried looked straight at Simonson.

"You can cover him now, Mordred."

Lupo

His better judgment tossed out the window, Lupo watched helplessly as the glass-protected CEO grinned at him condescendingly.

He stared at Simonson, who stood stock-still—a statue.

"Simonson? What the hell?"

A range of emotions washed over the big military guy, and his expression cracked. As Lupo watched, his face seemed to sag as if he'd suffered a sudden stroke.

"Drop your gun, now," commanded Sigfried.

Lupo swung his muzzle from the CEO to Simonson, but

Simonson's face seemed to be changing, stretching and distorting. Except it wasn't, not really. His features weren't changing, but yet he suddenly looked like someone else.

"Mordred?" Lupo whispered.

"Drop the gun, like he said," Simonson said, his MP5K now covering Lupo. "I have a clip of silver ammo in here now."

"You're one of them?" Lupo shook his head. "If you're a wolf, that silver would be burning up your hand like a torch by now."

Sigfried answered. "Mordred is the first of a new strain of werewolves, Lupo. Unfortunate name, really, isn't it? Yours, I mean."

Lupo ignored him. He looked at his recent ally. "Were you ever Simonson?"

"Sure, that's Mordred's cover identity," Sigfried said, waving it off. "He just used it to convince you to go along."

"No," Lupo said, "I saw it in his eyes. He wasn't acting. He believed he was Simonson. Didn't you, Geoff?"

Simonson blinked rapidly, as if he were having trouble following. Sweat broke out on his forehead. His gun's muzzle wavered.

"It doesn't matter, Lupo. Simonson or Mordred, he's mine. He always was, since his first days in the lab."

Simonson/Mordred's eyes widened a fraction, and his breath hitched. Even though his features had not changed physically, he still looked different. He glared at Lupo as if examining an insect specimen.

"He is Mordred, my creation," Sigfried intoned dramatically. He mimed a small Prussian bow. "But my grandfather started the work during the war. He was the first scientist to study the werewolf in a laboratory setting, and he began experimenting with curing the beasts from their silver aversion."

"It's more than an aversion," Lupo said.

"Yes," Sigfried agreed. "It's a true Achilles' heel, isn't it? But the great Doktor Klaus Schlosser learned how to make werewolves almost immune to the metal. Didn't he, Mordred?"

Mordred's face reflected years of pain and torture, but he nodded once, his gun muzzle now covering Lupo again.

"I am Schlosser's grandson, though I changed my name legally to avoid the connection. After all, he was known as *der Schnitter*—the Reaper—and I have used his notes to take my grandfather's experiments farther. My results have been more consistent than what he managed in his primitive facilities."

Lupo showed his disgust. "He experimented on concentration camp inmates, didn't he?"

"Chelmno was a transit camp, and they were volunteers who were treated better than the rest."

"Whatever you say."

Schlosser went on, unfazed. "It's too bad my chief assistant was weak and eventually succumbed to his damnable conscience—"

"You mean Gavin, in Minocqua?" Lupo said, stalling for time. "Cowardly murderer of his entire family?" *Keep the megalomaniacs talking.*

Ghost Sam would approve.

Schlosser showed surprise. "Ah, you made the connection? Never mind. I relocated Gavin to Minocqua years ago to monitor *you*, Dominic Lupo."

He was pacing behind the wall now, fully engaged in his subject. In control of the situation, and clearly the victor.

Lupo's shock was apparent.

"Yes, that's surprising, isn't it? You see, there was a silly man who still made some strides of his own. He was a so-called *shaman* up there in your Indian lands, Joseph Badger. He tinkered with things well out of his intellectual range, that is certain. But somehow he stumbled onto something even I found fascinating. He managed to blend the old, European werewolf gene with a new world, magical version. I confess, I don't even know how he did it! But it led to *you*, Lupo, and you're different. You aren't immune to silver, not by a long shot, but you are more so than most other werewolves. Your hand is scarred from handling silver ammunition, but what you did on my Georgia compound should have killed you by all rights."

Lupo looked down at his hand, remembering the pain, the burning-scorching agony of it.

"Yes, I think studying you will definitely accelerate my future experiments. I created Mordred here, but he would probably admit the process was not, how shall I say it, *painless*. Eh, Mordred?"

"You're a bigger monster than he is," Lupo growled.

"Words, Lupo. Soon you'll be screaming when I start injecting silver-infused blood into your veins."

Lupo shuddered despite himself.

But he let the insane CEO continue to rant.

"You represent a quicker solution to my goal. My destiny. Wolfpaw has hundreds of werewolves in its ranks, Lupo, and a few are like Mordred. We have taken on a large percentage of this country's defense under various contracts, as you know. But—"

"And made a lovely fuck-up of it, too," Lupo blurted out.

"A mere distraction, those hearings. Soon those idiots in congress will cower when our name is spoken. We'll slowly take over more and more functions of the U.S. military, until we *are* the U.S. military. I already have numerous congressional stooges ready to introduce bills that will merge us with Pentagon-directed services. My super-wolves will do the rest."

"You're insane," Lupo said. "Fucking nutcase."

Ghost Sam would have laughed and called this bastard a wanna-be Bond villain.

"Except he's doing what he says," Ghost Sam said. The specter was standing between Lupo and Simonson. "Not all of this is new to you, is it?"

Meanwhile, Schlosser lost his cool. "Silence! You're not in a position to call me names. I need you alive, but I can send Mordred here back to your den and have that doctor lover of yours brought here minus a few key parts. To *inspire* your cooperation."

Lupo felt a jab of fear then, knowing he was in a precarious situation despite his preparations. Jessie was safe in the hotel, but not impregnable.

Schlosser calmed himself. *No doubt by thinking of himself as a supreme commander of werewolf armies or some such garbage.*

The descendant of Klaus Schlosser, the Reaper, smacked his palm with a fist. "Once in command and control positions, it will not be difficult to further infiltrate the government. The coup, when it comes, will be quick and briefly savage. My grandfather's vision of a Fourth Reich will be realized after all these years."

"What happened to him?"

Schlosser frowned, caught between talkative and ruthless. "He was caught in an air raid. He chose to stay in his Chelmno apartment one night near the end of the war. He had company, a weakness of his, and he stayed with her..."

Schlosser seemed to be far off in his mind. But then he recovered. "Your family history was also of interest to me, Lupo, with those very interesting daggers used against my countrymen's werewolf soldiers. Of course we wrested possession of those two weapons from some drunk old priest, and they were useful in some of my experiments. But that idiot Gavin had already started unraveling some years ago. He gave an elder of that...that *tribe*, one of the daggers as a gift—because he was conflicted about Badger's intentions. *Those daggers were not his to give away!*"

"I disagree," Lupo said. "My family's contact with them during the war makes them as much mine as yours."

Schlosser laughed derisively. "No matter, they are both mine again."

"You'll have to take one from me."

259

"I don't have to. Mordred will."

Lupo looked at Simonson. The man who was also Mordred had him covered, but his mind seemed elsewhere. His eyes were troubled.

"Simonson, come back to me." Lupo guessed there were complexities in the werewolf's brain that he could barely comprehend.

He'd studied enough psychology to remember the concept of dissociative identity disorder, stress-induced amnesia that affected identity and resulted in memory loss and distinct personalities. It was the basis of the so-called multiple personality disorder, and it was a safe bet that what Simonson—or Mordred, whatever his real name was—had seen in Iraq combined with Schlosser's torture had fucked him up royally.

For a moment, it seemed that Mordred's stone face was breached by Simonson's, the intense soldier who'd approached Lupo for help destroying Wolfpaw, his tormentor. The two faces flickered back and forth, even the eyes changing from the swirling spirals of the werewolf Mordred to the cold, soldier's eyes of Geoff Simonson.

"You committed those murders to warn me, didn't you?" Lupo said softly. "The wolf references were the Simonson identity's influence on you, which you hoped would raise my alarm like coded messages. I missed the reasoning, but they did get my attention."

"Ah, Mordred," Schlosser said with false sadness, "you let your Simonson cover take over your head?" He seemed intrigued by the concept.

"Apparently what you did to him shattered his mind into separate identities and caused him to try to both hurt and help me."

Schlosser sneered. "Impossible."

"Is it? Look at him."

They both did.

"Mordred, please overpower Lupo and bring him to the cage." Schlosser pressed a button on a remote he'd been hiding in his hand, and a panel slid open behind them. Inside a concrete cell stood a cell. The bars were silver-plated, Lupo knew—because he felt the intense heat from a distance.

But there was a war going on in Mordred's head, and he seemed to be alternating from one identity to the other.

Which identity would win?

Mordred

The liquid fire in his veins rendered him into a screaming mass of exposed nerve endings, the invisible flames licking their way through every limb, every muscle, and every individual hair on his body.

Memory of Schlosser's torture threatened to give Simonson the edge, but the CEO's presence was strong, and the soldier's identity was a fake, after all. Mordred's memory was full of gaps. Perhaps they represented when he'd been Geoff Simonson. Perhaps he was losing what was left of his mind.

But as he looked at Schlosser, he remembered that he was a soldier with a mission.

And he would be tortured again if he didn't follow orders. After so many years spent in a cage, he knew that soldiers followed their orders. And he knew what hurt werewolves.

He turned the submachine gun on Lupo.

Mordred was in charge.

Lupo

He had carried the silver dagger in his boot, but while entering the conference room he had stealthily slid it out and, protected by its magical scabbard, held it close to his leg.

The silver's proximity would have seared his skin like a torch, but the wooden scabbard's special qualities shielded him until he unsheathed the blade.

Which he did, at the same time dropping the Glock and whirling on the man who was the werewolf Mordred.

The blade glowed close to his hand.

The searing began...

Mordred, for his part, was caught by surprise because he thought he held the upper-hand weapon. But he dropped the HK when Lupo's sudden lunge speared his forearm and sliced a jagged cut toward his elbow.

He screamed. Apparently even Mordred wasn't altogether immune to the silver of the special weapons.

From the letter his grandmother had left, Lupo was now certain that it wasn't the silver alone, but the provenance of the silver that had its effect on werewolves.

His own hand shrieked in burning pain, but he kept the blade in motion and pierced Mordred's side. The blade slid into the muscular body without resistance, and Mordred screeched as the scalding hot tip pierced organ and sinew.

Lupo withdrew the blade and was in the process of seeking a new target when Mordred managed to unsheathe his own silver dagger, and though Lupo threw up an arm to block its trajectory, the blade's edge made a long slit on his forearm.

Lupo hissed as the blade sheared through his skin and flesh and scorched the wound like a propane flame.

They traded slices and stabbing thrusts as men, neither of them transforming to werewolf form. The clothes inhibited them, but Lupo also suspected the dagger in his hand was a better edge against Mordred's dagger than his wolf's jaws—after all, the daggers had proven astonishingly effective against werewolves in their animal form.

They squared off, thrusting and parrying like swordsmen of old, except the length of their blades necessitated coming in close, inside the enemy's reach.

Schlosser stared at the contest between the cop and the soldier from behind his protective barrier.

Lupo heard the Creature inside howling, urging a Change so he could wade into the fight. The wolf wanted to fight, lusting for blood.

But Lupo's control had improved, and he managed to overcome the Creature's influence.

Mordred went on the attack, and his thrusts and slices drove Lupo back toward the conference table, where he became tangled in the rolling chairs and almost fell sideways.

The slip was fortuitous, however, because Mordred's thrust would have been on target had Lupo still stood in the same spot.

Kicking the chairs out of his way and into Mordred's, Lupo grunted with effort as he heaved himself to his knees and thrust out blindly, feeling his blade tip find Mordred's lower belly and slip in even as the big man swept sideways with his own blade.

The silver edge scorched Lupo's hair and nearly scalped him, separating a flap of skin from his skull.

He screamed as the heat seared through his brain, and he nearly blacked out.

But instead he felt the bubbling warmth of magically heated blood gushing over the hand that held his dagger, which was buried deep in Mordred's body, pointed up. He felt the blade sawing upward like a jigsaw almost out of his control, as if the Creature had taken over, and then Mordred's intestines poured out, smoking as the heat cooked them.

Lupo retched and tried to withdraw the dagger, but he couldn't.

Then he looked up into Mordred's eyes and saw that Geoff Simonson looked back at him. Gone were the swirling, cold werewolf eyes.

"Thank you," the big soldier mouthed, blood bubbling out from between his lips.

Lupo understood then that Simonson had taken the thrust

intentionally and kept himself skewered on purpose, killing both himself and his evil Mordred personality.

Simonson folded over and died, his body twitching and his inner wolf attempting to Change, fluttering between human and wolf.

He collapsed at Lupo's knees, and Lupo finally withdrew the blade from the corpse, his own pain suddenly intolerable. Panting, he found the scabbard and sheathed his blade, his hand and arm and wounds overwhelming him. His vision blurred.

He drew himself to his feet with the help of a chair and fixed his eyes on Schlosser, who was still behind the glass.

He was no longer smug, seeing that his champion had been vanquished.

Lupo advanced on the glass wall, trying to think past the pain.

How to get at the fucker?

"You're still vulnerable, Lupo," Schlosser said, his eyes betraying his sudden fear.

"No," Lupo spit out. "*You* are vulnerable. And you're mine."

"Not quite, Nick."

Lupo was startled by the familiar voice.

"Margarethe?" Schlosser said. "What are you—"

"Heather?" Lupo said, his hands on the glass.

Heather

She had waited until the opportune moment to take Sigfried-Schlosser by surprise.

Her stolen cards had provided access. After all, the CEO himself had given her unparalleled freedom in his house, trapped by his own weaknesses, the sadistic lust that had undone his family throughout the ages.

Now she had sneaked up behind him and snatched the remote out of his hand from behind.

"What the hell?" Lupo's voice came through the speaker.

He was staring at her as he held his wounded arm, blood streaming down his face.

He was staring because she was nude—magnificently nude and incredibly alluring, waves of lust cascading off her glowing skin.

"Margarethe?" Schlosser said again. "What—I don't have time to—I don't know what you—"

His tongue tied itself up and he backed away from her.

She smiled at Lupo. "I told you I had sources," she said. "I was the source."

"You?" Lupo shook his head, wishing he could break down the glass partition and tear the CEO limb from limb.

"He knew me as Margarethe, the woman who bought his favorite dom business. I became his personal dominatrix, Nick, at his beck and call twenty-four seven, and he was so besotted with me that I managed to break his security from the inside."

"So that's how you—" Lupo nodded. Her calls made sense now. He thought she'd been using her investigative journalist skills, but actually she'd been using her body. And her own lusts.

Schlosser's face now showed that his confusion had been replaced by rising fear. Maybe some latent lust, too, as he eyed the formidable woman before him.

But she was backing him toward the cage. She knew her eyes were changing, colors swirling.

And that he saw, and understood.

She pressed a key on the remote.

The glass partition began to retract.

"No!" Schlosser shrieked, turning to run, but there was nowhere to go because now Lupo was standing on this side of the room. And the remote, with which he could have summoned help, was in Heather's hand.

She smiled widely.

And her body shimmered, turning into a sleek and muscular gray wolf.

Lupo caught the remote in his good hand and studied it.

The cage door opened, but Lupo stopped it. They were only two yards from the cage, but the heat from the silver bars was becoming intense.

"I can't put him in there," Lupo said, his voice cracking with pain. "It'll protect him."

The she-wolf looked at him. She understood. He pressed a button and a section of wall closed, hiding the cage from sight and shielding them from the silver.

Lupo left Heather's wolf guarding the trembling CEO.

"Margarethe, I'll give you anything you want," he pleaded.

The she-wolf growled and showed her fangs.

Chapter Twenty-Seven

Lupo

He went back to where Simonson lay dead in a puddle of gore and closed his eyes, one at a time. He tucked both sheathed daggers into his belt. Then he picked up his silenced Glock left-handed. His right hand was a mangled mass of melted, seared skin, and the pain was so intense he could barely stand.

He checked his watch.

DiSanto, the cavalry, should be at the gates now, having made the trip with the department's chopper as Lupo had instructed. A trip to the local law enforcement, a warrant signed by a friendly Milwaukee County judge in his hand, should have stimulated their interest. Lupo's phone hadn't vibrated in his pocket, so everything must have gone according to plan. A convoy of cop cars should have been driving through the gates, the guards held at gunpoint.

The werewolves stationed here would make themselves scarce.

Live to fight another day?

He turned back to where Heather guarded the Wolfpaw CEO he had known as Sigfried. Schlosser sounded more like a remnant of the Nazi party, though.

He brought up the Glock and unsnapped the suppressor.

"What are you doing? *Do you know who I am?*" Schlosser demanded.

That old chestnut? He'd have to tell DiSanto.

He glanced at his watch. Probably less than five minutes now.

He nodded at the wolf, who growled at Schlosser. It blurred, and then it was Heather standing there again. She put her long hand on Lupo's mangled arm and hissed in sympathy.

"God, Nick, this looks terrible. Painful."

"You have no idea," he said, not taking his eyes off Schlosser, who seemed to be measuring his distance to the door.

"We almost done here?" Heather asked.

"Almost."

"You got DiSanto leading the charge again?"

"He's getting really good at it," Lupo said.

He smacked Schlosser with his mangled arm and the CEO cringed, crying out.

"That's for what you did to Mordred, or Simonson, and all the other people you and your family tortured through the decades. *The Reaper*, huh? Something to really be proud of."

"Nick, the time." Heather said.

He noticed for the first time her Nazi tattoos. "Those real?"

She grinned. "Yeah, had to be convincing. But I'm going to have them lasered off, and then the scars'll heal back to normal."

He shook his head. "You really are crazy. Dominatrix!"

Had to be good at it, he thought.

She tapped his watch.

"Okay, time to pay up, you sonofabitch. You and your mercenaries and murderers have had your way with too many good people. Here, overseas, you name it. With your threats gone, I'm sure the congressmen you silenced will go back on the attack. Wolfpaw is no more. As of now."

He pushed Schlosser to the door through which Heather had come. "Is that one okay?"

"It's like a study with a connecting door to a sort of secret apartment. There's a desk."

"Good." Lupo shoved the shuddering CEO through the door bodily, eliciting a grunt of pain. He pushed him down in the chair behind the desk.

There was a pad and an expensive pen on the old-fashioned blotter.

"I'll keep watch," Heather said, backing out. She closed the door.

"Write," Lupo said to Schlosser, handing him the pen. He held the Glock in his left. He thought he saw Ghost Sam standing in the room's shadows. When he looked again, the specter was gone.

"Write what?" All fight had leaked from the CEO like bitter water.

"What I tell you."

"Wait, I know something about your family...your father..."

Lupo rested the Glock's muzzle on Schlosser's forehead, staring into the frightened eyes below.

"Talk first, then," he growled.

Heather

She thought she heard sirens outside, far away. Many of them. Coming closer. She looked at the door.

Come on, Nick. Come on.

Looked like DiSanto had come through. The information used to request the warrant couldn't be ignored by any judge, anywhere. What she had culled from Sigfried's—*Schlosser's*—files had probably yielded several roads of inquiry.

Lupo was going to have a time of it, what with the missing cop and psychologist. But she never underestimated Lupo's ability to shield himself. And Jessie.

It's over.

Too bad, she thought. Being a dom had been...fun.

Too bad about Simonson, too. He'd been exciting.

She heard a single shot from behind the door.

She grinned.

It *was* over.

Minutes later, two wolves made for the woods backing the Wolfpaw compound as a file of official vehicles fanned out. They were ignored by almost everyone as escaping guard dogs.

DiSanto, wrapped up in a police kevlar vest, gave them a tentative little wave and watched them go.

Chapter Twenty-Eight

Two weeks later...

Heather

She let herself into her huge Washington condo and closed the door behind herself, kicking off her heels and allowing her toes to sink into the shag carpeting. It was retro, it was decadent, and she'd had to have it.

She still felt the ache of where her tattoos had been removed—shouldn't they have healed by now?

Then she flicked on her dim lights and turned.

And stopped, startled.

Her eyes widened a fraction, but she could hide her feelings easily enough.

"Hello, Jessie," she said, smiling as if they were friends and Jessie had stopped by for a sociable cup of coffee or tea with cake and scones. "I didn't expect you, or I would have prepared something."

"Cut the pleasant bullshit," Jessie said from where she stood, leaning against the massive, oblong desk set at one side of the wide living room. Behind her were floor to ceiling bookshelves. Heather's laptop, a silver Mac, was open on the desk. Jessie tossed a tiny flash drive up in the air and caught it.

"Thanks for your files," she said. "Should do the trick."

"Trick, what trick?" Heather said, looking down while sidling closer. She took her hand away from her side. Appeared to be checking for her discarded shoes.

"Prove to Nick that you've been keeping files on him, on me, on all of us and what we do and why. You have enough information to get us all charged with something, certainly to make our lives miserable. Maybe now Nick will believe that you aren't on his side after all, even though you seem to be obsessed with him."

Heather said nothing.

Jessie grimaced. "I saw through you from the start, but Nick—well, Nick is damaged when it comes to women. He's too easily led to the wrong conclusion."

"And you lead him to the right conclusion? When you're not busy pushing the slot machine buttons?" *Zing.*

"I never claimed to be the best thing he's ever had," Jessie said, tears squeezing from the corners of her eyes. "I never said he owed me anything. I never led him wrong."

Now Heather was slowly approaching her intruder. "Well, don't let the door hit you on the ass on your way out. I'll take that flash drive now." She held out her hand.

"Fuck yourself."

"Don't make me angry, Jessie. You don't want to make me angry."

Heather seemed to be touching herself in the dim light, but then her dress dropped off her shoulders, and she stepped out of it almost daintily. Naked now, her breasts thrust out at Jessie and, her exquisitely honed body glowing, she stepped closer.

Jessie spoke. "You shouldn't make *me* angry, Heather. I have what I need. Step aside. All you'll lose is Nick."

Heather couldn't help but laugh. "Jessie, I don't plan on losing anything. Now, if you want to leave here alive, hand over the drive."

Jessie shook her head. "No," she said. "You lose this time."

And didn't move from her spot.

Heather's features turned ugly. Her sneer became the basis of a growl, climbing up from the depths of her throat.

Long runs of light-colored fur started to sprout along her back and shoulders and on her belly. Her manicured nails turned to claws. Her teeth became fangs. Another growl erupted from her throat. Her eyes swirled and changed colors like kaleidoscopes.

Jessie seemed mesmerized for one second.

But then she showed what her other hand held. It was one of the twin Longinus daggers from the wooden case they had taken from Mordred's car. Its blade glowed as she slowly unsheathed it from the shielding wooden scabbard.

Heather's body blurred and she was now on all fours, a sleek giant gray wolf poised to leap and maul her intruder.

The dagger's point cleared the end of the scabbard and Jessie held it, much more expertly than Heather would have expected, and approached the threatening wolf.

The wolf lunged.

Jessie's hand became a blur in motion, the bluish glow of the blade marking the arc of her attack.

They met in the middle of the room.

About the Author

W.D. Gagliani's *Wolf's Trap* was a finalist for the Bram Stoker Award in 2004. His novels *Wolf's Gambit* and *Wolf's Bluff* and the novella *Wolf's Deal* also feature Homicide Detective Nick Lupo. His novel *Savage Nights* introduces a new character, Rich Brant. Gagliani is the author of numerous short stories published in anthologies such as *Robert Bloch's Psychos, Undead Tales, Dark Passions: Hot Blood 13* and *Malpractice* (both with David Benton), among many others. "The Great Belzoni and the Gait of Anubis," also a werewolf tale of sorts, is available from Amazon.com, as are *Shadowplays* (a story collection) and *Mysteries & Mayhem* (with David Benton).

His fiction has also appeared in various e-zines such as *Wicked Karnival* and *Dead Lines*. His book reviews have been published at the Stoker Award-winning Chiaroscuro (*www.chizine.com*) since 1999, plus *HorrorWorld* and *Cemetery Dance*, as well as *The Milwaukee Journal Sentinel, BookPage, The Scream Factory, Science Fiction Chronicle*, and others. He has had nonfiction in *On Writing Horror* (WD Books), *The Writer* magazine (October 2011), and written about author Wilbur Smith in *Thrillers: The 100 Must Reads* (Oceanview).

When not writing, reading, or reviewing books, he listens to old and new progressive rock, plays with vintage synthesizers and his Theremin, and collects interesting weaponry. Visit him at *www.wdgagliani.com, www.facebook.com/wdgagliani*, and follow him on Twitter at *@WDGagliani*.

See how the terror started.
Read the first book in the Nick Lupo series!

Wolf's Trap
© *2003 W. D Gagliani*

Nick Lupo is a good cop—a bit of a renegade at times, with the instincts of a great detective...or maybe a wolf. Lupo has a lot in common with wolves, which is only natural considering he's a werewolf. He's battled the creature inside him for years, but now there's another predator in the area. A bloodthirsty serial killer is leaving a trail of victims, and it's up to Lupo to track him down and stop the slaughter. Will Lupo dare to unleash one beast to stop another?

Available soon in ebook and print from Samhain Publishing.

It's all about the story...

Romance

HORROR

www.samhainpublishing.com